Choosing Sides

"I've bought you an extension on life," Aren says, leaning against the porch column. His casualness and the intensity in his silver eyes make an odd combination. I don't like the way he's observing me. I like even less the way the moonlight glows behind him, making him seem mysterious, almost debonair.

"Do you want me to thank you?"

"You'll help us eventually." He sounds so certain.

I shake my head. "No. My allegiance is to Ky— King Atroth."

He smiles a little. "I'll earn your trust."

"I'll doubt everything you say."

He chuckles, pushes away from the column, and crosses the porch to stand in front of me. He takes my right hand in his. As he pulls me to my feet, I make the mistake of looking into his eyes. This close, I can become lost in them, especially with the heat of his *edarratae* traveling up my arm. He dips his head, staring down at me with mirth on his lips.

"You will be an interesting challenge . . ."

THE SHADOW READER

Sandy Williams

ACE BOOKS, NEW YORK

THE BERKLEY PUBLISHING GROUP
Published by the Penguin Group
Penguin Group (USA) Inc.
375 Hudson Street, New York, New York 10014, USA

Penguin Group (Canada), 90 Eglinton Avenue East, Suite 700, Toronto, Ontario M4P 2Y3, Canada
(a division of Pearson Penguin Canada Inc.)
Penguin Books Ltd., 80 Strand, London WC2R 0RL, England
Penguin Group Ireland, 25 St. Stephen's Green, Dublin 2, Ireland (a division of Penguin Books Ltd.)
Penguin Group (Australia), 250 Camberwell Road, Camberwell, Victoria 3124, Australia
(a division of Pearson Australia Group Pty. Ltd.)
Penguin Books India Pvt. Ltd., 11 Community Centre, Panchsheel Park, New Delhi—110 017, India
Penguin Group (NZ), 67 Apollo Drive, Rosedale, Auckland 0632, New Zealand
(a division of Pearson New Zealand Ltd.)
Penguin Books (South Africa) (Pty.) Ltd., 24 Sturdee Avenue, Rosebank, Johannesburg 2196,
South Africa

Penguin Books Ltd., Registered Offices: 80 Strand, London WC2R 0RL, England

THE SHADOW READER

An Ace Book / published by arrangement with the author

PRINTING HISTORY
Ace mass-market edition / November 2011

Copyright © 2011 by Sandy Williams.
Cover art by Gene Mollica.
Cover design by Lesley Worrell.
Interior text design by Tiffany Estreicher.

ISBN: 978-1-937007-01-0

ACE
Ace Books are published by The Berkley Publishing Group,
a division of Penguin Group (USA) Inc.,
375 Hudson Street, New York, New York 10014.
ACE and the "A" design are trademarks of Penguin Group (USA) Inc.

PRINTED IN THE UNITED STATES OF AMERICA

10   9   8   7   6   5   4   3   2   1

*For Trey. Thank you for putting up with me . . .
even when I'm "too much."*

ACKNOWLEDGMENTS

•-•-•

My writing would have forever remained buried on my computer if it weren't for the support of some amazing people. First and foremost, my husband, Trey, who believed in me before I believed in myself. I couldn't have done this without you. And to my friends and family: thank you for not thinking I'm crazy when I spontaneously drop everything to run and grab my notebook.

A special thank-you goes out to my beta readers, David Bridger, Tina Everitt, Katee Robert, Shelli Richard, and especially Reneé Sweet, who has been this book's number one fan from the very beginning. I'd also like to thank two people who made this story the best it could be: my agent, Joanna Volpe, for being awesome from the very beginning, and my editor, Kat Sherbo, whose wisdom and editing prowess have truly amazed me.

ONE

◆

M Y SKIN TINGLES a moment before a slash of white light flashes at the front of the lecture hall. I grit my teeth and keep my eyes locked on my scantron, refusing to acknowledge the fae entering my world through that fissure. I don't give a damn if it's the king himself; I will pass this test tonight.

I darken in *C* on my answer sheet and then read the next question.

"McKenzie."

It's Kyol. Of course the Court would send *him*.

"McKenzie," he says. "We must go." No one else can hear or see him even though he towers over my professor, who stands less than two feet to his left. All the other students remain bowed over their desks, completely focused on their final exams. I grip my pencil and bubble in another circle.

The fae climbs the steps to my fifth-row seat. Still not meeting his eyes, I shake my head. I told him—I told all of them—not to call on me this week, but none of the fae understand why I need this degree, not when the Court takes care of all my needs. I tried to explain I'm human. I have human dreams and need a human life, and it shouldn't take anyone eight years to earn a bachelor of arts in English. They hadn't listened. At least, Kyol hadn't.

Not now! I want to scream, but even the softest whisper

will disturb the quiet in the lecture hall. I stare down at my exam, letting my long hair brush the top of my desk. It forms a brown curtain, cutting off my view of Kyol as I reread question ten. The Court's war can wait until I finish.

Kyol lays a hand on my shoulder, and a pleasant warmth expands beneath the thin strap of my purple cami. If we were alone, I'd lean into his touch, soak in his heat, his scent—soak in *him*—but not here, not now, in the middle of a test I *have* to pass. I shift, trying to get away. When his hand remains, I slam my fist down on my desk.

My classmates turn their heads to stare and Dr. Embry frowns. Fantastic.

"Number ten," I say with a nervous laugh. "It's a doozy." It isn't. It's on the works of C. S. Lewis. Easy. I bubble in *A*.

Kyol pulls on my shoulder and I squirm again. There's no way in hell I'm flunking this course a third time. I need it to graduate, and I don't care if Kyol drops his invisibility in front of all my classmates; my ass isn't budging until I finish my test and triple-check my answers.

"We've no time to waste," Kyol says. "The rebels have found you."

I suck in a frigid breath, hold it as I close my eyes for one brief, fragile moment, then I exhale, stuff my pencil into my backpack, and stand.

"I'm sorry," I say to my surprised professor. "I have to go."

By the time I turn to hurry up the steps, Kyol's already waiting by the exit. I brace for the surge of emotion I know is coming and finally meet his silver eyes. Most people don't see past his hard, unyielding scowl, but I do. I've seen his eyes soften and sparkle in the moonlight. I've seen a smile crack those lips, heard a laugh ring from that broad chest. And yet, even in those few, untroubled moments, there's always a certain gravitas to him, like he could stand in the middle of a battle and part the enemy's line with one cool glare.

He reaches for the door. I lock down my feelings and cut him off, not wanting my classmates to see it swing open seemingly on its own. He glances down at me, and a bolt of blue lightning skitters from his jaw to his temple before disappearing into his dark hair. Another bolt zigzags across the hand he rests on his sword's hilt. They're chaos lusters, visual reminders that the fae don't belong in this world, and they're beautiful, mesmerizing. With his quiet, strong confidence, *he's* mesmerizing.

"Where should I go?" I ask after the door thumps shut.

"The River Bend." He seizes my arm and pulls me after him. God, he's really worried. Just how close are the rebels? I scan up and down the hallway, but there's only one other person in sight, a student asleep against the wall, newspaper pillowed under his head. I wish I could be oblivious like him, but I can't. If the rebels don't kill me on sight, they'll use me to hunt down the Court's officers one by one, just like I've hunted them down over the years.

My skin tingles again. I tense, then relax when three fae wearing the Court's *jaedric* armor join us, stepping through fissures to take up position around me. Escape would be easy if I could travel through one of those strips of narrow light, but I'm only human. I can't use a fissure unless it's opened at a gate and a fae escorts me through: not if I want to survive the trip.

Kyol speaks to his soldiers in their language. They nod, acknowledging his orders, and we set off down the hall. I shove my worry aside and hurry to keep up with their quick strides, telling myself everything will be okay, Kyol will take care of me. He *always* takes care of me.

Outside, a faint orange and pink haze smears the lowest portion of the sky. The growing darkness triggers the campus lights. They clank on, illuminating the faces of the students sitting on cement benches or walking alone or in groups of two or three. Even after dusk, this part of campus is always crowded because of the library. The River Bend Gate is about a mile northeast of it, past the construction for a new engineering building.

I hitch my backpack up on my shoulders. It's not heavy. I left most of my books at home and brought only the essentials: my English Lit notes, sketchbook, cell phone, and the small, drawstring pouch that contains a handful of imprinted anchorstones. I'll need the latter to pass through the gate unless Kyol gives me a new stone to use.

I jog to keep up. When students start to stare, I try to free my hand from Kyol's. It's not completely unusual to see someone run across campus, but my gait is awkward because he's pulling me, and I'm sure they're wondering what the hell I'm doing with my arm.

"Kyol," I whisper.

His gaze darts to the humans who don't see me holding his hand; they see me clutching wildly at the air. His jaw clenches before he lets me go. "I'm sorry, *kaesha*."

I catch my breath. *Kaesha*. It's a term of endearment he calls me only when we're alone. I don't think he knows he said it—there's no hitch in his stride as he leads me across the courtyard—but if his soldiers overhear, if they report back to the king . . .

An unnatural wind cuts through the previously still air, rustling through the trees and skittering a soda can across the cement. The hair at the nape of my neck stands on end and goose bumps prickle across my skin. The rebels are here. They're watching. They're hiding. They're—

Arrows whistle through the air. Light erupts around me as the Court fae vanish into their fissures. The arrows disappear when they touch the light, too, swallowed up by the In-Between. Only one hits its target: the shoulder of a fae who reacted an instant too late. With a grunt of pain, he escapes through his fissure. He's the only one who doesn't return. The others reappear with reinforcements as the rebels release another barrage.

"Go!" Kyol shoves me forward, but I spin to run back to the English building. No way am I running across the open courtyard.

More arrows fire through the air. I don't see if any hit the fae—I'm struggling to get past Kyol—but I hear the sound of more fissures opening. Each time the bright lights slash through the atmosphere, it sounds like someone's ripping a thick cloth in two. Add to that noise the fact that my heartbeat is thudding in my ears, and I almost don't hear Kyol's words.

"You must make it to the gate, McKenzie. You must!"

Instinct screams for me to get inside the building, but I trust Kyol with my life, so I stop fighting and glance over my shoulder. Arrows still fly through the air. A few seconds after they leave the rebels' bows, they'll become visible to normal humans, so if a fae misses his target or doesn't hit a fissure, people will see the bolts embed in trees or the ground or skidding across the cement. None of the students are reacting, though. The rebels are being careful.

I take a small step forward. Some of the Court fae have fissured to the rooftops to fight; others remain on the ground, darting in and out of their fissures in smooth, defensive dances. They're drawing the rebels' attacks, but it's a long way to the gate. They'll tire before I get there. Some of them might die. *Kyol* might die.

"I'll be fine," he says, reading the concern in my expression. He cups my cheek in his hand. "As long as you're safe, I'll be fine."

I bite my lip and nod. Of course he'll be okay. He's the king's sword-master. He can take care of himself. Besides, the fae will need me if any of the rebels are illusionists. Only a human with the Sight can see through that magic.

Ignoring the stares students throw my way, I take a deep breath, grit my teeth, and run. Kyol and I have worked together for ten years—we're tuned in to how the other moves, how we think and react—so when a rebel charges straight toward us and Kyol doesn't turn his way, I know he can't see him.

"Ten o'clock. Now!" I say.

Kyol swings as ordered, forcing the rebel to parry. Touch breaks a fae's illusion, so as soon as their weapons clash, Kyol can see him. His blade cuts into the rebel's arm three moves later, but it's not a killing blow. The illusionist fissures away.

Kyol returns to my side. I flinch when an arrow almost hits him, flinch again when another one whizzes past my face, disappearing into another Court fae's fissure. I want to duck and dodge the rebels' attack, but that will slow us down and draw even more attention from the humans. I've already lied my way through one psychiatric evaluation; I don't think I can lie my way through another.

We sprint past the library. Ahead, a metal fence blocks off the construction site to the new engineering building. I veer left to go around it, but a wall of fissures forms in my path. Six fae appear. All rebels.

I tell Kyol their number. None of them must be hidden by illusion because he doesn't hesitate. His blade carves through the air as he charges the rebels, but he can't occupy all six at once. Two of them break away from the others and move toward me.

I turn and run. To hell with going around the fence. I leap up and grab its top. My tennis shoes struggle for a foothold in the metal links, and the wire cuts into my palms. I manage to pull myself over the top, but I land hard on my right hip. Ignoring the sharp burst of pain, I scurry back to my feet and sprint forward again. When a fissure opens in front of me, I almost run into it, but Kyol steps out, stopping me. Saving me.

He extinguishes the fissure and then shoves me behind him. Metal clanks against metal as he takes on my pursuers. I dash under the exterior scaffolding and through the doorless entrance to the engineering building. The construction company's already erected the interior walls on the first floor. I run through what will be the common area, almost make it to the other side, but five fissures open in a semicircle in front of me.

Five rebel fae appear. I'm no military genius, but this is clearly an ambush. I've been herded here, lured like a sheep to the wolf's den.

"McKenzie."

Even if the fae in the center of the group hadn't spoken, my attention would be riveted to him. He's tall, taller than Kyol, but not as thickly muscled, and his silver eyes, while intense, have a lighter, livelier hue to them. He's wearing a poorly made, dark *jaedric* cuirass over a once-white tunic, loose gray pants, and scuffed black boots. His golden-blond hair looks like it's been chopped off with a knife or, perhaps, the sword in his hand. Despite his haphazard appearance, he's confident, he's alert, and he's completely focused on me, his prey.

"McKenzie Lewis." A bolt of blue lightning flashes down his neck. He cocks his head slightly. A moment later, his sword-point dips and *something* changes in his posture.

"Are you hurt?" he asks.

I follow his gaze down to a dark stain on my purple cami. I press a hand against my stomach. It's warm, wet.

"Are you hurt?" the rebel asks again.

No. I'm not. I don't know where the blood came from. No one's touched me. No one but Kyol . . .

Kyol. Oh, God. He's hurt.

I spin toward the exit, trying to get back to him, but two rebels move to block my path, their swords held ready to strike.

"I don't want to hurt you," the fae's leader says. "I'd like to talk to you."

He takes a step toward me. I take a step back.

"Look." He sheaths his sword, then holds his hands out, palms up like he's harmless.

Screw him. I won't let them take me. I sprint for my only remaining escape route, the metal staircase in the building's northeast corner.

My backpack bounces as I run up the steps. I reach the second floor before I hear the rebels coming after me. I pause to consider my options, realize I have none.

"Shit!" I have nowhere to go but up, and once I'm up, I'll have nowhere to go at all. I sprint to the next floor because I don't know what else to do. I can't turn around. I can't stop. They're right behind me.

"Shit, shit, shit!"

My legs are burning by the time I reach the fourth level. I can't make it up the next flight of stairs so I run across this floor instead, watching my feet as I step over stacks of two-by-fours and through the wooden frames of the building's future walls. The sun's set. It's dark, but I'm able to make out the outline of a piece of machinery in what will eventually be a hallway. I duck down behind it, praying I'm out of sight in time.

Soft footsteps walk across the cement.

My hair clings to my face and neck. I swipe it out of my eyes and search for some way out of this. There's an opening at the end of the hallway for what I assume will be a floor-to-ceiling window. An orange plastic safety fence runs across the gap, and seven or eight feet away from the edge of the building is the white, moonlit arm of a tower crane.

Seven or eight feet. Can I jump that?

"You're making this more difficult than it needs to be."

I flinch at the voice. He's close. He knows I'm here.

I grit my teeth and refuse to panic. I don't think the rebels will kill me immediately. They'll try to use me. They'll try to turn me against the Court, make me read the shadows. They

probably won't hurt me until they're certain I won't cooperate.
I should have a few seconds to make my move.

I wipe sweat from my face and focus on the crane outside
the building. *Seven or eight feet.* I *have* to jump that.

I don't give myself time to second-guess my decision. I
sprint the distance to the plastic fence, scramble over it—

"No, wait!"

—and jump, but the rebel grabs my backpack.

I slip. I scream.

My fingers tangle in the plastic fence.

I fall.

I hit the side of the building and keep screaming.

My throat's raw by the time I realize I'm not dead. I'm
hanging between the third and fourth floors, holding on to the
plastic fence like my life depends on it because . . . well, it
does.

A chuckle draws my attention upward. The damn fae peers
over the edge, looking all jolly and relaxed.

"I can't believe you held on," he says.

The moonlight highlights the planes of his face, and even
though I'm dangling three and a half stories above the ground,
I'm suddenly more pissed than afraid. I don't recognize him,
but my gut tells me who he is: Aren, son of Jorreb, the false-
blood who's determined to overthrow the king. And he's laughing at me.

The plastic fence stretches. My fingers cramp, but I'm
determined to hang on forever if it keeps me away from the
killer above.

Something snaps loose from the wall and I drop another
foot.

"Whoa, easy there. Easy," Aren says.

"Back off!" I mean to yell the words, but they come out as
a hoarse croak. I know I should be begging for his help, but a
part of me believes Kyol will rescue me. I choose to ignore the
part that believes he's dead.

"Sure," Aren says in an infuriatingly devil-may-care voice.
"No problem, but how about you give me your hand first?
There's no need for you to fall."

"I won't help you!"

"I'm not asking for your help. Just give me your h—"

The plastic rips free from the wall. I scream again and tense, bracing for impact.

"McKenzie. Hey, look up here, McKenzie. I've got you."

Heart thudding, I look up. He does have me. Sort of. He's dangling over the edge of the building, his left hand wrapped in the fence, his right hand grasping the opening's frame.

"Stop kicking," he says. I stop, not realizing I was moving at all.

"Good. Now, you're going to have to grab my legs. I think the fence will rip if I try to pull you up. Can you do that?"

I nod. I don't care who he is anymore. I don't want to die. I want to live. I want to be normal, graduate college, get a real job, and spend time with some real-life friends. Hell, I want to have sex at least once before I croak.

The thought of death pulls my gaze toward the concrete.

"No, don't look down, McKenzie. Look up here. Look at me."

I do as he says. His eyes are bright but soft, like silver sand with tiny shards of diamonds, and his expression is serious but not strained. The last part impresses me. I might be thin, but I'm not dainty, and he's supporting both of our weights.

"Pull yourself up." There's a bit more urgency in his voice now. He must feel the plastic stretching, too.

I muster the strength to reach up and grab his legs. As soon as I wrap my arms around him, he releases the fence. With a grunt, he pulls himself up and over the edge. I scrape along the side of the building until he grabs my arm, dragging me to safety.

I lie facedown on the cement floor. My arms feel like spaghetti and I'm shaking, but I can't be weak right now. The rebels will demand a high price for saving my life, and I have no intention of sticking around to pay it.

I lurch to my feet, but my knees buckle.

"Are you okay?" Aren asks.

I ignore him and rise again. This time, I manage to keep my balance. It doesn't matter, though. Three rebels block the staircase. One of them speaks in Fae.

"The police are coming," Aren translates behind me. No doubt my screams have brought them. I consider screaming again, but Aren grabs my arm.

Lightning flashes from his skin to mine. I can't shake loose. He wrestles me to a corner and, when he presses his lean body against mine, my brain stops functioning. The lightning between our skin increases, becoming almost volatile, and my body flushes with heat.

"The police can't help you," Aren says. I'm sure that smirk on his face is due to my obvious discomfort. He feels the electricity between us the same as I do, but he's not bothered by it.

"Let go!" I demand, trying to free my arms.

Flashlight beams precede the cops up the stairs.

"Be quiet. Be still," Aren whispers.

I twist. I almost slip free, but one strong arm locks around my waist. He covers my mouth with his other hand.

Stupid move on his part. I bite down hard.

He doesn't grimace, but his smirk vanishes.

"Sorry about this," he whispers in my ear.

Pain explodes above my temple. I totter, but don't black out. My knees aren't working, though. Aren's holding me up. I'm able to focus on his face well enough to see surprise in his eyes. Then the surprise disappears. His lips thin as he raises the weapon again. It's a dagger. He swings its hilt down a second time.

TWO

◆━◆

MY HEAD'S KILLING me. I'm alone in the backseat of a van. A human is driving, slowing down, stopping. I don't want to move from the floor of the van, but the side door grinds open and I'm yanked to my feet. Black splotches dance in my vision. They're much like the shadows I read for the Court, but these don't form patterns and no one's opened a fissure here, wherever here is. Before I'm able to focus, I'm yards away from the vehicle, which is already pulling back onto the road. At least Aren isn't the fae who's trying to dislocate my shoulder. He's a man the rebels call Trev. I can barely feel the electric thrum of his touch because his fingers are cutting off my circulation. He doesn't hesitate when I stumble or lag behind. Humans can't move as quickly as the fae. He knows this. He's a total asshole for not slowing down.

We don't go far. That's good because walking makes the world wobble, but bad because this means we've reached a gate. It's invisible when I look directly at it, but if I turn my head to the side, it's there in my peripheral vision. A thinness in the world. A subtle blurring of the atmosphere.

I blink, trying to figure out where we are. I manage to read the numbers on my digital watch. It's a little after midnight. I know the locations of every gate within a three-hour radius of my campus, but we've driven beyond that boundary. I don't recognize the tiny pond in front of me or this patch of trees, which appears to be in the middle of some farmer's cow pasture.

Aren steps to the pond's edge. Gates are always located on water, so I understand what he's doing when he reaches into the dark pool. He makes a connection with the gate, then stands, lifting his cupped palm toward the sky. But instead of a sprinkling of water, light spills over his fingers one drop, two drops, three drops at a time until the unending rain forms a bright, solid downpour. When this fissure breaks through the In-Between, it grumbles like a raging thundershower.

"I'll take her through," Aren says, taking a long strip of indigo cloth out of his pocket.

"Is that necessary?" I ask.

His silver eyes meet mine. "If the rumors about you are true, then yes. It's very necessary."

Having a reputation sucks sometimes.

Trev holds me in place while Aren ties the blindfold around my head. I guess I shouldn't have expected them to make a stupid mistake, especially since the only reason I'm in this situation is because of what I'm able to see. If I wasn't blindfolded, there's a good chance I'd learn our location after we fissured. Basically, I'm a glorified cartographer. When fissures wink out of existence, I see the topography of the earth written in the shadows left behind. It's like looking at a bright light for too long. When you look away, it takes a while for your vision to clear. The same thing happens with fissures, but where everyone else sees random blurs and blotches, I see the curves of rivers, the edges of mountains, and the slopes of the land. I sketch out these shadows so the Court fae can hunt down their enemies, and I'm pretty damn accurate; a fact that has obviously pissed off the rebels.

Aren says something in his language and a moment later, I hear normal, ungated-fissures opening. I assume the other fae are going directly home or to their base or camp or wherever the hell it is they stay. That leaves me alone with Aren, one on one, mano a mano. Not that my odds of escaping are that much better but, hey, I'll take what I can get.

Aren presses something warm and smooth into the palm of my right hand. I don't have to see it to know it's an anchor-stone, one that's probably still glowing from his imprint.

"Do you know what will happen if you drop this?" he asks.

"I'll be eviscerated into a hundred billion pieces of flesh and plague your nightmares." I let the stone slip through my fingers. It hits the ground with a light thump. I wait for him to bend over to retrieve it, but I don't hear or feel him move.

"If you're suicidal," he says after a long moment. "There are less painful ways to die."

"You need me alive." My voice is steady. My heart rate, however, is not. The lightning from his touch radiates up and down my arm.

"You're sure about that?"

"You wouldn't have saved me if you wanted me dead." That's the only thing giving me courage right now. He went to a lot of trouble to keep me from going splat. He has to want me to shadow-read for him, for the rebels. As long as he thinks I might do it, I should be okay. I think.

His hand slides from my elbow to my shoulder. "Pick up the anchor. It's by your left foot."

I sink down to get away from the tingling heat of his touch and pat around the dew-covered grass until I find the stone. It's so very tempting to chuck it as far away as I can, but I'm *not* suicidal and Aren, son of Jorreb, is the Butcher of Brykeld.

"You won't be eviscerated if you let go of the anchor," he says, pulling me upright. "You'll be lost in the In-Between."

And with that, he yanks me into the gated-fissure.

My breath whooshes out of my lungs and crystallizes. It feels like I've dropped through the surface of a frozen lake. It's so cold here my heart stops beating, my blood stops flowing. Only my mind functions, and it can only focus on the heat of the anchor in my left hand and the heat of Aren's palm in my right. I don't remember taking his hand, but I squeeze it tight. I'd rather be squeezing his throat.

Supposedly, traveling via fissure, whether gated or not, is instantaneous, but I swear it lasts ten to fifteen excruciating seconds. That's plenty of time for me to know I do *not* want to stay in the In-Between one moment longer than necessary. I hate going through gates, especially without Kyol.

As soon as the ice releases me, I know we're in the Realm. The air here is different. It's . . . crisp, like biting into an apple, and the atmosphere is lighter. Or maybe it's me that's heavier. I'm not sure. All I know is I'm human. I don't belong in this land any more than the fae belong in mine. I feel big and awkward, like I stick out. And I do. Here in the Realm, chaos lusters originate from humans, not from fae, and the bolts of lightning are white instead of blue. I'll get used to them and this world in an hour or two, but right now I'm more than uncomfortable. I'm pissed.

As I turn toward Aren, I reach up to take off my blindfold. He stops me, takes both my hands in one of his, and holds them to the hard *jaedric* armor protecting his chest. We're so close his cedar-and-cinnamon scent dances its way into my lungs. My thoughts hitch for a moment as his touch triggers more lightning. It shimmies through my fingers, over my palms, and up my arms. It would be so easy to forget myself in the addictive sensation, but I've had ten years to steel myself against a fae's touch and I won't be distracted.

"Never, ever pull me through a gate unprepared again!" I try to jerk away as I snarl the words. I'm unsuccessful, of course, and I think I hear a chuckle beneath the rumble of another gated-fissure opening.

"I brought you through in one piece." He takes the anchor-stone from my hand, returns it a moment later. It's hot with the imprint of a new location. "Hold your breath."

Already? I start to ask, but he pulls me into the fissure and the question is whipped from my mouth.

I've never traveled this quickly before. Fae can fissure over and over again as long as they don't move far from their original location, but we just jumped between two worlds. Even if we stayed on Earth, the most conditioned fae would have to wait two to three minutes before opening a second fissure. No wonder the Court's never been able to capture Aren.

My world's warmth wraps around me. I try to listen between my gasps for air for the voices of people or fae, for the sounds of traffic or construction. Something, anything, to give me a clue as to where I am. The birds twittering overhead aren't helping me out. I could be anywhere.

Aren re-imprints the anchor-stone. "Again."

"Again?" I yelp, but this time I hold my breath before he takes me through. That helps. My lungs don't feel the bite of the frost, but I've never, ever been through more than two fissures in an hour before.

We stay in my world. I'm shaking now, and it's not entirely due to the ice that seems to have replaced my bones. Journeying sucks energy from travelers. When Kyol takes me through a fissure, he absorbs most of that drain himself. Unless he's exhausted or injured, I only feel a little disoriented on most trips. I'd undoubtedly feel more if we crossed through three fissures, but there was never a need to. Besides, I'm pretty damn sure what we just did was dangerous.

Aren releases my hands to rub his palms up and down my arms. The electric tingle warms me some, but I shove away from him. With the cloth still blinding me and my head still pounding from being knocked out, I'm off-balance. I'm sure my knees would have buckled if he didn't steady me, but I don't want his help. As soon as my dizziness subsides, I pivot on my right foot and swing my left knee up and into his groin. He harrumphs but doesn't let go, and he has no trouble catching the fist I blindly aim for his nose.

I kick and twist and struggle. "Let me go!"

I try to swing my head into his, but he's ready for me now. His arms encircle me, pinning my arms to my sides. I spin until my back is pressed into his chest and stomach, and I keep squirming until I wear myself out, which doesn't take long since the gated-fissures siphoned most of my strength.

"Are you finished?" he asks.

I slam my heel into his shin one last time. "For now."

A short pause, then, "I'm going to take your blindfold off. *Do not* turn toward the shadows."

I can feel them lingering just a few steps away, and when Aren removes the cloth from my eyes, it takes all of my self-control not to glance over my shoulder. It's always difficult not to be sucked in by the shadows. They tug on my consciousness, calling to me like the whisper of a siren's song. I've gotten better at resisting their lure over the years, but Aren's order not to turn has made them even more tantalizing.

I dig my fingernails into my palms, trying to distract myself. Then, instead of a forbidden glance over my shoulder, I tilt my head back to peer through the treetops to the sky—the *sunlit* sky.

Wait a second. It was pitch-black when Aren took me through the first gate, and he was so freaking impatient to get through the next two that no more than three or four minutes could have passed. My watch says it's only ten minutes after midnight.

"Where the hell have you taken me?" I demand.

A tiny smirk pulls at the corner of his mouth. He should have left the blindfold on because I'm seething now that I can see the smug expression framed by his tousled blond hair. He pulls off disheveled-sexy very well, and the fact that I notice he's good-looking pisses me off even more. A killer should be ugly and scarred. He shouldn't have a face like his.

I yank my gaze away to scan my surroundings. I think there are mountains to my right, but I don't get a clear look because Aren's hand locks on the back of my neck.

"I told you not to turn."

"I wasn't looking at the shadows!" His fingers *hurt*. He must have found a pressure point because I'm on my knees in an instant.

"I'm trying to be kind to you, McKenzie, but I will not allow you to learn anything that might hurt my people."

"I'm sorry," I say because my left shoulder is going numb. I stare at his scuffed boots and remain as still and docile as possible. His hand relaxes but remains on my neck. I can feel him staring. After a long silence, I risk a glance up.

His silver eyes turn a mirthless, steely gray as he appraises me, and fear shimmies down my spine. His words really sink in now, and I'm afraid he's starting to think keeping me alive isn't worth the risk.

"Good," he says with a nod that tells me he knows I understand how precarious my situation is. He takes my hand and helps me to my feet.

"This way." He gestures to a path that might loosely be considered a trail. "We have a long way to walk."

Because I'm exhausted, it takes a hell of a lot of effort not to ask him why he didn't just open the last fissure directly to our destination. I have to enter a fissure at a gate, but I can exit anywhere, as long as I have an anchor-stone imprinted for that location. Besides, I think I know the answer to my question. He's paranoid. That's why he took me so quickly through three gates, and that's why he's watching me now like I might suddenly grow eyes in the back of my head and see the shadows behind us. I want to tell him I'm not *that* good at my job—the shadows are too old, too faded, for me to read—but I keep my mouth shut.

I glance at the sky as we walk and wonder if we could be in California or maybe Oregon. There's a two-hour time difference between my home near Houston and those states, but no, that distance isn't enough to account for the sun. It's on its way up, not down, so we can't be on the West Coast. I don't think we can be anywhere in the western hemisphere.

Great. Just great.

Critters skitter in the underbrush as we follow the pseudo-trail. Aren stays close by my side. I want to ask about Kyol. I know he could have escaped if he tried, but he's never abandoned me when I've needed him, and I can't shake the feeling that he died for me.

My steps falter. I bite my lip, forcing myself to focus on that pain instead of the fear gathering in the pit of my stomach. I don't want Aren to learn how much the king's sword-master means to me. I don't want him to know how much I mean to the sword-master.

Grimacing, I duck under a low-hanging branch. Hiding my feelings isn't anything new; I should be used to it by now. Kyol and I aren't supposed to want each other. We've both tried not to. We've tried to keep our relationship professional, to touch only when necessary, but Kyol's stronger than I am. He's the most honorable man—human or fae—I've ever met, and he was honest with me from the beginning: we'll never have a happy ending. Even if he doesn't lose his life fighting for his king, the laws of the Realm keep us from being together.

I know I need to move on. No woman in her right mind would wait ten years for a man to become more than just a friend, but that's the thing about love—it makes you do stupid shit. I live for the moments when Kyol's control breaks, the moments when we're alone and we kiss, and when I can pretend everything is right in both our worlds.

God, what if we never have another moment like that?

When the trail ends, I force my worry aside. Aren and I step from the woods into a clearing that's about the size of a football field. Enough trees are scattered about the glade for their outstretched branches to create a fairly solid canopy above us. Sunlight flickers through the leaves, tossing shadows over dirt, trampled grass, and a broken wooden sign. The paint on the sign is cracked and faded, but I'm pretty sure it's welcoming visitors to the illegible name of the guesthouse that's just ahead. It's a three-story structure with a peaked roof and brown trim crisscrossing its once-white walls. Cracks zigzag up its side and the whole place looks weakened by age, but I can imagine what it might have looked like in its youth. There's a certain storybook feel to it. More precisely, there's a Hansel and Gretel feel to it. Hmm.

I look back at the dilapidated sign and scrutinize the barely there words. It's not exactly welcoming visitors to the guesthouse; it's *willkommen*-ing them to the *gasthaus*.

I stop suddenly and turn to Aren. "Germany? Seriously?"

The corner of his mouth quirks up. "Why not?"

He places his palm on the small of my back and urges me forward. Maybe I should count myself lucky he isn't upset I've learned what country we're in, but honestly, it's not like we're in Luxembourg, which is about the size of the average mall in Texas. If I'm ever in trouble, I'm supposed to call Paige, my best friend—okay, my *only* friend—and tell her where I am. She doesn't know the fae exist, but she's met Kyol. She'll pass on my message if I ask. Problem is, even if she passes it on today, it would take the Court months to search all the remote areas of Germany. Aren and his rebels would be long gone before they found me.

Speaking of the rebels, there are more than a dozen here. It's a decidedly strange sight—medieval, I guess I should say—but it's a sight I've become somewhat used to over the years. They're dressed in typical non-noble fae fashion. Men and women both wear white or pale-brown tunics over dark pants that are stuffed into black boots. A few wear armor similar to Aren's. It's made from the bark of a *jaedric* tree. The Court treats theirs with a substance that darkens and shines it, but the rebels don't. Theirs is dull and splotchy. Small drawstring pouches are tied to the weapon belts cinched around their waists. They're the same kind of pouches as the one I have stuffed into my backpack, which I haven't seen since Aren knocked me out. Those pouches hold anchor-stones the same as mine does.

The fae notice me and a whisper passes through the camp. When their silver eyes meet mine, they end their conversations. Pretty soon, everyone's staring. No one's muttering a syllable.

Blue lightning flashes over their skin, and the hair on the back of my neck prickles. These people despise me, especially the trio sitting on logs several paces to my right. Swords lie in scabbards on the ground at their feet, and two of the men's shirts are stained red. They're the attackers Kyol engaged when they tried to block my escape. At the time, there were six of them. Some didn't survive. That bothers me even though it shouldn't. Those deaths are their own fault. When I track fae for the Court, Kyol always tries to capture our targets. He only kills if it's necessary. These rebels made it necessary when they attacked me.

"Aren!" A female voice shatters the silence. She closes the inn's front door, then hurries down the porch steps, and the entire camp is suddenly in motion welcoming Aren back. It's clear everyone here respects him, and I have to admit he has a certain amount of charisma. I watch him grin and shake hands, and though I don't understand what's being said, I get the impression he's shrugging off what he's just done. That's irritating. Abducting me might not have been difficult, but there *will* be repercussions. I'll make sure of it.

The woman who called Aren's name rushes forward and throws her arms around his neck. He returns her embrace, but turns his hips away in a safe-hug. It's a platonic hug between friends, though I'm positive she wants it to be more. With shells braided through her gold-blond hair and stone bracelets clinking together on her wrists, she's beautiful. And important, too, if her clothing is any indication. She's dressed in a bright blue tunic and clean, snug-fitting pants. The material looks expensive, like only-affordable-to-nobles expensive, and her collar and the tunic's flowing hem are adorned with chips of gemstones. Everyone notices her. Aren does, too, I'm sure, but maybe he has a prettier girl tucked away somewhere?

While he's distracted with his homecoming, I experiment with a small, almost insignificant step backward. No one seems to notice, so I retreat another inch. I can't outrun the fae. I guess I'm hoping I can put some distance between me and the camp before anyone figures out I'm gone, but I don't make it one full stride before Aren turns. I freeze and don my best innocent expression.

"This is the *nalkin-shom*," he says to his audience.

I frown. I've never learned the fae's language—humans aren't allowed to—but I'm pretty sure what he called me is an insult.

"You didn't kill her," the pretty female says. She scrutinizes me with obvious contempt. I don't like her either, and it's not just because she's beautiful. The only reason she spoke in English was to unsettle me, to let me know that killing me had been a very real option. The reminder *does* bother me, but I manage to keep my chin up and glare.

"This is Lena, daughter of Zarrak," Aren says to me. "She'll show you to your room."

Her scowl deepens. "*She* gets a room?"

"Yes. Make sure it's one on the third floor. She needs to get some rest before we decide what we're going to do with her."

"You mean, before you decide if you're going to kill me." A moment passes before I realize I spoke those words out loud.

Aren smiles. "And, Lena, make sure the room's not near one of the oak trees. I think our *nalkin-shom* has an affinity for jumping out of windows." He winks at me. "Enjoy your stay, McKenzie."

"Come on," Lena snaps as Aren unbuckles his weapon belt and walks toward a trio of waiting fae. I consider ignoring her until she folds her slender but toned arms across her chest and raises an eyebrow, looking all too ready for a fight. We might be close to the same height and weight, but I'm pretty sure the daughter of Zarrak can kick my ass—I'm pretty sure all the fae here can.

THREE

❖

NEAR AS I can tell, the camp is divided into two groups: those who want to kill me and those who want to use me. I'd like to say a majority is taking my side, but it's not even split down the middle. Two-thirds of the fae voted with Lena, who seems to be the biggest advocate for my death.

I'm standing on the inn's front porch with the rebels staring up at me like I'm on some kind of auction block. The sun's almost gone, and I have to squint to make out the faces in the growing darkness. I know better than to ask them to turn on a light, though. Not only can fae see better than humans in the dark, but I highly suspect they've had someone cut off the electricity to the inn. The room Lena shoved me into for twelve hours was stripped bare of everything except a rickety old bed. Not even a lightbulb was left in the single socket in the ceiling. They gutted the house of human technology.

Honestly, I'm surprised they risked transporting me in a vehicle last night. Even if the van was the most basic model, it was a complicated piece of tech, and tech screws with a fae's powers.

They call what they do *amajur*. I call it magic. Almost all fae are able to manipulate the atmosphere—that's how they create fissures between our worlds. Others can create illusions, animate small, nonliving objects, suppress sound, control the elements . . . Everyday things we do on Earth with our technologies, they do in the Realm with their magic. The thing is, because of human influence, some of those magics have become extinct. Fae are no longer able to build gates or glimpse the future. Other magics like healing and empathy are endangered. That's part of the reason why the Court is at war with the rebels. Aren and his people ignore the laws against bringing human artifacts and culture into the Realm. King Atroth has to take action to protect the fae's magic.

I refocus on the lynching party. Oddly, I'm more annoyed than afraid. Maybe it's shock. Maybe it's foolishness. Or maybe it's Aren. He's sitting on a wooden bench a few paces to my right with his boots propped on top of the porch rail. He's on the "use me" side of the debate, and though he hasn't said a word in my defense—he hasn't said anything since this trial began—I figure his vote has to weigh more than the others'. I hope it does, at least.

Lena says something in their language and the fae go quiet. Seconds tick by. As the silence stretches, my discomfort grows.

"It's decided, then," Lena says in English, laying a silver-eyed glare on me.

My heart slams against my chest. Tension gathers in my shoulders and my leg muscles tighten, ready to run, but nobody moves. I think that's a good sign. A majority may have voted to kill me, but maybe no one wants to do the deed.

The scowl on Lena's pretty face deepens. She unsheathes a dagger from the leather scabbard at her hip, climbs the porch steps, and holds the weapon out toward Aren. "It needs to be done."

She doesn't have the guts to do it herself. I think she's a coward for that, but I'm also relieved. Maybe these people do have some type of moral compass. I imagine it's a hell of a lot harder killing someone in cold blood than killing them in the middle of a fight; not to mention it's wrong. The Court wouldn't do this.

Aren doesn't look like he's going to accept the dagger. He's still lounged back on the bench, his arms folded across his chest, his eyes locked on me. I return his stare while I wait with the rest of the fae for his decision.

He takes his boots off the rail, leans forward. My heart drops when his gaze shifts to the weapon in Lena's hand.

No. Surely this is a ploy. He isn't going to kill me. He needs me. He's just trying to scare me into cooperating. Right? *Right?*

When he takes the dagger, I dig my fingernails into my palms to keep my hands from shaking.

"Sure you don't want to read the shadows for us?" Aren asks. None of his usual mirth is in his voice. He's completely serious. He's going to kill me if I don't do what he wants.

"Trade me," I blurt out.

He cocks his head to the side and his eyes leave mine to travel slowly down to my feet and then slowly back up. The tiniest smirk tugs at the corner of his mouth.

"How much do you think you're worth, *nalkin-shom*?"

"She's stalling," Lena interjects before I can answer. "We can't let the Court have her back."

Damn right, I'm stalling. She would be, too, if she were surrounded by people who wanted to slit her throat.

"Maybe we can get Roop and Kexin back," Trev speaks up to my left.

"Or maybe Mrinn," another says. Others chime in with more suggestions. There's no doubt I'm valuable—few humans have the Sight; fewer still have the ability to read the shadows—so maybe this will work. I let out a pent-up breath and imagine my chance of survival cranking up to 30 . . . 40 . . . hell, maybe even 50 percent.

Lena looks at the fae gathered on the lawn. "We don't know if any of them are alive."

"The Court doesn't know *she's* alive," someone says. It's a good point, and I think about recommending they take a picture of me to send to the king, maybe with me holding the *Frankfurter Times* or whatever the hell the local paper is called.

I snort. Like they have a camera here. Even if they did, no one would dare touch it.

Aren leans forward, rests his forearms on his knees, and clasps the hilt of the dagger between his hands. The world's waiting on his decision. Again. Must be nice to have that much influence.

His face is expressionless when he stands. I feel cold and detached, like I'm someone else watching the end of my life play out. I'm half a second away from a desperate, destined-to-fail escape attempt when Aren says, "Care to make a wager?"

I blink, then frown. "Wager?"

He hands the dagger back to Lena. "Yes. A wager."

Okay. I'll play this game. For now. "Depends on what you're bidding."

His smile is full of mischief. "There's only one thing you're interested in, *nalkin-shom*. I'm willing to offer it."

I pause, consider a snarky response, decide against it. "You're offering me my freedom?"

He crosses his arms over his chest and leans a shoulder against the porch column. "If you can map one of my fae to within a hundred feet, yes."

A hundred feet. Shit. That's accurate. I've done it before—twice, in fact—but I'm pretty sure luck played a role in both of those readings. My luck has sucked these last twenty-four hours. I doubt I've had a sudden change in fortune.

"What do you want if I can't do it?" I ask, though I know what his answer will be.

"You'll shadow-read for me," he says. He's in all-out mirth-mode now, and it's getting under my skin. Even though he knows my reputation, he's certain I can't do it. For good reason, too. The best shadow-readers usually map their targets to within three, four hundred feet. I routinely do it in half of that. That's why I'm an asset to the Court. When a fae fissures to the location I mark, he's almost always within arrow-range of his target.

Lena steps forward. When Aren doesn't look at her, she touches his elbow. "Even if she's half as good as the rumors suggest, we can't trust her."

That's true. I don't know why he's willing to make this bet. Does he think I'm less likely to send him into an ambush this way? Like if I lose a wager, fair and square, I'll willingly work for them, and not pull any tricks?

It doesn't matter. If there's a chance to earn my freedom, I have to take it.

"If I lose, I'll read one fissure."

Aren's eyes don't leave mine. "You'll read as many as I need."

"Two," I offer.

"All of them until I'm satisfied, McKenzie."

I fold my arms. "If you're going to be like that, then I'm back to offering one."

His perma-smirk doesn't waver. "I'm offering you your freedom."

"You're asking me to hurt the Court."

"They're not your people."

No, but some of them I consider friends. I don't have many of those. If I'm counting only humans, there's just Paige. She overlooks my odd behavior and frequent, unannounced absences. She's like a sister to me, and since I cut ties with my mom and dad, she's the only family I have.

Kyol's not family. He's something else entirely.

I ignore the ache in my chest and straighten my shoulders. There's only one solution here: I won't let myself lose the wager. "Fine. I'll do it."

"Good." Aren turns his silver gaze on the gathering of fae who've been watching our exchange, and then he trots down the steps. He pulls Trev a few paces away and whispers something—a location, I presume—into his ear. They're standing by an old, wooden picnic table that sits on a bed of white rocks. My attention locks on to something resting on the end of one of its benches. My backpack.

I'm not sure if I'm allowed off the porch, but the closer I am to Trev when he fissures out, the more details I'll be able to see in the shadows, so I take a chance and walk down the three steps. Plus, my backpack is right *there*, just a few more feet away. My cell phone is in its inside pocket. My wallet. My collection of anchor-stones.

None of the fae stops me as I walk forward, but hands move toward sword hilts. Worry is etched on some of their faces. Aren and Lena might not think I can pinpoint Trev's location, but many of the others aren't sure. A quiet murmur passes through them. I overhear *nalkin-shom* muttered more than once. They say the word like I'm some kind of monster.

"Ready?" Aren asks. Two more steps and I'll be standing

over my backpack. I want to fish out my phone, turn on its GPS,
and call for help, but I stop short. There's no way the fae are
going to stand there and let me dig through my bag. There's no
way I can grab it and run. Attempting it might get me killed.

I plant my feet in front of Aren and nod. "I'm ready."

Trev rips open a fissure. The slash of white light makes me
squint, but it's only there a few seconds. As soon as Trev
enters it, he becomes lost in the brightness. It winks out of
existence a moment later, leaving only its afterimage behind.
I blink until that image blurs and shimmers, darkens and
twists. Shadows creep in from the edges of my vision. They
start out as large, elusive outlines. Continents. A continent. I
blink again and the shadows shift, shrink, then narrow to a
bony spine. A mountain range. East Coast, I think. Yes. Definitely East Coast. Trev's traveled to a region of the Realm
known as Mashikar.

"Give me pen and paper," I say.

"We don't have any," is Aren's languid response.

I scowl, but don't look away from the shadows. When
I read for the Court, Kyol always has a fae carry what I need.
I know there's paper around here somewhere, but Aren's being
difficult, stalling, because the shadows will stay in my memory for only so long.

"I have a notebook in my backpack."

"Oh," Aren responds. "We cleaned out your bag. Got rid of
your tech and things."

This time, I do glance at Aren. He smiles, and Lena laughs
behind him. I clench my teeth, close the distance to my backpack, and lift its flap. Two big, bright blue eyes stare back at
me. A *kimki*. It's sort of a cross between a ferret and a cat with
a long, supile body and mouselike ears. When the moon's light
touches its curled front paws, it crinkles its nose and a ruffle
runs through its silver-tipped fur.

Aren lowers his hand to the bag, palm up. The *kimki* stares
at me a few seconds more before it scurries up Aren's arm and
perches across his shoulders. Another ruffle runs through its
sleek fur and the silver fades until the animal is snow-white.

Aren reaches up to scratch behind its ears. "His name's
Sosch. *Kimkis* flush silver when they're near gates or other
things they're attracted to, so he must really like you. He

curled up in your backpack the moment he caught your scent in it."

Sosch blinks innocently at me.

I glare at Aren. "I . . . You . . ." The bastard's tricked me. This is why he was willing to make a bet. He set me up to fail, and now he looks so . . . so *entertained* by my reaction.

No. No way. I am *not* losing like this.

I reach down to the bed of rocks beneath the picnic table and pick up the largest one I can find. It's sharp on one end, and as I straighten, it takes all my self-control not to chuck it at Aren's head. I don't have time for that. My memory of the shadows is fading fast.

I face the two fae sitting on the table. "Move."

They glance at the rock in my hand, at each other, then back at me. I'm about to shove them both off the table when they scoot off its edge and stand out of the way. I fist my rock pointy-side down in my right hand and begin to carve the shadows. The wood is old and damp with humidity. It gives way to my makeshift knife. I sketch quickly, seeing the shimmers and shifts of the shadows in my mind's eye. I draw the curve of a river down the craggy side of a mountain. A village lines its west bank, but that's not where Trev fissured to. He's somewhere in the farmland on the opposite bank.

My map's scale changes when I narrow his location down to a smaller area. I focus in on that, trying to remember distinguishing features in the shadows. There was an orchard, I think. Right there.

I mark the spot, but I have no clue if Trev is in the orchard or in the farmhouse half a mile away. Where is he? *Where?*

The shadows tell me nothing, and a moment later, they vanish from my memory. Shit. In frustration, I stab my rock into the orchard.

Wait. I focus on my map.

A rock in the orchard.

Yes.

I pick up my rock to scratch an *X* near the edge of the orchard.

"He's there." I point. "Near Carbada."

As soon as I voice the name of the city, Aren's grin vanishes. I don't know which of us is more surprised. He's visibly stunned, but I'm downright astounded because I know the location that magically locked into Aren's mind isn't just within a hundred feet of Trev's location; it's practically underneath his boots.

Holy crap, I'm good.

I push away from the picnic table, and with an unwavering gaze and a little attitude, I tell Aren, "That's what I'm worth."

He sets Sosch on the ground. The whole camp must be shocked, because nobody says a word, not even Lena, who's still staring at my scratched-out map.

"Have a nice life," I say, and then I turn on my heel and head for the narrow trail that brought me here. I keep my spine straight, my chin up, but I'm half expecting a dagger to be thrown at my back. I listen for the sound of metal sliding free of a sheath, but hear only the wind, the chirping of crickets, and the shuffling of feet. I'm almost to the tree line when Aren finally speaks.

"Stop her."

I wince but continue walking until a fae cuts off my path. He reaches for my arm, but stops just short of touching me. I can't outrun him. I can't fight him. With a sigh, I return to Aren.

I meet his eyes. "Glad to know you're a man of your word."

"I said I'd give you your freedom and I will. Eventually." He pauses to pass his silver-eyed gaze over me as if he can't quite figure me out. I don't like the scrutiny, especially not when something in my chest tightens in response. "But I can't let you go right now. Especially not after seeing what you can do. You're amazing." A small smile finds its way back to his mouth. "I'm sorry, McKenzie, but you're going to have to stay with us until this war ends."

"The war's never going to end."

He shrugs. "I guess you're going to be here awhile, then." His gaze shifts to the fae beside me. "Take her up to her room, then find Sethan. We need to talk."

Aren takes one last look at the map scrawled into the picnic table and shakes his head as if he still can't believe it.

"Aren," I call when he starts to walk away. I don't want to say another word to him, don't want to look into his silver eyes a moment longer, but I have to know.

He turns.

"The king's sword-master," I say past the lump in my throat. "He'll kill you for taking me."

If Kyol's dead, I have no doubt Aren will boast about it. I hold my breath and my heart shatters and mends a thousand times while I wait for his response. I'm too terrified to hope, too desperate not to. Finally, after what seems like millennia, Aren dips his head in acknowledgment.

"It will be an interesting fight."

FOUR

◆▪◆

AS SOON AS the door to my room closes, I waste no time stripping the sheets off the bed. I test their strength. Both are ratty but they're strong enough to resist my attempts to rip them. Whether they're strong enough to hold my weight, I don't know yet, but I'm not sitting here for another twelve hours alone with my thoughts.

I walk to the window. My room faces a bright, full moon. Its light struggles through the treetops, mottling the surface of the picnic table. The rest of the lot is deserted. I don't know if that makes me lucky or the rebels careless, but I plan to take advantage of the situation. Problem is, I'm three stories up and two sheets aren't going to make a long enough rope.

I try again to rip the cotton. I don't break a single thread. At least it's stronger than it looks, but I need something sharp, something that will cut.

The bed is the only piece of furniture in the room. Kneeling beside it, I inspect underneath for anything that might snag the fabric. The mattress rests on a network of metal links. It's too dark to see anything useful, so I pat around until I feel a loose link. I work it around until one end pulls free from the bed frame. Once that's accomplished, I stab the metal through the center of one sheet, brace both my feet on the bed, lean back, and pull.

"Ha!" I gloat to the empty room when the sheet rips perfectly down the middle. I repeat the process with the other sheet, ending up with four halves. Tying each of these together, I take my makeshift rope to the window and peek out. Still no patrol.

I test each knot. When they all hold, I clamp down on a sudden surge of anxiety. I have to do this. I won't wait around for Kyol to save me.

Kyol's alive.

I close my eyes, silently say a quick prayer of thanks. Our relationship—if you can call it that—has been awkward these past few months. It's my fault. I'm trying to be a normal human. I've concentrated on my studies. I've looked for a real job. I've even let Paige set me up on a number of blind dates. The guys have all been nice, and I've tried to like them— really, I have—but, so far, I haven't been interested in a second date.

Frustrated, I shove open the window. Christ, it's loud. It screeches like it hasn't been opened in decades. I hold my breath and listen. No footsteps sound from the hallway; no voices shout from outside. I breathe again, but count to a hundred just in case. After one last scan of the inn's yard, I tie one end of the rope around the radiator bolted beneath the window and then toss the other end outside. Even with the knots, it reaches almost to the ground.

It's a heck of a lot harder climbing out than I imagined, and I'm not sure how to go about it without getting myself killed. I end up straddling the ledge, a difficult thing to do since the window isn't that big. Slowly, carefully, I let myself slip down until my left leg, which had been inside the inn, pulls over the edge and scrapes down the side wall. I have no idea how much noise I'm making, but at this point, I can't do anything about it.

I grab the rope with my right hand, then let go of the windowsill with my left. As soon as I do, I start falling. I tighten my hands around the sheet, but I'm sliding too fast. My palms burn until I hit my first thick knot and yelp—softly, so as not to draw attention. I glance up at the window, wonder if I should try to get back inside. Shaking my head, I decide against it, grit my teeth, then let the next sheet sear through my palms. I meet another knot. Then another.

There's blood on the white cotton now. I'm still half a story above the ground when it hurts too much to hold on. I manage to land on my feet, but a sharp twinge of pain shoots through my legs and I crumple over. As I'm down on all fours drawing cold air into my lungs, it occurs to me just how big an idiot I am for trying a stunt I've seen done only on TV. I could have broken my neck.

But I didn't, I remind myself. I'm alive. I'm outside. I'm alone.

Careful to keep my blistered hands off the grass, I push to my knees and stand. I wait a second for a wave of dizziness to pass—God, I need some sleep—then quietly move away from the inn.

Thump.

I stop, glance over my shoulder.

Aren. Shit. He must have heard the window opening after all and followed me down. He stares up at my makeshift rope, gives it a little tug, then turns his silver eyes on me.

"You're certainly resourceful," he says. "I must give you that."

His hands don't look sheet-burned. Mine are on fire. I try to hide them, try to appear unconcerned that he's interrupted my escape attempt, but when he strides forward, I tense. What if I've made him change his mind? What if he thinks it's too risky to keep me alive?

He doesn't hit or scold me. He takes one of my hands between his and flares his magic. Blue lightning skitters down his arms and his palm is suddenly a warm compress against mine. After a few uncomfortable seconds, the achy warmth changes. It feels good now. So does the electric tingle pulsing toward my elbow. I allow him to touch me longer than I should, long enough for some of the jagged blue lines to leap from his skin to mine. They're bright in the moonlight. I watch them pirouette around my forearm, very aware Aren's watching them as well.

"Edarratae," he says. "Chaos lusters."

"I know what they are," I tell him, trying to ignore the sensations the lightning, the *edarratae*, sends careening through me.

"You can let go." I try to tug my hand free.

"You could have killed yourself." He releases my right hand to take my left, carefully avoiding the watch strapped around my wrist. This palm isn't hurt as badly as the other, but he heals the skin with another warm touch.

"That would have made Lena happy."

His gaze meets mine. "Yes. Yes, it would have."

I don't like the way he continues staring into my eyes. It reminds me of Kyol and how mesmerized he always is by them. To me, they're nothing extraordinary, just a plain brown color a few shades darker than my hair. My features are slightly different from a fae woman's—my cheekbones aren't quite as prominent, my nose not quite as sharp—but Aren's not analyzing the rest of my face right now. I wish he would because the intensity of his gaze coupled with his chaos lusters triggers a warm, simmering sensation in my stomach. It's not right to feel like this, especially not with Aren, son of Jorreb.

I break eye contact, willing my body to cool and berating myself for reacting to those soft silver eyes. I try to tug my hand free again. I need his *edarratae* gone so I can think clearly.

After another moment, he releases me. I fold my arms across my stomach without looking at my mended palms. Healing is an endangered magic, and it seems wrong that a killer should be gifted with that ability.

Aren motions toward the front of the inn. "Come, *nalkin-shom*. We need to talk."

I keep my feet rooted to the ground. "I have a name. You don't have to insult me."

"Insult you?" He cocks his head. "*Nalkin-shom* is one of the least insulting titles you've been given."

I frown. "Titles?"

"Yes, titles. *Nalkin-shom* means shadow-witch. Lena prefers to call you *traep-shom*. Shadow-bitch. Some of the other names lose their sting in translation, but there's also shadow-scum, map-whore, kin-killer." He pauses. A grin bends a corner of his mouth, and I swear moonlight twinkles in his eyes. "What? You didn't know you have the reputation of a killer?"

"The Court captures most of the fae I track," I say, trying not to let his smirk get under my skin.

"Fae children have nightmares about you." He grabs my

wrist, waits until his *edarratae* leap up my arm. "Parents tell them if they're bad, the *nalkin-shom* will come for them in the night, sear them with her lightning, and drain them of their magic."

My heart beats in time with the energy pulsing through me. "You're exaggerating."

"Am I?"

"You're the false-blood. If the fae tell stories to scare their children, then they're telling them about you." False-bloods are like cult leaders on crack. They gather a following of the gullible and disillusioned, then wreak havoc on the Realm, claiming to be the chosen progeny of the *Tar Sidhe*, the magically superior fae who ruled the provinces centuries ago. I've hunted down half a dozen false-bloods over the years, some more successful than others, but all of them violent. Aren's the real monster here.

To my surprise, he chuckles. "Come, *nalkin-shom*. You need to meet someone."

He doesn't give me the opportunity to protest. He lets go of my wrist, places his hand on the small of my back, and ushers me forward. We round the corner of the inn. Either the rebels have all fissured out or they're holed up inside the house, all except for Lena, who's on the porch speaking to another fae. He's new. I'd certainly remember if he was one of the onlookers during my sentencing. His blond hair is long and straight, falling over broad shoulders covered by a burgundy cloak. His tunic and black trousers look rich and clean, and the leather scabbard at his hip is in pristine condition, almost as if he's never had to draw his sword. He's either a criminal or a noble. Either way, he has access to *tinril*, the currency used in the Realm, and I can't help but wonder if he's the fae funding Aren's rebellion.

He ends his conversation with Lena as we climb the porch steps.

"This is Sethan, son of Zarrak," Aren says. Lena's brother? I hate him already. "Have a seat, McKenzie."

He places his hand on my shoulder, guiding me to the weathered wooden bench beside the front door. I sink down, partly to get away from his touch and partly because I'm so damn tired. My stomach growls a reminder that I haven't eaten anything since a few hours before my final, and a headache pounds behind my eyes. The least the rebels could have done was given me a scrap of bread when they locked me inside that room.

The fae remain standing. I hate having to look up at them, but I cross my arms, lean back, and wait for Aren to speak.

"Tell us what you know about the Court."

Even though my stomach twists into knots, I keep my gaze steady and—I hope—defiant.

"It's your system of government," I say, sticking with a universally known fact. Well, universally known in the Realm, at least. "It's led by King Atroth, a Descendant of the *Tar Sidhe*, who was elected by the high nobles of the thirteen provinces. The king's—"

"The king told you there are thirteen provinces," Sethan interrupts. It's not quite a question.

"He's shown me maps," I say, then immediately wish I hadn't.

"What kind of maps?"

"Paper ones," I snap. I know what he's fishing for. He wants to know if gates were marked on those maps. That's what this war is about, after all. Control of the gates means control of the Realm's commerce. While fae may be able to fissure from whatever point they choose, they can't drag along wagons full of goods unless they open their fissure at a gate. Anything more than what they can carry will be lost in the In-Between. Several decades ago—long before I first met Kyol—King Atroth's predecessor began regulating their use, requiring merchants to pay a tax to fissure their wares throughout the Realm. The merchants didn't like that, of course, and it doesn't take a genius to figure out why so many have started searching for an alternative Descendant.

Sethan remains unperturbed. "How many gates were there?"

"None," I lie. There were thirty-one, over a dozen more than are marked on the Realm's public maps.

"Then why were you shown the maps?"

"For the same reason he"—I nod toward Aren—"probably shows maps to his shadow-readers: geography." I needed to memorize the Realm's provinces and regions. Without knowing the name of a place, my maps might as well be random scratches on a page. I have to say the name of the region out loud for the magic to lock in, and for the fae I'm with to be able to fissure to the location I mark. It's the one teensy bit of magic that shadow-readers like me can claim.

Lena pushes off the wall. "She's lying. She knows where the Missing Gates are. She's used them."

"I've used the *Provincial* Gates," I tell Sethan. I'm not sure why I feel like I have to explain myself to this fae. He's important—of that, I'm certain—but why haven't I heard his name before?

"We monitor the Provincial Gates," Lena says. "We would have abducted you long before now if you used only those to travel."

I keep my expression neutral, trying not to give any indication that she's right. The Realm used to be made up of hundreds of small kingdoms, each with its own gate, but three thousand years ago, almost all of those gates disappeared in the *Duin Bregga*, a brutal war that translates roughly into "The Dissolution." According to Kyol, the Missing Gates were said to be destroyed, but there were always rumors that some of them remained, and that the locations had just been wiped from the minds of the fae using a magic that's extinct today. When one of King Atroth's aids, with the help of a silver-flushed *kimki*, stumbled upon a gate not marked on any map, those rumors were confirmed. Ever since then, Atroth has been searching for—and finding—other Missing Gates.

"If you want to extend your life," Lena says, taking a step toward me, "you'll give us those gates."

"Lena," Aren cuts in. Then he speaks in their language. She fires something back. Calmly, he speaks again. Whatever he says, she's obviously not happy about it. Sethan barely has time to move out of the way before she yanks open the front door and storms inside, grumbling a litany of what I'm betting are fae curses under her breath. Most likely, they're directed at me.

Whatever. I'm glad to see her go.

Sethan turns his attention back to me. "I'm truly sorry you've been brought into this war. We never wanted to involve humans, but Atroth made it necessary when he began employ-

ing your kind against us. His shadow-readers, you in particu-
lar, have almost destroyed us. We had no choice other than to
take you away from him." He pauses, his silver eyes boring
into me as if he can read my thoughts. He can't. Telepathy isn't
one of the endangered magics; it's one of the extinct and forever lost ones. "We would like your help, McKenzie. And we'd
like to help you."

"Help me?" I snort. "The only thing I need from you is permission to leave."

"And allow Atroth to continue using you?" He shakes his
head. "That's not an option."

"What if I agree not to work for the Court again?"

Sethan's brow wrinkles as if he can't comprehend my question. His eyes narrow and he studies me. I hope he can't read
my expression. I hope he sees my offer as the biggest conces-
sion I can make and not as something I've been planning to do
for several weeks now. Next Saturday, the day I was supposed
to graduate if I hadn't flunked my final exam—and I'm certain
I *did* flunk it—I planned to announce my retirement to the
Court. Avoiding the Realm and everything fae is the only way
I'll be able to live a normal, human life, and in anticipation of
my degree, I filled out an application for an entry-level editor
position in a suburb outside of Houston. I made plans to make
new friends, to join a book club, to go to movies and concerts
and clubs and all the other places normal people have time to
go, but that's not going to happen now, not unless I escape
these fae and discover some way to convince my professor to
let me retake my final.

Thinking about escape makes me turn my attention to the
dark forest. A gentle breeze blows, and I half expect Kyol to
step into the clearing, a silent, deadly figure in the night. A
little tug of longing pulls at my heart.

Aren speaks over the rustling leaves. "She thinks they'll let
her go."

I shift my gaze to the false-blood. "Of course they'll let me
go. They're not the ones who've kidnapped me. They're not
the ones who are trying to blackmail me into working for
them. I'm free to leave whenever I want."

Aren gives Sethan a pointed look. "See."

"See what?" I demand.

"Your ignorance." He grins as if he's just delivered the punch line to a grand ol' joke. He crosses the porch and rests a hand on the knob of the front door. "Talk to her, Sethan. Then tell me what you decide."

The door clanks shut behind him. My stomach twists and turns, but this time, I'm not sure if it's because I'm starving or because Aren's left me alone with an unfamiliar fae. It makes no sense, I know. Aren's the man who's abducted me, who's brought me halfway across the planet, and who's responsible for the massacre at Brykeld. The thing is, other than knocking me unconscious to keep me quiet in the engineering building, he hasn't hurt me. In fact, he's been almost kind. He could have—probably *should* have—ripped into me for my escape attempt. Instead, he healed me.

Sethan leans against the rail. "Aren thinks the Court has misled you. He thinks if you learn the truth of this war, you'll work with us."

"I already know the truth." The knots in my stomach tighten. I'm not completely delusional. I know how easy it would be for the Court to mislead me. I don't speak their language. I don't understand their politics. I know only the history that's been told to me. But I've *seen* what these rebels have done and Kyol . . . Kyol wouldn't be on the wrong side of the war. He's a good man, and even though I want him to be more, he's a friend. Has been for the last ten years. He couldn't have faked every moment he's been with me.

"The king's told you there are thirteen provinces," Sethan says. "He's lying. There are seventeen. I'm sure he's also told you we want complete control of the gates. We don't. We want equal access to them and reasonable tariffs."

Who *is* this guy? "You could have discussed that with Atroth years ago—he gave you the chance—but all Aren's concerned about is taking the Silver Palace. False-bloods are power-hungry like that."

Sethan gives me a smile that he probably intends to be patient and pleasant, but I find it patronizing. "Aren doesn't intend to sit on the throne, McKenzie. I do."

I sit very still, trying to keep the reverberations of shock from making their way to my face. *Sethan* is the false-blood, not Aren? The king has no clue about this. If he did, Kyol or

Lord General Radath would have had me searching for him every time we hunted a rebel, just in case he was around.

"I'm not a false-blood," Sethan continues. "The Zarrak bloodline is purer than Atroth's. Other fae's are even purer than mine, but they have all been killed, appeased, or made *tor'um*."

Tor'um is a word I know. It translates roughly to "walkers," a derogatory name given to fae who don't have enough magic to fissure. Most fae who are that weak are born that way, but some lose their magic later on in life. When they do, they don't exactly stay sane. Scary thing is, the numbers of both are on the rise. Even with Atroth regulating the Realm's gates, he's been unable to reverse the slow decline of the fae's magic. Despite laws against it, fae take human plants, animals, sometimes even technology, into the Realm. The big problem is that there are literally hundreds more gates on Earth than there are in the Realm. The Court doesn't have enough soldiers to guard them all, so some merchants have set up shop in my world to avoid taxes and regulations. Those fae don't care what they fissure into the Realm so long as they make a profit.

"You don't believe me," Sethan says.

"That you're a Descendant of the *Tar Sidhe* or that you have a stronger claim?" I'm not sure what to believe, but I sure as hell am interested in finding out more about him, Aren, and the rebellion. This can be my last hurrah before I retire. I'll do a little espionage, plan a little escape, report my findings to the king, then get myself a job and a real life on Earth.

I keep my gaze steady. "If either of those were true, the high nobles would have voted for you to become king."

"They would have if all seventeen provinces had been permitted an opinion."

"Nine of the thirteen voted for Atroth," I say, even though I'm not sold on the seventeen province thing. "Do the math. He still would have won."

"The high nobles would have voted differently," he says, confident. "There are two sides to every war, McKenzie. The king has told you only one version of our conflict's origins."

And you're only telling me your version, I want to point out, but a deep, repetitive banging distracts me. I scan the clearing, see nothing. It sounds like it might be coming from inside the inn. Sethan doesn't appear concerned about it, and I wouldn't care much either except for the fact that my head pounds with each erratic beat. I pinch the bridge of my nose, hoping to find some relief.

The front door opens and Aren reemerges carrying a leaf-lined basket of fruit and cheeses topped by a circle of flatbread. He holds the basket out. It takes all my effort not to wrench it from his hands and dig in. The Realm's fruits are decadent—more luscious and sweet than any Earth-grown apple or melon I've ever tasted—but I force myself to fold my hands in my lap.

He frowns. "You haven't eaten anything in almost a day."

"I don't know what you put in it."

His laugh startles me. "You're incredibly stubborn, *nalkin-shom*."

"My name is McKenzie." I manage to refrain from rolling my eyes, but this *nalkin-shom* crap is getting old.

Aren pops a purple slice of fruit into his mouth, holds the basket out again. I stare at it, my stomach rumbling.

"Do I need to try the cheese as well?" he asks.

When I realize it doesn't make sense to poison me, I heave a sigh and take the basket. He doesn't have to be devious if he wants to kill me. A knife across the throat would do the trick and none of the rebels would complain. Most likely, they'd celebrate.

My fingers bring a wedge of soft white cheese to my mouth. It touches my tongue, triggers my taste buds. If Aren and Sethan weren't watching me, I'd sink back against the bench and moan. The cheese is absolutely delicious, but then, in my half-starved state, I'd be content even with the bitter-bark the fae are so fond of.

I chew and swallow and reach for another wedge, ignoring Aren's satisfied expression as he turns to speak to Sethan in Fae. I tear a strip off the flatbread and fold it around an orange-tinted cheese. Before I finish that one, another is on its way to my mouth. I save the fruit for dessert and try to slow my pace. Even so, I devour the whole basket in a few minutes. Now, if I could just get some sleep, I'd feel so much better. Even a five-minute nap would be heavenly.

The two fae finish their conversation as I set aside the basket. Sethan doesn't look happy.

"I trust your judgment, Aren, and I hope you're right. McKenzie." He gives me a shallow bow before he trots down the porch steps. I watch him walk into the forest. A blink of light indicates he's fissured out. Unfortunately, his shadows are unreadable behind the foliage.

"I've bought you an extension on life," Aren says, leaning against the porch column. His casualness and the intensity in his silver eyes make an odd combination. I don't like the way he's observing me. I like even less the way the moonlight glows behind him, making him seem mysterious, almost debonair. When he doesn't say anything else or look away, I shift on the wooden bench.

"Okay," I say slowly, because the silence *needs* to be broken. "Do you want me to thank you?"

"You'll help us eventually." He sounds so certain.

I shake my head. "No. My allegiance is to Ky— King Atroth."

He smiles a little. "I'll earn your trust."

"I'll doubt everything you say."

He chuckles, pushes away from the column, and crosses the porch to stand in front of me. He takes my right hand in his. As he pulls me to my feet, I make the mistake of looking into his eyes. This close, I can become lost in them, especially with the heat of his *edarratae* traveling up my arm. He dips his head, staring down at me with mirth on his lips.

"You will be an interesting challenge." He draws a finger along the line of my jaw and lightning floods inside me, shooting down my neck and into my core. I'm lost for a moment, unbalanced, and burning with a need I'm afraid to identify.

Finally, Aren steps back. He opens the front door. "Come, *nalkin-shom*. I'll tuck you in."

When at last I regain my composure, I give the bastard my coldest glare. For some reason, he finds my defiance amusing.

FIVE

◆

I BECAME AN insomniac ten years ago. I was a sophomore in high school, president of my class and enrolled in every advanced course the school offered. My teachers loved me, my friends respected me, and my parents were proud. Meeting the fae changed all that. At first, I wasn't sleeping because I thought I was going crazy, hallucinating because no one else could see the lightning-covered people searching the corridors and classrooms. And it was clear they were searching for something. For someone. For me.

A false-blood named Thrain realized I had the Sight and dragged me into the Realm. He used me to wage a war against the king. When I refused to read the shadows for him, he starved me. He hit me. He threatened my friends and family. I had no choice except to help him. No choice, that is, until Kyol freed me. He returned me to my world, and I couldn't sleep because my blood burned in my veins when I lay down at night. Kyol intrigued me. He protected me, and when King Atroth asked me to help him capture Thrain, I didn't hesitate to say yes. That was when the nightmares began. Some of Thrain's fae didn't run or surrender. They fought. They killed. They died, and I couldn't sleep because I was haunted.

Now I can't sleep because I might never see Kyol again. I was sixteen when we first met and he was . . . older. The

Realm ages people—both fae and humans—slower than Earth. Kyol looked like he was somewhere in his twenties, but he could have been twice that for all I knew. He wasn't Atroth's sword-master yet, but he was his friend. He became my friend, and we eventually became *something*. In the last decade, the only nights on which I've had a peaceful, restful sleep were the nights when Kyol watched over me. Despite my resolution to lead a normal fae-free life, that hasn't changed.

I've been staring at the ceiling for hours, surrounded by my fears. Occasionally, they loosen their stranglehold and my heavy eyelids close, but the creaks and groans of the inn wake me no matter how soft they are.

Footsteps stop outside my room. I feign sleep as the door creaks open. Someone walks inside, clears a throat. I keep my eyes shut and refuse to twitch.

"McKenzie."

Even though the sheetless slab of springs beneath me could double as a torture device, I still don't budge.

"McKenzie," the someone says, louder this time. I don't recognize the voice. It's female, but it's not Lena.

"McKenzie Lewis."

I crack open my lids to glare. I end up frowning instead. The light coming in from the doorway is just bright enough to see that the fae staring down at me is wearing human clothing: jeans paired with a tight red top, jingling bracelets, and a triple-layered black-beaded necklace. It's hard to be sure in the dim room, but it looks like a string of garnets and *premthyste*, a pearllike stone found in the southernmost province of the Realm, is braided through a lock of her dark, silky hair. I think I recognize the pattern the stones make. If I'm right, she's a daughter of Cyneayen, Tayshken Province's ruling noble.

"The sun is up," she says, nodding uselessly toward my boarded-up window. Not even a crack of light peeks between the wooden planks. The banging that gave me such a headache last night was Lena going to town with a hammer and nails. I'd have better luck clawing my way through the wall than through the layer of wood covering the window.

"It's time to get up."

"Not back home, it isn't." I close my eyes, willing her to go away.

She huffs out a breath. "I have instructions to place you in Lena's care if you're uncooperative."

Well, there's nothing like a threat to get you going in the morning. I sit up . . . and barely manage to suppress a groan. Despite not sleeping well, I didn't toss and turn much, and damn, my body's stiff. I guess jumping fences and dangling off the sides of buildings will do that to you. I rub my neck, trying to massage out some of the pain.

"Aren said you might be sore." The fae holds out her hand and uncurls her fingers to reveal two little white pills.

"What's that?"

"Ibuprofen."

My eyes narrow. "Fae don't take human medications."

"They're not for me."

Fae anatomies aren't all that different from humans', but they're not supposed to have anything to do with our food or culture. Not that the medicine is directly hurting her. If it was, lightning would be circling the pills in her palm like writhing blue snakes, but nontech items from my world are gradually weakening the Realm's magic. Of course, we're not in the Realm right now so the only one hurting here is me.

After reminding myself that poisoning me doesn't make sense, I pluck the two tablets from her hand. It takes a moment to work enough moisture into my mouth to swallow them. Unfortunately, it'll take another twenty minutes or so before they kick in.

"Who are you?" I ask.

"I'm . . . Kelia."

Interesting hesitation there. I've never met a fae who, on their first introduction, doesn't tell me who they're a son or daughter of. Are we hiding our ancestry, perhaps?

"Is that *premthyste* in your hair?" I'm sure I recognize the stone now. Only a few prominent bloodlines wear name-cords these days. She has to be a daughter of Cyneayen. If I remember Lord Raen, elder of Cyneayen, correctly, he's notoriously anti-human. He doesn't speak a word of English and every time I've run into him he's scowled as if I've put a bad taste in his mouth. This girl—Kelia—has impeccable English. She's perfected an American accent and could blend in with a crowd of humans so long as no one around her has the ability to see *edarratae*.

Her lips narrow into a thin line. "Aren wants me to teach you our language."

I might have called her out for avoiding my question if her statement didn't give me pause. Teach me to speak Fae? Why the hell would Aren want that? He speaks English. So do Sethan and Lena and anyone else who might need to work with humans. I wouldn't be surprised if half the rebellion has mastered my language. Plus, won't I be more of a liability if I can eavesdrop on their conversations? As it is now, they could detail their entire war strategy and I wouldn't have a clue what they were saying.

"The king's forbidden that." It's not that I don't want to learn to speak Fae—I'd love to—but I'm used to not knowing it. I'm used to keeping our cultures as separate as possible.

"He's also forbidden us from learning the languages of your world," Kelia says without missing a beat. "That hasn't stopped us. It shouldn't stop you, not unless you're afraid of the Court."

Afraid of the . . . Oh, I see his angle now. "Aren starts big, doesn't he?"

Kelia's eyebrows rise. "What?"

"Never mind." This is a devilishly clever move on his part. He's making a statement with this offer: the Court might not trust me enough to learn their language, but he does, or so he wants me to believe. Nice try, but I'm not stupid. The only way I might—*might*—have believed his intentions were pure is if I learned their language, then he let me go. Unfortunately for him, he and Sethan both made it clear that's not an option, not until this war's over. I won't fall for Aren's manipulations.

But I will take advantage of them.

"Okay. I'm game," I say, standing too quickly. My muscles protest the movement and my vision blackens around the edges.

She stares a moment. "After breakfast." She starts to turn, then suddenly she grabs my hand.

I ball my other hand into a fist, ready to defend myself.

"Is that a watch?" she asks.

I hesitate. "Um, yeah." It's a cheap digital watch, $14.99 at Wal-Mart.

Kelia's silver eyes widen. "Can I wear it?"

I pull my hand free from hers, rubbing it against my jeans to chase out the tingle of her *edarratae*. "It's tech."

"Small tech," she says dismissively. "Please? I'll give it back."

What the hell is wrong with her? Kyol hates it when I wear my watch, and I'm honestly surprised Aren didn't demand I take it off so he could send it to whatever tech graveyard my cell phone ended up in.

"Please?" she says again.

Well, it's her magic. I unstrap the watch and hold it out. Chaos lusters spring up her arm when she takes it. Not bothered by their increased activity, she tries to fasten the band around her wrist. It's obvious she's never done this before—why would she have?—so I help her insert the metal hook into a hole in the rubber. Beneath the strap, her skin glows a faint blue.

She rotates her wrist, staring mesmerized at the digital face. The light coming in through the door wasn't quite enough for me to make out the time, but she's fae. She can probably see the numbers.

"Thank you," she says without looking at me.

"There's a . . . You see that little button on the right? If you press it, the face will light up."

"Really?" She presses it and a trio of needle-thin *edarratae* rush up her finger and spread over the back of her hand like tiny blue spider veins. They disappear when she releases the button and then reappear when she presses it again. After lighting up the watch a dozen times, she finally drops her hands to her sides. The intrigue leaves her face when she realizes I've been studying her.

She clears her throat. "It's time for breakfast."

I close my eyes and press my palms into my temples. After three solid days of nothing but repeating everything Kelia says and naming everything she points to, I've reached my breaking point.

"Enough!" I yell.

"*Na raumel e'Sidhe,*" she responds calmly. *In the language of the Fae.*

"No. No more. I need a break." Plus, I can't remember the

Fae word for "enough," and I'm exhausted. The only times I've been left alone since Aren brought me here are when the rebels lock me inside my cell.

Okay. Room. And the rebels haven't exactly been awful to me. They've made sure I have plenty to eat and drink, and no one's outright threatened me since that first day, but they're *always* around. They're always watching, scowling, judging. They might as well have me shackled because I haven't had a single chance to escape.

Kelia folds her arms and cocks her hip, waiting, but if she thinks she's even half as stubborn as I am, she's wrong. I've been the perfect student since we began these lessons. I've never in my life crammed so much information into my head in so short a period of time, not even the evening I returned from shadow-reading in the Realm and was forced to pull an all-nighter for an exam I should have spent days studying for.

Kelia lectures me in Fae. I don't have to understand what she's saying—her tone makes her meaning clear—but at this point, I don't care if she turns over my supervision to the daughter of Zarrak. I can't learn one more new word. I won't.

Kelia finally realizes her words are hitting a wall—a very tired, grumpy, unmovable wall. Her shoulders slump as the fight whooshes out of her.

"Fine," she says, a petulant purse to her lips. "You hungry?"

"No." We ate lunch no more than half an hour ago and had a snack a little before that. Besides, I suspect this might be a scheme to get me to start naming foods and cutlery, and I'm serious about not learning another word of Fae today.

I walk to the picnic table and stare at my rock-carved map. My shadow-readings always look like they're drawn by a schizophrenic. This one is worse than my others, bigger and messier with a series of lines that cut off abruptly only to begin again a few inches to the right when my mental map scale zooms. To a normal human, the final sketch probably looks like a kindergartner's drawing, but to a fae who hears me name a city or a region, it's as good as having an imprinted anchor-stone. Without an anchor-stone or a shadow-reader naming the location on his or her map, fae can only fissure to places they've memorized. It's sort of like humans and phone numbers: they *can* remember dozens upon dozens of locations, but if they don't think about them often or dial in on occasion, they tend to forget them completely.

I plop down on top of my map's orchard, rest my elbows on my knees, and stare down at my boots. While I ate breakfast my first morning here, Kelia fissured out. Twenty minutes later, she returned with an armload of clothing. Most of it was for her, but she gave me two pairs of jeans, three new tops, and a pair of black leather boots—*high-heeled*, of course, because comfortable flats would make running away far too tempting. The jeans are just a smidgen too tight. Kelia's assured me they look fine—not that I asked or cared—and that the neckline of my azure blouse isn't too low, but this is definitely not my normal attire. I shop sale racks and wear T-shirts. This look is way too trendy for me. But not too trendy for Kelia.

She sits beside me on the tabletop, fingers the drawstring pouch tied to her belt, and gazes at the overgrown trailhead cutting through the dense tree line. She's been doing that for three days now, gazing at the trail. At first, I thought she was waiting for Aren to return. I haven't seen him since he deposited me in my room and, despite burning curiosity, I haven't asked where he is. Now I'm not so sure he's the reason for Kelia's constant head-turning, not unless she has a crush on him. I'm pretty sure Lena's in love with the guy—I suspect there are very few fae who wouldn't want to jump into bed with him—but Kelia never sounds love-struck when she mentions Aren's name. Maybe she's worried about the Court finding this place? I can only hope.

As I pick at a thick splinter on the edge of the table, my mood plummets. This is one of the reasons I've managed to endure three full days of language cramming. If I let my mind go idle, inevitably I get depressed. It's been four days now and I'm certain no one misses me back home, not even Paige, who is used to my long, sporadic absences. Those absences are the reason why I live alone in an apartment a couple miles from campus. I tried the dorm thing back when I was a freshman, but after being caught one too many times talking to myself— fae almost always choose to remain invisible to normal humans—my roommate requested to be transferred.

I flick the splinter I tore from the table away and search for a distraction. Anything to take my mind off my life.

"Aren," I say, grabbing hold of the first image that pops into my head. "Will he come back?"

Kelia snorts. "Probably."

"Where did he go?"

"The Realm." Her response is short, like she's closing the door to future questions about the false-blood. Or rather, the false-blood's decoy, if I'm to believe Sethan.

"How long have you known him?" I ask.

She stops fiddling with the pouch on her belt and eyes me. "You haven't mentioned his name in three days. Why the sudden interest?"

I shrug.

"Do you miss him?"

This time, it's my turn to frown. "Of course not."

"Most women fawn over him," she says.

Is she actually suggesting I like his company? "He *kidnapped* me."

She tilts her head to the side. "You don't think he's attractive?"

"He's fae." The words tumble out. Not agreement or denial, but they're as heavy as a lie on my tongue.

Kelia's face darkens. "What's that supposed to mean?"

"We don't belong in each other's worlds, let alone each other's beds," I recite, my voice sounding as desolate as Kyol's the day he made the same statement to me.

"You believe that?" she asks.

I force out an empty, "Yes."

Kelia's tone turns acidic. "You're just like the others." She rises off the picnic table. "If you need a break, you can take it in your room."

She starts to walk toward the inn, but stops midstride and pales. I follow her gaze to the trailhead.

A bruised and bloodied Trev limps into the clearing. *Edarratae* flash beneath a thick layer of dirt to disappear under a ripped and blood-soaked tunic. I haven't seen Trev since the night I read his shadows. Including Kelia and Lena, only five fae remained at the inn. They've been watching me like hawks from the front porch all afternoon, but now they abandon their posts and sprint to the wounded rebel.

Kelia reaches him an instant before the others. Her words are panicked. Trev shakes his head, his expression grim. I understand a few words . . . *Court* . . . *heal* . . . *gate*, but then they're all talking at once and too quickly for me to decipher. It doesn't matter, though. The important thing is they're 100 percent engaged in their discussion. No one's so much as thrown a glance in my direction, and the eastern edge of the clearing is no more than ten little-itty-bitty feet away from me.

I don't think. I run. Three long strides and I'm engulfed by the forest.

Adrenaline kicks in as I leap over a rotting tree trunk. I know the fae will have wards surrounding the camp, but I'm a human who has the Sight. I won't exactly see the magical trip wires, but I'll feel them, so I let my skin listen for a hum in the air. When a slight vibration runs across my left arm, I follow my instincts and veer right. The ward won't stop me, but if I run through it, the fae will know exactly where I am. I ignore the branches whipping at my face and arms and push on, faster and faster.

The forest floor plunges beneath my feet. I shuffle-slide down the steep incline in a waterfall of dead leaves, and just manage to regain my balance when the land levels out. I have no idea where I'm going—everywhere looks the same—but I don't slow down. I can't. I've got to get away, to put as much distance as possible between the rebels and me, and find some way to contact Paige.

I run full-steam for two to three minutes before my skin tingles a warning. I skid to a stop, staring into the forest. It's not a ward I'm sensing now. It's them.

The thick canopy blocks out most of the sun's light, and when the wind moves the treetops, shadows dance on the forest's floor. I can't see the fae, but I'm certain they can see me.

Shit. What am I supposed to do now? Run? Fight? Beg for mercy? None of those options appeals to me.

I turn in a circle. My boot heels sink into the damp ground as I glance from one thicket of trees to another, trying to predict the direction of their attack. A movement catches my attention. Lena. She steps toward me, sword drawn. Not good.

It doesn't matter that she's a woman. All the fae know how to fight. She could kick my ass even if I were the one holding the weapon.

Okay, then. This narrows my options down to one—run—because I won't beg.

I turn and flee. Branches whip my face and snag my clothes. I raise my arms to block the forest's attack. Ahead, the ground dips sharply again. Despite burning lungs and a stitch in my side, I push on.

The underbrush rustles behind me, to my left, and to my right, and just before I reach the hillside, I trip on the wind.

There's no other way to describe it. One second my legs are swinging out in front of me; the next my shins slam into air as solid as steel. I'm able to keep my balance long enough to grasp that Lena's an air-weaver—an incredibly strong air-weaver—then another burst of impermeable wind slams into my shoulder. I pivot from the blow, my ankle catches in a thicket of thorned weeds, and I land hard on my butt. I might have slid to a stop then, but a third shot of wind hits my chest, throwing me backward with enough force to carry my feet over my head, again and again until I'm gaining momentum, not losing it.

The forest slashes at my skin and flips through my vision. Suddenly, there's a tree directly in my path. I stretch out my arms to ward it off. A mistake. My right arm absorbs the full force of my weight. I hear a crack, feel a sharp explosion in my forearm, then I'm lying facedown in the dirt.

As the world grows fuzzy around me, I roll to my left side. My right arm flops as if I've grown an extra joint between my wrist and elbow. I try to ignore the white bone stabbing up through my flesh. I try to rise to my knees, but I'm nauseated. Dizzy. My vision blurs. Then, as Lena steps to my side, everything goes black.

SIX

◆•◆

"THERE'S A NEW false-blood."

I tear my gaze away from Kyol's shadow-trail. It's been months since we've seen each other, but time hasn't dulled my reaction to him. My stomach does a little flip. He looks the same as he did the last time we were together, the same as he did when we agreed things would be easier if we stayed in our own worlds. We were right. The way he keeps his expression carefully neutral makes my chest ache.

I sink down on the couch. My parents are out. This is the first time they've left me home alone since I went missing for three days straight. I wouldn't tell them where I was—really, what would the truth accomplish?—and they only ungrounded me a couple of weeks ago, after I got my grades up.

"A new false-blood?" I echo. The first one nearly killed me, but the fear I should be feeling is buried under a more potent emotion.

"You're safe," Kyol assures me, sitting on the couch as well. Even though there's a good foot between us, the air warms with his body heat.

"Then why are you here?" I ask.

His gaze slides to meet mine. He doesn't have to say a word. He's not here for the reason I want him to be. Nothing has changed. The king hasn't revoked the laws keeping us apart and Kyol has no intention to break his oath.

"I asked Atroth to send somebody else," he says.

"Because you didn't want to see me."

"No." His jaw clenches, then his gaze drops to the floor. "Because I wanted to see you."

I hate the way his admission flows out on a wave of guilt. I hate the way I want to comfort him, to tell him it's okay—that *I'm* okay—and I understand. I don't want to understand, but he's the king's sword-master. He swore to protect the Descendants of the *Tar Sidhe* with his life, and even if being around me and my world's technology didn't damage his magic, he's a man who doesn't break his promises.

Damn it, time was supposed to prove these feelings were just a crush.

"What's his name?" I ask because my mind will start contemplating what-ifs if I don't focus on the real reason Kyol is here.

"Betor, son of Jallon."

Déjà vu hits me so hard my head aches. No. This can't be déjà vu. I can predict what happens next.

"Is he worse than Thrain?" I hear myself ask.

"Not yet. We hope to capture him before he organizes another attack." Kyol doesn't meet my eyes. There's no inflection in his voice.

"You don't want my help."

"No."

"Then why did you come?"

"Atroth thought I could convince you to map a few fae. I'm to tell you that you won't be in any large-scale battles. You'll be used . . . covertly?" He looks up. At my nod, he continues. "When we learn the location of one of the rebels, my swordsmen will attempt to arrest him. I'll escort you, and if the rebel fissures out, you will map his shadows."

It sounds safe enough. It's better than being used to see through fae illusions in a full-on confrontation.

"I can do that," I say.

Kyol's hands tighten on his knees. "When Thrain found you, you had to help us. But this false-blood doesn't know who you are. This isn't your war. If you help us, it's because you choose to and . . . and, McKenzie, there can be nothing between us."

I close my eyes. That's not what I want to hear. I want to hear that there's a chance the king might change his mind or make an exception.

"I'm sorry," Kyol says as he rises.

I force a smile and stand as well. "It's no problem. I get it. I'm probably better off dating my own kind, anyway."

"Yes," he says, peering down at me.

We're standing closer than we should. We both know it, yet neither one of us takes a step back. Kyol brushes my hair from my face, lets his fingers linger alongside my cheek, and without conscious thought, my chin tilts up.

Time slows.

Our lips meet.

It's supposed to be a last kiss, and if we were both human or both fae, it might have been, but the moment before we separate, chaos lusters explode through me. The jerk of his body, his sudden inhalation, tells me he feels them, too, and instead of moving apart, we move closer. So much closer.

One kiss turns into two, two into three, then there's the brush of his tongue and I can't concentrate enough to count. He cups the back of my neck—gently, as if my humanity makes me fragile—but if this is the last time we touch like this, I don't want to hold anything back.

I wrap my arms around him when he would pull away, and another strike of lightning ricochets through us. That's the end of his restraint. When he kisses me now, it's like being caught in the gale of a storm. I'm completely swept away as he lowers me to the couch, as his hands slide up my arms, as they drop to my hips, then slip under my shirt.

Something happens with the chaos lusters. With *our* chaos lusters. We're on Earth but white bolts of lightning sear across my body. They tangle with his, and a fire sizzles through us.

Both our lips are parted, our breaths shallow. He knows what he's doing; I try to act like I do, too, but the intensity of the chaos lusters build, and I'm not sure I can handle this.

He must see that moment of uncertainty in my eyes. "You're untouched?"

A part of me realizes this is a dream, and if it's a dream, I should be able to change my response.

I can't. I hear myself tell him yes, hear him say he can't take this away from me. I protest, but he smoothes down my clothes with an apology and a light kiss on my cheek. His fingers slide from my skin, and the heat of his lightning fades away. It feels like a part of my soul fades, too. I'm still breathing hard, but the air I draw in is cold and empty. When he fissures out, I want to be angry. I want to hate him for his self-control, for leaving me when I'm craving more than his touch, and for not being a typical, human male. But I don't hate him. If anything, his restraint makes me love him more.

YOU'D think the agony stabbing through my right arm would eclipse any discomfort caused by my bed, but there's a spring or a knife—I'm not entirely sure which—digging into my spine. I'm unwilling to shift away from it. My arm might be splinted and wrapped in strips of cloth, but the slightest movement sends me careening toward the edge of consciousness. I don't want to fall asleep again. I can't stand the loneliness that descended at the end of my dream.

Hours pass. My muscles stiffen and I grow bored of staring at the ceiling. The cracks zigzagging through it make me frown. I shouldn't be able to see them, not with the door closed and the window boarded up. Slowly, I turn my head to the right and find the source of the room's light: an upside-down mason jar sitting on the floor. Bright swirls of white and blue mists battle for dominance within the glass confines. That's how the fae light their world after dark. Of course, they don't usually use mason jars. The Realm's glassmakers make lamps, wall sconces, and hanging orbs that the fae can light with a touch of their magic. That's all fine and good if you're fae. If you're human, not so much.

I experiment with lifting my head a few times. When that's tolerable, I bend my knees until my feet rest on the mattress. This puts more of my weight on my spine, though, so I finally try to scooch ever so slightly to the side.

I squeeze my eyes shut as pain shoots down my arm. God, running was a bad idea. What made me think I could escape?

The fae outnumber me. They're faster and more familiar with the terrain. Even if they didn't have magic, I'd have little hope of slipping away.

The throbbing in my arm slowly fades. I think I'll feel better if I sit up, so this time, I go all in. I hold my breath, spin my feet toward the side of the bed, and use my good arm to push up.

Nausea grips me as the room spins. I focus on breathing. Sweat breaks out on my forehead as a chill creeps into my bones. Panic's edging in on me, making my chest ache, my throat burn. I shouldn't be here, shouldn't be involved in this war. I was going to get out of it. If the rebels had waited just three days, I would have graduated and retired from the Court. Aren's shadow-witch would have faded to a myth and I'd be safe. Safe and unhurt.

I swallow back my emotions and force myself to deal with the pain radiating up my forearm. After a few minutes of deep breathing, the room settles.

Okay. So the escape attempt didn't work. I can't give up. I'll just have to plan my next move better. I'll have to—

The door clicks. It opens inward and Kelia enters. She's carrying a waterskin and a second magically lit mason jar. When she sees I'm awake, she crosses the room to stand in front of me.

"That was a stupid thing you did."

"Yep," I manage, though my voice sounds strained.

"You're lucky Aren was adamant about you being kept alive."

Lucky? Lucky would have been me escaping. Or me not being captured in the first place.

Kelia pauses, cocks her head to the side. "How's your arm?"

"Feels great."

She mutters some Fae word I haven't learned yet and then reaches into her pocket. "Hold out your hand."

Lifting my good arm takes a hell of a lot of effort. The tendons in my shoulder are tight and I feel weak, like I've swum for hours in a pool and now have to bear my full weight again. Kelia drops two pills onto my open palm. Even they feel heavy.

"I don't think ibuprofen's going to help," I tell her.

"These are a bit stronger than that."

My gaze returns to her and I lift an eyebrow. "Robbing pharmacies now, are you?"

"A few pills won't be missed," she says dismissively.

I pop them into my mouth and Kelia hands me her water-skin. When I nearly drop it, she helps me tip it back. I swallow the pills, not really caring what they are so long as they ease the pain in my arm.

"Thank you," I say when she takes the skin away.

"If you're thankful, don't try to escape again."

I snort. "Sure. No problem."

Her eyes narrow as she leans forward to set her mason jar down, but her glare lacks real scorn. I think we're both trying to hate each other. And we're both failing.

The creak of the door opening draws both our attentions. I hear Kelia suck in a breath and then she's suddenly across the room and in the newcomer's arms.

"Naito!" she cries out.

I blink a few times. I try not to let my mouth hang open, but she's *kissing* the guy and despite the sound of his name, *he's not fae.*

Kelia takes a tiny step back, but keeps her hands on the man's chest, touching him like he might not be real. Now that they're not lip-locked, I note his disheveled black hair and the sharp planes of his face. He's at least half Asian, but 100 percent human.

Kelia kisses him again, longer, more deeply this time, and a chaos luster flickers from her face to his, shimmying down his neck to disappear under the bloodstained collar of his shirt.

"What happened?" she asks. "Are you hurt?"

"I'm okay," Naito says. "The blood's not mine."

She falls into his arms again. He holds her tight, but his eyes are locked on me. I'm too stunned to look away. He's human, she's fae, and I can't help but wonder what would happen if Kyol joined the rebellion. Could we be together then? I want him more than anything, but I've never asked him to abandon the Court. Would he if I asked?

Guilt spikes through my chest. I've no right to ask that. No right at all.

Naito eases Kelia back a half step, then runs his hands down her arms. When he reaches her wrists, he stops, scowls, and drops his gaze to the watch I let her borrow.

"What the hell is this?" he demands.

She hops back like she's been stung. Her right hand darts to cover her left wrist. "It's nothing."

"We've been over this," he says. At least, I think that's what he says. Apparently, I'm not the only human the rebels have taught to speak Fae. He continues scolding her, but his words come too quickly now for me to follow. Kelia's lip twists into a pout, but she lets him unlatch the watch from her wrist.

He crosses the room and holds it out to me. "Yours, I presume."

I nod, still a bit dumbfounded.

He tosses the watch onto my bed. "Don't give that to her again. That or any other tech."

I don't know whether to be annoyed for Kelia's sake at his overprotectiveness or to find it endearing. Honestly, she shouldn't have touched my watch, let alone wear it. A pale circlet of blue shades her wrist as if her skin's been bruised, though the coloring is too phosphorescent for that. Most likely, such a simple piece of tech won't do lasting damage to her magic.

Naito's still watching me. I think he's waiting for a response until he says, "So. You're Aren's shadow-witch."

I barely refrain from rolling my eyes. "I'm not Aren's anything."

"Sure." The corner of his mouth quirks up. "I heard you're better than the rumors."

"I'm better than you." When the words slip out, I suppress a grimace. I shouldn't have said that, even if it's undoubtedly true.

"What makes you think I read the shadows?"

"Why else would you be here?" I can't help but look at Kelia when she steps to his side.

"Maybe I just have the Sight," he says, intertwining his fingers with hers.

"Maybe." I'm not jealous of the two of them. I'm not.

Kelia's hand tightens around his as she peers up at him. "What happened?"

His smile fades and he looks suddenly weary. "The Court's arresting fae who sympathize with us, hoping they'll have information on her." He nods toward me. "The people they took didn't know anything, but Aren stepped in anyway. We freed most of them. Almost captured another one of Atroth's shadow-readers, but the sword-master showed up." His gaze settles on me. "The son of Taltrayn isn't happy he lost you. He's personally leading the attacks against our people."

"*Your* people?"

"I'm as much a part of the rebellion as you're a part of the Court," he says, pausing to study me. "But I think my people might respect and include me more than yours respect and include you."

"I get plenty of respect."

"But they don't include you, do they? Don't tell you their plans or the consequences of what you do for them. They've even forbidden you to speak their language."

I raise my chin, trying to appear confident. It's not an easy thing to do with a broken arm and bruised body, but his criticism gets my hackles up. "They've never locked me in a room and threatened my life."

"Just because you don't know you're a prisoner doesn't mean you aren't one."

"And your injuries are your fault," Kelia tosses in.

I throw her a quick glare before returning my attention to Naito. "The Court takes care of me. It takes care of the Realm. It doesn't burn families to death behind silver-painted walls."

Naito's nostrils flare at the reference to Brykeld, but he doesn't say anything, so I press on. "It doesn't hide in the homes of innocent fae or starve people to try to get its way."

His eyebrows rise. "Starve people?"

"That's what happens when you attack the gates. You're disrupting commerce. Merchants are afraid to travel because of you."

"You think *we're* starving people?" He throws back his head and laughs. "You believe everything the Court tells you, don't you?"

Oh, big mistake, buddy. Nothing sets me off like a condescending laugh. Not that I can do anything about it but simmer from my roost on my bed, but I'll be damned if I ever help these people. Aren is responsible for the massacre at Brykeld, and I've seen the consequences of the rebels' other actions. Their sporadic attacks on the gates have forced merchants to hire guards or journey solely by road to reach their destinations. The cost of that is passed on to the rest of the Realm, and not all the fae can pay the higher prices. Those who can't, go days, sometimes weeks, without food.

"We're not the reason people are going hungry," Naito says when his laughter subsides. "People are going hungry because of Atroth and his taxes."

"Taxes he has to charge to protect his people from Aren," I retort. "False-bloods have always hurt the Realm. Your leader's no exception."

"Aren's not a Descendant of the *Tar Sidhe*. Sethan is."

"Look," I say. "The lords of the provinces voted for King Atroth. He *is* a Descendant—nobody disputes that—so unless you have some aversion to democracy, he's the rightful king."

His expression darkens. "This isn't America—"

"No, it's Germany," I interrupt, suddenly tired and more than a little cranky. "And if you don't mind, I'd like to go home."

He shakes his head. "Aren should have killed you."

So much for getting sympathy from my fellow human. The rebels have completely brainwashed this guy.

He says something in Fae to Kelia. She responds, but I'm suddenly too distracted to decipher their words. Aren glowers in the doorway. *Edarratae* flash across a tensed jaw, briefly erasing the shadows on his face. They don't lighten his mood, though. I can feel him seething from across the room. He strides forward, his hand strangling the hilt of the sword at his waist. He's holding himself back. Barely.

"Leave," he barks. He's staring at me, but it's clear he's talking to Naito and Kelia. I want to beg them both to stay, but Naito takes Kelia's arm. They're walking out of the room already, leaving the door open by only a tiny crack.

Okay. Stay calm. There has to be something I can do or say to get out of whatever he plans to do to me. Should I apologize for trying to escape? Offer to read shadows for him? That's why he's kept me alive so far, for that and my knowledge of the Missing Gates, but giving in seems shameful. Kyol wouldn't give in. He'd resist as long as possible, then . . .

Aren pulls a knife from his belt.

. . . or maybe he'd think me a fool for not doing whatever it takes to stay alive.

I open my mouth to make an offer that might buy me more time, but my words catch in my throat. Pain strikes through the right side of my rib cage when I cough, trying to clear an airway suddenly constricted with fear. Aren crouches down in front of me, silver eyes locked on mine.

"I'm not going to hurt you." Despite his low growl, he's gentle when he slides the knife's blade through the bandages wrapping my fractured arm. I suck in a breath when the splint and strips of cloth fall to the floor. It hurts, but not as much as it would if I hadn't taken Kelia's pills.

Carefully, Aren wraps both his hands around the break and awakens his magic. I grit my teeth to hold back a scream. Fire. That's what his touch feels like. Hot, molten fire. If I weren't staring at my arm, I'd swear my flesh was turning black and crisp beneath his fingers.

When the agony increases, my left hand darts out to grip Aren's shoulder. I dig my nails into his muscle, squeeze my eyes shut. Instinct begs me to shove him away, but I've been through this before. King Atroth has three healers in his Court, and I almost died that first year I read the shadows, trying to track down the false-blood Thrain.

The pain vanishes. Oh, yes, the arm still aches, but the fire's gone and I'm able to breathe again.

Aren's hands are still on me, though. I can't help but notice his knuckles are swollen and dirty, the skin over them broken. Blood, sweat, and dirt invade a deep gash running from his wrist to his elbow. He needs to take care of that. Before it becomes infected.

He finally releases my arm, and then lays his hand on top of mine, which still clings to his shoulder. I loosen my grip and pull back, my fingers sliding out from under his.

I swallow once, twice, then find my voice. "Why not?"

An *edarratae* flashes across his jaw. "Why not what?"

"Why aren't you going to hurt me?"

His eyes meet mine, linger a beat too long, before he looks away. "Lena's already done that."

"You didn't do anything when I climbed out the window, either," I point out.

He sits beside me on the bed. "You want me to hurt you?"

"No." I drop my eyes to my injured arm in time to see a pair of blue lightning bolts flash across my skin where the break had been. That's freaky. Aren's no longer touching me. The chaos lusters shouldn't still be there. I rub my hand over my arm as if I can wipe them away.

"I've left the *amajur*, the magic, in you," he says. "It's still working to mend the fracture. It'll fade in a few minutes. Where else are you hurt?"

"I'm fine." I don't remember the magic of the king's healers doing that, but then, I was only half-conscious at the time.

"Where else are you hurt?" Aren demands more forcefully this time.

I hesitate, then say, "My ribs and back."

His gaze travels down to my shirt. Uh-uh. No way am I taking it off. When he moves toward me, I grab the front hem, holding it down tight. He pauses, then leans behind me to lift the back of the material.

"You may keep your shirt on."

"Thanks," I snap, but I let my shirt rise enough for him to slide the back up to my shoulders. His fingers skate lightly down my ribs and then slowly back up, inspecting my injuries. He does the same to my left side even though I'm not hurt there, and I shiver under his touch.

"Not fractured," he says. "This won't hurt like mending bone." He presses his palm against the worst of my bruises and the heat of his magic seeps into me. A blue glow fans out just above my hip and a luster flickers across my bare stomach. No, it doesn't hurt. It tingles in an unpleasantly pleasant way.

Behind me, Aren breathes deeply. He leans forward. When I feel his breath hot on the back of my neck, I stiffen. I'm a girl, he's a guy, and we're alone in this room. He's ten times stronger than I am. He can do whatever he wants and even if I scream, it's unlikely anyone will come to my rescue.

"You're still afraid of me."

My heart thuds in my chest. I don't dare look at him. "Shouldn't I be?"

He takes a long time to respond and when he does, I get the impression he's choosing his words carefully. "You can't help us if you're dead. You won't want to help us if you're hurt. Lena and the others don't understand that." He moves away.

I smooth down my shirt. "You seem more angry at them than me."

"Because they know . . ." He stops. "I expected you to try to escape."

"You did?"

He nods, and the glimmer of a smile appears on his lips. "Why do you think I left so many fae to guard you?"

I shrug—and am relieved when the motion doesn't hurt. "You're afraid the sword-master will find me."

"Ah, yes. The sword-master. I think you would be dismayed to learn the things he's doing to get you back."

Unease churns in my stomach, but I don't move, not until Aren's laugh startles me.

"You won't even ask what he's done? Too afraid to learn something you won't like?"

My glare does nothing to erase the teasing glint in his eyes. His previous melancholy is gone, the burden lifted from his shoulders, and he's once again the mirth-filled kidnapper who held me dangling three stories above a concrete pavement.

"Aren?" A fae peeks in from the doorway. He mentions Sethan's name along with a string of other words I recognize, but I can't make sense of their order or meaning. Aren responds as he rises off the bed, then he smiles down at me.

"Are you feeling better?" he asks.

He expects me to be grateful, to feel like I owe him. "I was coping before."

He chuckles. "You're stubborn to a fault, *nalkin-shom*. I *will* win you over. Eventually."

The door closes and locks behind him. I'll never admit it out loud, but his healing does make it difficult to hate him.

SEVEN

◆◆◆

SOMEBODY SHOULD TELL Naito and Kelia to get a room.
They might be swinging swords at each other's heads, but
there's something suggestive about their sparring. They're
both drenched in sweat and their chests heave almost in sync
as they stare into each other's eyes. Kelia's toying with him.
She moves slowly enough for Naito to think he might have a
chance, then she coyly ducks or flits back just out of reach. She
stays mostly on the defensive, but on the occasions she chooses
to attack, her dulled practice sword always scores a hit.

The clash of metal on metal rings again across the clearing.
Naito manages to block one of Kelia's offensives. He grins,
catches the playful punch she swings, then pulls her into his arms,
slanting his mouth over hers. Chaos lusters spark between them.

"Curious?"

I nearly fall off the picnic table when I spin toward Aren.

"What?" I squeak, my heart leaping into my throat. When
Aren smiles, my heart stays lodged there. Damn him for being
this devilishly attractive and damn him for reappearing now.
He vanished a second time after healing my arm four days
ago, and I just stopped looking over my shoulder for his return.

"You're watching Naito and Kelia," he says. "You want to
know how it feels to kiss a fae."

I know how it feels to kiss a fae. That's the problem.

"Back to stay this time?" I crane my neck to look up at him when he steps in front of me.

"I'd be happy to satisfy your curiosity." His grin grows even more mischievous. My stomach somersaults, and I have to fight to keep my expression blank.

"Kill anyone while you were gone?" I ask.

He leans toward me, lowers his voice. "It would be an interesting experiment, don't you think?"

Unwilling to cower away from him, I keep my back rigidly straight as he eases closer. I try to appear bored, but my heart beats a quick staccato against my chest. I'm not afraid of kissing him. I'm afraid that I'll like it. In fact, I'm certain the *edarratae* will make me like it, and there's something downright disturbing about that.

Aren's gaze drops to my mouth. I panic when he begins to close the distance between us. Before his lips touch mine, I raise my hands to shove him away. He laughs and dodges aside.

"I wouldn't touch you without permission," he says as he hops up to sit on the table beside me.

What the hell? "You *always* touch me without permission."

"I . . ." He stops, chuckles. "Well, yes. I guess I do."

A chirpy squeak makes us both look toward the ground. Sosch, the adorable but villainous *kimki* I found curled up in my backpack a week ago, scurries to the picnic table. He stops, lifts his front paws off the ground, and perks his ears forward.

Aren picks him up, but as soon as he sets him in his lap, Sosch chirps again and stares at me. I keep my arms folded. No way am I letting him near me. He belongs to Aren, and I will not let his nose-crinkling turn me into a vulnerable puddle of goo.

Aren clucks. Apparently, this is all the permission Sosch needs to leap into my lap. He nudges my crossed arms. His nose is soft, damp.

"You're going to hurt his feelings," Aren says, reaching into his pocket.

I don't move until he tosses something to me. I catch the drawstring pouch—*my* drawstring pouch—in the air. The anchor-stones inside grind against one another when I tighten it in my grip.

"You're giving this back to me?" He might as well. Without a fae to take me through a gate, the rocks are useless.

"I've spent the last two days fissuring to those stones' locations," he says, watching Sosch slip under my arm. The *kimki*'s fur feels like silk against my skin. I let the thing stay in my lap, but I don't pet him.

Aren's mouth curves into a slight smile before he refocuses on me. "Most of them were predictable: your home in Texas, several Provincial Gates, and a few of the Realm's major cities. One took me to a Missing Gate we hadn't found yet. Useful, that one."

A chill settles over my skin. I tear my eyes away from Aren and drag my hand over Sosch's back, making his fur turn silver.

"There's only one location I couldn't fissure to."

Damn it, damn it, damn it.

"I had to find a stone-reader to be sure." He takes my right hand—*without permission*—uncurls my fingers, and presses a semitransparent rock into my palm. He closes my fingers over it. "She told me where it goes."

Damn it!

It was stupid to keep it, but I wanted to remember the night Kyol fissured me to the *Sidhe Cabred*. Fae can only enter the Ancestors' Gardens with the king's permission; humans aren't allowed to enter at all. The *Sidhe Cabred* is the closest thing to holy ground in the Realm, and Kyol . . . he wanted to take me there. Because the gardens are located within the silver walls of Corrist, the Realm's capital, the only way to get me past the heavily guarded entrance was to use a *Sidhe Tol*, a special type of gate that allows fae to fissure into areas protected by silver.

It doesn't hurt fae to come into contact with silver; it simply prohibits them from fissuring wherever the hell they want. The homes of the rich are protected by the metal. So are prisons, military installations, and any place that holds something of value. The Realm's kings have kept the locations of the few *Sidhe Tol* they've found a secret, but since Kyol is Atroth's sword-master, he knows where they are. He fissured me through one to get me inside the gardens.

I don't know if any place on Earth can compete with the beauty of the *Sidhe Cabred*. As Kyol led me down its seldom-trod paths, I felt like I was walking through a paradise, some cross between a rain forest and the Hanging Gardens of Babylon. Maybe it's because even without magic sculpting the vegetation, all the trees and plants and flowers were exotic to me. A river cut through the center of the gardens before it crashed over a steep, rocky cliff into a clear pool at the base of Corrist's northern wall. It's there where Kyol led me, there where we almost . . .

But we didn't. Again, I was completely willing, and Kyol was so close to breaking, but he held himself back. It wasn't a surprise. I was used to not crossing that line, used to being satisfied with kisses that stole my breath and *edarratae* that electrified my skin.

Beside me, Aren reaches up. With two fingers along my jaw, he turns my face toward him. "You've been through a *Sidhe Tol*, McKenzie."

The evidence is fisted in my hand. I can't deny it.

"I was blindfolded," I say.

"I don't believe you." He doesn't remove his hand from my jaw. Instead, he slides it back until his fingers weave through my hair, until his thumb slides over my cheek. "If you tell me where it is, I'll let you go."

His touch is too intimate. *Edarratae* flow into me, spiking down my neck and into my chest. I swallow and clench my teeth, trying my damnedest not to enjoy the sensation. I make the mistake of looking into his eyes. He doesn't look like a killer. The way his hand cradles my head makes me feel safe. I feel like I can trust him. I feel like he . . .

Son of a—

I shove Sosch into his lap and stand. "That won't work."

He keeps the seduction charade up another moment before flecks of silver glitter in his eyes. He sets Sosch on the table. "You can't blame me for trying, can you?"

"I can. I do."

He laughs. "Of course you do. I meant what I said, though. Your freedom for the *Sidhe Tol*. A fair exchange, I think, but the offer won't last long."

"Your offers aren't worth shit anyway."

The light leaves his eyes. "You really do hate me, don't you?"

"Yes!" I turn away, searching for Kelia in hopes that she's finished sparring with Naito so we can resume my language lessons. Neither of them is in the clearing, though. They must have taken my unspoken advice and found a room.

"Do you not doubt the Court at all?" Aren asks.

I turn back to him and snap, "Not since Brykeld."

He flinches as if I've just taken a swing at him. He recovers quickly, though, steeling his expression. "Brykeld was—"

"An accident?" I demand.

He slowly stands. "I wasn't there—"

"Liar."

"—when it was burned," he finishes, his eyes narrowing. "I wouldn't have allowed it."

"Were you there for the rapes, then?"

A muscle twitches beneath his right eye. "No."

"Convenient!"

Kyol apologized a thousand times for taking me to Brykeld. He said he never would have done so if he knew how bad it was going to be. I had nightmares for weeks afterward. Even now, more than two years later, I sometimes hear the screams. The rebels locked entire families inside shops with silver-painted walls. They boarded up the windows and doors and then set the structures on fire. The Court fae tried to help, but they were occupied fighting the rebels. I did what I could, ignoring the flames to hack at the buildings with a dead fae's sword. I came away with deep, ugly burns on my hands, arms, and face. It took one of the king's healers to repair the damage, and I only saved one fae.

"I gave you the person responsible for Brykeld," Aren says.

"*You* were responsible for it." And I can't stand here talking to him a second longer. I turn abruptly and head for the inn.

"Madin, son of Vinth," he calls after me.

I recognize the name immediately, but I don't stop walking, not until Aren grabs my arm and forces me to face him.

"You know who he was," he says.

"One of your fae. So?"

A chaos luster flickers over his clenched jaw. "I leaked his location to the Court the week after Brykeld. I handed him to you because of what he did."

I lift my chin.

His eyes narrow. "Since you've been with me, have I done anything that makes you think I'd condone a massacre?"

"No. You've been on your best behavior," I tell him. "When you're around me. I don't know what you're doing when you're gone."

"I'm fighting a war. *Honorably* fighting it." He lets go of me with a little shove.

I snort. "You don't know a thing about honor. You allow rapists and murderers to fill your ranks."

"I don't have direct control over every single fae who supports the rebellion."

"You should!"

He opens his mouth to retort, stops. He scans the clearing. So do I. Lena and two other fae watch us from the front porch like our argument is some source of entertainment.

Something bites into the palm of my right hand. I glance down at my fist and force my fingers to relax around my anchor-stone. Yes, I was a fool to keep it. Eventually, Aren's patience is going to run out. He'll start listening to Lena and the other fae who want to get rid of me, but he won't kill me without prying the location of the *Sidhe Tol* from my lips.

I've heard rumors of what he and his people do to get information out of the Court fae they capture. I don't know how long I'll be able to resist Aren's interrogation, not when he decides it's time for me to talk. I have to escape before then. If I don't, if they can get to the *Sidhe Tol*, the rebels will be able to invade the Silver Palace. They might even be able to kill the king.

OVER the next two days, I design and dismiss several dozen escape plans. If the rebels weren't so damn vigilant, one of them might have worked, but even though I've pretended to be resigned to my captivity, they haven't let me out of their sights. My time is running out—I know it is—so when a fae's shadow falls over me early in the afternoon, I tense thinking Aren's finally decided to force me to give him the *Sidhe Tol*. But it's not Aren. It's Sethan, who I haven't seen since the first night I met him.

"Kelia tells me you're learning our language quickly."

I shrug. I'm learning it quickly because all my two- to three-day jaunts into the Realm over the years have added up. The sound and cadence of their speech is familiar; I just needed a little formal instruction to begin understanding the words and phrases.

Sethan pushes aside the *jaedric* cuirass I had set on the picnic table to dry and sits on the cleared edge.

"Thank you for your help," he says with a nod to the piece I'm working on now. I use my thick-bristled brush to spread a clear, quick-drying glue over the strips of black bark I've stretched over the leather. The bark is tough and nearly impossible to cut. The fae harvest it by pulling off whole pieces from the *jaedric* tree. Once the paper-thin, lightweight strips dry over the cuirass, they can stop arrows as effectively as police vests stop bullets.

Yes, there's a certain irony to my making armor for the Court's enemies, but it gives me something to do. Plus, every so often I stretch only four layers of bark over the shell rather than the five Kelia told me to. Despite her random inspections, I haven't been caught yet.

"No problem," I say and pick up another strip of *jaedric* from the dwindling stack at my feet.

"The Court has treated you well, hasn't it?"

I stretch the bark across the middle of the cuirass, using my knee to keep one end held in place. Without looking up, I say curtly, "Yes."

"The king provides for you."

"Yes," I answer again. Shadow-reading is my job. The king gives me just enough cash each month to pay my tuition and bills, to buy groceries. I could probably live in a three-thousand-square-foot house if I wanted to—Atroth would pay me more if I asked—but I live cheaply because I don't want anyone asking where my money comes from.

"We could provide for you, too," Sethan says.

This time, I do look up. "Are you trying to *buy* me?"

"It's preferable to other methods of coercion, is it not?"

I keep my expression blank. "My loyalty's not for sale."

Sethan's lips thin. I don't think he likes me much more than Lena does. I'm surprised he's letting Aren have his way instead of his sister, who still wants me dead. But then, from what Kelia's told me, Sethan and Aren are practically brothers.

Speaking of Sethan's family, Lena's voice carries across the clearing. I miss what she says, but she's striding toward us carrying a cloth sack. An unfamiliar fae trails behind her, his face drawn and ragged.

Sethan stands, but I don't move from my perch straddling the picnic bench, not until Lena overturns the sack and a severed head thumps onto the table.

I leap away. My boots slip on the rock bed and I crash down on my ass. The stench hits me a second later. My stomach lurches, but I can't take my eyes off *its* eyes. The head rests on its left ear. The right eye is open, but the silver iris and gray pupil are nearly invisible beneath a white film. I can't see the iris and pupil in the left eye because of the stake jammed into the socket. A part of my brain registers the fact that the metal also spikes through a bloodstained note. The other part of my brain registers nothing.

Aren pulls me to my feet. I don't know where he came from. I hear his voice, but can't make myself understand his words. He's not talking to me anyway. He's speaking in Fae to Lena and the man who followed her.

I make myself focus on them, on Aren actually, hoping his face can block out the image of the thing on the table.

He glances at me. "Is the Court not as benevolent as you thought?" he asks.

My gut tightens. I've heard of the rebellion sending heads with messages, but I've never seen it before. When fae die, they disappear in a flash of light and their soul-shadows—white mists visible only to humans with the Sight—dissolve into the air. Kyol calls it "going into the ether," which I guess is their equivalent to going to heaven. Severing a fae's head prevents that, though, and it's considered exceptionally malicious.

"You do it, too," I say quietly.

Lena snorts. "So of course that makes it okay for them to do."

No. It doesn't make it okay. A trace of doubt snakes through my confidence. What if I'm wrong about the Court? What if I've spent ten years reading shadows for the wrong people?

Lena rips the note from the spike and shoves it in front of

my face. "This is a threat. The Court wants you back. If we don't give you to them, they're going to begin random raids on cities and encampments until they find you. They'll kill or capture anyone who puts up resistance, even if they have no connection to us." She slaps the bloodstained paper down onto the picnic table. "We should send you back to them dead. That's what the king would do."

She strides away before I can say a word. Not that I know what I would have said. I can't defend this. It makes me sick, but it doesn't fit with what I know of the Court. Kyol goes out of his way to capture the rebels, even when it would be easier to kill them. The swordsmen he trains are the same. I've never seen them do something cruel or ruthless.

But I don't monitor them constantly. Uncertainty churns through my stomach.

"You're pale," Aren says at my side. His voice is soft, maybe even concerned.

"I'm just . . . I just need to sleep."

I hate the way he nods, like he's assessed my condition and determined sleep is exactly what I need in order to think clearly.

Before I head toward the inn, I force myself to look again at the note. I can't read the words, but I'm certain it's not Kyol's script.

My next breath comes a little easier. This is just one instance of cruelty committed by one of the king's supporters. If Kyol finds out about it, he'll punish the fae responsible.

I glance at Aren as I pass by. Immediately, I jerk my gaze to the ground. I think I caught a hint of satisfaction in his eyes. It was so brief I almost missed it, but I'm sure *something* was there.

A new wave of uneasiness runs through me.

He wouldn't . . . ? No. Surely not even Aren would do this to one of his own fae. He wouldn't commit this crime just to plant a seed of doubt in my mind.

Then again, how do I know the head belongs to a rebel?

EIGHT

·◆·

A CACOPHONY OF gunfire jars me from sleep. I bolt upright and blink the room into focus.

Wait. Gunfire? The fae don't use guns.

A single mason jar bathes the floor in a dim light. I must
have been dreaming. For a moment, I don't hear anything
except the distant rumble of thunder.

Pow-pow-pow.

What the hell? That's definitely gunfire.

I whip off my thin blanket and lurch out of bed. Shouts ring
out from within the inn. The hallway comes alive with creaks
and groans as fae rush past my closed door. There's too much
noise for me to understand the rebels' words, but I don't need
to. The shooters *have* to be human.

Bullets splatter against the outside wall—somewhere
below me, I think—and I swear the inn shudders like it's in
pain. I hurry to the boarded-up window and pound on the
planks.

"Help! There's a human up here!" I scream. Ridiculous
words in any normal situation, but the people outside have to
be able to see the fae to shoot at them. They'll understand.
They'll help me. "Hello!"

Another volley of gunfire drowns out my plea and the inn
quakes again. I crane my neck to stare at the ceiling, fairly

certain it'll come crashing down if the humans keep up this barrage. I've never suffered from claustrophobia before, but the air filling my room tastes stale and the walls press in too close.

I abandon the window to pound my fist against the door. "Let me out!"

No one answers.

My heartbeat races in time with the stuttering of gunfire. I'm blind up here. I have no idea what's going on outside, how many humans there are, or why they're here. I'd like to believe they've come to rescue me, but they're pelting this building with so many bullets they can't possibly be aiming to get me out alive. They don't know I'm here.

Damn it, I will *not* die like this.

I grab my jeans, pull them on under the satin slip Kelia gave me to sleep in, and then stuff my feet inside my boots, not wasting time putting on socks. I hurry to the door. It takes four awkward, half-balanced kicks to break off the doorknob, but the damn thing still doesn't open.

I'm about to pound on the door again when it flies open. A dagger-wielding fae bursts inside, rushing past me. He uses his blade at the boarded-up window to pry up the lengths of wood, one by one. While he works, two more fae sprint inside carrying crossbows and quivers of arrows.

Crossbows and arrows against guns? I don't wait around to see how effective they are. I escape into the hallway and run for the stairs. It's not until I reach the second-floor balcony that I stop to question where I'm going. Maybe it's safer to hide and let the humans come to me? Their gunfire is relentless now, almost as if they're attempting to mow down the inn with their bullets. The muted *thunk*s of the fae's crossbows are much more disciplined in comparison. If the inn doesn't fall, the humans could run out of ammo before they kill all the rebels and . . . Is that smoke?

I peer over the rail to the floor below. A gray cloud of something smears the air. It doesn't smell like anything's burning. It smells . . . metallic? I don't think it's poisonous, but I'm torn on what to do now. Hide out up here or go downstairs? I try to picture myself cowering in a dark corner somewhere and realize I'd go insane not knowing what's happening. I'll go down. I can always run back up if it's necessary.

I quick-trot down the stairs and am halfway to the bottom floor when someone shouts. I glimpse a pair of humans in camo at the inn's front door, see their guns firing, spraying bullets across the greeting room in a line that begins to arc up toward me. Instinctively, I cover my head with my arms and dive. But I'm on the stairs; it's not level here. I tumble. Flowered wallpaper twirls around and around before I slam into the L-shaped banister at the bottom of the steps.

When I'm able to focus again, my eyes lock on an arrow-pierced head staring at me from the other side of the rail. The crossbow bolt goes straight through the human's blood-filled mouth, pinning his skull to the wall behind him. The memory of the fae's severed head superimposes itself over the human's. I close my eyes, trying to block out both images.

Someone wrenches me to my feet. I'd cry out a protest if the sharp twinge of pain in my lower back didn't drive the air from my lungs. Black spots murk my vision as I'm dragged away from the inn's front door. I'm thrown to the ground before I can suck in a breath.

Freaking hell, I hurt. The pain radiates up my spine and into my neck. Nauseous, I force myself to my hands and knees and wait as my stomach tries to empty itself. A few dry heaves, but nothing comes up, and after another minute, the pain ebbs, becomes more manageable. I settle onto my haunches and try to get my bearings.

I'm sitting on the kitchen floor. Naito and Kelia are crouched down by the cabinets, too. They're both smeared with the soot in the air. She's wearing a very thin, baby blue nightie but Naito has on nothing but a pair of jeans. Long, red scratch marks curve over his shoulders and down his chest. They're clearly not the result of this attack. Kelia's cheeks are flushed and the *edarratae* scurrying over her flesh quiver with pent-up energy.

"Who's outside?" I ask them, though my gaze is drawn to the window in the breakfast nook where Lena and another fae crouch, bolts nocked and ready in their crossbows. A few boxes, a couple of swords, and an extra crossbow are lined up against the wall beside them. My backpack and some other bags are thrown there as well.

"My father," Naito responds. The acid in his voice could corrode iron.

"Vigilantes," Kelia clarifies. "Humans who kill fae."

My frown triggers a headache behind my eyes. Humans who kill fae? "Why?"

"Because they hate," Naito all but snarls.

"They have the Sight?" I press. Kelia nods. "Are any of them shadow-readers?"

"It doesn't matter," Naito says. "They can't follow fae into the Realm without a fae to take them through a gate."

Kelia lays her hand on his shoulder. "The vigilantes won't touch us."

Something in her voice tells me that "us" is really a "me." The vigilantes won't touch *her*, or so she's trying to assure Naito. Sounds like there's an interesting story there. Could it be?

I turn my attention back to Naito. "You used to be one of them."

The tension in his clenched jaw indicates I'm right. I sniff. How Romeo and Juliet of them.

I glance in the direction of the front door. The humans seem to be concentrating their fire on the upper floors. Whether that's because the fae up there are drawing their fire or because a few humans invaded the ground floor, I don't know, but that's not what's worrying me. The humans have slowed their attack. The spluttering of gunfire is more intermittent now. They're taking their time to aim. What if they *are* running out of ammunition? If they have to retreat, will they return? I don't want to miss this opportunity to escape, but if I make a mad dash out the door, will the fae upstairs take a shot at me?

"Don't think about it," Naito says, reading my mind. "The vigilantes will kill you just for being here."

I throw him a quick glare. "I'm not with the rest of you."

"They won't care. You work for the Court. A fae is a fae to them."

"Then I won't broadcast my job," I snap. It's been a week since Aren healed my arm, and this is the first, possibly the last, chance I might have to escape.

"Listen to him, McKenzie," Kelia says. "These people are the worst of humankind. They'll kill you on sight."

I stifle the "whatever" I want to snap out when a flash pulls my attention back toward Lena. Out of arrows, the fae beside her has set his crossbow aside. He rises to his knees now, holding a handful of flames.

"*No fire,*" Lena orders in their language. After a brief hesitation, the fae makes a fist, extinguishing his small blaze. Almost all fae have the ability to create and manipulate fire, but having enough skill and power to throw it—as I assume this fae was about to do—is impressive. I wish Lena hadn't stopped him, though. A forest fire would undoubtedly draw more humans here. *Normal* humans. I won't admit it, but Naito and Kelia's claims about the vigilantes make me nervous.

I can't stay here, though.

I rise into a low crouch, prepared to sprint for the front door, when another niggling thought causes me to hesitate. Something's not right here, something aside from the vigilantes and the fae. I'm not sure what it is until I glance again toward the breakfast nook. Lena's staring back at me, her face pinched.

"Go ahead and run," she says. "We need a diversion."

They're fae. They *shouldn't* need a diversion.

"Why isn't anyone fissuring?" I ask.

"We *can't* fissure," she says as if I'm the densest person she's ever met.

"You can't fiss . . ." My voice trails off. I survey the kitchen, the countertops and floor, then my jeans and my palms. It's not soot in the air; it's silver dust. Everything's coated in it.

Shit. The rebels are totally screwed. These humans are brilliant. Not only are they keeping the fae from escaping, they're severely limiting their ability to fight as well. The fae rely on their fissures to avoid and initiate attacks. They're crippled without use of that magic.

Their problem, not mine. I'm getting out of here.

I don't want to get a crossbow bolt in my back, so I wait until Lena takes aim outside the window before I make a dash for the kitchen's exit. I don't get far. A mass of intertwined arms and legs barrels past me. I spin around as Aren and a human crash against the counter. Both men grapple and curse, but Aren's stronger, more agile. He wraps his arms around the struggling human and body-slams him to the linoleum.

Something skates across the floor. A gun. Naito grabs it on his way to help Aren; then, together, they wrestle the human across the kitchen and heave him into a chair.

"How did you find us?" Aren demands, inches from his captive's face. I think the man's one of the two humans who charged inside when I tumbled down the stairs, but I didn't get a good enough look to be sure. Besides, he's been roughed up so badly he's barely able to sit upright. His nose looks broken, his mouth and chin are covered in blood, and his cheek is so swollen he can't open his left eye.

Aren's face looks better, but he's hurt, too. Blood runs down his back and chest from a bullet wound in his upper left shoulder. He's not wearing a shirt. I'm pretty sure the round went straight through his muscle. If it had struck a few inches lower, he'd most certainly be dead.

"How did you find us?" he demands again. He doesn't give the man time to answer before he swings a fist into his face.

"Answer his question, Tom," Naito says, stepping forward and running his hands over the human's camouflaged pants. He finds something in a pocket on the man's thigh. I don't recognize the black rectangle until Naito snaps it into the magazine well of the gun.

"Naito," the captive responds, drawing out the shadow-reader's name. "Your father thought you might be with this group."

"So he's throwing all his firepower at us? How'd he find out about the silver?" He tucks the pistol into the waistband of his jeans.

"It's old legend, Naito. We just discovered a way to deploy it." He nods toward the remains of some twisted-up piece of metal. It looks like it might have been an old Maxwell House coffee can. The vigilantes must have stuffed it with silver dust and some type of explosive and then launched it into the inn. There are other twisted pieces of metal scattered around, too. Probably dozens more outside.

"Bullshit," Naito says. "Who told you?"

Tom shrugs as if he hasn't been beaten to a bloody pulp. His gaze takes an inventory of the kitchen, finally rests on me. "You're with them?"

"No. They kidnapped me."

He's about to say something else, but Aren cuts him off. "How did you find us?"

"Go to hell," Tom says. I have to give the human kudos. If

Aren interrogated me with that expression on his face, I wouldn't talk to him like that.

Aren towers over the vigilante. His voice is ice when he speaks. "You know what I'm capable of?"

Tom straightens and meets the fae's eyes.

Aren's temple pulses when he clenches his jaw. He glances at Lena as if asking her for permission. Her lips thin, but she gives him a curt nod.

"Very well," he says. Then he wraps his hands around the human's forearms. Tom screams and jerks. His chair tilts back on two legs before crashing over. Aren follows him down, his hands burning through Tom's camouflaged sleeves and searing his flesh. The scream and the acrid smell trigger the memory of Brykeld, and my stomach churns.

"Okay!" Tom screams. Aren releases him. Sweat glistens on the man's face and his chest rises and falls as he sucks in air. He stares at his arms, which are both an angry red from the fire that seared him, then he raises his eyes to meet mine. There's so much pain in them. I have to do something. I can't let Aren hurt him again. Silently, I open the cabinet drawer behind me.

"How did you find us?" Aren demands once more.

I peek into the drawer. No knives. Not even a freaking fork.

"We"—Tom heaves a raspy breath—"tracked her cell phone."

I hip the drawer shut before Aren and Naito swivel their gazes toward me. I know I look guilty. Hopefully they misinterpret the reason why.

Naito turns to Aren. "You didn't crush it?"

"I did," the fae answers. "After we fissured here." His voice is low, angry. I doubt he's used to making mistakes.

He returns his attention to his captive. "How did you know to track her?"

I hesitate before checking the next drawer, partly because I want to know the answer to Aren's question, but mostly because Kelia's watching me now.

Tom shakes his head. "I don't know."

"How?" Aren lowers his hand until it hovers just above Tom's face.

"I would guess it was an anonymous tip," Sethan says,

stepping into the kitchen. Since everyone's being careful to stay away from the windows in the breakfast nook, it's getting crowded in here.

Aren glares at the son of Zarrak. "You shouldn't be in here."

"Neither should you," Sethan responds. "If you die, we fail."

Aren fires back something in Fae. I don't try to translate his words. Tom catches my eye. He holds my gaze a moment, then deliberately looks at Naito. Or, more specifically, he looks at the pistol in Naito's waistband.

Ah, hell. He wants me to grab it. Grab it and then what? I glance at Aren and Sethan, at Trev, Lena, and the other fae by the window, at Kelia, who's stepped to Naito's side. I can't possibly shoot them all. To be quite honest, I don't know if I want to.

Tom's eyes plead with me. I swallow. I was looking for a knife seconds ago. A gun is a more efficient weapon. I can do this. I *will* do this.

I give Tom a little nod. He manages a small smile; then, a second later, he springs to his feet.

I lunge for the pistol and manage to get it out of Naito's waistband. Naito spins, but Tom grabs him before he can wrench the weapon from my hands. Aren tackles the vigilante, and all three men crash to the floor.

I point the gun. "Stop. Stop!"

They don't stop. Fists fly and I'm afraid Aren and Naito will kill Tom before I get their attention. I point the barrel toward the floor, try to pull the trigger. Nothing happens.

Shit. I've never touched a gun before in my life. I only know what I've seen in the movies and . . . Hold on. Don't guns have safeties?

I check the side, find some little toggle and flick it, aim the weapon at the floor a second time, and shoot.

The gun jerks hard as the shot rings out. My heartbeat restarts a second later. I have everyone's attention now.

Aren straightens and steps away from Tom. He turns toward me.

"Stay where you are." I point my weapon at his chest. I know the gun puts me in charge here, but I feel less safe with it in my hand. It makes me feel dangerous, and rightly so. I could take someone's life if I pull the trigger.

"You don't know what's going on here," he says. His voice is soothing, his expression softer than it was seconds ago.

"I know enough," I say. "Let him up."

Naito's still holding Tom down on the floor. He holds his hand out, palm down as if to calm me. "McKenzie, I know these people. They'll shoot you the moment you step out the door. Don't do this."

I point the gun at him, manage to hold it steady. "Let him up, Naito."

"McKenzie." Kelia's voice cracks as she steps toward her human, her silver eyes wide with fear. Guilt twists in my gut. Killing Naito will destroy her and, damn it, I don't want to hurt either of them.

"McKenzie," Aren says softly, taking a step forward. He pauses when I re-aim at him. God, there are too many people in here. I can't keep them all in my sights.

"You're not going to shoot me," he says. I clench my teeth as he takes another step. "Put down the gun, *nalkin-shom*."

He's right. Why the hell is he right? I *should* want to kill him. He *kidnapped* me. He has no plans to let me go. Killing him might be the only way to get back to Kyol.

"You won't shoot me," he repeats.

I readjust my sweaty grip on the pistol. *Think, McKenzie. Think!* My gaze flickers around the breakfast nook, finds inspiration, returns to Aren.

"You're right," I tell him. "But I will shoot her."

Aren freezes when I point the pistol at Lena. Oh, yeah. He knows I have reason to want *her* dead.

"How 'bout you let him up now."

To my surprise, Lena laughs. Her crossbow rests in her lap. I watch for any twitch that might indicate she's about to use it, but she appears 100 percent relaxed in her position beneath the window.

"Let them go, Aren," she says with a smile. "Your *nalkin-shom* is responsible for what happens to her."

Well, shit. If Lena's willing to let me walk away, then Naito's telling the truth. These humans aren't interested in helping me. But then, I have Tom. He'll tell them what I've done here. That has to count for something.

"Shoot them," the human says, trying to sit up. Naito shoves him back down.

"Sethan," I say without taking my eyes away from my target. "If you want your sister to live, you'll let me and Tom go."

It's too quiet while I wait for Sethan's response, and gravity seems to be toying with the gun in my hand, adding to its weight little by little until my shoulders ache. I'm barely keeping it trained on Lena's chest.

"Very well," Sethan says. "Naito."

When Naito moves, my eyes flicker to Tom. My mistake. The moment I look away from Lena, Aren darts forward. He knocks the pistol from my hand and captures my wrist before my brain registers he's moved. He advances and I stumble until he presses me against the wall. My arm is caught between my sweat-soaked slip and his silver-dusted chest. As his *edar-ratae* leap into me, I use my free hand to try to push him away, but my palm slips across his blood-slick shoulder. His grip on my wrist tightens.

"You're becoming increasingly difficult to keep alive," he says, his voice low, his eyes burning inches from mine. "Stay here. Do not move."

My knees are jelly when he lets me go. He returns to Tom, who's staring at me with more than a little disappointment. I don't blame him.

"Sorry," I mouth.

"Never hesitate," he says. "If you have another opportunity, you take it."

Naito retrieves the gun off the floor, flicks the safety back on, then stuffs it deep into the pocket of his jeans. "She won't have another opportunity."

Tom focuses on him with his one good eye.

"Kill these demons, Naito. Kill them and your father will let you come home."

The corner of Naito's mouth quirks up into a mirthless smile. "I think I'll pass."

"We outnumber you. We can wait you out. Your fae can't fissure away for food or help. They're going to die here. Don't waste your life."

Naito turns his attention to Sethan. "You think they're working with the Court?"

"I think the Court is using them to find McKenzie," Sethan says. "Atroth would rather have her killed than risk her helping us."

"Atroth knows I'll never help you," I say. Aren throws a warning look my way, but I haven't moved an inch from where he ordered me to stay.

"You're mistaken." Sethan's words are punctuated by a rumble of thunder. His statement is so matter-of-fact I can't come up with a response. A tiny kernel of doubt chips away at my faith.

"I'll make a deal," Tom says. I'm relieved when all eyes turn back to him. "I'll talk to Nakano about letting you surrender. He might let some of you go. The women maybe."

Naito snorts. "Clemency from my father? I'm not a child anymore, Tom. I know what kind of man he is."

Tom wipes his sleeve across his face, smearing blood from his nose and mouth across his cheek. "But what kind of man are you? You're going to let your girl and the human die when you might be able to help them? You prolong this fight and your father won't have any choice but to kill all of you."

Aren takes a step toward the vigilante. "Why are you so eager for our surrender? You have us surrounded. You said yourself you can wait us out."

Tom crawls to his overturned chair. He rights it and then slowly pulls himself into the seat. He settles in with a grimace. "We can."

I want to throw myself between Aren and the human. Tom's hurt too badly. I don't want Aren to rough him up more. I don't want to hear him scream or smell burning flesh again, but I stay in my assigned spot by the kitchen counter.

"Something's going to happen," Aren says. "What?"

I start to interrupt, but a cough wracks through my chest. I cover my mouth with the back of my hand and notice my skin's become coated with silver dust. It's thick in the air down here and it's probably doing some serious harm to my health. There's no escaping breathing it in, though.

Another rumble of thunder shakes the inn. That's when the vigilante's lie clicks.

"It's going to rain," I say.

The kitchen's inhabitants stare. I wait for one of them to ask why the hell I'm concerned about the weather, but one by one, they get it, too.

Tom bursts from his chair. "You fae-fucking bitch!"

NINE

◆•◆

A REN LEAPS INTO Tom's path. The human comes to a sudden stop, his one good eye widening over Aren's shoulder. I don't realize he's dead—no, dying—until Aren gives him a firm shove back. His dagger makes a sucking sound as it slides from Tom's chest. A fountain of red spurts from the wound and splatters on the linoleum floor.

Tom collapses, and I can do nothing but stare as his life ebbs away in a puddle of crimson. This is my fault. I should have kept my mouth shut.

I'm only able to wrest my eyes away from the dead human when Naito grabs Kelia's arm, pulling her to the kitchen sink. He twists on the faucet, cups a handful of water, and then splashes it over her shoulder, wiping at the gray dust coating her skin.

"If we clean you up and wait for the rain to settle the silver, you should be able to fissure out."

Aren steps over Tom's body. "If we know the storm's coming, they know it's coming, too. They'll make their move before then."

Naito cups another handful of water. "You have to hold them off. They won't stand a chance once you can fissure. Don't conserve your arrows. Kill anything that moves." He abandons his method of bathing Kelia, grabs her hands, and thrusts them into the sink.

She sucks in a breath. "It's cold, Naito."

"I know, baby, but we need to get the silver off you."

"A shower will be quicker," Sethan says. "We'll need to change into clean clothes, too, and wash the dust out of the inn."

Aren nods. "We'll clean up in shifts. You three first. Take McKenzie with you."

I don't like being shuffled up the stairs—I just want to be left alone—but I'm relieved to get away from Tom's body. I hunker down in the hallway in the middle of the second floor, hug my knees to my chest, and listen for rain. All I hear is intermittent gunfire. I half expect to feel the pierce of bullets, but there must be enough walls and piping to keep them from passing all the way through the inn.

The fae shower and change clothes. Aren's the last one who comes upstairs. He's carrying a *jaedric* cuirass, a clean wool shirt, and pants. He doesn't glance at me as he shuts himself inside the bathroom. I stand and start to walk farther down the hall, not wanting to be near the door when he exits. The idea of finding a closet to hide in appeals to me more than it did earlier. It's probably the safest place for me.

"You'll fissure out as soon as you're able to," Naito's voice carries down from the third floor.

"You know better than that." Kelia descends the stairs after him.

"They won't kill me."

"That's a lie. If you shoot at them, they'll shoot at you."

He reaches the second-floor landing, grips the rail. "Then get out of here so I don't have a reason to shoot."

"Not without you."

"Damn it, Kelia," Naito explodes. "My father will take his time slaughtering you!"

A throat clears. I glance to my right, see Aren standing in the bathroom doorway. "You two will have to fight about this later. I need you at the back door, Naito. Kelia, you stay with Sethan." He holds up his hand when she starts to protest. "Just until he fissures out. After that, do as you please. McKenzie." He turns to me, opens his mouth to say something, stops. He clears his throat again. "Stay away from the windows."

"They're coming!" someone shouts from downstairs.

Aren sprints for the staircase.

"You'll fissure out," Naito says, then he grabs Kelia by the nape of her neck and pulls her into a fierce kiss.

She looks breathless when he releases her, slightly disoriented when he rushes off to chase Aren down the stairs. After a moment in which she masks her emotions, she turns to me. "Sethan's upstairs. Come on."

By "upstairs" Kelia means the attic. We climb the ladder to the low-ceilinged loft. Lena's up here, too. She hands Kelia a sword, then gives me a glare that seems to trigger a rumble of thunder. The soft pitter-patter of rain begins on the rooftop. It'll wash the silver dust out of the air and off the inn's outside walls.

I take a half step away from Lena, afraid she'll *accidentally* open a fissure right where I'm standing. Her *edarratae* flare, but no slash of light breaks through the attic's dim glow.

"It might take some time," Sethan says.

Lena paces. "We don't have time. The humans' guns are more accurate; they have more ammunition. Aren's not invincible—"

"I know that."

"He takes too many risks. He never should have brought *her* here."

Stress doesn't do good things for my patience. I cross my arms and meet her glare. "This isn't my fault."

"They're your people," she says. "It was your tech that led them here."

"Your people." I make the words sound like a racial slur. "Kidnapped me. And the vigilantes are no more my people than they are Naito's."

"Yet you were going to shoot us all so you could escape."

I snort. "No, not all of you. *Just* you."

A flash to my right cuts off Lena's retort. A fissure rips through the air beside Sethan. After a moment of stunned silence, he nods to his sister, steps into the light, and disappears. Lena opens her own exit a second later and vanishes, too. My fingers itch to draw the shadows, but I have no pen or paper. Without sketching what I see, all I know is they've fissured to the Realm, to a province in the west, I think.

Kelia taps her sword on the ground and stares at the space where Sethan stood.

"Naito will never forgive himself if you die," I tell her. Her silver eyes rise to meet mine. *Edarratae* flash across a tensed jaw.

"Then I better not die," she says softly. Then, more firmly, "Let's go."

She gestures to the ladder. I'm tempted to refuse to leave, but I saw the rage in Tom's eyes when he sprang at me. If the other vigilantes are as mad as he was, reasoning with them won't work.

I heave out a sigh and make my way down the ladder, then the stairs. I almost slip when I reach the ground floor. The entryway is wet. All the first floor is. There's still some silver glistening in the water, but the rebels managed to wash most of it away.

"This way," Kelia says.

I follow her toward the back of the inn, ducking beneath the windows we pass. Naito's at the back door. Aren is, too. He yanks me to the floor as soon as I enter the narrow washroom.

"Stay low," he orders.

"I am staying low," I snap back.

A flicker of some unidentifiable emotion shines in his eyes when I move away from him.

He says something in Fae to Naito. A second later, he and Kelia open fissures and disappear.

"They're going to create a diversion," Naito tells me. "When they start fissuring in the clearing, we'll run for the trail. Aren and a few others will try to keep our path clear, but don't stop moving."

He rises up a little to keep a watch out the small window in the back door. Tom's pistol is in his hand. His fingers are wrapped tightly around its grip. The firm set of his jaw indicates he's willing to use it if necessary.

"Would your father really kill you?"

He glances at me, gives a short nod. "Yeah. He would."

"You were a vigilante when you met Kelia?"

His expression softens at the mention of her name. "Yeah."

Gunfire strafes our side of the inn and pings off pipes in the wall. I flatten myself on the ground, close my eyes, and pray for it to stop. In a few, long seconds, it does.

Naito shakes glass from his hair. The door's window is completely blown out now.

The silence that follows makes me uneasy, especially when it stretches out over several minutes. I want to throw open the door and take my chances, but the rational part of my brain tells me to wait. To distract myself, I ask, "You two are happy together?"

"Yeah." He rises to peek outside again.

"Even though most fae don't like humans?"

"Most *Court* fae don't like humans," he corrects me. "That's the king's fault. He thinks we're destroying their magic."

"We *are* destroying their magic." We're at least damaging it.

"No. It's cyclical. The Realm's magic grows stronger in some centuries, weaker in others." Naito sinks back down and studies me. "Why so many questions? You thinking about getting involved with a fae?"

"Of course not," I say quickly. I've heard Naito's theory before; fae use it to excuse the little souvenirs they take back to their world.

"I highly recommend it," he continues. "Sex with the *edarratae* . . ." He shakes his head and a small smile tugs at his lips. "Trust me, you'd love it. You'd never want to be with a human again."

I glance away, hoping Naito doesn't notice my cheeks flushing with heat. That's when I see two big, unblinking blue eyes staring at me. Sosch. He's huddled in the gap between the hot-water heater and the wall.

I stretch my hand out. It's the only invitation he needs. With a chirp-squeak, he darts into my arms. The poor thing is covered in silver dust and trembling.

"He'll slow you down," Naito says.

He's right. I should leave him behind, but the grudge I've been holding since I found him hiding in my backpack is gone. I won't abandon him just because he belongs to Aren.

And speaking of my backpack, it was on top of the fae's supplies in the breakfast nook. Carrying the *kimki* in that will be easier than running with him in my arms, so I set Sosch on the ground, ordering him to stay.

He doesn't. As soon as I crawl away, he chirps and follows me. Fortunately, the laundry room and breakfast nook share a wall, so I have my backpack in hand within seconds. Sosch darts into it before I return to my spot by the back door.

Naito watches me zip the bag. "The vigilantes probably wouldn't find him."

I shrug, then reopen the zipper a little, leaving Sosch enough room to breathe and get out if he wants.

"How much longer?" I ask, slipping the backpack on.

He doesn't need to answer. My skin tingles an instant before a fissure opens just outside the laundry room.

"Now," the fae says.

Naito pulls me to my feet. "Stay close."

I don't have time to worry about jostling Sosch. We burst from the inn's back door and into the night. Or what's supposed to be night. The clearing is lit with fissuring fae. The white slashes of light reflect off the pouring rain. It's like running through a field of fireworks—the grand finale—on the Fourth of July. Gunfire accentuates the *shrrip, shrrip, shrrip*s of the fae's fissures as they leap in and out of this world, over and over again, faster than I can track.

"Keep moving!" Naito shouts.

My vision is blurred with light and smudged with shadows. I can barely see where I'm running, and I'm terrified I'm going to sprint straight through a fissure. Where's the damn tree line? Rain pelts my eyes, and I swear the clearing lengthens as we cross it.

"Down!"

The moment I realize I've been shoved to the ground, I'm yanked back up.

"Go!"

I recognize Aren's voice this time. He pushes me after Naito, who's scrambling to his feet. I ignore the stitch in my side, the squirming *kimki* in my backpack, and keep running.

We make it to the trail, but if I thought the forest's cover would ease some of my panic, I was wrong. I can't see the vigilantes, but I can hear them. I hear their guns, their heavy breathing, their movements in the wet underbrush. They're closing in on me. From my left. From my right. Shit, a camou-flaged man steps right in front of me.

I skid to a stop as he raises his gun. Aims.

Aren fissures between us. A shot rings out. There's a flash of steel as Aren's sword cuts through the rain, cuts through the human.

Aren reaches back, grabs my arm, and thrusts me forward. "Follow Naito!"

I stumble over the gurgling vigilante, try to ignore the gaping slash angling from the top of his shoulder through his chest. My body wants to shut down, to stop moving. I've seen too much blood tonight, too much violence.

I crawl forward and then notice the little blue cell phone sticking out of the vigilante's pocket. I tug it free—oh, God, I'm stealing from a dead guy—and bury it deep in my pocket.

Flipping my wet hair out of my face, I glance up. Naito's just ahead. He peers over his shoulder, sees me down on all fours in the mud. I make a decision, scramble to my feet, spin, and run back toward the inn. After a few strides, I veer off the trail and carve my own path through the forest.

"McKenzie!" Naito shouts, but I'm sure he won't follow me. He loves Kelia too much to risk her waiting for him at the gate. And Aren's preoccupied. I should be able to escape long enough to make a phone call.

The underbrush entangles me. I shake loose, continue on, slipping and sliding over leaves and wet grass. I don't know what direction I'm heading in, but I don't care as long as it's away.

The gunfire fades, and I no longer see fissures in the thick green of the forest. A hint of light peeks through the canopy above, and my pace slows when the trees thin up ahead. Cautious, I flatten myself against a thick oak and study the clearing. The inn isn't located as deep into the forest as I imagined. An honest-to-goodness *paved road* lies just on the other side of the field. But running without cover makes me decidedly uneasy, especially when I'm not sure where I can find a safe haven.

I wrap my hands around the straps of my backpack and scan the road again, wondering how much traffic it gets on any given day, when, finally, God throws me a bone. To my left, no more than twenty yards away, an empty BMW is parked half obscured by an outcropping of trees. As an added bonus, I can get to it without crossing the field. I'm sure it belongs to the vigilantes. Hopefully, I can get to it before they return. If the fae leave any of them alive to return.

The rainwater drenching my hair and clothes weighs me down as I pick my way along the edge of the forest. With each step, I pray the humans left the keys in the car. I don't know what I'll do if they haven't—I can't hot-wire the thing—but as I draw near, I hear the engine purring beneath the sound of the falling rain. They've left it idling.

Taking my backpack off, I hurry to the driver's-side door, open it, and fall inside. Sosch squeaks when I swing the bag into the passenger's seat, but there's no time to see if he's okay. This seems all too convenient to go off without a hitch, but I'm already committed. I shift the car into reverse, then slam down the pedal. Too hard. The BMW fishtails in the wet grass before its tires catch. I curse and ram the gearshift into drive.

The back windows explode the next instant. Glass rains through the air. I duck behind the wheel, blindly steering as bullets thunk against the car's sides. I accelerate over uneven ground, away from the attackers and toward where the road should be, before risking a quick peek over the dash.

Aren's there. I slam on the brake as he cuts down a vigilante who had a gun aimed at me. He fissures, reappears behind another armed man, and strikes again. Three more vigilantes replace that one.

This time, Aren moves more slowly when he attacks. Two of the newcomers get shots off. Aren stumbles back. He loses his footing, slips, and lands hard on his back.

Maybe I could have driven away if he hadn't caught my eye just then. I freeze, one foot hovering over the accelerator. The vigilantes will kill him. I shouldn't care. I should let him die—he's killed hundreds of fae—but leaving him here is too close to murder. I can't do that, not when I'm in a position to help.

Cursing my conscience, I slam down the accelerator. I ram into the two humans, hard enough to knock them off their feet. Before they have a chance to recover, I pull up beside Aren and shove open the passenger door. "Get in."

TEN

◆•◆

"YOU OKAY?" I ask, even though I don't care. Really, I don't. I'm fulfilling my humanitarian obligation by giving Aren a lift. After we put a few more miles of asphalt between us and the vigilantes, I'm kicking him to the curb and he's on his own.

I glance at him. His right hand is wrapped around the pommel of his sword and he's huddled against the car door as far away from the radio and air controls as he can get. His *edarratae* flash erratically, and he's noticeably uncomfortable. When tech messes with a fae's magic, it disorients them. Not much, at first, and they can ignore the dizziness for a while, but Aren's weak and he's injured. His cuirass is mottled with dents, and aside from his other scrapes and bruises, there's that hole in his shoulder from the vigilantes' first assault on the inn. His armor covers it up right now, but blood trickles down his left arm, dripping off his elbow and staining the seat's upholstery.

Carefully, he begins to loosen the cuirass's laces. I tighten my grip on the steering wheel so I don't give in to the urge to help him struggle out of it. It takes a while, but he finally manages to get the armor off and shoved to the back of the car. The effort takes its toll. His chest heaves as he leans back against the seat and closes his eyes.

Great. I can't kick him out when he's hurt this badly.

Well, he can stay in the car for all I care. Once we reach some type of civilization, I'm out of here.

"Turn the heat off?" he asks.

I'm already cold with the back windows blown out, and we're both still soaking wet, but a deep frown creases Aren's forehead.

I sigh and kill the heater.

"Your *edarratae* don't look *that* bad," I tell him as the last of the warm air vanishes. It's only a half lie. The tech is obviously screwing with his lightning, but I've seen worse reactions.

"That's because I'm not operating the vehicle." There's a soft squeak when he shifts in his seat. He frowns down at the floorboard.

Oh, no. Sosch.

"Is he okay?" I ask as Aren bends down to retrieve the *kimki* from my backpack. Sosch is alive, at least. He chirps when Aren holds him to his chest, but Aren doesn't answer for a long time. Maybe Sosch would have been better off if I left him at the inn.

"You saved him," Aren says.

His tone draws my gaze. The raw gratitude in his expression makes him seem all too human. That's not good. It makes it hard to remember he's a killer.

"I didn't do it for you," I snap, staring out the windshield again. Don't they have road signs in this country? I haven't seen a single one, and we've only passed one car. That was too close to where we started out, though, and I didn't blink my lights or try to flag it down because I couldn't be sure it wasn't a vigilante. Plus, I know more Fae words than I do German. Communication with the locals might not be so easy.

I glance at Aren, wondering just how badly the tech is affecting his magic.

"Can you fissure out?"

He hesitates before answering. "Yes."

"Good. Do it."

The way he looks at me causes a jolt of something to flutter through my stomach. *Apprehension,* I tell myself, because there's regret in his eyes. He's going to say something I don't like.

"I still can't let you go."

Yep, there it is. I don't like that at all. "You don't have a choice. I'm driving, you're the passenger, and I just saved your ass. Fissure out."

He runs his hand over Sosch's back, and a small smile tugs at his lip. "That doesn't make us even."

"I'm factoring in the fact that you kidnapped me."

The bastard actually laughs. "Come on. It hasn't been that bad an experience, has it?"

He's got to be kidding. "I just got shot at."

"I took care of you."

Something clenches in my stomach again. I stare at the road so I don't have to see the way he's looking at me. There's no desire inside of me. None. Zilch. Zero. And I am *not* thinking about what sex with the fae and their *edarratae* would be like. Hell, I haven't had sex with a human. I probably couldn't handle it with—

I shake my head and grip the steering wheel. Why the hell did I invite him into this car? He's my *kidnapper*. I should be trying to kill him, not help him, but even now, I'm concerned about his injuries. That shoulder wound doesn't look good, and even though he's trying to hide it, I can tell he's hurting. He needs a doctor or, rather, a fae healer.

Damn it. Why the hell do I care?

"Do you know where you're going?" he asks.

"I'm following the road," I answer tersely.

"Can the humans follow this car?"

I check the rearview mirror. "There's no one behind us."

"No," he says. "With tech. Can they track us using tech?"

Oh. I study the panel of gauges behind the wheel. How can you tell if a car's rigged with OnStar or something?

"There's a second gate to the north of the inn," Aren says. "Sosch can help us find it."

He must not know exactly where it is. Without Sosch, we could walk right past it.

Wait. We? What the hell am I thinking? I need to ditch this fae. I'm about to insist he fissure out again when he pushes Sosch into the backseat, then takes off his shirt.

"What are you doing?" I swivel my eyes away from him and stare at the road, trying not to remember the way his body looked when his torso was covered in nothing but silver dust.

"Bleeding," he responds. He tears the shirt down its center.

I give in to temptation and glance over when he tears the shirt again. He wraps the strips of cloth around his injured shoulder. His abs clench when he pulls the bandage tight. Damn.

I focus on driving. He's *not* attractive. He can't be, not when he's covered in blood and bruises. *And not all the blood is his,* I remind myself. I don't know how many humans he's killed. That alone should make me want to get rid of him as soon as possible. The thing is, I'm comfortable with him sitting beside me. It's insane, but he makes me feel almost as safe as Kyol always has.

I frown, thinking about that. Then suddenly, it all makes sense.

"Stockholm syndrome," I whisper, my knuckles turning white on the steering wheel.

Aren looks at me. "What?"

The Stockholm syndrome. It explains everything. I'm identifying with my kidnapper, forming some type of sick, emotional bond with him. That's why I saved him and why I'm concerned about his well-being now. It's probably the reason I'm feeling drawn to him. My mind magnifies every little kindness he shows me, making me believe he cares for me when he really doesn't.

"You okay?" Aren asks.

"No," I snap. "I'm not. I'm psychologically impaired."

He lifts an eyebrow.

"Fissure out."

"McKenzie," he says, sounding as if he's disappointed in me.

"Now, damn it." I swing my arm at him, hit his shoulder.

He grunts. "I can't go anywhere while we're moving."

I slam on the brake, shove the gearshift into park, and then wait, but he doesn't budge. He just sits there staring at me. "I'm not kidding, Aren. Fissure. Out."

He sighs and I think he's finally going to comply when he says, "I'm very sorry about this."

"Sorry about wha—"

His hand darts out, grabs the keys, and pulls them from the ignition.

I lunge across the center console, reaching for them. I'm screwed if I don't get them back, but Aren fends me off.

"I can't let you go," he says.

"Give me the fucking keys!" I make a second attempt to grab them. He holds them away and bats my hands down. I manage to catch his wrist, but my momentum and a small jerk from him causes me to half fall into his lap. A smile starts to appear on his lips, so I slam my fist into his injured shoulder.

"*Nom Sidhe*," he groans, squeezing his eyes shut. When the keys fall to the floorboard, I reach between his legs to grab them. Before I straighten, he wraps an arm around my waist and then kicks open his door.

I throw an elbow toward his gut. He blocks it, pulls me across his lap, and nearly throws me out of the car. I drop the keys to grab the oh-shit handle above the door with both hands as Aren rises out of the car, keeping his arm around me.

"Let go of the handle."

"Let go of *me*!" I yell back. He pulls harder, lifting my feet off the ground. The handle is my only anchor to the car, but my grip is weakening. I kick, but he's holding both my legs now.

"McKenzie." He gives a final jerk and my hands slip. My teeth slice through my bottom lip when I land face-first on the damp roadside.

Aren flips me over and pins me to the ground. I buck and twist and try to shimmy out from under him.

"Relax," he orders.

My left arm slips free. He recaptures it.

"Enough, McKenzie. Enough!"

I let my body go limp beneath him and force myself not to react when *edarratae* scramble from his hands into my arms. I fail miserably in the no-reaction department. I don't move, but chaos lusters pulse under my skin, and the longer he touches me, the hotter they become. They're not painful; they're stirring and addictive.

"I hate you," I whisper. His silver eyes follow a luster as it tickles over my shoulder, up my neck, and across my cheek.

"You're bleeding," he says, and then he gently presses his thumb to my bottom lip. I suck in a breath when he flares his magic to heal the small cut there, and it feels as if a thousand chaos lusters crash together in my stomach.

I fight back my frustration, turning my head to the side so I don't have to look at him. "Will you let me up now?"

"Will you try to run?" When I don't respond, he breathes out a warm sigh on my neck. "Stupid question. Of course you'll try."

Aren rises and pulls me to my feet. When he turns to open the car's back door, I swoop down, grab the keys lying forgotten on the ground, and shove them into my pocket.

He searches the backseat a moment and then straightens. "This is a . . ."

I peek around his shoulder at the metal box in his hand. "It's a first-aid kit."

He nods, opens it up, and stares at its contents.

"You can't heal yourself, can you?" I ask.

"No." He sits on the edge of the seat, facing me. "Do you sew?"

I still, and a hint of nausea churns in my stomach. "No. I don't."

"My shoulder needs to be cleaned and closed."

"No." I look away, into the forest. He's hurt, but I don't think I can outrun him. Maybe he'll grow weaker on the way to the gate? Then I can sprint back here and escape.

"McKenzie," Aren says, a plea in his voice.

"I'm not sticking a needle into you," I say, refocusing on him. Stitching a wound shut is a little too much for me. I can clean it, though. I look into the open kit on his lap. The vigilantes must have brought it with them. Everything is labeled in English. I spot a few butterfly bandages and pick them up. "I can use these to hold the wound together."

"I'm bleeding too much for that."

"Well, it's that or nothing."

His expression hardens. "Is this your new escape strategy? To let me bleed to death?"

"It's not a bad idea." In fact, that'll be my backup plan if I can't lure him away from the car.

"Fine." He peers into the kit. "Which one of these will disinfect the wound?"

"The antiseptic wipes."

"Which ones?" He takes off the ripped-up shirt he wrapped around himself no more than ten minutes ago. It's dyed completely red now.

"They're on the left."

He tosses the shirt to the ground and pins me with a frustrated glare. "I can speak your language, McKenzie, but I can't read it."

I huff out a breath and grab one of the white packets. "It's this one." I rip the top off and take out the wipe. "You're going to need more of these than we have." He's covered with dirt, sweat, and blood.

"Just clean it as well as you can."

I run the towelette across the hole in his shoulder and down over his incredibly firm chest. God, he's in shape. He's thinner than Kyol, but has the same mouthwateringly toned physique. I try to ignore the hard muscles beneath my hand as I clean his wound. Mostly, the towelettes only smear the blood around. This isn't going to prevent an infection. "You need a doctor."

"I'll be fine once we rejoin the others."

"So fissure out. We're not driving anymore. You can send someone back to this location in two minutes." Two minutes would be enough time for me to jump into the driver's seat and speed off.

He shakes his head. "I'll be fine."

I stop cleaning his shoulder to frown suspiciously into his eyes. "You can't fissure, can you?"

"I can." His jaw clenches. "I just can't fissure very far, right now. The tech's poison will fade by the time we reach the gate."

"In your condition, you won't make it to the gate."

"It's not far."

"You can't judge distances when you're in a car." Kyol can't, at least. "We might be miles away from the river."

"I'll make it."

"You'll bleed to death."

A smile breaks through his fatigued expression, and damn it if those chaos lusters don't spring to life again in my stomach. You'd think my awareness of the whole Stockholm syndrome thing would make me immune to its effects, but no. It's worse than ever.

"Your concern for my well-being is heartwarming," he says. He *oomph*s when I slap a new wet wipe against his wound.

Sosch drapes himself across the ledge behind the backseat.

His blue eyes blink, watching me work. I clean Aren off as well as I can, but don't feel like I'm making any progress. Every time I put pressure on his shoulder, a new river of blood pours out. When I'm down to my last two towelettes, I decide it's time to do what I can for the exit wound. The exit wound's on his back, though, and short of sitting in his lap, there's no easy way to get to it.

"Get out of the car." I move so he can stand.

He grips the edge of the BMW's roof, hefts himself to his feet, then turns and leans his forearms on the trunk. Damn, he has a beautiful back—minus the bullet wound and blood, of course. His shoulders are broad and the muscles to either side of his spine ripple when he adjusts his position. A chaos luster zigzags down his right rib cage and disappears beneath the waistband of his pants. The urge to trace its path with my hands is despicably strong, but I force myself to focus on the hole in his shoulder.

When I toss the last blood-soaked wipe into the backseat, Aren dips back into the car. He rummages through the first-aid kit for a needle and a spindle of something that looks more like floss than thread. He holds both up to me.

"I didn't volunteer for that," I say, keeping my eyes on his face.

He watches me a moment, then says softly, "You didn't volunteer for any of this, did you?" He strings the thread through the needle himself, then, without hesitation, sticks it through the flesh beside his bullet wound. I grimace and look away.

"You're not what I expected," he says.

I keep my eyes on the dirt under my feet. He's not what I expected either, but I won't admit to that.

"I thought you'd be heartless," he continues. "Cold, like Sword-master Taltrayn. You're not."

"The sword-master isn't cold," I say before I think better of it.

He pauses with the needle sticking through his skin. "Do you ever get tired of defending the Court?"

I shrug off the question. He almost has the wound closed, but his blood-slick fingers struggle to hold the needle and he can't see what he's doing anymore, no matter how far down he tries to tilt his chin. He won't be able to sew up his back either.

"Here," I growl and take the needle. Before I can back out, I stab it through his skin. I tug the thread tight, slip it under a few of the other stitches, then tie it off. "Turn around." I grab his arm and spin him to face the car again. A few minutes later, he's all stitched up. I wipe as much of the blood off him as I can before I tape gauze over the bullet's entry and exit points.

Aren smiles. "That wasn't so bad, was it?"

"It was horrible," I say, letting my gaze travel over him. He's lost a lot of blood. Surely that'll weaken him, slow him down some. "You sure you can make it to the gate?"

"I'm sure." He leans inside the car, grabs my backpack, and then clucks to Sosch. The *kimki* darts inside the bag.

I step to the side and motion for Aren to lead the way. He slips one strap of the backpack over his good shoulder, then holds out his hand.

"I don't need my hand held."

"McKenzie," he says, his tone ever so patient.

I grind my teeth when I realize what he wants. Rolling my eyes, I take the keys out of my back pocket and chuck them at his chest.

ELEVEN

◦•◦

WITHIN THE HOUR, I'm wearing the Sosch-filled back-pack and half carrying Aren through the forest. He resisted my help at first, and I watched him stumble along our weed-clogged "trail." When the underbrush became too thick to pass, he used his sword to carve us a path. It wasn't until he overswung and almost hit me that I finally ignored his protests and took the sword from him. He managed a weak laugh and said he was worried I'd strike him down with it. He's not laughing anymore. He hasn't said a word in more than twenty minutes, and I'm too exhausted to attempt conversation.

He rests his weight across my shoulders. My arm encircles his waist. His body is hot. I can't tell if that's from his *edar-ratae* leaping to my skin or from a fever. Most likely, it's the latter. How long does it take for an infection to set in? His lips are pale and he's sweating. I'm sweating, too, and my back aches from supporting his weight. My boots sink into the wet earth and I'm seriously regretting not taking the time to put on socks. I feel like I'm shuffling ankle-deep in broken glass, my feet hurt so badly. Aren's not complaining about the hole in his shoulder, though, so I endure the pain.

Sometime later, I hear the murmur of a river. Sosch must hear it, too. He shifts in the backpack; then, with his signature chirp-squeak, he climbs onto my shoulder before leaping to the ground.

The forest thins enough to see the morning sun glittering across the river's surface. Sosch scurries to its edge and then laps at the water.

"Is it safe to drink?" I ask, hobbling to the bank.

"It shouldn't hurt him," Aren says, but he doesn't look anxious to try it himself. Is he not as thirsty as I am? I'm absolutely parched.

He takes his arm off my shoulder, stands on his own. "We're not far from the gate. Once we fissure, we'll have water."

I plop down on the damp ground beside the river. It might not be a good idea to drink the water, but I can't pass up the opportunity to dip my feet beneath its surface.

"Which way is the gate?" I ask as I unzip my left boot.

He looks downriver. "That way." He doesn't sound certain.

"How far was it on a . . ." Jesus, my foot looks worse than I thought. Oozing red blisters cover my heel and almost all my toes. The fresh air makes them sting and now I'm not so sure I want to plunge them into the water.

"*Nom Sidhe*, McKenzie," Aren says, staring down at my foot. "Why didn't you say something?"

"I didn't know it was this bad."

He sinks to the ground beside me. When he reaches toward my toes, I pull my foot back.

"You don't have the energy to heal me."

"You can't walk like this."

"You won't be able to fissure."

Silver eyes meet mine. "And that's bad for you because?"

Good point.

"Fine," I say.

He encases my foot between his palms. Chaos lusters quiver over his hands, flow into my toes, the arch of my foot. I tense and hold my breath, but I can't help it. I giggle like a schoolgirl.

Aren looks up from his magic, eyebrows raised, and Sosch perks his ears forward.

"Tickles," I explain. My leg jerks when an *edarratae* darts from my heel to my pinky toe and another snicker escapes me.

The weariness leaves Aren's face and the left edge of his mouth curves up.

"What?" I demand.

"I've never seen you smile before," he says.

I plaster on a frown despite the butterflies rioting in my stomach. "Don't get used to it." I pull my foot out of his hand. Damn this Stockholm syndrome. There's got to be some cure for it.

"You haven't tried to run," he says quietly.

"You see my feet?" I wisecrack, but I'm gritting my teeth. I don't need him to point out my lapse in judgment, my inconsistency. Maybe I should leave him now? I'm sure I can outrun him, but he obviously still has the ability to use some magic. He might be able to fissure short distances or stop me some other way. He's a healer, but that doesn't mean he doesn't have other skills.

Oh, who am I kidding? None of that stopped me before. I'm making excuses to stay by his side. Weak excuses. The real reason I'm still here is because I don't want him to die. Plus, if I abandon him, it'll be like I'm sliding a sword through his chest, and executing someone who's injured and in need of help isn't something I can do.

"Take off your other boot."

I swallow back my frustration and comply. Crap, this foot is worse than the other one.

Aren just shakes his head and sends his magic into me. I bite my lip to prevent another giggle from escaping. Thank God, he finishes his work quickly. Laughing makes me feel too vulnerable.

I pull my foot out of his grasp and then submerge both my blisterless feet in the river. Its cool current is invigorating.

Beside me, Aren awkwardly tilts back until he's lying flat. He closes his eyes. I watch his chest rise and fall. The crinkles at the corners of his eyes betray how much his shoulder hurts. I'm worried about it. He's not bleeding anymore, but maybe we shouldn't have stitched it shut. Maybe it needs to drain or have air or something.

"Talk to me," he says. "It'll distract me from my shoulder."

I doubt that, but say, "What do you want to talk about?"

A chaos luster shoots across his abs. Is it dimmer than usual? It's hard to tell under the dirt and sweat.

"How long have you worked for the Court?"

"Ten years." I pause, considering how much I should reveal. When one of his breaths turns ragged, I add, "I was planning on retiring."

Silver peaks between his lashes. "Really?"

I nod. "I was supposed to graduate a week after you kidnapped me. I was going to be a normal human, ignore the fae, and never set foot in the Realm again."

He smiles. "You could never be a normal human."

I glare at him, but he's closed his eyes again.

"Ten years?" he says after a moment. "You were young, weren't you?"

"Not that young."

"You still lived with your parents?"

I definitely don't want this conversation to go *there*. I lift my feet out of the water and rest them on the bank to dry.

He turns his head to look at me. "Will they be searching for you?"

"No," I say in a way that should end that conversation.

"Will any humans be searching for you?"

"Yes." Not a lie. Another couple of weeks and bill collectors will be calling. And it's possible Paige is missing me. Her sister's getting married this month and I promised . . .

Ah, hell.

"What?" Aren asks.

"I missed the bachelorette party."

"The what?"

"A party," I say. "My friend's sister is getting married on Saturday." Paige has never gotten along well with Amy, but she's the maid of honor. She has to play nice until the wedding, and I gave her my word I'd be at both events to help her keep her sanity.

This is why I don't have many human friends. Something always comes up with the fae, and I end up breaking my commitments.

Aren stares up at the tree-blocked sky. "Tell me why you started working for the Court."

I pick up a rock from the bank and blow out a sigh. He still needs a distraction? Fine. "What human girl would turn down the chance to be part of a fairy tale? I was sixteen. I wanted excitement and adventure." And love, but I won't tell him that. "The Court offered me all of that. They told me I was special, that I could help them, and that they'd keep me safe."

"Safe? From who?"

I watch Sosch slide into a rocky, shallow section of the river. "From the false-bloods. Thrain found me."

"Thrain?" Aren says, as if the name puts a bad taste in his mouth.

I raise an eyebrow. "I thought you false-bloods would stick together."

"I'm not a false-blood." He sits up. Too quickly. I can tell he's light-headed by the way his eyes lose focus. It takes a moment for him to stop swaying. "Sethan's not a false-blood either."

"So you say." I won't argue with him. If—no, *when*—I make it back to the Court, I'll have Kyol look up the Zarrak bloodline for me.

I stare downriver, the direction Aren indicated the gate was in. "I think you're wrong about the gate. Did you see it marked on a map? How far was it from the inn?"

"About thirty *yraka*." He blinks, focuses on me. "That doesn't help, does it?"

"It does. Kyol's maps are measured in *yrakas*."

He tilts his head to the side. "Kyol?"

Too late, I realize my slip. Aren's eyes meet mine, and, hard as I try, I can't keep him from learning the truth. He sees it in me, and a thousand emotions collide on his face. Amazement. Confusion. Horror. I manage to mask my feelings the same instant he does.

"You're in love with Taltrayn." It's not a statement, not quite a question, and I don't know how to respond. My grip tightens around the rock in my hand. He'll see the lie if I deny it. If I admit it . . .

What's Aren going to do? Run off and tell the king? Not likely.

He shifts beside me. "Taltrayn may be my enemy, but

he . . . he has principles. He'll never go against Atroth's wishes. He'll never disgrace himself with you."

"I know that!"

He grimaces. "I'm sorry. That came off wrong. I didn't mean—"

"The gate's that way." I jab a finger upriver, wondering why Aren's words hurt so much. Is it because he used the word *disgrace*? I would disgrace Kyol?

No. I can't let Aren get inside my head.

"McKenzie."

I stand and chuck my rock into the river. "If you don't want me to leave you here, get up. Now."

Slowly, carefully, he struggles to his feet. I keep my hands fisted by my sides. I won't help him. I don't care how much his face pales or how heavily he leans on his sword. I'll get him to the gate where it'll be easier for him to fissure and then I'm out of here.

His knees manage to hold his weight. "You're smart, McKenzie. You must see—"

"Don't."

"He's manipulated you."

"Just shut up." I turn away.

Aren turns me back. "He's agreed to be bonded to the daughter of Srillan."

I stop breathing. My heart shatters. It shouldn't. Aren wants to drive a wedge between me and the Court. Between me and Kyol. He's making up lies to lure me to his side of the war. I have no reason to believe him except . . . I know the daughter of Srillan. She's a beautiful fae named Jacia, and she's been around Kyol often the past few months.

Cold, damp air clings to my skin. I'm not shaking, but I feel like I'm breaking apart on the inside. Could it be true? And if it is, why wouldn't Kyol tell me? Did he deliberately hide it from me? I drop my gaze to the ground, unwilling to let Aren see the questions in my eyes.

Aren lifts my chin with a finger. His *edarratae* flare out over my jaw. I feel a bolt of lightning strike across my lips. Aren's gaze focuses on it, then on my mouth, then back to my eyes.

"He doesn't love you," he says.

I slap him. I don't know why. Maybe it's because all my doubts, all my frustrations, surge over me like a tidal wave. I don't want to face them. Not now.

"I see," Aren says quietly.

I shouldn't have slapped him. It's such a weak, girly thing to do. I should have balled my hand into a fist and launched it at his nose.

"Come on," he says. "We'll search for the gate upriver."

I had every intention to shove him through the fissure without me, but as we near the gate, I realize that's not going to be as easy as I thought. Aren must have been conserving his strength for this last leg of our journey. As soon as Sosch's fur begins to turn silver, Aren's grip on my arm tightens. His face is pinched and he's bathed in sweat, but he doesn't feel weak at all right now.

He digs into the pouch tied to his belt and takes out an anchor-stone. It glows briefly when he imprints it with a destination.

"You should let me go," I say, the first words spoken between us since we started upriver.

"And leave you alone so far from civilization? And with no boots? No, *nalkin-shom*. You'll come with me."

My barefootedness is an issue. The boots would have quickly rubbed my feet raw again, so I didn't put them back on. I took care to walk along the softest parts of the riverbank, but still they're sore and sensitive. They shouldn't be a problem for long, though, not once Aren is gone and I can use the cell phone that's burning a hole in my back pocket. I haven't had an opportunity to make a call yet. Aren hasn't strayed from my side once since we left the car.

Sosch's coat is completely silver now. He chirps and then scurries back and forth along the bank. If I don't look directly at the spot in front of him, I can see the blur in the atmosphere.

"We're here," Aren says. He keeps a tight hold on my hand after he presses the anchor-stone into it, then he carefully steps to the edge of the river and dips his palm into the water. I sense the gate before the light trickles between his fingers. *Edarratae*, dozens of them, flash to life, darting over his deltoids, across his firm chest, and following one side of the V that dives from his lower abs down to his . . .

I realize where I'm staring, tear my gaze away.

Aren looks back at me. "You ready?"

It would be such an easy betrayal to melt into his warmth. It's tempting. Aren, the son of Jorreb, the Butcher of Brykeld, could be my rebound guy. He could kiss me and touch me and do all the things I've wanted Kyol to do. He could fill the hole in my heart.

Until I give him the *Sidhe Tol*. What happens after he gets what he wants from me?

"McKenzie?"

This is ridiculous. I don't trust him, and even if—*if!*—Kyol agreed to a life-bond with Jacia, Atroth is still the rightful king of the Realm. The Court fae have saved my life dozens of times. They take care of me. I will *not* let Aren make me forget that.

Without warning and with all the strength I have, I yank back on my hand. Aren's grip slips, but his other hand is quick. He grabs me by the nape of the neck and pulls me against his chest.

"No." The growl rumbles against my cheek. His heartbeat thumps in my ear. "You don't want to go, McKenzie. You're running from me out of habit."

"I'm not."

"If you'd bend your will just a little."

"No!" That's how it starts, a little give here, a little give there, until I've given everything to him. I push away. He lets me take a step back but takes a tight hold on my wrists.

He sighs. "This fissure . . . it might not be comfortable."

"They never are," I retort.

"I've lost a lot of blood. My magic isn't strong. I'll take on as much of the drain as I can, but it'll be hard on you. Hold tight to the stone and to me. It'll be over quickly."

He holds both my wrists in one hand and then holds out his arm. "Sosch. *Up*," he says in Fae. The *kimki* leaps to his forearm, then to his shoulders. As soon as Sosch is settled, Aren pulls me into the ice.

No, not ice. Fire. My body convulses when we step into the In-Between. I nearly lose my grip on him. Everything is wrong at once. I'm outside my skin, not floating but falling. Falling fast. Fissures are supposed to be filled with piercing white light, but this one isn't. Everything here is black. All black.

TWELVE

❖

M Y DOORBELL RINGS. They're early. Great.

I run a brush through my hair, wondering yet again why I let Paige talk me into a double date. I should be studying or sleeping or doing any number of things other than going to dinner and some dance club with a guy I don't know. Besides, I'm not feeling quite . . . right.

I try to shake the fog from my mind as I toss my brush on the couch and walk to the door.

"Hey!" Paige says when I open the door. She bounces on her toes, causing her beach-blond hair to swing just above her shoulders. It's shorter than usual because she's twisted small tendrils into thin braids, braids that are pulled and twisted in a dozen different directions. On me, the style would look like one gigantic rat's nest. On Paige, it's some kind of organized chaos—edgy and sublime.

"Hey," I return, just as an electric thrum tingles across my skin. It takes everything in me not to turn around to see who's fissuring into my living room. My guess is it's Kyol. Fabulous timing.

"This is Ben," Paige says, nodding to one of the two guys on my porch. "And you know John."

I don't know John. The boyfriend I met last month was called Mark or Matt or something like that.

"I'm McKenzie." I shake Ben's hand. He has a strong grip, a nice tan, and, as promised, a killer smile.

"I told you he's hot," Paige says at the same time a voice behind me says, "I'll come back later."

I give a little shake of my head to answer Kyol. The world moves more than it should. Weird. It takes a few seconds for it to settle. That's when I notice Ben's raised eyebrow and Paige's frown.

"I mean, yeah. I was just . . . remembering I forgot something."

"No problem, psycho," Paige says, dragging her date inside. "I forgot to call ahead to the restaurant."

"Um." I look over my shoulder, see Kyol standing at the far end of my couch. His *edarratae* flicker a little more than usual—nothing too serious—but it's hard not to reach out and turn off the living room lights.

"I'll come back later," he says again.

I motion Ben inside. "I need to run to the restroom."

"Hurry," Paige says as she picks up my phone.

Kyol's gaze lingers on Ben before he follows me to the bathroom. When I close the door behind us, it's dark. Too dark. I rub my eyes until my vision clears. I almost wish it didn't. A jagged bolt of lightning flashes across an expressionless face. He's never this closed off when we're alone.

"I just met him," I say. "Paige talked me into a double date and . . ."

His eyes soften. "No, it's okay. You should see your own kind."

"That doesn't mean I *want* to."

"Neither do I," he says quietly.

"But you should, too?" It's a stupid question. Of course he should. We both know this can't go on forever. The king will find out. Some other fae will be assigned to escort me when I read the shadows. Kyol assured me the worst that will happen to him is that he'll lose his position as Atroth's sword-master, but I think there's more to it than that, more he doesn't want me to know about.

"There are reasons I should," he says. "And a reason I shouldn't."

The way he's looking at me makes my stomach flip. I

wonder if there's any way I can get out of this date. I can tell Paige I'm sick. It wouldn't be a complete lie—I do feel disoriented.

"I'll tell Radath you're busy," Kyol says.

I sigh. Never mind. Kyol won't let me out of it. "Radath won't like that."

"No," he agrees.

The lord general expects me to be at his beck and call, go where he wants, when he wants, no matter how dangerous it might be. Sometimes I wonder how much hell Kyol gets when he makes excuses for me.

He opens a fissure. The bright light makes me squint, and a sharp lance of pain strikes behind my eyes. I rub my forehead until it goes away.

"Hey," I say to stop Kyol before he disappears.

He turns away from his fissure.

"I'm not interested in that guy."

He smiles down at me. "You just met him, *kaesha*."

The smile and the *kaesha* undo me. I throw my arms around his neck. He wraps his around my waist. Some days we're better at staying away from each other than others. This isn't one of those days.

His kiss burns through me. I run my fingers through his dark hair, then let them linger on the sensitive spot just below his left ear. I want my lips there, but I'm too absorbed by what he's doing with his tongue. His chaos lusters rush into my hands, into my mouth, into every place we touch.

I must forget to breathe. I'm light-headed, but I don't want to stop. I press my body into Kyol's, pull his bottom lip gently between my teeth, and do everything I can to break his self-control. It's become a game, teasing and testing him. It's one I always lose, but one I never grow tired of playing.

He grips my shoulders and smiles against my mouth.

"Try to have a good time," he says, ending this game *way* too soon.

I rest my head against his chest. I don't want to have a good time. I want to stay right here in his arms, sleep forever in them.

"No. Don't sleep, McKenzie."

"I'm not." I close my eyes. He's warm. Hot, really.

"You need to wake up."

"Mmm," I murmur against his heartbeat.

"McKenzie. Please."

He sounds worried. That's strange. He hardly ever worries. Always so in control. More in control than I want him to be. But that's okay. It's comfortable here. Quiet. Peaceful and . . .

I'M dropped into a vat of scalding water. I lurch up, trying to evade the blistering heat, but my shoulders are held submerged beneath the surface.

"Easy, McKenzie. You need this."

The room spins and blurs as I awaken. *Focus,* I order. *I need to focus.*

Chaos lusters slither from a fae's hands into my skin. "Kyol?"

After an eternal pause, the voice says, "Aren."

"Aren?" I repeat, confused. I squeeze my eyes shut once, twice. Ah, yes. Aren, the Butcher of Brykeld, my captor. Of course it's him. Kyol would never hurt me like this.

I struggle to get out of the vat—no, the *tub*—again. "It's too hot."

"It's fine, McKenzie. You're too cold. Stay still."

His hands don't unlock from my shoulders. My *bare* shoulders. His *edarratae* flow unhindered into me. I glance down as a bolt flashes from his fingers to my skin. It zigzags below the water's surface, disappears briefly beneath my bra, then reappears before it skirts along my hip.

My attention snaps back to Aren. "I'm naked."

"Not completely," he says, and some of the tension leaves his face. His grip loosens. I try to sit up, to get out of as much of the water as I can, but he won't let me. When the room spins again, I stop struggling. It feels like I'm waking up from a bad hangover. I swear to God, I'm never letting Aren take me through another gate.

I open my eyes and take a quick inventory of my surroundings. I'm sitting just high enough in a Jacuzzi to see the rest of the bathroom. There's a separate, glass-encased shower on the other side of twin sinks. The white countertop is bare except for a magically lit mason jar. There are no bath mats, no towels that I can see. There's a vent for central air and heating, though, which makes me hope we might be somewhere in the U.S. Maybe this is some kind of rebel safe house? I want to part the blinds of the window over my left shoulder and peek outside, but turning doesn't seem like a good idea just yet. My equilibrium is still off.

"What happened?" I ask.

Aren's focus drops to the water rippling above my bare stomach. "I . . . You took more of the drain than I intended. I couldn't wake you."

I hug my knees to my chest, partly to hide my body and partly because I'm suddenly numb. Cold, but sweating. I clench my hands into fists, trying to squeeze away the prickling sensation in my fingertips.

"The In-Between's made you sick," he says. He reaches down to his side of the tub, then brings up a bottle filled with some deep red liquid. "Drink this."

"What is it?"

"It will make you feel better." He raises the bottle to my lips.

As soon as I take the first sip, I try to spit it out. He grasps my chin and tilts my head back. "Swallow."

His fingers dig into my jaw. The bitter drink floods my mouth and I can either choke or do as he says. The first gulp burns down my throat, sinks and sizzles in my belly. I grab his wrist, try to force him and the bottle away, but he doesn't budge, not until he's satisfied I've choked down enough of the liquid. When he finally lets me breathe again, I sit up in the tub, coughing and spluttering. I scoop a handful of water to my mouth and try to rinse the taste away.

"Are you finally trying to poison me?"

The faintest smile appears on Aren's lips. My stomach burns with something hotter than the flames of the concoction he forced down my throat. Damn him for being so attractive. Damn him for keeping me with him, and damn him for gazing at me with that stupid, sardonic grin.

"We've already discussed this," he says, setting the bottle aside. "Poisoning you would be inefficient, my *nalkin-shom*."

"You shouldn't have taken me through the gate."

He shrugs. The motion draws my attention to his chest, to

the scar beneath his collarbone. That's where the bullet hole was. The stitches are gone now. There's not even a scab anymore. The wound looks like it's been healed for weeks.

Holy crap. "How long was I out?"

"Only a half hour or so," he assures me. "Lena healed me."

"Lena." Her name puts a bad taste—one worse than that horrible drink—in my mouth. "She's a healer, too?"

Aren nods. "She's a stronger one than I am."

And she locked me in a room with a broken arm when she could have fixed it. Bitch.

"So the rebellion has at least two healers," I say. "I guess those endangered magics aren't so endangered, are they?"

"Ah, you've bought the Court's propaganda." He rests his forearms on the edge of the tub. "Atroth wants the Realm to believe anything human-made is destroying our magic. He likes to pretend it spreads like a disease, following carts of human goods through the Realm. If fae are afraid, they don't mind their king regulating the gates. They even think it's necessary for their welfare, but it's not."

"How do you explain the increase in *tor'um*, then?"

He hesitates just long enough to be noticeable and then he goes for a not-so-subtle subject change. "Here." He retrieves the bottle of poison and holds it in front of me. "Another sip."

I bat it away. "No." No way in hell. "Tell me about the *tor'um*."

"Just one, McKenzie." He grabs the back of my neck and an *edarratae* tickles down my spine. That pleasant heat explodes inside of me again. It's ripe and stirring and so completely wrong.

My frustration with him, with me, with us, boils over. Before he forces the horrible concoction down my throat, I grab it from his hand and chuck it against the far wall. It shatters in a satisfying spray of glass and crimson. "I said no, Aren."

He stares at the stained wall, then back at me. I swear he looks amused. "Your color's returning. And your spark." His hand grazes my calf when he reaches into the water to unstop the drain.

"Sorry," he says with a grin.

He's not sorry. He's deliberately messing with me, *teasing* me even.

"A towel would be nice," I snap.

He dips his head in a shallow bow. "Of course, *nalkin-shom.*"

He steps over my dirty clothes. They're stained with his blood. I hope I don't have to wear them again. I hope Kelia's stolen something new. I hope—

My heart stutters when my eyes lock on my jeans. The vigilante's cell phone. Could it still be in my pocket? I can't tell by the way the jeans have been thrown to the floor, but wouldn't Aren have said something if he found it?

He returns before the last of the water gurgles out of the tub. I make every effort not to look at my discarded clothes as he hands me a towel, which I wrap around myself as I stand.

"Where are we?" I ask innocently.

Aren crosses his arms, watching me. "Somewhere safe. You'll have to wear your old clothes until we get you new ones."

"Okay," I say, still not looking at the jeans. I'll have to find out where we are another way. It shouldn't be too difficult. I just need Aren to get out of here. My skin feels the touch of his gaze. Self-conscious, I pull my towel tighter around me.

Aren's hand at my elbow keeps me balanced when I sway. "You should have drunk more of the *cabus.*"

"I'm fine," I force myself to lie. "Can you give me a few minutes to get dressed? Please?"

The "please" is almost too much. His eyes narrow.

He glances at the window behind me. "We're on the second floor," he says. "Can I trust you not to jump out?"

"This towel won't reach all the way to the ground."

My quip dispels his suspicion. He laughs. "I'm glad you're feeling better, my *nalkin-shom.*"

"I'm not yours," I fire back, but he's already left the bathroom.

"Jerk," I mutter, but as I wring the water from my hair, I realize I'm smiling. Not good. Not good at all. *You can't have feelings for him.* He's manipulating me, twisting my emotions around and around so that whenever they stop spinning, I'll be malleable in his hands. I have to get away from him. Now. Before I start believing everything he says.

I frown. Am I believing some of the things he says? I've stopped thinking of him as the false-blood. I don't even know if I think *Sethan* is one. If Aren's telling the truth about that, it's possible some of the other things he's said aren't lies.

Like Kyol's life-bond.

My dream comes back to me. It's fuzzy. It would be even fuzzier if Paige didn't really talk me into that blind double date. I almost forgot Kyol encouraged me to see other people, other humans. Maybe he did so because he was seeing Jacia? But surely he'd tell me if he'd agreed to a life-bond. I mean, I'd tell him if I was getting married. The life-bond is similar to that, but much rarer because it's permanent. A bond-weaver ties the magics of two fae together, linking them for life. There aren't any divorces in the fae world; I'm fairly certain death is the only way to break the bond.

My head pounds behind my eyes. I don't know if Aren's lying, or if I'm lying to myself. I hate this doubt. I *need* to talk to Kyol.

I step out of the tub and, holding my breath, I scoop up my jeans. The cell phone is there in the back pocket right where I left it. I hold down the On button. When the screen lights up, I let out a breath. Hallelujah, it works.

I need to leave a message with Paige. Problem is, I don't know where I am, and I don't know how long it'll take my message to get to the Court. Will Kyol check with her daily? Does he have someone shadowing her?

I grip the phone and stare at the window. A dim light glows behind the blinds. I walk over and peek outside. The light is from a streetlamp. I check the time on the cell, see that it says it's midnight, but I have no idea what time zone I'm in. Paige always keeps a crazy schedule. She could be out partying or she could be home dead asleep.

Okay. We'll start with Plan B. I turn on the sink for some background noise and then dial the cops.

"Nine-one-one, please state your emergency."

"My name's McKenzie Lewis," I tell the woman as I step into my jeans. "I'm being held by . . . some people. Against my will. I need help."

"Can you tell me where you are, ma'am?"

I pull my damp jeans up over my undies. "Uh, no. I'm sorry. Can you tell me? Can you trace this call?"

"We'll have your location in a few minutes. You said people are holding you against your will? How many people?" She's calm and, I think, more than a little skeptical.

I grab my satin slip off the floor. I wish I had a T-shirt. "I'm not sure."

"Do you know any of their names?"

I glance back at the door. "No, I don't. Can you tell me what city I'm in?"

"You've called Cleveland nine-one-one dispatch."

"Ohio?"

"Cleveland, Georgia, ma'am. Are you being threatened? Are you hurt?"

"No, I'm . . . Just send someone here. Please." I hang up, hoping they had time to trace the call.

I dial Paige's number as I pull the slip over my head, hold my breath when I hear a click.

"Yeah?" a groggy voice answers.

"Paige, it's McKenzie. You awake?"

"McKenzie?" She sounds confused. Great.

"I need you to wake up, Paige. I'm in Georgia."

"What?"

"Has Kyol come to see you?" Silence greets my question, and for a moment, I'm afraid she's hung up.

"McKenzie, is that you?"

Finally. "Yes, have you seen—"

"Where the hell have you been? You promised you'd be at Amy's bachelorette party."

I grimace. "I know. I'm really sorry, but this is important. Have you—"

"You're coming to the wedding," she says, her tone daring me to say otherwise. "I swear, McKenzie, if you abandon me—"

"I'll be there!" I whisper-shout into the phone. "I'll be at the wedding if you'll just listen for a second. I need you to tell Kyol that I'm in Cleveland, Georg—"

The phone is ripped from my hand. I whip around to grab it back, but Aren launches it against the wall, hitting the center of the red stain I made earlier as if it's a target.

His hands latch around my arms. "I can't leave you alone for one minute, can I? Who did you call?" His fingers dig into my shoulders. "Who?"

"Aren, you're—"

"Naito!" he shouts.

"You're hurting me," I say. His grip doesn't loosen.

"What's wrong?" Naito demands, running into the room. Kelia and Sethan are right on his heels.

Aren nods toward the cell phone, but his eyes remain locked on me. I want to shrivel up and disappear. This is the expression he wore when he tortured Tom, and—and oh, crap—what if he does the same thing to me? What if he demands I tell him where the *Sidhe Tol* is? If he *truly* threatens me, will I give in?

"Aren, please."

"She called nine-one-one," Naito says, scrolling through the calls on the phone. "And another number."

"Every time I think I'm making progress with you . . ." Aren closes his eyes and lowers his head. I feel him shake, trying to control whatever's raging inside him. His hands are bruising my arms. Even the chaos lusters seeping into my skin seem angry.

"Aren," I try one last time.

Cold silver eyes meet mine. I don't dare breathe. He's not Aren right now. He's someone else, a fae capable of being the Butcher of Brykeld.

"This ends now," Sethan says from the doorway. "We're taking her to Lorn."

A muscle twitches in Aren's cheek, then he nods once, accepting Sethan's pronouncement. That's what it sounds like, a formal proclamation deciding my fate.

"We don't need to go to Lorn." Naito drops the cell phone and then slams his heel into it. "We can make her talk."

"She'll lie," Aren says. He pushes me into the wall.

"We'll take her to Lorn," Sethan says again. He walks to the sink and turns off the water. "I won't risk her sending us into a trap."

Naito's jaw clenches. "Lorn won't help without something in return."

Kelia rests her hand on his arm. "It'll be fine."

"I'm going with you."

"Naito—"

He pins her with a glare. "You're not going without me."

Kelia's lips thin, but she doesn't protest again.

THIRTEEN

◆

ICE FISTS AROUND me, squeezing, cracking, then shattering apart when we emerge from the gated-fissure. I suck sweet, crisp air into my lungs and waver unbalanced while I adjust to the Realm's atmosphere.

Lena releases my arm. That's how I know Aren hates me: he ordered *her* to bring me to this place. It's dark except for a thread-thin tendril of light peeking around what I assume is this building's door. I step back and my heel hits something . . . a wall. I lay my hands flat against rough wood planks. The structure feels small and crowded. I'm pretty sure we're in the middle of a village or city. Fae speak on the other side of the wall. Their voices aren't stationary. They're moving along a street, probably dodging around the carts I hear bumping over cobblestones.

The room brightens when Lena sends her magic into the glass sphere hanging from the ceiling. The blue-white light shines on wooden crates and barrels. Between me and a stack of cloth sacks, shadows from our fissure dance. They bend. They lengthen and shrink. My hand itches to draw them out. I think we're in a coastal city, but without pen and paper, I can't be sure which way is up or left or right. If I could just make one line, one tiny scratch on a page, I'd be able to orient myself.

"Put that on," Lena orders, gesturing to the cloak in my arms. She thrust it into my hands just before she pulled me into the fissure. I'm no longer wearing my ruined jeans and bloodstained nightie. Kelia gave me fae-made clothes before we left Georgia—clinging beige pants made of soft leather, an embroidered blue top, and black, knee-high boots that match Lena's. It's cold here, so I'm actually grateful for the addition of the cloak, but I refuse to follow Lena's command without at least a little resistance.

When I don't immediately do what she says, she arches a perfect eyebrow. "Aren won't be upset if I hurt you."

"He was upset when you broke my arm," I point out, even though I know things have changed between us.

She shrugs a shoulder. "Only because he wanted you to willingly read the shadows for us."

My stomach knots. I shouldn't let her bother me. She's just confirming what I already know: Aren's been manipulating me, using his *edarratae* to tease and tempt me to his side of the war.

The silver in her eyes seems to brighten. "Oh, it worked, didn't it? At least a little?"

I use the cloak as a distraction, unfurling it more aggressively than necessary. I don't like her seeing a crack in my loyalty to the Court.

"He was certain he had you after the vigilantes' attack," she continues. "But when you made those phone calls . . . Well, Aren's patient, but he can pretend for only so long."

I find the top of the cloak and swing it on. Forcing myself to keep my composure, I meet Lena's eyes. "Don't we have somewhere to be?"

Sethan would have been a much better escort, but at the last moment, Aren told him it wasn't safe to come. I'm not sure if Lena is here because they need an extra sword or if she's needed for some other reason. It doesn't matter, though. I don't see a way out of this mess.

Lena has no trouble returning my gaze. She crosses her arms, taps a finger idly on her elbow, then says, "Rumor has it you're in love with the sword-master."

If I look away, it will be an admission of guilt. Somehow, I manage to return her stare, though I don't think I'm breathing anymore. I'm cold, as cold as if I'm passing through the In-Between. I'm not used to people knowing how I feel about Kyol. I've spent the last ten years hiding it from the Court.

"So it's true." Lena shakes her head in mock pity. "The Court bought your allegiance with a kiss. Or was it more than that? No, Taltrayn would never lie with you, not unless his king ordered it, and there was no need to when you were purchased so cheaply."

I blink. I think she just called me a whore. Anger sparks deep in my chest, but before I can do or say something I'll undoubtedly regret, my skin tingles. I press flat against the wall as a fissure splits the air. A second later, Kelia and Naito emerge from the light. I try to focus on the shadows even though I know I won't be able to read them without sketching a map, but Naito distracts me. I rarely encounter other humans in the Realm, so it's odd seeing the white chaos lusters on anyone's skin except my own.

The storage room's door opens. Aren slips inside and shuts it quickly. He looks at Kelia. *"Is he still here?"*

"Yes. Near the herev," she says. I don't recognize the last word.

"How far from the gate?"

Kelia's brow wrinkles as if she's concentrating. I assume they're talking about Lorn. I also have to assume she can sense where he is. That's odd. And disturbing.

I watch an *edarratae* skitter across Naito's clenched jaw. His movements are jerky, angry, as he pulls the flaps of his cloak around him. Well, huh. My suspicion must be correct. Unless Kelia possesses some type of magical ability I've never heard of, the only way she could sense another fae's location is if she has a life-bond with him.

"Near enough," Kelia says.

"Good," Aren says in English. "That will make things simpler. You and Naito will lead the way. McKenzie and I will follow. Lena, you'll stay five to ten paces back. Don't look like you're with us. If anything goes wrong, fissure out. Understood?"

His gaze travels over them as they each agree. He doesn't look at me. He hasn't so much as glanced in my direction since he entered.

He gestures toward the door. "Go."

Naito dons his hood and follows Kelia out. Lena leaves next. Aren's going to have to say something now. He's at least going to have to acknowledge my existence because I'm not walking out of here without more information.

"Who's Lorn?" I ask.

He stares at the crates stacked against the wall. "Pull on your hood."

"Where are we?"

"Somewhere you shouldn't be seen. Your hood, McKenzie."

"Are you worried the king's soldiers will recognize me?"

He finally turns. If my back wasn't already pressed against the wall, I'd retreat from those eyes. They're angry, miserable, and judging all at once. I don't breathe as his gaze follows what I assume is a chaos luster across my face. Another one flashes across my hand.

Aren steps toward me. His expression doesn't soften, but his lips part slightly as if he's about to say something. He takes a second step, then another. He's within an arm's length. I can feel the heat of his body, smell cedar and cinnamon.

He jerks my hood over my head. "Keep your skin covered."

Aren's seriousness scares the shit out of me. I force myself to breathe again and try to slow my heart rate. "Where exactly are we?"

He grips my arm through the cloak. "We're in Lyechaban."

"Lyechaban!" So much for slowing my heart rate; it triples its pace. "Are you crazy?"

He harrumphs. "Indeed."

"These people will kill me, Aren."

"I strongly advise against an escape attempt." He pulls my hood lower, puts an arm around my shoulders, then forces me out the door.

I'll draw attention if I struggle, so I stay pressed against his side. I wish my *edarratae* could be hidden by illusion, but that magic doesn't work on humans so when a stout wind lifts the edges of my cloak and threatens to pull off my hood, I cling to the woollike material, desperate to hold it in place. I'm careful to keep my hands unseen, and to walk casually, to look like I belong in the Realm and this city when I very much do not.

There are certain places where humans aren't welcome in this world. Then there are places like Lyechaban.

I try not to let the memory surface. I try to focus on the shacks lining either side of the road, on Kelia and Naito, who lead the way east, toward the briny scent of the ocean. We're in a poorer district of the city. You can always tell by the amount of silver on the buildings. These are made of wood and brittle stone and none are painted with a coat of silver.

A fae crosses my path. His booted feet pass within my hooded vision. I lean into Aren. The one and only time I was in this city, a full guard of Kyol's swordsmen escorted me. Lyechaban is the capital of Derrdyn, one of the provinces that did not vote King Atroth to the throne. It's always been—not a lawless place, but a place with its own laws. After Kyol rescued me from Thrain, Lord General Radath learned Lyechaban's magistrate and his council were sheltering the false-blood. Since I was young and new to shadow-reading, I wasn't the first reader they sent in. I came after two others were . . .

No. I won't think of that.

Aren's arm tightens on my shoulders as he guides me around a corner. Beneath my cloak, I can see little of the city. I feel it, though. It always takes time to adjust to being in the Realm. Being in the Realm in Lyechaban takes even longer. Every movement I make feels so human and so wrong here. It's hard to convince myself I don't stick out in this cloak, but it's not like I'm walking down a street in my world. Capes and cloaks are common here, especially with such a cold wind blowing. I blend in. Probably.

We take another right turn. Aren keeps me between him and the buildings lining the road. I try to calm my heart rate and force my feet to continue at Aren's pace. It's artificially slow for a fae, but it's all I can do to keep up, especially when I have to be careful of my steps. The streets of Lyechaban are full of potholes and gaps.

Fortunately, this street is better than the last. Plus there's silver on the front doors of some homes and shops.

Ahead I hear rather than see the street becoming more crowded. I want to run, but we're deep within a city that is smashed between the Realm's tallest mountain range and the Kerrel Ocean. The gate is my only way out of here. How is

Aren planning to take me through it? It'll be regulated by inspectors and surrounded by Lyechabanians.

Oh, God. Maybe he's not planning to take me through it. Maybe he's planning to leave me here after we talk to Lorn. Maybe he's planning to turn me over to the locals.

Panic settles like a heavy weight on my chest.

No. *Don't overreact, McKenzie.* Naito's here. Aren has to have a plan to get him out of the city.

But I can't shake off the fear slithering over my skin, especially not when I recognize the structure at this twist in the road. A high silver fence adorned with intricate metalwork, effigies depicting the *Tar Sidhe*, surrounds the building. Black spikes make it look more like a medieval church than a political house. This is where the city's soldiers will take me if I'm found. If the Lyechaban citizens find me first, they'll skip the formality of an appearance before the magistrate and take me directly to the city center. Like criminals sentenced to the stocks in my world a century ago, I'll be put on display in the middle of the marketplace.

What if a human is on display there now?

My steps falter, stop. Someone bumps into me from behind. I tense, but they mutter an apology in Fae and keep moving.

The warmth of Aren's arm encircles me again. He speaks through my hood into my ear. *"Keep moving."*

He forces me forward a step. Two steps. I want to beg him to go another way. I can imagine rounding this corner and entering the city center. The last time I was here, two people were bound back-to-back to a pole on the central dais. I was halfway across the marketplace before I recognized them as human. I thought for sure they were dead. Then one of them twitched.

Aren leans down to peer into my hood. "McKenzie. *What's wrong?"*

"I can't—" I stop because I realize I'm speaking in English and I can't think of the words in Fae.

Get a grip, McKenzie. It's just a memory. No one will be on the dais. Every human who's ever entered the Realm knows better than to come to Lyechaban, and I'm not a coward. I can walk through a freaking marketplace without losing my composure.

"Nothing." I start forward again. Aren remains close by my side. With his arm around my shoulders, I know he feels my body tense as we round the corner. I know he feels when I let out my breath a moment later. Not that I've relaxed. No skinned humans are on display on the dais, but the market-place is crammed with Lyechabanians, or whatever the hell they call themselves.

Honestly, I'm not sure how I do it. I must brush up against a dozen different fae as we squeeze through the thickest part of the crowd. Even though I keep my skin covered, I'm terri-fied my *edarratae* will somehow leap through my cloak and into them. They won't be able to ignore the heated kiss of the lightning if that happens. I won't be able to run.

By the time we leave the marketplace, I'm shaking and sweating. I can't get any closer to Aren without him carrying me.

"We're almost there," he speaks through my hood again.

Is he trying to comfort me? I wouldn't be here if it weren't for him.

I throw him a glare he doesn't see. He hangs on to my arm as if he's afraid I'm about to run. Idiot. I'm not suicidal. In this city, I'm as good as chained to his side.

Aren leads me to where Kelia and Naito wait in front of a modest, two-story structure made of *tewar*, a pale red stone abundant on the east coast of the Realm. At first, I don't note anything special about the place. Its nondescript, flat façade blends in with the others on the street. The only difference between it and the buildings on either side is the glittery coat of silver painted over its walls.

Lena joins us at the door. No one says a word as she steps forward and taps the wooden planks with her fingertips. I don't notice the magical ward until its soft hum fades away at her touch, alerting whoever's inside that they have a visitor. I oscillate between feeling claustrophobic and overexposed in my cloak. It seems to take forever for someone to come to the door. When a fae finally cracks it open, he levels a crossbow at Aren's chest and wears a scowl effective enough to make me retreat a pace. Aren grabs my arm, keeping me from fleeing farther. At least he isn't thrusting me in front of him. On the other hand, death by crossbow appeals to me more than death by the hands of the Lyechaban citizens.

"We're here to speak with Lorn," Lena says.

"He knows I'm here, Versh," Kelia adds.

A hint of amusement touches the fae's silver eyes. *"Kelia,"* he drawls. *"You've been absent for months. It's good to see you again."*

"Let us in."

A smile curves his lips. He nods toward me and Naito. *"I need to see their faces first."*

"You know Naito," Kelia says. *"You can see McKenzie inside."*

Versh's eyebrows rise just perceptibly, causing a current of unease to run through me.

"A moment," he says and closes the door.

Aren's grip tightens on my arm. *"He recognizes McKenzie's name. He shouldn't."*

Kelia says something about Lorn. I don't understand all her words, but I think she's saying he has friends or servants or sources throughout the Realm. Aren's expression makes it clear he doesn't accept that explanation. Apparently, it took a lot of digging for the rebels to learn my name. Aside from Atroth, Radath, Kyol, and a few other trusted members of the king's Inner Court, no one knows who I am. No one's supposed to, at least.

Versh returns after a few minutes. He opens the door wide enough for us to enter. As we step inside, he says, "Only Kelia and the son of Jorreb need to disarm."

If fae had the guts to use tech as outdated as a record player, it would have screeched to a halt just then. Never mind that Versh spoke in English; he's deliberately insulting every one of us but Aren and Kelia. Not asking a guest to disarm when they enter your home is akin to giving them the finger. They're saying you have so little skill with your weapons you could never be a threat to them. Since I'm human and honestly can't fight worth a damn, the snub doesn't bother me. It bothers Lena, though, and from his stance, I think Naito might even be insulted.

"Nom Sidhe," Kelia curses. Without disarming, she brushes by Versh. "Lorn! Lorn!"

Versh lets her go and waits while Aren unbuckles his weapons belt and hangs it on something that looks like an extravagant coatrack. The rack is the only piece of furniture in sight besides a couch with a broken back in the large room to the right of the entryway. It's pushed up against a wall that is covered in . . . graffiti, I guess. Fae symbols are scrawled from the baseboard up almost to the—

I duck my head. There are at least two fae armed with crossbows peering down at us from the balcony. Even if they aren't Lyechabanians, I'm not eager to let them see my *edarratae*.

"This way," Versh says. He leads us toward the corridor Kelia vanished into. We take one right-hand turn and then Versh leads us down a narrow staircase. I have trouble seeing in the dim light, but I move toward the blue-white sphere hanging ahead. Four armed fae sit in the room at the bottom of the stairs. They don't say a word as we follow Versh through another doorway, but I feel their eyes watching us. Watching me.

I hear Kelia before I see her. She's ripping into a fae seated casually on the edge of a red wood desk. He's not bothered by her lecture. Neither are the two guards holding their crossbows at ease in the room's back corners.

Unlike the graffitied walls and dilapidated condition of the front of this building, the basement is painted a deep burgundy and has plush white carpet underfoot. A number of silver-framed paintings hang on the walls. I recognize the *Sidhe Cabred* in one, the Silver Palace's sculpture garden in another.

Naito brushes back his hood and steps to Kelia's side. The fae on the desk—I assume he's Lorn—steeples his fingers.

"Naito." He greets the human with an insincere smile before shifting his gaze to Aren. "I'm surprised you've allowed him to come. From what I hear, you don't have enough spare shadow-readers to risk losing another one." He glances at me. "Or two."

"You know why Naito's here," Kelia says.

I don't know why he's here. Maybe it's a male thing, a competition or something. If so, it's stupid. Naito doesn't trust Lorn—that much is obvious—but he should trust Kelia. She didn't leave him when the vigilantes attacked. She loves him. There's no need for him to risk coming to Lyechaban.

"That was over a year ago." He turns back to Naito. "And

my *kaesha* insisted I apologize. Surely even humans don't hold grievances this long?"

"It's a lack of trust, Lorn," Naito says. It's clear the fae is trying to get under his skin, but he does an admirable job of keeping himself together, especially with Lorn calling Kelia his *kaesha*.

"Ah, yes. I suppose that's not unfounded." With a flick of his fingers, he straightens his cuffed white sleeves and stands. "At least I can make this a short trip. I have no intention to increase provisions to the rebellion. Atroth is already quite peeved I've supplied you with silver, as minuscule as the amount was. You'll have to find somebody else to bribe."

"We're not here for silver," Lena says. Even though Lorn has been speaking English, I feel like I'm missing part of the conversation.

"No?" His gaze shifts to me. "I had an interesting visit yesterday. Few things take me by surprise, but when the king's sword-master himself comes knocking on your door . . . Well, even someone like me couldn't have predicted that."

Kyol's still looking for me. Why does that make me feel more nervous than relieved?

"What did Taltrayn say?" Aren asks.

"Why don't we have a seat?" Lorn motions to a shiny table to our left. It looks like it might be made out of *jaedric*. If so, it seems like an extravagant waste of money. This whole room is.

Lorn takes a seat at the table. Lena sits across from him. Kelia and Naito remain standing. I want to follow their example and lean against the wall, but Aren places his hand on my shoulder. "Sit, McKenzie."

I shrug his hand off but sink down onto the chair.

"Is she shy?" Lorn asks, staring at me.

"Most likely she's plotting an escape attempt," Aren replies. Then he brushes my hood back. With my face exposed, I feel naked, but I manage to keep my expression blank. I hope I do, at least, because Aren's right. I'm beginning to formulate a plan.

"Ah, there you are." Lorn smiles. "And the *edarratae*. Quite beautiful. Taltrayn is very concerned about you. Odd, that. I've never seen the sword-master unsettled, but he very nearly slit my throat when he didn't like what I had to say."

"What did you tell him?" Lena demands.

Lorn's eyes don't leave me. "I told him, quite honestly at the time, I've never seen nor heard of a McKenzie Lewis. May I?" He holds his hand out, palm up.

I glance at Aren, searching for some kind of direction, but his face remains impassive.

Okay. Fine. I reach out and lay my hand in Lorn's. I'm prepared for the hot lick of lightning, but Lorn sucks in a breath the second my *edarratae* seep into him

"Hmm," he murmurs. "I'd wondered . . ." His grip tightens. The *edarratae* surge with the prolonged contact. Three bolts spiral around my wrist, then through his palm and up his arm. His coal gray pupils dilate, and I'm not sure if he's going to let me go. Touching him feels strange and piercing, but I won't tug free. I don't want him to know how much this sensation affects me.

Aren straightens. Lorn's gaze flickers to him briefly and then he releases my hand. "Well, that answers a few questions."

I rub my palm over my pants leg, erasing the pleasant tingle. It's easier to work with the Court, where no one but Kyol ever touches me.

"We need you to read her," Lena says.

Lorn props his arm on the edge of the table. "She's the Court's toy. Certain people will be unhappy if she's hurt."

I glance between Lena and Lorn. Does she mean . . . Is Lorn a mind reader? Telepathy is supposed to be an extinct magic.

"I have money," Lorn says after a moment. "I have silver. I have excellent informants and a good deal of influence throughout the Realm. What could you possibly offer in exchange for this service?"

"She knows the location of a *Sidhe Tol*." Aren's quiet words fall like a noose around my neck.

Lorn's eyebrows go up. "Now, that's interesting. Tell me, however did you learn that? I wouldn't think Atroth would trust a human, not even his *nalkin-shom*, with that information."

"I'll work for you." It's a shot in the dark, I know. "Protect me, and I'll read the shadows for you."

"An intriguing offer," Lorn says. "But I have no need of a

shadow-reader, even one of your renown. You humans are tools for the Descendants, not for businessmen who stay out of wars for the throne."

"If you force me to give them the *Sidhe Tol*, you'll be taking sides. The king won't let that slide."

"I presume you'd disappear afterward." He lifts an eyebrow in Lena's direction. After she nods, he smiles. "The king will never know I was involved."

I swear if I found some way to kill Lena, most of my problems would go away. Okay. I only have one more offer to make. "Protect me from the rebels and I'll give the *Sidhe Tol* to you. You'll be the only fae who knows its location."

"Me and the king's Inner Court, of course," he says without missing a beat.

I feel a muscle twitch in my cheek. "Of course."

Lorn glances at Aren, who's standing over my shoulder. "I must say I'm tempted, Aren. I think you've captured more than you can handle."

Aren ignores him, takes a parchment from his pocket, and unfolds it on the table. I stare at the blank sheet, knowing what he wants. I remember where the *Sidhe Tol* is. I can imagine the lines I need to draw, the curve of the shallow creek as it merges into the river.

"You've no reason to remain loyal to the Court, McKenzie. They've used you all these years." Aren wraps my fingers around a pencil. "Help us." My *edarratae* leap into him as he places the lead tip on the center of the page. "Please. I don't want Lorn to have to pry it from your mind."

My chest tightens. He looks and sounds so sincere, but damn it, I shouldn't believe the word of my captor. Kyol didn't make me fall in love with him just so I would help him fight his king's enemies. He didn't agree to a life-bond. He's the man I think he is. Aren's the one who's been putting on an act. Lena came right out and said so.

I look at Kelia, how she's relaxed into Naito's arms by the opposite wall. They're not putting on an act, though. Neither one is bloodthirsty or disillusioned.

"Negotiate." I intended to make the word sound like an order, but it comes out more as a plea. If the rebels and Court fae would just agree to stop fighting, everyone would win.

"We've tried, McKenzie," Aren says, tucking a lock of hair behind my ear. The tender gesture is a stark contrast to how he's treated me since I called Paige. "We asked Atroth to restore the four provinces he absorbed into their neighbors. We asked him to stop invading our homes and to stop setting his *nalkin-shom* on us." He kneels beside me and rests his hand on the back of my chair. "The only thing he agreed to was lowering the gate taxes. He did that within days of the meeting . . . for his friends and supporters. We didn't want this war. Draw the map."

My hand trembles as I drag the pencil down the page. The line is nothing but a delay tactic. Even if he's telling the truth, I can't give him the *Sidhe Tol*. It will only add to the violence.

"I wonder," Lorn says above the soft scrawl of lead on paper. "Why did you side with the Court?"

I raise my eyes.

"Atroth is quite antihuman," he continues. "He makes exceptions for those of you with the Sight, but still, you must feel the hostility. The king's men aren't like Lyechabans—they won't cut the *edarratae* from your skin—but they don't like you, do they?"

Atroth is antihuman? The Court hates my kind? They're cautious around me, but I've never felt hatred. They've taken care of me.

"Do they?" Lorn asks again.

So it wasn't a rhetorical question.

"Some of them do," I say. Some of them are my friends. They speak with me and are curious about my life and my world. At least, I thought they were. Nothing makes sense anymore.

I return my attention to my sketch. My map will have to be a real one. Otherwise, they'll know I'm not cooperating when they aren't able to fissure when I name a city. But where to send them?

"There's rumor of scandal in Atroth's Inner Court."

My pencil stills on the shore of a river, a river that's nowhere near the *Sidhe Tol*.

Aren, kneeling by my side, says, "Finish it, McKenzie."

"My informants say Taltrayn has fallen for a human."

Silence takes over the room. I stare at Lorn. His lips curve up almost imperceptibly, but the smile is obvious in his eyes. Beside me, Aren doesn't move.

"I ignored the rumor at first," Lorn says. "After all, Taltrayn was entering a life-bond with the daughter of Srillan."

I close my eyes, gripping the pencil tight. It's true. Oh, God, it's true.

"Then I learned he refused the bond."

My heart stops midbeat. "What?"

Aren curses.

"Taltrayn never agreed to the life-bond," Lorn says. "Apparently, the sword-master loves you."

I'm cold, numb, confused. My pencil trembles in my hand.

"He's lying," Aren says, still kneeling beside me. Lightning sparks along my jaw when his fingers touch me there. Gently, he turns my face toward his. "Ten years, McKenzie. You've waited for him for ten years. Do you honestly think he's changed his mind? That he suddenly wants you now?"

There's tension in his jaw and the glimmer of something else in his eyes, but I'm too angry to figure out what it is. The bastard. The son of a bitch. He knew Kyol refused the life-bond.

I spring from my chair. Before I even think about turning my pencil into a weapon, Aren wrenches it from my hand. He yells at Lorn in Fae.

"I was curious," Lorn responds with a shrug. "She doesn't have any more choice now than she did before. Sit her down. Make her finish the map."

I pin him with my darkest go-to-hell look. "Screw you."

Aren's hand tightens around my arm. "It will hurt if Lorn has to pull it from your mind."

"I don't c—"

The door slams open. Versh bursts inside. "The Court! Taltrayn's men, they're—"

An arrow thuds through the fae's back.

FOURTEEN

∙═◆═∙

AN UNNATURAL GUST of wind slams the door shut.
Lena's most likely responsible for it, but everyone's moving at once. I flatten myself against the wall as Lorn's two guards rush to his side. Naito swings Kelia around behind him, and Aren sprints to the door, shouldering it shut when it cracks open. He locks it before they're able to get inside.

Lena throws a barbed glare at Lorn. *"Tell me you have a hidden exit."*

"Of course," he says, hurrying behind his desk. He touches a spot high up on the wall. A blue glow fans out beneath his palm, then a vibration fills the room as the slab of painted stone slides aside.

Something rams the door.

"Kelia!" Lorn shouts from the hole in the wall. He motions her to join him.

"Go!" Naito pushes her forward. She doesn't let go of his arm.

Kelia eyes Lorn. "Does it go to the gate?"

Exasperation takes over his expression. "You can't stay with him, Kelia. The Court fae will—"

"Does it go to the gate!" she demands.

He winces as the door creaks. *"Nom Sidhe.* Yes! Yes! Come on!"

Naito shoves her toward Lorn. "Take care of her."

"Naito, no!"

"Both of you go," I find myself saying. "I'll slow them down." I mean it. I don't want Naito or Kelia to get hurt. Somebody's fairy tale has to have a happy ending.

"We all go," Aren says. "Now. Run!"

After Lena disappears into the black hole, Lorn grabs Kelia, then Naito, propelling them both out of the room before following. I back away from the exit, but Aren catches my arm. An instant later, I'm half falling down a staircase.

Aren keeps me on my feet. He's moving too fast and I can't see a damn thing. I slip, landing hard on my left knee. No time to feel the pain. Aren wrenches me back to my feet. I catch sight of a flash of white lightning as *edarratae* brighten Naito's cheek. He's no more than a few feet ahead. Behind us, wood splinters as the king's soldiers finally burst through the door. They'll be inside this tunnel in seconds.

I try to tug my arm free. "They're here for me, Aren. I'll stall them."

His grip tightens. "No."

"You'll have time to get away."

"No!"

Damn it, why won't he leave me behind? Dragging me with him only slows him down, and I have no clue how he expects to get past the inspectors at the gate. If they don't turn me over to the Lyechaban citizens, they'll call the guards. They'll hold me until Kyol gets there and they'll arrest or kill Aren.

"I'm trying to help you!" I yell.

"You can help by running faster."

Okay. Fine. I don't know why I'm worried about him anyway. He lied to me. If his insistence to keep me destroys him and his rebellion, so be it.

I stop fighting him and run. It's not an easy thing to do blind. I trail my fingers along the damp stone wall and hold tight to Aren's hand. We're still not fast enough. The soldiers are gaining ground.

"Hurry!" Lorn's voice breaks through the blackness. A second later something intangible breaks. It feels like the snapping of a cord. The tension in the air shatters and the temperature plummets. A deep rumble vibrates through the tunnel.

Aren stops running. He shoves me against the wall, pressing his body against mine and tucking my head under his chin.

It's going to cave in on us. Whatever magical trip wire Lorn activated, he did it too soon. The ground lurches beneath my feet. My knees buckle. I cling to Aren, praying he has some kind of magic that can save us as the thunder grows louder and louder.

He swings me away from the wall. Something slams down on my shoulder. I stumble and lose Aren as I fall. When the ceiling hails down, I cover my head and pray.

An eternity passes before the quake subsides. I'm skinned up and bruised, but still alive. Nothing's broken.

Rocks skitter across the ground. I have no idea which way I'm facing, but it has to be Aren making his way to me. I consider playing dead until I choke on a breath. My lungs are so filled with dust and micro-debris it feels like I'm coughing up an avalanche.

Aren kneels beside me. "You hurt?"

"Yes," I force out between coughs.

Maybe his ears are ringing as badly as mine because he says, "You're fine," and lifts me to my feet. He starts to lead me down the tunnel, but my cloak drags me backward.

"I'm caught."

"Take it off." He unhooks the clasp holding the cloak together and shoves it off my shoulders. I look down when it falls and see an *edarratae* flash over my forearm. Short sleeves in Lyechaban. Not the greatest idea.

"I can't go out like this."

He tucks my hand against his side. "Just stay close."

I have no choice but to follow. My lungs itch, my shoulder aches, and I feel so beat-up the heat of the *edarratae* spiraling from me to Aren doesn't bother me.

"Watch your step here," he says, and I'm hit with déjà vu. I've done this before, stumbled along blind and hurt, depending on someone else to get me to safety. Kyol's always taken care of me, but little by little, Aren whittled away my faith in him. That shouldn't be possible. I know Kyol—I've always trusted him—and he . . .

He refused a life-bond because of me.

Guilt cuts through my gut, sharp as a dagger. It's this Stockholm syndrome. It's totally screwing with my common sense, making me doubt things I've always known to be true. Everything will be better as soon as I get away from Aren.

I hold tight to his arm as I trip. Since it's sudden, I almost take him down, too. He catches me before I hit the ground. I turn in his arms, sliding a hand behind his neck and letting my other hand drop to the ground.

"Are you okay?" he asks.

God, his lips are close. A part of me doesn't want to do this, but as soon as my fingers find a loose rock, I swing it toward his head.

He curses. Blind in the darkness, I swing again. This time, he catches my wrist.

"Stop," he snarls.

He might be pissed, but so am I. "You lied to me. *Deliberately* lied!"

"I didn't know he refused it."

"I don't believe you."

"I didn't know!" He shoves me away.

"You've manipulated me from the beginning," I accuse.

Somewhere to my left, he laughs. "*I've* manipulated *you*? I've kept you alive and safe. I haven't hurt you. I haven't lied to you. In a few days, you've learned more about this world and this war than you have the entire time you worked for the Court. Kelia's taught you our language. I've saved your life. I've healed you. You repay me with nothing."

"You kidnapped me!"

"I should have killed you!"

There's so much emotion in his voice, I swallow back my retort. I'm not sure if it's all anger. Is he hurt? I only hit him once. Maybe he was injured when the ceiling caved in? I refuse to believe the undertone of pain is from anything else. He feels nothing for me. And I feel nothing for him.

He sighs. "I can't let the Court have you back, McKenzie. If you want to live, stay by my side."

He pulls me forward, and I stumble along in the dark, trying to convince myself I have no reason to feel guilty. Aren hasn't killed or tortured me only because he needs my willing cooperation. I'm useless as a shadow-reader without it. I'd lie, I'd stall, I'd fissure the rebels into a trap. But shouldn't he know by now that I'll never turn against the Court? There's no reason to keep me alive anymore.

Chaos lusters mark a shadow ahead. Naito. Before we reach him, a sharp *shrrip* cuts through the air. Kelia steps out of the fissure, tosses a sword to Aren. She hands another one to Naito, saying, "Hurry. The Court fae are coming."

"Lena?" Aren asks.

"She'll fissure back with help."

We're only a few steps from the end of the tunnel. A faint light from above allows me to see Naito's and Aren's silhouettes and the wooden ladder climbing the wall beside us. Naito goes up first. I follow, grimacing each time a chaos luster flashes over my hands and arms. By the time I slide out a narrow crack in the rock, I'm shaking. I know better than to expect the street to be free of Lyechabans.

A fissure opens to my right. I recognize Aren's scent, the warmth of his touch, as he steps out of the light and helps me to my feet. Squinting, I take in my surroundings. We're on a narrow strip of land between the city and its river. Behind us, shops and residences are built almost on top of each other. Vendors have opened kiosks along the bank. I'm able to translate most of their shouts. Fortunately, they're selling their fish and produce, not pointing fingers at me and Naito. Yet.

Aren pulls me in front of him. I stumble forward, toward another group of merchants who are standing with their carts and *cirikith*, beasts of burden that look like a cross between a horse and a stegosaurus with small, opalescent plates as skin. Their bridles and the carts they pull are inlaid with imprinted anchor-stones to ensure nothing gets lost in the In-Between when they fissure. We're close to the front of the line where a thick band of silver plating covers the ground. The merchants have to pay a toll to cross the silver and reach the semicircle of bare earth, right on the river, where the gate is located. That's where the inspectors wait. When one of them looks up, looks right at me, I suck in a breath.

The next instant, his attention snaps to his left. A dozen fissures rip through the air just beyond the band of silver. Rebels charge out of the light, swords drawn and bellowing. A second wave appears behind them with Lena in the lead.

I'm astounded when the merchants don't run. They *always* run, saving their hides by abandoning their wares and *cirikith*. The rebels have been successfully attacking gates like this for years, but maybe the merchants have finally had enough of being caught up in the cross fire. Only a few of them flee. The rest draw their weapons and move between their carts and the approaching rebels.

"Sidhe," Aren mutters under his breath. One glance at him, though, and it's clear he's not worried about a bunch of merchants with swords. I follow his gaze behind us, down a street that leads toward the city center. The Court fae—about two dozen of them—sprint toward us. All at once and midstride, they open fissures and disappear.

"Go!" Aren shoves me forward. I skid across the silver plating. Fissures open up behind me—the Court fae are reappearing—and metal rings against metal.

Some of the king's swordsmen run by to intercept the rebels. As I push up to all fours, a second wave arrives at the edge of the silver. Then there's a third wave. Lena is in the midst of the chaos, vanquishing every Court fae who encroaches within the reach of her sword. Bodies drop around her. Some enter the ether before they hit the ground. Their soul-shadows float up and mingle with others. So many others. The bank looks like it's covered in fog.

Anxiety pools in my gut. I peer over my shoulder, looking for Aren. He's outnumbered, but okay. No, he's more than okay. In seconds, he fells two of his opponents, turns, and blocks an attack from a third. Holy hell, he can fight. He's surrounded by soul-shadows, too, and I realize there's a damn good reason why this rebellion has lasted so long: its leaders wield swords almost as well as the king's sword-master.

The sword-master. I climb to my feet and search the faces of the fae as they rush by, but I don't see him. There's too much chaos for me to recognize anyone.

"To the gate, McKenzie!" Aren yells. He's stepped onto the silver.

"Watch out!" The warning escapes my lips as a bleeding

fae on the ground pushes up to an elbow and swings his sword at Aren's ankles. Aren jumps over the path of the blade and then plunges his sword into the fae's gut.

"Go!" Aren orders.

Frozen, I stare at the dying fae until he disappears and the white mist of his soul-shadow rises into the air. What did I just do? My warning killed him. I killed a *Court* fae. I back away from my crime, clench my hands into fists so they don't tremble.

Someone runs into me. Then someone else.

"*Tchatalun*," a voice whispers. The word means "defiled one" but it's practically synonymous with "human."

"*Tchatalun*," the merchant says again, louder this time. I leap back when he swings at me, realize he's holding a dagger only when he strikes again. Aren kills him before he can cut me a third time. Numb, I stare down at the red stain growing across my stomach.

Aren's hand is there a second later, slipping under my wet shirt and flaring with magic. Lena comes to his aid, fighting off fae as he heals me. He eases me closer and closer to the gate, but there are too many people closing in on us. When a fae lunges toward us, Aren shoves me toward a merchant's cart.

I lose traction on the silver underfoot and land hard on my side. Pain, white-hot and nauseating, shoots across my middle. My stomach's not completely healed. Gritting my teeth, I ignore the wound, crawl to the cart, and slide underneath.

It takes a moment to catch my breath. When I focus on the blood and chaos beyond the shadow of my shelter, I see him—Kyol, conquering his way through the rebels. A rush of emotion fires through me. I want to shout his name, to be at his side again, but I keep my silence because I'm afraid I'll distract him. I don't think he knows I'm here. If he did, he'd be searching past the fae he's fighting, looking for me near the gate or the edges of the battle to make sure the rebels don't take me away from him. Instead, he wears an expression of cold indifference as he cuts through his opponents. It's a mask. He shuts off his emotions when he fights. I think Atroth and I may be the only ones who know how much the killing bothers him, but Kyol will do anything, slay anyone, for his king.

He'd even kill Aren.

I don't know why the thought pops into my head. Maybe
it's because my stomach hurts and needs healing. Maybe it's
the Stockholm syndrome reasserting itself. Or maybe it's
because . . . because I don't want Aren to die. Whatever the
reason, I find myself searching the throng, seeking his tall
frame and wild, disheveled hair.

I find him close to Kyol. Too close. They're fighting practi-
cally back to back. If Aren turns a few degrees to his left and
Kyol turns a few degrees to his right, they'll see each other.
They'll attack each other. And one of them won't survive.

It'll be Aren who's struck down. I'm sure of it.

Only two clashing men separate them now. One of those
men is Naito. He hasn't made it to the gate and, holy crap, his
sword cuts through a Court fae's defenses, cleaving deep into
his cheek and jaw. I don't know if the swordsman felt it,
though. The blow itself was hard enough to snap his neck. The
fae's body crumples. It's replaced by his soul-shadow a second
later.

"Naito!" Kelia screams a warning.

Another Court fae swings his sword at the human. Aren
turns, intercepting the blade before it finishes its arc.

"Go!" Aren shouts.

Naito sprints toward the gate, toward Kelia, who's waiting
for him in the circular area that's free from silver. She dodges
attacks while he closes the distance between them. When he's
almost to her, she dips her hand into the river. Stands.

A cry to my left. I turn in time to see Kyol pull his blade
free from a rebel, in time to see him take three long strides
toward Kelia. Her fissure splutters out when she staggers back
and lifts her sword.

"No," I whisper.

She deflects Kyol's sword, but doesn't duck under his fist.
It slams into her face. Naito's there the next instant, screaming. Kyol effortlessly parries the human's enraged attack. By
the time Kelia hits the deck, Kyol's disarmed Naito. Within
seconds, he opens a gated-fissure, wraps his arm around Naito's neck, then vanishes into the slash of light.

"No," I whisper again.

"Naito!" Kelia screams.

Aren skewers his opponent, turns toward Kelia, sees her

crawl to her knees and stare helplessly at the twisting shadows.
But she can't read them. She doesn't know where to go.

I do.

With a start, I look away, but Aren's already seen me.

The next minute passes in a blur. Before I can scramble out
from under the merchant's cart, Aren takes hold of me. He
pulls me out, holds me down on my hands and knees, and
grabs a handful of my hair, wrenching my head back so I'm
staring at the shadows.

"Read them!" he orders. He takes the paper, the map I
started in Lorn's basement, and unfolds it on the ground.

I shake my head.

"Now!" He jams a pencil into my hand. When a Court fae
rushes us, Lena leaps into his path, thrusting her sword into
the man's gut.

I don't move, don't even flinch, when the body drops down
beside me and disappears. I won't read the shadows. I won't
send Aren after Kyol.

"Either she maps them or you kill her!" Lena snaps,
deflecting another fae's attack.

Aren raises the bloody edge of his sword to my neck.
"Don't make me do this, McKenzie."

My breath empties out in a quick puff. No. He healed the
gash across my stomach—or started to, at least. He's not going
to kill me now. He's bluffing.

I close my eyes so I don't see any more of the twisting
shadows.

Aren yanks on my hair. "Look, damn you!"

His blade slices into my neck. My eyes snap open.

"I'll do it," he snarls into my ear.

The metal presses deeper. I'm too terrified for it to hurt, too
surprised to manage a protest or a plea. Warm, thick liquid
bleeds down my throat.

"Read them!"

I stare at the shadows. My hand moves. I don't know what
I'm doing until my map's scale changes.

Red splatters on the paper, marking the edge of a forest on
the west side of the Derrdyn Mountains. Kyol's there. My
reading is accurate enough for Aren to reach him before he
fissures again. I can save my life with just one word.

Another drop of red hits the map. I don't feel the blade at my neck, just the warm wetness that proves Aren is willing to kill.

He might be willing, but I'm not.

It's suicide, my next action, but I carry it out nevertheless, ripping my shadow-reading in two. Seconds later, I'm engulfed in darkness.

FIFTEEN

❖

I HAVE TO be dead. People die when their throats get slashed. They drown in their own blood. I'm pretty sure I'm not breathing. I'm cold, numb, and I don't hurt anymore.

IT'S oppressively heavy here. Vaguely, I remember the bite of the In-Between, but I don't know how I got from the merchant's cart to the gated-fissure or who took me through it. All I know is I'm not where I was before. I'm walking next to lightning. Stumbling next to it, really. My coordination is shot. I'm weak and tired. And cold. Why can't I get warm?

The lightning holds out a hand. Something warm presses into my palm. It's not enough to keep me going, though. My knees buckle. This time, I'm carried into the ice.

LUCIDNESS returns slowly, sane thought by sane thought. I realize my hand is pressed to my neck. I feel the cut beneath my fingertips. The blood's almost dry now, but I don't dare move. I'm afraid of opening the gash again. I have images of my throat splitting apart, of feeling my windpipe whistling red spittle. But Aren must not have cut deeply enough to sever whatever tissue protects my airway. Any more pressure, though . . .

We're in a suburb of Vancouver, somewhere called Lynn Valley. I must have overheard the fae name this place when we fissured here. I honestly can't remember. Shell-shocked, I think they call this. But we're definitely in my world. Only the fae have chaos lusters on their skin, and the house in front of me with its shingled roof, arched windows, and white siding is definitely Earth architecture.

"You need to rest." A voice to my left.

I slowly turn my head toward Sethan, see him standing behind Aren. I'm sitting against a wooden fence. So are a dozen hurt fae. Aren moves from one rebel to the next, laying his hands on them, easing their pain and healing their injuries. Even from this distance, Aren looks exhausted, and I wonder how long he's been at this. From the slump of his shoulders and his shakiness when he rises, I'd say he's trying single-handedly to heal everyone here.

Everyone but me.

He looks my way. Our eyes meet. The weariness in his gaze changes just perceptibly, growing heavier with something that might be a plea. My throat suddenly hurts, inside and out, and I glance away.

Too quickly.

The backyard spins. I close my eyes a moment, willing the world to settle.

"HEY."

Someone nudges my leg. I force my eyes open, see a fae in jeans and a white sweater squatting in front of me. At first, I think it's Kelia, but no stones are braided into this girl's hair. Plus, her eyes are unnaturally dark, and something feels *off* about her. When a chaos luster flashes across her face, I realize what that something is. The lightning is pale, so pale it looks almost white, not bright blue like a normal fae's. She's a *tor'um*, a walker. Born that way, I presume, because she doesn't look crazy.

"We need to move you inside," she says.

Maybe my head isn't completely clear yet, because it makes no sense for *tor'um* to be in my world. Fae aren't supposed to come to Earth unless they have permission from the Court.

I realize that doesn't stop all of them. Every false-blood I've hunted has come looking for shadow-readers and humans who have the Sight. Merchants fissure here as well, either to avoid the gate taxes or to take back Earth-made goods to sell. But the *tor'um* can't do that. They can't fissure.

"Here," she says, holding out a bottle of water. "Drink."

I'm afraid to swallow, but my lips and throat are parched. I reach for the water. My arm is heavy and my hand shakes so badly I accidentally brush hers.

I jerk back, dropping the bottle, as a chaos luster leaps into my skin. Instead of a hot, tingling sensation, the lightning is cold, almost numbing. My gaze shifts between my hand and her face, which has turned stony. She picks up the bottle and thrusts it at my chest. "*Tor'um* aren't contagious."

That's not why I recoiled. I'm human—it's not like she can damage my magic—but I haven't met many *tor'um*. I certainly haven't touched one before. They tend to keep to themselves. Whether that's by choice or because they're outcasts, I don't know. The ability to fissure is deeply embedded into their culture. Taking that away is a huge handicap no fae wants. It doesn't matter that some of the *tor'um* are able to work small magics; they're not able to instantaneously travel from one point to another on their own, so fae society has left them behind.

"You have half an hour," she says, standing. "Be ready to move by then."

An apology is on my lips, but my voice refuses to work. I take a sip of water. It doesn't give me more energy, though, and the back door to the house seems so far away. I don't know why she wants me inside. The other fae have been healed, but they don't look like they're going anywhere soon. They're sitting farther away from me than before, far enough that I can't hear their conversations, and someone's brought them food and water. Someone's taken care of them.

I rest my head back against the fence, letting my eyes droop shut again. I swear it's only seconds later when I feel someone watching me. Aren. I wonder how long he's been there, sitting with his arms propped up on his knees. His posture makes it seem like a while, and that makes me uncomfortable. So does his silence. I close my eyes again, hoping he'll go away.

He doesn't.

"May I heal you now?" he asks quietly.

"You're the one who cut me." My voice is weak, hoarse, and the wound across my neck stretches with each word, but at least I can speak.

Aren doesn't respond for a long time. I stare at the dew-covered grass. I should feel afraid or angry right now, but I don't. I don't feel much of anything until Aren says softly, "I'm sorry."

I pull my lower lip between my teeth. I don't want to believe him, but there's so much regret in his voice, in his gaze, even in the air around him.

"I didn't like hurting you," he says.

"You could have healed me hours ago." I want my words to come out angry, but I'm too tired, too hurt, to hate.

He tilts his head slightly. "I tried."

At first, I think he means he tried and didn't have enough magic. After all, he healed a dozen fae during the night. Then a memory surfaces. It's fuzzy but I remember Aren kneeling at my side and reaching out to me, and me, kicking and screaming and demanding he stay the hell away.

I shrug in response.

A minute passes in silence before Aren says, "The *tor'um* want you inside before their neighbors wake up."

Next door, the upper story of a house rises over the fence. Above it, the stars are fading from the sky. It's almost morning. Is that why the *tor'um* wanted me inside? Someone might look out and see me here, covered in blood? If I screamed, would someone hear me? Help me?

My throat won't handle a scream, though, so I ask, "Why are they here?"

"They choose to be," Aren answers. "To survive in the Realm, they have to rely on other fae, and they're considered . . . *enthess*." He pauses, searching my eyes to see if I understand.

"Second-class citizens?"

He nods. "Most fae don't want anything to do with them, but they can blend in here. The tech doesn't affect them much. They don't have to hire a fae to freeze their food basements. They can use refrigerators. They don't have to find someone to fissure them from one city to the next. They can use cars. They can find jobs that don't require the use of magic, and humans don't shun them. Here, they can be normal."

"What if someone sees their *edarratae*?"

"They'll let us know," he says. He moves toward me now, raises a hand toward my neck. "May I, *nalkin-shom*? I don't want to move you before you're healed."

I focus on the house. The Sight, like shadow-reading, is an inborn trait, but I made it through the first sixteen years of my life without running into a fae. Kyol and the rest of Atroth's soldiers don't stay longer than necessary, so the idea that any fae would choose to live on Earth confounds me.

"McKenzie?" Aren's hand is still raised.

"Okay," I say, brushing my hair away from my neck. He inches closer and lays his hand against the wound.

It burns, not as much as when he healed my broken arm, but enough that I grab a handful of his shirt and twist it in my fist.

"It's not deep," he says.

"It feels deep."

He shakes his head. "Your life-blood runs through here." His thumb presses against the heartbeat to the right of my windpipe. "If I'd severed that, you'd have bled out. I was careful."

"Careful, my ass," I say through gritted teeth. It doesn't hurt anymore. Now it feels good. That's almost worse than the pain. "I blacked out from blood loss."

"That was from your stomach wound, I think." He removes his hand and inspects my throat. "You've scarred."

"Great."

"If you'd let me heal you when I first offered, you wouldn't have."

I raise an eyebrow. "Do you really want to discuss who's at fault for all of this?"

When he traces my scar with his fingertips, it takes all my effort not to shiver.

"Lift your shirt, *nalkin-shom*."

I hesitate, but he didn't have a chance to completely heal the two gashes across my stomach. They were much deeper than the comparative scratch on my neck so I pull up the

bloodstained cotton. Looking down at the ugly, almost paral-
lel lines now, I figure I'm lucky to be alive.

"I suppose those are going to scar, too," I say.

He nods. "But these definitely aren't my fault."

I lose my battle with my smile. Aren sees it, and I swear his
mood lightens. All sorts of funny feelings shoot through me
when I realize I've relieved a little of his stress, lessened a
little of his burden. I wish . . . Yes, I wish he wasn't part of this
rebellion. I wish we could be friends.

I swallow back my smile. "Could you do this quickly,
please?"

"I could heal you with a kiss." Mischief sparks in his silver
eyes, and a thousand chaos lusters ricochet through my stomach. Heat flows into me. It's more intense between my legs.
Shit. *Shit*. What the hell is wrong with me?

"Just do it."

His chuckle tells me my reaction to him doesn't go unno-
ticed. Thankfully, he places his hands, not his lips, on my
stomach. I grit my teeth when he flares his magic. Pain strikes
across my middle, and I lurch into him.

"Shh," he soothes. "Almost got it. It's deep on your side."

My fingers dig into his biceps. His muscles tremble. He's
exhausted. He hides it well, but he needs rest. *I* need rest. My
stomach hurts worse than when I received the cuts.

"Aren," I hiss out.

"Done," he says quickly. He runs a gentle hand across my
stomach, back and forth as if he can rub away the memory of
the pain. Sweat beads on his forehead.

"Are *you* okay?" I ask.

He tilts his head a little to the side, and I regret voicing my
concern. The way he's looking at me, it makes me feel like he
wants me. I'm stubborn, but I'm not a complete idiot. I know
I want him, too. How could I not when his touch triggers lightning under my skin? With his devilish grin and mussed-up
hair, he's incredibly sexy, but I need a hell of a lot more than
a good-looking face to fall for a guy. I need someone like
Kyol, someone who knows me, *really* knows me. Kyol's concerned not just with my physical well-being, but my emotional
one as well. He protects me as much as he can from the violence of his world, and he worries about my other life. When

my parents cut me off, when they refused to speak to me until I got "help" in a mental institute, he was there for me. I can depend on him. And Aren? Well, he's proven I'm disposable if the situation is right.

I push away the hand he left resting on my stomach. "We're going inside?"

"Yes," he says, rising. He helps me to my feet, holds me steady while the world settles. "We'll talk, then you can clean up."

Aren's tone is sober. Too sober. He said he was sorry, that he didn't like hurting me, but where does that leave us? When I thought he was going to kill me, I didn't read the shadows for him. He knows I'll never help him.

When he starts to walk toward the house, I stay where I am. He doesn't pull me along. He turns to face me.

"You win, McKenzie," he says. "We're sending you back to the Court. We're trading you for Lena."

"Lena?" I can't possibly have heard him right. Naito's the one who's been captured.

"She was taken in Lyechaban," Aren says. He tenses with his words, as if he needs to guard himself against my reaction. Does he expect me to celebrate? To rub it in? I should—this is a victory for the Court—but I recognize Aren's mood now. I've heard this tone, seen this weight on a fae's shoulders before. He feels responsible for what happened to Lena.

"It's not—" I stop myself just short of telling him it's not his fault. I might not be willing to gloat, but I won't offer sympathy either. This is good for me. I finally get to go home.

I get to see Kyol.

My stomach flip-flops. Most of what I'm feeling is anticipation, but there's some nervousness twisting through me as well. I *need* to see Kyol. I need him to reassure me I'm working for the good guys, Atroth is the rightful king, and the rebels' claims about the number of provinces, the gate taxes, and the Court's transgressions are all lies.

"When?" I ask Aren.

"Tomorrow." He must notice my surprise because he raises an eyebrow and adds, "Too soon?"

"No. Not soon enough," I say, not wanting him to know how uncomfortable I am with . . . Well, with everything.

He looks away briefly, then says, "Your friend Paige. Her wedding is tomorrow night."

I feel my eyebrows go up, surprised he remembers that part of our conversation in the forest. He was hurt and bleeding at the time, and I was just talking to fill the silence. "It's her sister's wedding, yes. Why?"

"Taltrayn and I will meet there unarmed and visible. It's a public place. People will know you."

"There will be tech there," I warn. "Electricity. Lights. Music."

"It'll handicap Taltrayn the same as it handicaps me." He places his hand at the small of my back, guiding me forward. "Come inside. I won't give you back to Taltrayn looking like this. You can clean up and rest."

My first steps are wobbly. I cling to Aren, waiting for my fingertips and lips to stop tingling.

"You okay?" he asks.

As soon as the dizziness passes, I focus on him. "You do realize you're going to have to wear a suit, right?"

He tilts his head to the side. "What's a suit?"

SIXTEEN

—•—

IT'S MAY IN Texas. The night isn't cold, but it's not quite warm enough to chase away the lingering chill of the In-Between. I'm not sure that's why I have goose bumps, though. Maybe they've sprouted across my arms because of the lightning-covered fae sitting on a tombstone to my left. I told Lorn it was rude to sit there, but he didn't believe me when I said humans bury the dead under the ground.

I guess this cemetery is as good a place as any to wait for Aren. A thick hedge separates it from the road behind us and from the palatial building lit up by landscaping lights at the top of the hill ahead. There's a twenty-acre garden between the cemetery and the mansion's side entrance. That's where we're supposed to meet Kyol and Lena. I just wish Aren would hurry up and get here already.

"Eager to return to your little scandal?"

I don't give any indication I hear Lorn's words.

He chuckles. "Don't worry, McKenzie. I'm a master at keeping secrets. Why, you could give me the location of the *Sidhe Tol* and I wouldn't tell a soul."

I give a short laugh and finally turn his way. "I was wondering why you were here."

He puts a hand to his chest and looks wounded. "What? I just wanted to contribute to the cause."

"Forget it," I say. "You lost your chance in Lyechaban. I don't need anything from you anymore."

"Everybody needs *something* from me. You just have to decide—"

A new set of goose bumps spreads across my skin. Lorn mutters something under his breath about timing as the cemetery is lit by a flash of light. Aren steps out of a fissure, and my stomach does a little flip. He looks good. More than good, actually. He's wearing an expensive suit, probably stolen from Neiman Marcus or some other high-end store. The pants hug his butt and his jacket all but begs for hands to slide underneath it, over his firm chest and up to his muscled shoulders.

He's staring at me. At first, I think he's watching my reaction to him. Then his silver gaze lowers to my chest, to my silk-wrapped stomach and hips, then finally to my bare legs and peep-toed heels. I shift. I rarely ever wear dresses—I never know when Court fae will pop into my life and ask me to read the shadows—and I feel vulnerable and exposed.

Aren's eyes snap back to mine. He blinks once, clears his throat, then holds up a shimmery blue tie. It doesn't quite match the color of the chaos lusters striking across his hands and face, but it comes close. "What do I do with this?"

"I believe it goes around your neck."

Aren whips around to face Lorn. "What are you doing here?"

He rises from the tombstone. "Just keeping the *nalkin-shom* company."

Aren turns back to me. His gaze travels over me again. This time, it's almost as if he expects to find an open wound. "You're okay?"

"Yeah," I answer, frowning. Lorn met me at a gate a few miles north of the *tor'um*'s home. A rebel named Kian escorted me there, then handed me an anchor-stone. He left me with Lorn. I assumed that was because he was supposed to fissure me here. Maybe I was wrong?

"He didn't hurt you?" Aren asks.

A snippet of conversation comes back to me, Aren saying it would hurt if Lorn had to pull the location of the *Sidhe Tol* from my mind. Lorn's reaction was strange back in Lyechaban. I assumed that was because he hadn't touched a human before, but his touch also felt odd. It felt odd again, penetrating, when he took my hand at the gate.

I twist around to face him. "You invaded my—"

"It didn't work," he says with a sigh. "Apparently, humans are immune to my magic."

Aren gently squeezes my arm. "You're sure you didn't feel any pain?"

A chaos luster, hot and enticing, travels to my shoulder, so I pull free of his grip. "No. It didn't hurt."

"Don't overstress yourself, Jorreb," Lorn says. "If it worked, I would have had the *Sidhe Tol* from her in Lyechaban. I came only to make sure it wasn't a flute."

"Fluke," I mutter. I don't know if I believe him.

"We'll talk later," Aren says, his tone firm. Lorn shrugs in response.

"This goes around my neck?" Aren asks me, holding up the tie. "Like a noose?"

"Yeah, well." I turn my back on Lorn and take the tie. I've never in my life put one on a man. "It's suppose to go around like this"—God, he smells delicious—"and hang like this. But I'm not sure what to do with the knot. And these need to be fastened."

The top two buttons of his shirt are undone. My fingers brush his skin when I button the bottom one. I start on the top.

Aren's hands cover mine. "Is it important?"

If this was anyone but Paige's sister's wedding, I'd say it doesn't matter, but Amy's marrying a lawyer who comes from a family of lawyers. He's paying for this shindig tonight, and Paige swears he doesn't know how to tell her sister no. Thus the formal dress and the booking of the Marbarrage Mansion.

"You'll draw attention without it." I pass the tie behind his neck. A shudder runs through him when the silk sweeps across his nape. I manage to ignore it and the heat of an *edarratae* as it tingles up my fingertips.

While I'm working on the tie, I use the added height my heels provide to peek at the tag on his jacket. Armani. Figures.

"You fae have expensive tastes."

"*Kelia* has expensive tastes," Aren says.

"She went shopping?" *Stealing* is the more appropriate term, but I've never been one to worry much about semantics.

"She needed a distraction."

Lorn steps up and frowns at my work. "You're doing it wrong. That goes under, I think."

I slap his hand away. "When did you become an expert?"

"Even a fae can tell that's a mess."

I glare at him. Then I whip the tie off and start again.

Aren lets out a frustrated breath. He's having trouble standing still and his muscles are knotting up like he's prepping for a fight, and maybe he is. Kyol might already be here somewhere, waiting for us. For me.

"Are you finished yet?" Aren asks.

I undo my sorry excuse for a knot and restart. "This would be easier if you wouldn't move."

Lorn says something in Fae that I don't understand. When Aren chuckles, I make the knot exceptionally tight.

In the end, I give up. I decide it's better to have no tie than one that's atrociously looped and crooked.

"Just forget it," I say and stuff the blue silk into his pocket. Maybe Paige can fix it later.

"Thank the *Sidhe*," Aren mutters unfastening the top button of his shirt. He looks at Lorn. "You can leave now."

Lorn responds with an indulgent smile, then turns to me. "McKenzie, if you should need anything when you return to the Court, please do send a message." With a wink, he steps back and opens a fissure.

Shadows dance when the slash of white light disappears. Aren doesn't give me time to read them. He pulls me toward the gate that leads into the mansion's gardens. It's locked. He places his hand over the bolt and flares his magic. The metal glows red from the heat of his touch. Then, with one firm tug, the melted lock falls to the ground.

When the gate screeches open, he extends his hand. I accept it, but only because I have zero experience walking in high heels.

"One thing," he says before I enter the garden. He reaches into his pocket.

I open my mouth. Close it. I don't know what to say because the necklace is stunning. The chain is white gold, delicately linked and long enough to put the strand of thirteen diamonds right below my collarbone. The diamonds are smaller on the ends, but about the size of a nickel in the center, and, even on this moonless night, they sparkle like drops of light from a gated-fissure.

"Why are you giving me jewelry?" I manage after a moment.

A smile tugs at Aren's lips. "It's Kelia's. She says you can keep it if you send Naito back to her. Otherwise, she's promised to plant evidence linking its theft to you."

Oh, hell. This isn't like stealing a suit or a dress from some department store. This necklace has to cost hundreds of thousands of dollars. Not that I'm worried about Naito. Kyol would never hurt a human, not on purpose, and I'm almost certain I saw him press an anchor-stone into Naito's palm. I told Kelia this. She just stared at me blankly until I swore I'd make sure he's okay and that they would be together again. Guess she's holding me to my oath now, but I don't need the necklace as a reminder.

I push Aren's hands away. "I don't wear pretty things."

"That dress is pretty. I've always thought dresses were impractical but this . . ." He lets his fingers trail down my side. "It clings just right. I think I like impractical."

He makes sure he brushes my skin when he reaches behind me to fasten the necklace. His breath is warm on my neck. I don't know if he's having trouble with the clasp or if he's lingering on purpose, but my body reacts to his touch. My eyes drift shut.

"Stop," I say suddenly. "Aren, stop this."

He fastens the clasp and removes his hands. "Stop what?"

"I don't know why you're doing this."

"You want to stay with me." He says it as if it's fact.

I shake my head. "It's your *edarratae*, Aren. That's all. It manipulates my emotions, makes me think I want things that aren't good for me."

"I agree."

"And it doesn't matter what you . . ." Wait. "You agree?"

"Taltrayn's not good for you." He moves toward me. I back through the open gate and into the gardens. "The Court's not good for you. *They've* manipulated you."

The earth gives way to my heels. Aren reaches out, taking my arm to keep me balanced. Frustrated, I shake him off.

"What do you want from me? You want me to refuse to go? You need me to get Lena back and to have any hope of the Court letting Naito go."

"I want you to admit I'm not the monster the Court's made me out to be. Admit that you trust me."

"Trust you? Are you kidding me?" I sweep my hair away from my neck and jab a finger at my scar. "You almost killed me!"

"Humans will hear you if you continue to yell." He closes the distance between us again. "And I apologized, *nalkin-shom*. I'm sorry I hurt you." He runs his fingers through my hair, combing the dark locks back over my scar. "I'm very sorry."

"We should get to the reception." I need to walk, need it so badly I'm shaking. He regrets what he did—I know he does— but I can't meet his eyes when he looks at me like this. His emotions are too raw, too strong. Too confusing.

His thumbs slowly move to my pulse. "I wish we'd found you first. Your loyalty to Taltrayn . . . It's astounding."

"Aren—"

"I know," he says, taking a step back. "I know."

He doesn't press further. He keeps his distance, staying a foot or two away as we turn and walk through the gardens. The night air cools the heat in my skin. I keep my eyes off Aren and focus instead on the wedding guests who are outside enjoying the weather. I try to watch them without looking like I'm watching. I'm always paranoid when I'm with a fae around humans, even when the fae chooses to be visible. Since 99.9 percent of the population doesn't have the Sight, most people still won't be able to see his chaos lusters, but that .1 percent chance still worries me.

The landscaper who designed this garden could rival King Atroth's, but instead of being accented by magic, lights shine on bursts of colorful flowers, on meticulously shaped hedges, and the occasional tree or decorative boulder. A string of lights lines both sides of our footpath. The simple tech plays with Aren's *edarratae*. Not much. Just enough to draw my attention. I wish I didn't like looking at him. I wish I wasn't comfortable by his side.

A cool mist tickles my skin as we pass a stone fountain. A lion, its mouth open in a roar, plunges through a curtain of water. We walk behind it, heading to the steps that lead to the reception. It's not until the first notes of music reach our ears that Aren stiffens. He's still moving forward, but his gait loses some of its confidence.

"You can wait out here if you want," I say, climbing the steps, hoping I look somewhat steady and graceful in these damn heels.

"Would you wait with me?"

I reach the upper terrace, glance over my shoulder. He's standing at the base of the stairs, his hands stuffed into his pockets.

"I have to find Paige, tell the bride and groom congratulations."

I'm not sure if Paige will even count this as going to the wedding, especially since we missed the actual ceremony. The reception is supposed to last until midnight but by the looks of some of the guests, they've been here for hours, drinking and having a good time. It's honestly not my fault I'm late, though, and at least I'm here.

Aren climbs the stairs, his *edarratae* growing more chaotic with each step he takes.

"It should only take a few minutes," I say, hoping he'll stay behind. I don't like seeing the lightning this erratic. "I'll be right back."

"I'm coming with you."

He reaches the terrace, gives me a lopsided smile as if nothing's bothering him. He really shouldn't go inside, not with the lights, the cell phones, and other tech. The longer he's exposed to it, the more disoriented he'll become.

"We're meeting Kyol in the garden," I tell him. "He's not going to be in here, especially not with Lena."

"I don't want to take that chance."

But he'll take a chance letting the tech mess with him. That makes perfect sense.

I roll my eyes, turn, and enter the mansion.

I knew Amy's wedding was going to be extravagant when I Googled the location. This definitely doesn't disappoint. The ballroom is beautiful. The interior wall is painted with a mural of cherubim in the clouds while the outer wall is made up entirely of glass, allowing guests to look out over the gardens and fountains. A live band is playing a cover of a Bryan Adams love song—*not* the one from *Robin Hood*—and the dance floor at the foot of the stage is packed with people. I glimpse the bride and groom in the middle of the crowd as I walk the perimeter, scanning the ballroom for Paige.

Aren stays by my side. He's careful not to come in contact with the other humans, but me? He brushes against me every chance he gets. I seriously need to relax. This is almost over. I just need to make it through the night.

"McKenzie," a familiar voice calls from behind me. "Where the hell have you been?"

I turn, an apology on my lips, but Paige throws her arms around me before I can say I'm sorry.

"You call in the dead of night and then you hang up on me? What happened?"

"I, uh . . ." I didn't prepare for this, didn't think about it at all. "I took a trip to see . . ." What's in Georgia? "Things. And the pay phone cut out."

Paige steps back. She clearly doesn't believe me, but she lets it go for now, choosing instead to turn her attention to Aren, who's standing quietly at my side, hands once again shoved into his pockets.

"You're not Kyol," she says. Blunt, that's Paige.

Something flickers across his face. "No. I'm not."

Paige looks at me. "I thought if you brought anyone, you'd bring Kyol."

"No. This is Aren. He's . . . an acquaintance." I can't bring myself to say more than that. I should have, though, because Paige is inspecting him with new interest now. I might as well have jumped onto the band's stage and shouted, "Aren's available!" into the microphone. Paige is cute and spunky, even in a long, pink satin bridesmaid's dress. It's actually not that hideous, and with her blond hair pulled into messy but chic pigtails, she pulls it off.

Aren doesn't say anything. I'm not sure he's even paying attention. He's looking behind Paige more than at her, scanning the wedding guests, searching for Kyol and Lena, I presume. It's a waste of effort. If Kyol was alone, he might come in here looking for me, but not with Lena, who I'm sure will probably freak out when she sees the tiny lights lining the garden's walks.

"We were just going to tell your sister congratulations, then step outside for a while."

Paige rolls her eyes. "Amy's on the dance floor. Still. She's been on my case to dance all night." She focuses on Aren, who I just so brilliantly labeled only an acquaintance, not a love interest or even a friend. "Do you want to dance? It'll spare you having to meet Bridezilla."

He'll have to take his hands out of his pockets to do that, and one touch between human and fae will send his *edarratae* into her. Paige won't see the lightning, but she'll feel it. She'll assume the electric tingle is evidence of their chemistry, and since she isn't anything close to a virgin, she wouldn't hesitate long before finding a place where they could be alone.

"He's germophobic," I blurt out.

Paige raises an eyebrow and I wince. That's what I told her when she and Kyol first met and he refused to shake her hand.

"Jesus, McKenzie. What do you do, raid OCD support groups or something?"

This is why people think I'm crazy.

"It's just a coincidence," I say lamely.

Beside me, Aren relaxes. It's an odd thing for him to do in the midst of humans and tech. I glance at him, see his expression is just as unstressed as his posture, almost lazy even.

"He's here," he says.

My gut clenches when I follow his line of sight and see Kyol, dressed in a suit, holding Lena's hand just inside the open glass doors leading out to the garden. I'm momentarily startled because they look good together. They look like a couple. I never thought that when he stood next to Jacia. Maybe that's why I never suspected there was something between them. Only a fae as beautiful as Lena can be a match for him, not someone like me, someone who's plain and human.

Stop it, McKenzie. He's here for you.

Kyol has to be aware I'm standing beside Aren, but his eyes don't leave the rebel. He's wearing what I've always referred to as his soldier's face. It's hard as stone and impossible for most people to read. I can tell he's uncomfortable, though, being so near to the ballroom's tech. But he keeps his shoulders straight, his posture confident, almost aggressive. He'd walk through an electronics store without a hitch to his stride if I stood at the opposite end.

That thought brings a small smile to my lips. A familiar, peaceful warmth settles over me.

Something unspoken passes between Kyol and Aren before Kyol turns and leads Lena from the ballroom.

"Who's the chick?" Paige asks. She's staring at the departing fae, too.

"She's just a girl. I need to talk to them. I'll be back in a minute. I—" I almost said, "I promise," but with the way my life's been going lately, there's no need to make commitments I might not be able to keep.

Paige sighs. "I still think you're better off without him, McKenzie."

For the first time, Aren seems to really notice Paige. He gives her one of his sexy, lopsided grins. "I couldn't agree more."

Paige raises her eyebrows, giving me a look that says she approves of him. Yeah, well, she doesn't know a thing about him.

"We'll be back." Aren takes my arm and leads me through the crowd. By the time we step outside, his *edarratae* are spiraling up my arm.

Kyol's not happy about that. He knows how it feels to touch me and how I feel when I'm touched by fae. He's waiting with Lena at the edge of the lower terrace, a rare scowl breaking through his usually impenetrable expression.

Aren notices his reaction, too. He stops before we descend the stairs, leans down close to my ear, and whispers, "This could be an interesting evening."

I manage not to shiver. "Don't provoke him." Aren would lose in a one-on-one match against the sword-master. I'm sure of it.

He responds with a chuckle.

My descent down the stone steps would be clumsy and awkward in these heels if Aren wasn't keeping me steady. I manage to make it all the way down with something resembling grace. We wait for a pair of humans to pass before we walk toward Kyol and Lena. Aren stops me about ten paces away.

"Are you okay?" Aren asks Lena. She doesn't look injured,

but she doesn't look good either. She's not comfortable being around tech, even tech as simple as a string of lights. Of course, part of that discomfort might be because she's wearing a dress. It's a pretty dress, low-cut and . . . Wait a second.

I take a closer look at the familiar chiffon fabric, the soft, pale violet that falls over her slender frame, stopping just an inch above the ground.

I gape at Kyol. "You gave her my dress."

As a hello, my statement lacks much, but it's *my* dress and she's *Lena*.

Kyol's eyes shift to me, soften, and then turn to steel when he looks back at Aren.

Aren doesn't hold back, though. He laughs out loud. "I'm going to miss you, my *nalkin-shom*."

The night grows quiet as the music from the ballroom suddenly ends. Someone, a drunk cousin of the bride or groom most likely, takes over the microphone, calling for a toast. The humans in the gardens start to make their way inside. Only one couple lingers. They're sitting on the fountain lost in deep kisses.

"Let's do this," Kyol says, unlocking a bracelet of silver from around Lena's wrist.

Aren squeezes my arm. At first, I don't think he's going to let go. I contemplate trying to struggle free, but the couple at the fountain stands. I don't want to draw their attention.

"Walk to him," he says finally.

I keep an eye on Lena as we start toward each other. She does the same, her expression much more hate-filled than mine. She's not wearing any shoes. Lucky. I wish I weren't.

A woman giggles. I glance toward the fountain in time to see the couple run deeper into the garden instead of to the ballroom. They disappear around a high hedge, leaving me and the three fae alone.

"Go," Aren says the moment they're out of sight.

Lena opens a fissure and winks out of this world. Then, suddenly, Aren is back at my side, his arm around my waist.

"Jorreb," Kyol growls out. His hand goes to his hip, where, if he were armed, his sword would be hanging.

"Relax, Taltrayn. If I was going to back out of our deal, I'd have my people take her at the gate. We agreed on a midnight exchange. It's not yet midnight, and McKenzie has a wedding to attend."

Technically, it's a reception and, *technically*, Aren has no freaking idea what time it is. The days and nights are longer in the Realm than they are here, and he's certainly not wearing a watch. It *could* be after twelve now.

"What are you doing?" I hiss.

"I'm being selfish."

He's brave as hell, turning his back on Kyol like this. I peer over my shoulder as Aren leads me toward the mansion. Kyol is right behind us, a predator one second away from springing on his prey.

"Midnight," I tell him quickly. "It's okay. Really."

Only a pane of glass separates us from the humans inside, and Kyol knows how much I hate the fae causing scenes in my real life. If he fights Aren now, people will come running. But he doesn't seem to hear my words. His gaze locks on the back of Aren's head as he balls his left hand into a fist.

"Hey, McKenzie," Paige calls out.

Kyol freezes. I slowly turn to see her standing at the top of the stairs.

"You doing all right out here?" she asks, her blue eyes darting between Aren and Kyol. She looks more curious than worried.

"Um, I'm great," I say. Aren gives a short chuckle at my side.

Paige's lips quirk up. "There's a guy who wants to meet you, but if you already have two men fighting over you . . ."

"I'd love to meet him." I try to pull away from Aren, but he won't let go.

"She's occupied," he says. He's angled toward me now, and even though he's still looking in Paige's direction, I'm sure he's aware of the sword-master. He's not going to change his mind on this.

I turn back to Kyol. "Midnight. Please?"

His gaze drops to my face, and a chaos luster bolts across his clenched jaw. I hold my breath, praying he'll listen. He has no reason to trust Aren—I don't have much of one either—but I think he'll keep his word. If Kyol will just be patient . . .

"Midnight," he says, his tone a clear warning. "I won't let you out of my sight."

I give him a weak smile as a thank-you, but Aren's already pulling me up the stone steps. When we reach the top patio, I kick off my high heels. I'm tired of the damn things making me unsteady.

"Occupied, huh?" Paige asks, eyeing Aren's arm around my waist and not even trying to hide her grin. "I'll just tell Lee he'll have to meet you another day."

"I can meet him n—"

"Thank you," Aren cuts me off. "She appreciates that."

"No problem," Paige says. I give her a glare but she just responds with a shrug. Honestly, sometimes I question *her* sanity. After all, she has to be a little crazy to have put up with my quirks for eight years.

Aren's arm drops lower around my waist as he leads me inside the ballroom. I can't see Kyol, but I know he's watching.

"You're being an ass," I say.

Aren's single-shouldered shrug is full of fake innocence. "We had a deal. I'm honoring it."

Fuming, I grab a flute of champagne off a passing waitress's tray and down it while everyone else is still clinking glasses to Drunk Guy's toast. The music starts up again when I set the glass aside.

"Dance with me, *nalkin-shom*," Aren says, leading me toward the dance floor.

"That's hardly appropriate."

Predictably, he ignores me, and I find myself pressed close to him, surrounded by humans in the middle of an immaculate ballroom. Aren holds me close and mimics the movements of the people around us. I've seen fae dance before. They don't do it like this, swaying back and forth with no space between their bodies.

"This is ridiculous, Aren. I'm not Cinderella at a ball. And this . . . this isn't going to win my support, not even my sympathy. I won't—"

He places a finger over my lips. "I forget my responsibilities when I'm with you. It's nice. Peaceful." His hand slides behind my neck, beneath my hair. He plays with the clasp of my necklace. "I wish you'd let yourself forget things when you're with me. You'd be happier."

My heart thumps. I bite my lower lip, trying to erase the tingle the touch of his finger caused. I can't do anything about the lightning shooting down my spine, not unless I want to squirm and draw attention.

I swallow and scan the ballroom, looking for a clock. I find one high up on the nearest wall. It's huge and ornate with a frame of gilded roses. Its gold minute hand is only a few ticks away from midnight, thank God. I can't last much longer. Kyol can't either. He's standing there beneath the clock. I can see the battle inside him, his struggle to balance my request for patience with his desire to get me away from Aren. Aren's roving hands are making this so much worse than it needs to be.

"Are you trying to piss him off?"

He follows my line of sight. "He doesn't like me touching you, does he?"

"*I* don't like you touching me."

"I don't believe that." He smiles and, damn it, I flush with heat. The hand he splays against my bare back burns pleasantly and my knees seem to be weakening. My arms are wrapped around Aren's shoulders. We're too close. I should shove away.

"I'm curious, McKenzie. What will you do when you learn Naito's not fine? When you learn your precious sword-master killed him?"

"Naito is fine." My voice isn't as strong as it should be. That's not because I doubt my words; it's because Aren's chaos lusters are intoxicating.

His thumb traces the line of my jaw. "I'm sorry, *nalkin-shom.*"

I don't ask him why. I look away, staring at the clock on the wall because his silver eyes are too intense, his touch too intimate.

The minute hand snaps to twelve.

"Midnight," I say softly. I half expect to hear a deep gong toll the hour, signifying this moment.

Aren follows my gaze to the clock and then to Kyol, who stands beneath it, silent and ready. When the sword-master takes the first step toward us, Aren puts his hands on my shoulders, turns me to face him.

"McKenzie, listen. Don't let Taltrayn know you've learned our language. Think about what you hear. Look for the lies. The rebellion, we're not who they've made us out to be. You know us." His hands tighten on my shoulders. "You know me.

"Your necklace." He lets his thumb glide over the string of diamonds. "These stones, they have some of the same . . . *ekissrin*." He glances to his right, undoubtedly seeing Kyol is halfway to us now. "There's not a word for it in your language, but they're similar, diamonds and anchor-stones. They can both be imprinted. This one." He touches the largest diamond, the one in the center of my chest. "This one will take you to a safe place."

"Aren—"

"I'll be there every sunset I can. If you can't come yourself, send somebody else. Not someone you think you can trust. Someone poor. Someone who can be paid off."

Aren's crazy to talk like this, to leave me with this imprinted necklace. Kyol's only a few steps away and—

"Tell the fae a location outside the silver walls and I'll come for you."

My stomach knots. "I won't—"

"I'll come for you, McKenzie."

His kiss takes me by surprise. I'm aware only for a moment of Kyol's steps faltering, aware of him watching me, watching us. Then lightning pours from Aren's lips and there's only us.

My only defense is that the *edarratae* make me lose my discretion because I kiss Aren back. *Really* kiss him back. Chaos lusters tickle down my face and throat, bolt across my shoulders and down my arms. They shudder through my entire body, and I lean into him, press my chest against his.

His hand slides up my back, pulling me closer. Everywhere he touches is bliss. Complete, utter bliss. The hand on my shoulder sinks lower. It slides down my breast before resting on my hip. Only my thin, satin dress separates us, but if I close my eyes, if I let myself forget everything that matters in both our worlds, I can imagine it disappearing, imagine being skin to skin with him.

My eyes shoot open when Kyol grabs my arm. Aren holds on a moment more, his lips and hands lingering as if this is his last breath. As if this is the only breath in his life that has ever mattered. Then he locks eyes with the sword-master.

"You have competition now."

He backs away before Kyol can kick his ass and gives me a smile that sends hot aftershocks coursing through my body. I take a step toward him, but he disappears into the crowd.

SEVENTEEN

◆

"M CKENZIE?" KYOL'S HAND tightens on my arm. "Are
you okay?"

For a handful of heartbeats, I stare at the path Aren took.
Humans have blocked it off now, but I can almost see him
there. I can still taste him, still feel the lingering heat from his
touch.

An *edarratae* leaps up my arm. Kyol's *edarratae*. He lets
go of me quickly, as if he's unsure if his touch is welcome. Still
unbalanced, I stare into his face until my world stops spinning,
until the silver storms in his dark eyes ground me.

It's over. I wait for a rush of relief, but it doesn't engulf me.
Instead, it trickles in.

"*Kaesha?*" Kyol's brows are lowered with concern—
concern for me—but he should be worried about himself. The
tech in this ballroom is wreaking havoc on his chaos lusters.
They're all but constant on his skin.

I shake my head, dislodging the memory of Aren's kiss.
"You need to get out of here."

"McKenzie." My name comes out on the end of a shaky
breath. There's so much pain in his eyes I take a step back.
Could Aren have done something to him? He doesn't look
hurt. He looks more solid and stoic than ever.

"Come on." I tug on his hand again. This time, he gives me

a somber nod and follows. Walking seems to settle him. After only a few steps, he's the one leading me.

His pace increases once we're outside, half trotting down the stone steps to the lower terrace. A handful of humans are out here. We hurry past them, heading toward the back of the gardens, toward the cemetery where Lorn fissured me and where Aren fastened diamonds around my neck.

Shit. I have to get rid of this necklace. If the Court finds out it's imprinted, they'll find Aren.

Aren. God, he's a fool, trusting me with something like this.

Kyol's face is hard, troubled, as he scans the garden's shadows. I have to jog to keep up with his long stride.

"Kyol."

He doesn't slow down.

"Kyol, stop." I dig in my heels, forcing him to turn. "What's wrong?"

"I . . ." He sucks in a breath. "I'm sorry, *kaesha*."

That injured look is back, injured and . . . guilty?

"I'm okay, Kyol. Really."

"Jorreb," he forces out the name. "He hasn't . . . didn't . . ." He cups the back of my head, lowers his forehead to mine. His dark hair is cut manageably short, but it's still long enough to run my fingers through. I shouldn't, not out here where fae might be watching, but I want to comfort him, and I've missed his touch, his scent, his entire presence. He's broad and muscular—more muscular than Aren—and I feel small in his shadow, safe, even though he still seems off-balance. Beneath my hands, his muscles tighten as if he's bracing for a blow. "Did Jorreb force himself on you?"

It takes a moment to understand what he's asking.

"No," I say, almost offended by the question. "He never hurt me."

I realize those last words are a lie right after I say them and, seconds later—after Kyol tucks my hair behind my ear and his fingers slide down my neck—he discovers the truth. He frowns, his silver eyes dipping to my throat.

I pull my hair back over my shoulder, but it's too late. He felt the upraised skin.

"What did he do to you?" he demands, both hands exploring my neck, searching for other scars.

"It's nothing," I say quickly. "I was hurt. He healed me."

"Healed you?" He stops his inspection abruptly. "Jorreb is a healer?"

"Yeah," I say, wondering if I've just revealed information I shouldn't have. But then, why should I worry what I tell Kyol? It's not my job to protect Aren, and don't I want this war to be over? Don't I want the Court to win?

Ah, hell. This isn't good. My loyalties are so twisted up inside I don't know what I want anymore. The rebels have faces now, personalities. They're not so bad, and what if some of what they've claimed is true? Sethan might not be a false-blood. He might be a true Descendant of the *Tar Sidhe*. There could have once been seventeen provinces instead of thirteen. And maybe the fae's magic isn't fading as much as the Court thinks, and the gate taxes aren't entirely fair.

Maybe. I'm sure of so very few things these days. A head-ache pulses between my eyes.

"I want to retire."

Kyol grows very still. "Retire?"

I didn't plan to mention this so soon, but it's too late to take it back. Besides, this was my plan before Aren abducted me. It sounds like an even better idea now. I'll stay out of the Realm's war. I'll go back to campus, convince my professor to let me retake my final, and then I'll graduate and get a job. I'll be normal.

"Yes. Retire." I meet Kyol's eyes, but his mask is in place. I can't get a gauge on his emotions. "I was planning to before Aren took me."

He lowers his gaze as he runs his hands down my arms. He slips his fingers through mine. "I'll . . . I'll talk to Atroth."

There's a noise in the bushes behind me. Kyol spins, putting himself between me and the danger.

Fortunately, he doesn't need to prepare for a fight. A moan of pleasure accompanies the next rustle of the underbrush and two pair of bare feet scrape across the dirt. Humans.

"Take me home," I whisper.

Kyol's arm tightens around me. "It's not safe to go home. The rebels could find you there. I'm sorry. They should never have learned your name. We don't know how they did, but . . ." He draws in a breath. "I'm sorry."

It's obvious he feels responsible for what happened. That doesn't surprise me. He always takes his responsibilities seriously, and he hates to see me upset. This isn't his fault, though, so I smile and start walking, keeping our hands clasped.

"Where are we going, then?"

"Another human who works for us lives nearby," he says. "He's sending a car to pick you up. You can stay with him until you find a new home."

"Is he a shadow-reader?" The Court has five of us. We don't usually work together, but I've met the others.

"No," Kyol says. "He only has the Sight."

Which means the Court uses him in full-blown battles, the kind Kyol tries to keep me away from. Fortunately. I hate it when my shadow-reading expeditions turn bloody, when the rebels attack instead of run or surrender.

"My swordsmen are on the other side of that wall." He indicates the tall hedge we're approaching, and I let go of his hand. Just in time. A wooden gate cracks open, and a fae peers out. He's Taber, one of Kyol's officers.

"There have been no signs of the rebels," he says.

Kyol takes off his jacket, hands it to the other fae in exchange for his sword-belt. *"Jorreb was alone."*

My Fae is by no measure perfect, but I think I understand their words. Even if my translation is off, Kyol's tone suggests he expected trouble. At least, he expected more trouble than a dance and a kiss.

Kyol ushers me through the open gate. About a dozen swordsmen wait on the side of the road. They're dressed in *jaedric* armor. It's fancier than what the rebels wear, coated with a black polish and with the king's sigil—an *abira* tree with thirteen branches, one for each province—etched in gold over their chests. They're all invisible, I presume, because they'd look odd standing here beside the street otherwise.

Not that there's much traffic. Just one car so far, coming around a corner. I watch it, wondering if it's the one the human is supposed to send. But it's a limousine. Probably for the wedding. I turn back toward Kyol and Taber to concentrate on their conversation, but they're both looking at the limo, which is pulling to the curb.

The driver rolls down his window. I sigh. He probably

thinks I need help since it looks like I'm alone on the side of the road.

"I'm okay—"

"Are you McKenzie?" he asks.

"Uh, yeah." I glance at Kyol.

"He'll take you to Shane's home," he says, confirming this is my ride.

The driver climbs out of the car and opens the back door. Before I get in, Kyol cuts me off. He says something to Taber, then ducks inside.

"Ma'am," the driver says when I don't move.

I smile an acknowledgment and then slide onto the soft leather seat. Kyol sits across from me. As soon as the door closes, I say, "You shouldn't be in here."

"I'm not leaving you alone until you're safe."

"Aren can't fissure into a moving car." I would say more, but the driver climbs behind the wheel and the partition between his seat and our section of the limo is open.

"Do you need anything, ma'am?" the driver asks.

"How long until we get to"—what was the guy's name?—"Shane's?"

"About thirty minutes," he answers.

Thirty minutes. That's a little longer than Aren and I were in the car in Germany. He was injured and his magic came back. Kyol's completely healthy so he should be fine.

"Do you mind if I close this?" I ask the driver, indicating the privacy panel.

"I've got it, ma'am," he says. He presses a button on the limo's dash. When the panel slides into place, I sink into my seat, trying to relax. For some reason, I can't. Kyol and I are alone. We're together. But we don't say anything; we just stare at each other as if we've both doubted we'd ever see the other again. I know I doubted it.

Kyol's gaze drops to the floor. That's not like him. I'm more likely to glance away, either because I'm worried others will see the way I look at him or because it's too hard to stay apart.

He unfastens his sword-belt and lays it on the seat. I'm not used to seeing him like this, looking so unsure of himself. I watch his *edarratae*. If they start to look too frenzied, I'll tell the driver I don't feel well and ask him to pull over. Kyol looks fine, though. There's only a slight crease to his forehead. Whether that's because the tech is giving him a headache or because he's thinking about something serious, I don't know. Maybe both. The heavy silence suggests he wants to discuss something.

Nervousness coils in my stomach. I think he wants to talk about us. Every conversation we've ever had about our relationship ended one way, with him telling me we can never be together.

His gaze returns to me and, suddenly, it's very important we don't have that conversation.

"I flunked my final again," I say quickly. "I don't know if my professor will let me retake it. I'll never be able to explain why I ran out of class."

He blinks. Yeah, my topic is that random.

"I'm sorry. There wasn't time and . . ." He lets out a breath and his shoulders slump. "In the end, it didn't matter. I wasn't fast enough." He shakes his head and frustration leaks into his voice. "I took precautions. I always double-fissured you home and only a few fae knew your full name. Fae I trusted. If I'd known you were in danger, I wouldn't have let you out of my sight. I'd have kept you safe." His hand clenches on the sword lying at his side. Conviction shines in his silver eyes. "I *can* keep you safe, McKenzie."

Butterflies take flight in my stomach. Not good. My determination to retire wavers like it always does. I don't want to leave him. Ever.

He holds out a hand, but I pretend not to see it. Instead, I scoot along my seat toward the wet bar in the back corner of the limo.

"I missed Amy's bachelorette party," I say, scrutinizing the label on every bottle, one by one. "It's a human tradition, basically an excuse to go out and get wasted. I promised Paige I'd be there."

"McKenzie—"

"I think she's forgiven me, though," I continue, refusing to look at him. "She was worried when I didn't return her calls."

Kyol moves to sit beside me. I grab an individual-sized bottle of wine, twist the top off, and pour it into a glass. My hand shakes, mostly from the motion of the limo, but partly from nerves. I'm usually more together than this, more in control, but I'm tired of . . . of everything.

Kyol puts his hand over the glass before I raise it to my lips. "McKenzie." His *edarratae* quiver across his skin. "Talk to me. I need to know you're okay."

"I'm fine."

"Look at me." He lifts my chin, forcing me to meet his silver eyes.

"Kyol." I draw in a breath. "I can't do this. I can't go back to the way things were, sneaking touches when no one is looking." I won't live like that. Not anymore.

"Okay."

"I know Radath and the king will—What?"

He runs his hands down my arms, then back up, leaving a trail of heat in their wake. "These last couple of weeks . . . they've been the worst of my life. Jorreb sent a fae with your clothes. They were stained red and . . ." He swallows. "I thought you were dead. I thought I'd never see you again, and I hated myself for holding back when we were together. I remembered every time I told you no, and all I wanted was the chance to tell you yes. I have that chance now." His hands tighten on my shoulders. "I'll talk to Atroth, McKenzie. If you'll forgive me, if you still want me, I'll talk to him. I'll convince him you and I should be together."

Really? I want to ask, but I can't form the question. This is what I've always wanted, the hope I've been clinging to for a decade, and now, I'm terrified I might be trapped in a dream. Maybe Aren killed me when he cut my throat. Something has to be up because this is too simple, too easy, to be real.

"What about you?" I ask when I find my voice. "Won't Atroth want you to be with someone else? Someone like Jacia?" Even though Lorn said Kyol refused the life-bond, it hurts to say her name.

He frowns. "How . . . Who told you that?"

My lips tighten into a thin, apologetic smile.

"Jorreb," he says. He lets go of my shoulders. "Atroth wants that—the daughter of Srillan is a good match for me—but I will never make a bond. Never, McKenzie."

"The king knows why?" If Atroth knows Kyol loves me,

why hasn't he done something? Why hasn't he changed the law, made an exception to it, or assigned me to another fae?

Kyol lets out a sigh. "I'm sure he suspects it, but if I don't say anything and there's no evidence to support it, I think he'll continue to ignore us."

But if he does say something . . .

"Will you lose your position?" I ask.

"There is a chance of that. I would like . . ." He stops, closes his eyes. When he opens them again, there's an apology there. "I need a few days. You'll need to tell us what you know about the rebellion. We'll find its leaders and take them out. When the war is over, Atroth will be more willing to listen. If he doesn't . . . if he won't allow us to be together, I'll leave the Court. I'll stay with you."

Everything I want, dangled in front of me like a carrot.

"And if the war doesn't end?" I ask, my voice quiet.

"If we take out the son of Jorreb, it will."

I have the means to kill Aren, hanging around my neck. My heart constricts. I love Kyol—always have, always will— but I can still feel Aren's lips, desperate against mine. I hear his last words to me, making a promise to come for me, a promise that, somehow, I know he would keep. I've spent the last few weeks trying to get away from him, and now that I'm free . . .

Isn't this so freaking fantastic? I've spent ten years searching for someone to fill the spot in my heart meant for Kyol, and when I finally find a contender, he's an enemy and he's fae.

Why the hell can't I fall in love with a human?

I suck in a breath. No. No way. I don't love Aren. I can't because, damn it, I'm not one of *those* girls, the ones who have two men chasing after them but can't make up their minds who to choose. If you can't decide who you love more, you don't love either of them enough. So I don't have feelings for Aren. I won't.

But I don't want him to die.

I close my eyes. I don't know which is the bigger betrayal: giving the imprinted necklace to Kyol or keeping it to myself?

"McKenzie?"

"I want this to be over," I say.

Kyol lets out an audible sigh and tension drains from his shoulders. "I know. Come here, *kaesha*."

He sets my glass of wine aside and pulls me into his arms. *Edarratae* flicker across his skin. His fingertips trace up my back to the nape of my neck. Lightning tickles the tiny hairs there before shimmying down my spine.

"I've missed this," he murmurs. "I didn't realize how much I would." His thumbs move to the heartbeat on either side of my throat, and he gives me a rare smile, the one he reserves just for me.

"You should get some rest," he says, pressing a kiss to my forehead. A chaos luster strikes down the side of my face. His lips trail it, then hover millimeters away from mine.

I won't be able to sleep, not with this heat pulsing in my veins. I close the distance between us. He doesn't resist. His lips slant hard across mine, pouring lightning into me. My heart thumps, startled by the intensity of the kiss. I half expect him to stop. This is the point when he usually pulls back, unwilling to get carried away, so I brace myself, waiting for a cold rush of air.

He doesn't stop. His silver eyes turn stormy, and it sinks in that he really means what he said. When the war's over, we'll be together, with the king's blessing or without it.

Finally.

My dress hikes up to my hips when he pulls me into his lap. I press against him, and his chest rumbles with a low growl. A smile finds its way to my lips. I love him like this, when all his self-control shatters and he becomes vulnerable to my touch.

There's desperation in his movements when he lays me down on the long bench-seat, capturing me between the soft leather and his hard body. He lowers his mouth to my jaw, guides his lips slowly to my ear. I moan and he moves to the hollow of my throat and—oh, shit. The imprinted necklace. His lips brush over it, then stop, lingering on the scar on the side of my neck. I tense, but he only presses a kiss there. He doesn't notice the extra heat of the stone.

Slowly, his hand slides down my silk-covered side, over my hip and lower, until he finds my bare thigh. He draws patterns on my skin, tiny circles that send a bolt of *edarratae* up my leg.

His hands are tantalizingly hot. I kiss him brutally, knowing Naito was right. Being with a human will never compare to this.

Ah, hell.

"Naito."

Kyol's hands still, but his chest heaves with his breaths. "What?"

I close my eyes. I'm a friggin' moron for breaking this moment.

"Naito," I say, forcing myself to meet Kyol's gaze. "The shadow-reader you took through the gate in Lyechaban. Is he okay?"

A line creases his brow. "You're thinking about Naito?"

"No, not really. I just . . . I didn't see you give him an anchor-stone and, well, I was worried."

"I gave him an anchor-stone," he says after a moment, removing his hand from my thigh. "I didn't know you were there."

Damn, damn, damn.

"So he's okay?"

Another long pause, then, "He's fine." He smoothes back my hair, plants a kiss on my forehead. "I promise."

I grimace when he slides away, leaving me to the cold air.

"I'm sorry," I say, sitting up as well.

To my relief, he gives me a small smile. "It's okay, *kaesha*. We're almost to Shane's."

Still, I feel like crap—guilty—because I shouldn't have asked if Naito was okay. The Court fae go out of their way to keep humans safe. They saved me from Thrain ten years ago and have rescued others who were under the control of false-bloods. Aren's just messed with my mind. Give me a few more hours, and everything will make sense again.

EIGHTEEN

❖

I AWAKEN TO a kiss on my forehead. It's so tender, and I'm so cozy and comfortable, that I don't react until lightning skates across my brow.

Panicked, I lurch up and shove at the fae hovering over me.

"Shh, *kaesha*. You're safe here."

Kaesha, not *nalkin-shom*. If it was the latter, though, I think it would have calmed me just as much. I let out a breath, then sink back into a pillow and focus on Kyol. "What time is it?"

"It's morning," he says. "I shouldn't stay any longer, and I need to speak with Atroth."

Stay? I scan my surroundings. We're not in the limo; we're in a bed. I don't remember closing my eyes, but I must have and this must be Shane's house, a guest bedroom by the look of it. Has Kyol been here the whole time? His chaos lusters are agitated, much more than they were on the drive here. Even though the lights are off, electricity runs through the wires in the wall, and there's likely Wi-Fi or cordless phones around. With the wedding, the limo ride, and this house, he's been exposed to tech for far too long.

I sit up. "You shouldn't be here."

"I'm only a little disoriented," he says. "I'll be fine as soon as I return to the Realm."

I start to peel back the comforter.

"No." Kyol rests his hand on mine. "Don't get up. Sleep. I'll send Taber for you in a few hours."

He squeezes my hand and then lets it slide through his as he stands. Even if the tech wasn't bothering him, he'd still have to leave. I'm sure Atroth and Lord General Radath both want a report. They'll want to talk to me, too.

"Kyol?"

He peers down, waiting, but I don't know what I wanted to say. Something about Aren? The rebellion? The words that come to mind now all sound like I'm defending what they've done. That's not right, so I settle on, "Thank you."

The barest of smiles touches his lips as he opens a fissure. "I'll see you soon."

He steps into the bright light and disappears. Even in the darkened room, I can see his shadows. I can't get a precise read on them, though, not without sketching a map, but there's no paper in sight, just the queen-sized bed, a dresser, and a matching chest of drawers, all red oak in color. Jeans and a gray, long-sleeved shirt are folded on top of the dresser, and a pair of boots—human, not fae-made—rest beside it. Knowing it's unlikely I'll be able to go back to sleep, I climb out of bed.

The clothes and boots are the right size. I grab them, walk to the door, and peek out. It's clear, and the bathroom is right across the hall.

I start the water running, then shed my dress, unfasten my diamond necklace, and lay them both on the counter beside the tub. A few minutes later, I sink into the water and let the heat pull the stiffness from my muscles. Beneath the surface, the twin scars across my stomach wiggle. It's a good thing Kyol and I didn't go further last night. If he saw these scars, he'd have felt even worse about my abduction. And he would have learned where Aren's hands were.

My stomach clenches, remembering Aren's touch. Frustrated, I suck in a breath and sink beneath the water's surface. I need to drown out his memory, forget that one kiss. It was just another one of his manipulations. Aren and I are enemies. I know that. He knows that. He should never have given me that damn necklace.

I burst out of the water and suck in air. The diamonds

glitter from the edge of the sink, mocking me. I have to hand over the anchor-stone, don't I? Even though it'll feel like I'm twisting a knife in Aren's back?

I run my fingers through my wet hair. I just want this to be over. I want to live a normal, human life. With Kyol.

You could never be a normal human. Aren's words from the riverbank in Germany. He said them with a smile on his face, as if I was too extraordinary to be normal.

"Damn it." Before my thoughts settle on his kiss again, I stand, sloshing water over the side of the tub. I towel off, wring the water from my hair, then snatch the diamond necklace off the counter. I don't want it hanging around my neck, so I wrap it around my wrist a couple times and then fasten the clasp. It actually works as a bracelet, and with the long-sleeved shirt Kyol left for me, no one will see it unless I want them to.

A few minutes later, I'm dressed and exploring the castle. That's what it feels like, at least. The place is huge, two stories with a theater upstairs and half a dozen closed doors I'm too afraid to open. There had to be some type of party or get-together here last night. In one of the living areas, red plastic cups and beer bottles are scattered about the room, on the floor and tables, even the pool table, which I'm pretty sure isn't good for it. And someone's snoring on the couch. Not wanting to wake him, I tiptoe through the room, find the staircase, and then head down to the first floor, hoping I can find the kitchen.

The size of the house shouldn't surprise me. A limo picked me up last night. Shane obviously has money. But I can't help but wonder how he earned it. What does he do for a living? How does he keep a high-paying job? How does he keep the Court from interfering with . . .

I stop, scan the tall walls of the foyer and its arched ceiling. Surely the fae haven't paid for all of this. I mean, I know the king would give me more money if I asked, but I'm fairly certain they get the bundles of cash by fissuring in and out of bank vaults. I feel guilty for letting them pay for my little apartment—it is stealing, after all—but maybe Shane doesn't. Maybe he feels this place is his due.

"Lost?"

I turn. Shane—I'm assuming it's him because he's standing there like he owns the place—is a few years older than I am.

He's wearing an unbuttoned white shirt and jeans, which are slung low on his hips. His brown hair is mussed up, but he doesn't look like he's just woken up. He looks like . . . well, like he's just attended a party.

"I'm McKenzie," I say, just in case he thinks I'm some left-over guest from last night.

"I met you a few hours ago." At my frown, the corner of his mouth tips into a smile. "You were unconscious. Taltrayn carried you upstairs. You a heavy sleeper?"

"Not usually." It doesn't surprise me I slept so hard, though. My insomnia issues disappear when I'm with Kyol, and the last three days—hell, the last couple of weeks—haven't exactly been pleasant.

"He said you had a bad day." Shane crosses the foyer and then, as he walks past me, he says, "You hungry?"

"Starving."

I follow him to the kitchen where he starts a pot of coffee and nukes breakfast: frozen waffles from a box big enough to supply a small army. After the microwave dings, he takes the two plates to a table in a separate room. Tall, arched windows curve around the breakfast area, separating it from the ter-raced backyard.

"Know how long you'll be staying?" he asks while he floods his waffles with syrup.

It's a good question, one I'm not sure how to answer. I don't want to hunt for a new apartment, but I understand why I can't go home. The rebels traded me for Lena, but that doesn't mean they don't want me back. *Aren* wants me back.

"I'll leave as soon as I can."

"No rush," he says. "I have plenty of room."

"Yeah. This place"—my eyes take in the view outside, the stone archways inside, and the marble fireplace in the next room—"it's . . . big."

"Extravagant, you mean." His crooked grin says he's not ashamed of the fact. He cuts into his waffles. "The Court doesn't care where I live so long as it's near a gate, so I picked a place that suited me." At the look on my face, he adds, "What? I risk my life for them. I've earned this, especially lately."

No one *needs* a place like this, but I don't open that debate right now. Instead, I focus on the last part of what he said. "What do you mean by 'lately'?"

Around a mouthful of waffle, he says, "They've been keeping me busy these last few weeks."

"Busier than usual?"

"Yeah. They used to only need me when the rebels attacked, but they've started going on the offensive. Have you heard of the Butcher of Brykeld?"

Slowly, I nod.

"He abducted the Court's best shadow-reader. She's probably dead, but they stepped up the search for Jorreb a few weeks ago, started hitting every place the rebels are rumored to be, hoping to . . . What?"

I realize I'm scowling, but I assumed Kyol told him who and what I am. Is there a reason he didn't? He's always kept my name a secret, but the rebels know it now. I don't see why it matters anymore.

"I'm not dead," I tell Shane.

"You're not . . ." His eyes widen. "Shit. I thought you just had the Sight. I didn't know you could read shadows. Shit," he says again. "You're lucky to be alive."

Uncomfortable, I grab my fork. "Do you have people over here often?"

He doesn't resist the subject change. With a shrug, he slouches back in his chair. "I have people over all the time. As you said, it's a big house. It can get lonely."

"You're lonely, baby?" a groggy voice asks.

The brunette who enters the breakfast room is tall, model-pretty, and dressed in a black robe with, unfortunately, nothing underneath.

"Not with you here, sweetheart," he says, pressing a kiss to her bare stomach. I stare out the window while he reties her sash.

"Who's this?" she asks.

"McKenzie." He loops an arm around her waist. "She'll be hanging around for a while."

The girl takes in my long, damp hair, makeup-less face, and plain, long-sleeved T-shirt. "Cousin?" she asks Shane, as if it isn't possible for him to be interested in someone like me.

He laughs. "No relation. She's a . . . business acquaintance. Now, why don't you go get some breakfast?"

After she glides to the kitchen, I ask, "Is she over here often?"

"Carla? Nah. First time." He shovels a forkful of waffle into his mouth. When he lowers his hand, his cuff almost dips into the syrup on his plate. He shoves up his sleeves.

He has a scar on his right forearm. It's ugly, close to two inches wide and long, running from his wrist almost all the way to his elbow.

"What happened?" I ask.

His fork freezes halfway to his mouth. He glances at the scar, then at me, and shadows seem to dance in his eyes. His lips tighten. A few more seconds pass, then he says, "Our job is dangerous." He nods toward my neck. "Is yours from Jorreb?"

My fingers go to the upraised skin. It seems like there should be some residual pain, but the only feeling lingering from my time with Aren is his departing kiss. It's still screwing with my head.

Just like he intended, I'm sure.

I clear my throat. "Sorry. I didn't mean to pry."

Carla returns with an apple and two mugs of coffee. She hands one to Shane, keeps the other for herself.

"Kelly and Joe hooked up last night," she says, sitting in the chair next to him. He grunts in response. I wish he hadn't. She takes that as a sign of interest and launches into a gossip session on the sex lives of people at last night's party. She never once looks my way, but in the middle of an accounting of how many guys Kelly's been with, Shane gives me a roguish smile, and shrugs.

I'm about to excuse myself from the table when there's a flash outside the window. Before I can identify the face peering inside, the fae fissures into the breakfast room.

Shane stiffens but doesn't turn. He isn't pulled in by the shadows like I am. He doesn't see their peaks and curves and his hands don't itch for a pencil.

I squeeze my eyes shut, then focus on the fae. An *abira* tree is etched into the center of his *jaedric* cuirass, so he's with the Court, but he's not Taber, the fae Kyol said he'd send for me.

"Both of you are needed. Quickly." His English is thickly accented.

Carla stops talking. The timing makes it seem like she heard the fae's words, but a glance tells me she's frowning at Shane, not at the lightning-covered man standing beside the table.

"Are you listening?" she demands.

"Of course," he says smoothly, but his brow is furrowed in thought, probably trying to figure out why we're both being summoned.

Carla crosses her arms. "Then answer my question."

"I said I was listening."

"The question *before* that."

"Now, Shane," the fae says. Something in his tone tells me this isn't the first time he's had to urge Shane to hurry. They've worked together before.

"I need to go out for a little while." Shane scoots his chair back from the table. I'm not comfortable with fissuring out with a fae I don't know, but I want more information, and since I can't ask what's going on with Carla sitting here, I stand, too.

"Out where?" She transfers her glare from Shane to me, then back.

"For a walk," he says.

She stands. "A walk. Now? With her?"

Their argument is brief. She insists on coming with us. He tells her no flat-out and leaves her in the breakfast room, fuming. No more than three minutes pass before we're outside, but the fae isn't happy with the delay. He sets off at what, for him, is a brisk walk, which means Shane and I are jogging to keep up.

"Where are you fissuring us?" I ask.

He barely glances my way. "Haeth."

Haeth is a city in the southeastern corner of the Realm. It's near the Adaris Mountains. I've only been there once, several years ago, to use its gate. With the Kerrel Ocean to its north and the mountains to the east, it's a beautiful place, one I wouldn't mind returning to if bloodshed pretty much wasn't guaranteed. The Court must have received information saying the rebels are there. Whether they are or not, I don't know.

Shane's house backs up to a golf course. It's mid-morning

and the sky is crystal clear, so we aren't the only ones out. Groups of golfers are waiting for the people in front of them to play so they can take their turns. They're not happy when they have to hold their swings while we cross the course.

"Did the sword-master send you to get me?" I ask, glad Shane is with me so it doesn't look like I'm talking to myself.

"Radath," the fae answers.

"The lord general? He usually summons me through Taltrayn."

When we reach the woods on the far side of the course, I take the imprinted necklace off my wrist and slip it into my pocket. The fae will give us anchor-stones when we reach the gate, and if I fissured with two against my skin, I'd become lost in the In-Between.

"I'm following my orders," the fae says.

"Is Taltrayn in Haeth?"

When he doesn't answer, I stop walking. "I'm not going unless he's there." I've shadow-read with fae other than Kyol before, but not often, and it was always with someone I knew. Besides, I *just* escaped the rebels, and I told Kyol I want to retire. I don't want to be thrust back into the war.

Shane stops beside me. "I've gotta say I support her, Daz. Something tells me Taltrayn will be pissed if she ends up in Haeth."

Shane's backing surprises me. He doesn't seem like the type of guy who gets involved in things that don't really impact him.

Daz turns, impatience etched into his face. "We have no time to discuss this."

"You can fissure me to the palace," I say, "but I'm not going to Haeth."

Leaves crunch to our right. Another fae approaches through the woods. He's vaguely familiar, but I don't think he's one of Kyol's swordsmen. Most likely, he serves under Radath. Since one fae can't fissure two humans, his presence makes sense.

"What is wrong?" the new fae asks.

Daz tells him I'm refusing to go to Haeth. I stare at the ground, pretending not to listen as they discuss what to do with me. It's convenient, though, being able to understand most of what they're saying, but their conversation makes me uneasy, too. According to them, Radath thinks they can find the false-blood if they attack Haeth. Whether that false-blood is Sethan or Aren, I can't tell.

The new fae holds up a hand, stopping Daz midsentence. *"I will fissure Shane to Haeth. Do what you will with the shadow-reader."*

He motions to Shane, who gives me an almost sheepish shrug. "See you around."

When they leave, Daz studies me, not looking at all happy. Finally, he lets out a breath and says, "I will take you to the palace."

NINETEEN

◆·◆

THE FAE KEEPS his word. We fissure to the Silver Palace's heavily guarded western entrance. Behind me is the outlying city of Corrist and in front is a wall of silver that reaches high into the sky. The portcullis at its base is half-raised. A contingent of Court fae wait on the other side, crossbows nocked and aimed. They lower their weapons only after Daz says something about the deceit of *kimkis*. At least, I think that's what he says. It must be a pass-phrase because the guards let us enter.

The capital's wealthiest merchants have shops inside the walls. The streets are crowded, but we travel quickly—or rather, as quickly as I can since my human pace slows Daz down—and enter beneath the Silver Palace's southernmost spire. I've never toured any of Europe's castles, which is a shame since it would be easy to have Kyol fissure me over there, but I imagine the interiors are similar in some ways: the stone walls, the intricate tapestries, the woven carpets running down the length of the corridor. Not the orbs set into sconces, though. They cast a blue-white light over the stone walls, subduing the atmosphere, making it feel cool and quiet.

"Wait here," Daz says. He heads toward the king's hall before I have a chance to say okay.

There are worse places to wait, though. I'm in the palace's

sculpture garden. With its marble floor, glass ceiling, and chis-
eled stone statues, the place is beautiful. Serene, too. The
open-air courtyard is drenched with the morning's sunlight. It
spills over the fae sitting on stone benches or standing in
clutches, deep in conversation.

"McKenzie?"

I don't recognize the voice, wouldn't recognize the fae
either if he didn't have a braid of *premthyste* in his silky gray
hair. It's been a while since I've seen Lord Raen, elder of
Cyneayen, high noble of Tayshken, but now I see Kelia in the
slant of his nose and the shape of his eyes. Those eyes dart
around as if he's afraid someone will see him talking to me.
Every fae here *will* notice us—the *edarratae* make me kind of
hard to miss.

"McKenzie," he says again. He looks toward the sky as if
he can find an English translation for what he wants to say
written in the wispy clouds. *"My daughter, Kelia."* He takes
an unsteady breath, looks at me, and emphasizes, "Kelia. *Is
she okay?"*

I stand there, force a confused frown, and pretend not to
understand him, but a knot of sympathy tightens in my
stomach.

"Sidhe." He runs a hand over his face. *"You . . . you would
know her name, I think, if you had met her. I need . . ."* He
glances around the sculpture garden again. *"I need a transla-
tor, but it's unwise . . ."*

I can't follow the rest of what he says. Poor guy. I don't
know how long Kelia's been with the rebellion, but he's obviously distraught over it. I want to comfort him, to tell him
she's okay or she will be, once I find a way to make the Court
release Naito. Instead, I cross my arms and keep my mouth
shut.

"Walk with me a moment. Walk." Lord Raen moves his
middle and forefinger like miniature legs.

I'm uncomfortable with it, but I fall into step beside him.
Fae are looking at us now. Some of those clustered in conversation have switched the topic of discussion to us, I'm sure.
Raen ignores them, staring at the marble floor as we pass
another sculpture. I don't know what it's called, but Kyol told
me it represents the *Tar Sidhe*, the magically powerful fae who

ruled the Realm centuries ago. I think the figures look like they represent the elements, though I don't know why there are five instead of four. Earth, wind, fire, air, and . . .

"Her mother blames me," Raen says. *"I think she's right. I shouldn't have . . ."* He shouldn't have something. He'd be easier to understand if he wasn't mumbling to himself. *"But the human, he's not good for her. Or he wasn't. He would have destroyed her magic, made her* tor'um. *Kelia's always been too infatuated with your world."*

I think he needs to talk, so I listen, careful not to react to anything he says.

"Maybe she would forgive me if I could give him back to her. Impossible now. The sword-master's killed him. She'll never speak to me again."

Ice settles in my stomach. I stop walking. "What?"

Lord Raen meets my eyes, brow furrowed.

Maybe I mistranslated what he said. Kyol gave me his word—he *promised* me—Naito was okay.

"Naito," I say, needing him to repeat his words.

"The human?"

I nod. He shakes his head.

"Kelia is my daughter. Kelia. Did you see her?"

I open my mouth to speak, close it. There are too many fae around and if he's right . . . No. He can't be right. Kyol wouldn't lie about Naito being okay. He *wouldn't*.

Would he?

Without an explanation, I leave Lord Raen. I have to talk to Kyol. I have to ask him again if Naito is alive. This time, I have to be willing to see a lie.

DAZ intercepts me before I enter the king's hall. His lip twitches, but he doesn't call me out for not waiting where he left me. He turns, leading me to the huge, open, gilded doors. Four swordsmen, two on each side, guard the entrance. They let us enter, and we step onto a plush blue carpet. It stretches all the way to the far end of the hall, stopping at the foot of the massive, silver dais on which the king's throne sits. It's vacant. Only a dozen swordsmen watch me from their posts.

I force myself to continue. Even though the silver walls

surrounding the palace make it impossible for fae to fissure here, silver is the main decor. Some of it, like the sculpture of interlinked geometric shapes hanging on the wall, is infused with magic. It sparkles with a shimmery blue light similar to the fae's *edarratae* when they're in my world.

The hair on the back of my neck prickles, but I can't leave. I have to know the truth. If Kyol lied to me about Naito, he could have lied about other things. He could have lied about everything.

God, please—*please*—let Naito be alive.

Daz leads me past the silver dais and gestures to an opening in the back wall. "Through there."

Drawing in a breath, I command myself to relax and then I step inside

Sconced orbs light the narrow stairwell in a blue glow. The air's cool, almost chilly, but it warms toward the bottom of the stairs. There's no fire in the small chamber, but some fae can heat the air with a touch of magic. Radath and Atroth stand behind a wooden table, scrutinizing a map spread out in its center. Kyol isn't here.

My boots scuff on the stone floor when I suddenly stop. I don't want to talk to Radath and the king. I came to Corrist to talk to Kyol, but what if he isn't here? What if Daz never really knew his location and he's now in Haeth, waiting for me?

Atroth looks up. If I didn't know him, I wouldn't think him to be the fae's king. He's dressed like a noble—like Lorn was when I first met him, a crisp white shirt under a dark brown vest. The vest is made from *jaedric* and etched with a design similar to a fleur-de-lis. He doesn't wear a crown or any other markings to suggest he's a Descendant of the *Tar Sidhe*. He's shorter than Radath and thick around the middle since his body hasn't been toned by war. He gives me a smile that seems genuine.

"McKenzie," Atroth says. "Please, come in."

Atroth's always been kind to me. I don't get the feeling that he views me as a necessary evil like I do with Radath and some of the other Court fae. It's more like he's regretful I'm harmful to his people. That's why I've never hated him for forbidding relations between human and fae. He's king. He has a duty to protect the Realm.

"Have a seat." He gestures to a chair. "Would you like something to drink?"

"Water's fine." I'm not thirsty, but my hands need something to hold.

Atroth himself pours the pitcher. He smiles again as he hands me the glass. I can't picture him ordering Kyol to kill a human. The king needs us to see through illusions, and when his fae enter my world, they do everything possible to make sure they don't harm us, whether we have the Sight or not. The rebels are the ones who don't care who they hurt. Naito is alive. He has to be.

"Thank you," I say.

He takes the seat across from me. "We were concerned about you. We're glad you're back. Safe again. I assure you, Taltrayn did everything in his power to keep the rebels from finding you. Once you were taken, he did everything possible to bring you back."

You would be dismayed to learn the things he's doing to get you back. Aren's words echo in my memory. We were sitting on that sorry excuse for a bed at the time, and he'd just healed my broken arm. I didn't ask for details. I didn't trust Aren then; I trusted Kyol. I *still* trust Kyol, don't I? It's possible I misheard Lord Raen.

"Where's Taltrayn?" I ask.

The lord general replies. "You are supposed to be in Haeth."

That's typical Radath. Never a "hello, how are you" and always sticking with the subject at hand. I never quite know how to deal with him. He's a tall fae with shoulders just as broad as Kyol's. When I first met him a decade ago, he was heavier than he is now. Or maybe *bulkier* is the better word. He hasn't been on the front lines of a battle in years and his body's lost the muscle mass it once had. He's still intimidating, though, which usually isn't a problem since he rarely speaks with me, preferring to leave that duty to Kyol.

"Taltrayn said he was going to talk to you," I say to the king.

"Talk about what?" Radath asks. Atroth doesn't seem to mind the lord general speaking for him, but I do, especially since it feels like an extremely bad time to mention I want to retire.

"My lord."

Kyol saves me from answering. I let out a breath and turn to see him descend into the chamber. He doesn't look at me, only at his king, and his face is blank. Nothing unusual about that. It's our normal routine, pretending we mean nothing to each other.

"Sword-master," Atroth says, his tone upbeat. "I thought word would reach you quickly. Come. Join us."

He sits in the chair next to mine. "I left McKenzie with Shane."

"Shane is assisting us in Haeth," Radath says. *"That's where your shadow-reader should be as well, but she refused to go."*

After a long moment, Kyol says, *"She escaped the rebels only yesterday."* He sounds different. Not worried, exactly, but not at ease either. It could be my imagination, though, because he doesn't look agitated. He looks completely in control.

Radath clasps his hands on top of the table. *"You've always claimed she's not fragile."*

"That doesn't mean she's indestructible. She needs time to rest."

"And we need the false-blood—"

Atroth interrupts Radath with a raised hand. *"I agree with Taltrayn. Sending her to Haeth wasn't your wisest order."*

The lord general's eyes narrow briefly at the reprimand, but he recovers quickly and returns his attention to me. "Tell us what you learned about the rebels."

I stall by taking a sip of water. I'm sure he's asking about Aren, but Aren's not the false-blood. Sethan is, though I'm believing more and more that he *is* a Descendant.

"Did you overhear any names?" Kyol asks.

I manage a shrug, hope it comes off as nonchalant. "Trev, Mrinn, Roop, Sethan."

I watch for a reaction on the last name. I get one from Radath. His nostrils flare. *"The son of Zarrak took an interest in her."*

"Of course he did," Atroth replies. After a pause, he adds, *"But did he convince her of his claim?"*

"He has no claim," Radath grates. *"His province no longer exists. Deliver a few threats, and the people of Haeth will abandon him."*

The air tastes stale. I feel Atroth's eyes on me, but I don't dare look up. I don't want this conversation to continue. I'm terrified of where it's going.

The king taps his fingertips on the table. *"Zarrak is persuasive. He may have more support than we realize. Ask her about him."*

"This Sethan." Radath emphasizes both syllables of the name. "Who was he?"

Stall! my instincts scream.

"He claimed he was a Descendant," I say. They already know who Sethan is. My words won't hurt anyone. "He said he intends to take the throne. I think Jorreb is just a front."

The king's forehead creases.

Kyol speaks up then, explaining what a front is in Fae.

Atroth nods, understanding. "Yes. There is a trace of the *Tar Sidhe*'s blood in the Zarrak line, but it's only significant enough to allow the family to remain part of the aristocracy, not significant enough to sit on the silver throne."

"You knew about him?" I ask carefully.

"When we captured Lena, we knew he must also be involved," Atroth says. Then, in a soft, somewhat pensive voice, "The Zarrak bloodline used to be well respected."

His answer makes sense, but it doesn't make me feel much better.

"Did you read any shadows while you were with them?" the lord general asks. "Do you know where they took you? If we could find Zarrak or Jorreb, we could end this uprising."

"It would save lives," Atroth adds.

Is the saving lives part an afterthought? For Radath, I'm almost certain it is. The king? I don't know.

"They kept me blindfolded." The words make my head pound. Whose side am I on? I could help the Court. I could give Atroth my imprinted necklace. I glance at Kyol, needing some kind of reassurance, but his face reveals nothing. I wish I could talk to him alone, wish I could go back to when I had no doubts about him or the Court.

Radath lets out a breath that's almost a growl. *"She's useless. We shouldn't have made the trade."*

"Not useless, Radath," Atroth says calmly. *"It may take some time for her to remember everything. She's traumatized.*

Look at her neck." It takes everything in me not to touch the scar on the side of my throat. *"Her time with the rebels was not pleasant."*

"They threatened her," Radath agrees. *"One has to wonder why they kept her alive to begin with. What secrets did she tell them?"*

Kyol meets the lord general's eyes. *"She's strong. She'd never betray us."*

I stare down at the water rippling in my glass, afraid my expression reveals too much, afraid they somehow know I've understood everything they've said. Kyol believes in me. That should account for something. But do I still believe in him?

"Naito would know where to find them."

Silence, then Kyol, still as emotionless as ever, says, *"She doesn't know he's dead."*

I'm lucky the shock sinks in slowly. I have time to control my expression, to dig my fingers into my knees and order my lungs to continue drawing in air. I understood Raen's words, but I didn't believe them, not until now. Naito's dead. Kyol killed him. *Kyol* killed him.

God, I've been a fool, a despicable, wretched fool. Aren told me I was stubborn to a fault, and he was right. I let my love for Kyol blind me. I let him use me.

Aren. I call his name in my head as if he can hear me. I should have stayed with him, should have given him the *Sidhe Tol.*

"McKenzie?" Kyol says beside me.

"What?" I force myself to choke out. I can't freak out, not yet.

"You remember nothing else?"

I still can't read anything in his expression. Did he ever have feelings for me or was Lena right? He secured my loyalty with a kiss?

"No," I say, my voice more in control this time. "That's everything."

"She's holding something back," Radath says. I don't dare meet the lord general's eyes.

"If she knew anything useful," Kyol says. *"She would tell us."*

The diamond necklace burns a hole in my pocket.

"You're wrong, Taltrayn. You have until dusk to discover what she's hiding."

"And how would you like me to pry out what she doesn't know, Lord General?"

Radath smiles. *"Use your imagination. The girl's in love with you. Beat her, bed her, I don't care, but do what you must to make her cooperate."*

TWENTY

•◆•

I HAVE TO keep my face impassive, unreadable. It's easier than I expect because I'm dead inside. I can't feel anything but a cold, jagged iceberg surrounding my heart.

"McKenzie," Kyol says as soon as we exit the king's hall. "What's wrong?"

I don't answer, just keep putting one foot in front of the other. I thought I learned what a broken heart felt like when I thought Kyol died trying to protect me from the rebels. That pain had been cutting and deep, but at least I felt something then.

Numb, I turn toward the sculpture garden.

"No." Kyol ushers me the opposite direction. "This way."

He's taking me to his quarters, I realize. I should run, but where am I supposed to go? I'm trapped in the Realm unless a fae fissures me back to my world. I'll even need a fae to fissure me to Aren.

I stare straight ahead. I fell for the bad guy. It's such a typical, stupid, girly thing to do. But then, I was sixteen when I met Kyol. Maybe he was part of my teenage rebellion. I was too young, too naïve, to see past his manipulations.

God, I've been so wrong about him. He's not honorable; he's conniving. Every smile, every touch, every look of concern he's ever given me, it's all a lie. A *lie*, damn it! And everything Aren's told me is true.

We climb a staircase. This isn't all my fault. Kyol's the real asshole here. I may have spent the last decade reading shadows for the Court, but I can undo all the help I've given them in three short syllables. I'm going to find Aren. I'm going to give him the location of the *Sidhe Tol*.

By the time we reach Kyol's room, I'm not numb anymore. I'm pissed.

He gently closes the door. "McKenzie, talk to me."

I shouldn't say anything. I should pretend everything is okay, but something inside me snaps.

"Talk to you?" I snarl as I turn on him. "Why don't you talk to me, Kyol? Why don't you try telling me the truth?"

His silver eyes widen in surprise. He actually staggers back a step. "What are you talking about?"

"Everything," I say. "But why don't we start with Naito? You promised he was fine."

Confusion wrinkles his brow. "He is fine."

"Bullshit."

"I swear it."

I ignore his lie. "Maybe we should talk about something else? Like how you're going to convince me to cooperate? It's going to take a hell of a lot more than a kiss to manipulate me this time. You'll have to rape me because I won't sleep with you. Not willingly." I slam my hands into his chest.

Comprehension finally dawns on his face. "You understood."

"Damn right, I did."

"Everything?" He braces a hand against the wall. "You understood everything."

He looks so wounded. A part of me wants to reach out and comfort him, but no. It's only part of his act.

I hang on to my anger. "I gave up my life for you, Kyol. I haven't talked to my family in *years* because they think I'm insane. And they're right. I was crazy to ever listen to you. I should have a real job now. I should have graduated four years ago. I should be married or at least have had a boyfriend. But no, I never gave anyone a chance because they couldn't measure up to you. I didn't think they compared, but every one of them—*every one!*—was a better man than you."

I pace the room. "I thought Atroth's decree kept us apart.

Ridiculous. Did I make you sick every time you touched me? Did you have to hold your breath when we kissed? Did you!"

He shakes his head. "No, McKenzie, it's not like that. I—"

"You knew Aren was a front, didn't you? Sethan had to hide behind him because you'd go after his family if you knew he was leading the rebels. That's what you're doing in Haeth now, isn't it?"

"McKenzie, we weren't sure. Please." He takes a step toward me.

"Stay back!"

He winces, but drops his hand to his sword. I freeze, realizing how easy it would be for him to kill me with that blade. Humans mean nothing to him. We're only tools.

He releases the hilt quickly and lets his hand hang by his side. Softly, he says, "I'd never hurt you."

"You already have."

His Adam's apple bobs when he swallows. "There were things I couldn't tell you, but I've never lied."

I laugh, and tears begin to pool in my eyes.

"I haven't lied," Kyol insists. "I . . ." He stops, closes his eyes briefly and recomposes himself. "Okay. My omissions could be construed as lies, yes."

I dig my fingernails into my palms to keep my tears from brimming over. "What else haven't you told me? Aside from murdering Naito?"

Another grimace. He hangs his head, staring at the floor. "This war, McKenzie, it's complicated—"

"Yeah. I figured that out."

He ignores my interruption, continues. "I've been friends with Atroth since we were boys. When he took the throne, I supported him. He was a good king—he still is—but the rebels have caused him to make decisions nobody has liked. Yes, there've been some atrocities, but they've been committed on *both* sides, and none have been committed by the soldiers serving under me. *None.* I've tried to protect you from the violence as much as possible, but if you'd seen the extent of the rebels' cruelty—"

"The Court isn't innocent."

"The rebels are worse by far—"

"You've sent *heads* as messages!" I shout.

"McKenzie, please." He reaches for my arm, but I jerk back. I should have turned away, though, because I see the breath whoosh out of his lungs.

"He's turned you against me," he says, blindly reaching behind him for the edge of his desk.

I keep my spine straight, my chin up. "He's turned me against the Court. Yes."

He shakes his head. "You can't trust him, McKenzie. Please don't trust him. He's spoken mistruths, used your insecurities against you."

"Insecurities?" I echo. "Insecurities! I've waited ten fucking years for you, Kyol! Do you know how pathetic that is? No sane woman would wait on a man for that long, but I did because I was fool enough to believe I was caught in some kind of fairy tale. My delusions let you walk all over me."

"I've treated you well."

"No, you selfish bastard, you haven't. You've manipulated me. You kissed me when I was sixteen to seal my loyalty to the Court and now you say all the right things to keep me hanging on by the thinnest thread of hope. Well, screw you. You never gave a damn about me."

"You're wrong, McKenzie. You're wrong. I've loved you from the moment I first stepped into your world."

My heart throbs in my chest. I won't listen to this, won't let him manipulate me anymore. "I've wanted to hear those words for a decade. Convenient you say them *now*, when I'm threatening to stop reading the shadows for you."

He steps toward me. "I'm not saying it to—"

I back away. "I don't believe you anymore."

"If you'll just listen." He presses closer.

My heel hits the wall. "I've been listening. I've hung on your every fucking word for far too long and I'm through with it. I'm through with y—"

His mouth covers mine, silencing me. He pins me to the wall, pressing against me so hard I couldn't escape if I wanted to. I *should* want to. I shouldn't tremble like this, shouldn't let my knees go so weak he has to hold me up as he kisses me. The chaos lusters on my skin come alive in frenzied excitement, bolting up my neck, across my jaw, through my lips and into him. He sucks in a breath when the heat hits him.

Beat her, bed her, I don't care what it takes.

Kyol's lips leave mine, but he keeps my face cradled between his palms.

"Please, *kaesha*. You know me."

I place both my hands on his chest and shove. "No!"

He wouldn't have budged if he didn't want to, but he gives me space, moving to the opposite wall. He leans against it, looking defeated and devastated, and I have to turn away. It's difficult to fall out of love with someone. I don't want to hurt him, but he's not the man I thought he was. He's not Kyol. He's a stranger. A murderer.

I stare out the window behind his bed. The silver walls surrounding the palace rise up in the distance. Between here and the wall, Corrist's wealthier merchants and nobles have built their homes. The nobles have residences elsewhere as well, and most of the merchants probably haven't hand-sold a thing in years, but being permitted to step foot within the capital city means you're somebody. Maybe I picked up on that, thought I was somebody, too. Meeting the king, knowing Kyol and other members of the Inner Court, made me think I was important. And Kyol took me to the *Sidhe Cabred*. Most fae aren't naïve enough to dream of encountering so much as a leaf from the king's private paradise. Maybe my vanity put me in this situation.

I jump when Kyol slams his fist against the door. "No!"

Before I realize he's moving, he's at my side.

"It's not ending like this."

His hand fastens around my arm and he yanks me from his room.

Panicked, I pry at his fingers. "Let go, Kyol."

"Quiet," he snaps, ignoring the curious looks of the fae we pass. I'm tempted to plead for help, but no one will cross Kyol, especially when he's like this, looking like he'll slaughter anyone who breathes too loudly. His face is rigid, all hint of pain and uncertainty gone.

I've screwed up, pushed him too far. I should have kept my mouth shut and disappeared without a word. Now I might not get the chance because—holy hell—I think he's leading me to the basements. There's nothing down there but the dungeon and storage.

"Kyol, please."

He forces me down a staircase. A rack of unlit torches hangs on the wall. He passes his hand over one of them, sending magic into its glass orb, and takes it with us down the dark passageway.

It's cold and I can't see anything beyond the torch's blue-white glow. I feel like a rat in a maze, but Kyol knows exactly where he's going. I consider trying to buy my freedom with the anchor-stone in my pocket, but I want to give that to Kyol about as much as I wanted to give the location of the *Sidhe Tol* to Aren. It's ironic how things can so quickly be flipped on their heads.

Kyol stops before a heavy wooden door, knocks twice. We wait. If I wasn't terrified, I'd find the silence awkward. I've been comfortable with Kyol for the past ten years. I never thought anything could change that, but then, I thought he loved me. I thought I knew him.

"You're hurting my arm," I say. Immediately, his hand loosens.

The door cracks open, unmuffling the sounds of moans and murmurings beyond its threshold. A fae woman peeks out and frowns, seeing me first before opening the door wider.

"Sword-master," she says.

"We'll only be a minute." He pulls me inside.

It's too clean to be the dungeon, and while some fae are tied down to cots, most are free and sitting up. It's a large chamber, one that reminds me of the temporary shelters the governments in my world set up after a natural disaster. About a dozen workers tend to the sick. I focus on a man moaning and rocking near me. *Edarratae*, out of place on a fae in the Realm, fade in and out over his skin, casting him in an unhealthy pallor. His eyes are sunken, his face gaunt. It takes me a while to recognize him. I think his name is Kwinn, one of Kyol's lieutenants.

"This is the rebels' work," Kyol says. *"Jorreb's* work. When he captures Court fae who might have knowledge of our plans, he takes them to your world and locks them in a room with tech. For hours, for days, for weeks sometimes. As long as it takes to break them. When the rebels have what they need, they send them back like this."

These fae aren't like the *tor'um* in Lynn Valley. Those fae were born without the ability to fissure; they didn't live their whole lives normally only to have their magic crushed by human technology. Kyol's described this sickness to me before. He said the fae can't handle the loss, the damage to something that's so integral to their existence. Their minds break. Shut down. Close off. And they become . . . this.

Kwinn begins rocking and moaning. I close my eyes, trying to cope with the mix of emotions tangling through me. Aren's not innocent. He did this.

Kyol's hand slides down to grasp mine. "I've never wanted you to see the horrors of war. Your nightmares are bad enough without seeing fae waste away like this. I've kept certain things from you to keep your conscience clean and to keep you safe. Maybe that was a mistake."

I didn't need to be coddled. I needed to be given all the facts so I could make my decisions based on what was real, not on someone's twisted version of the truth.

"Is this not enough?" Kyol asks.

I say nothing. This . . . this torture is one of the things Aren kept hidden from me. He knew it would bolster my resistance to him. And it does. I swear the anchor-stone pulses in my pocket, urging me to hand it over. Are there no good guys in this war?

"Just take me back to my world."

Kyol's jaw clenches. "You need more evidence? Fine."

He pulls me from the room. The blue glow from his torch lights the corridor. We descend another staircase, take a left turn, and eventually stop in front of an iron gate guarded by two swordsmen. They acknowledge Kyol with nods and me with mildly curious glances. The fae on the left turns a key in the lock and swings the gate open.

Swords, spears, bows, and other weapons are propped up in racks against both walls while *jaedric* cuirasses, helms, and other protective gear I can't identify are layered in waist-high stacks down the center of the long room. They're covered in a fine layer of dust, suggesting fae rarely come down here for their gear. A waste. Aren could equip the entire rebellion with a third of the armor and weapons stored here.

Kyol leads me through the labyrinth of arms. At the far

end, the room takes a sharp left turn and a fae—I recognize him as Garrad, one of Kyol's swordsmen—rises from a chair. Kyol signals him to sit as he crosses to the stone wall on the right. He drags an old, wooden cart out of the way and then makes a fist with his right hand before flattening his palm on a stone high up on the wall. Just like with Lorn's escape tunnel in Lyechaban, blue light surrounds the rectangle, and a moment later, a three-by-five-feet section of the wall grinds aside.

Kyol wedges his torch into the groove in the stone floor and then pulls me beneath the low overhang.

"Now!" someone shouts from inside.

Kyol shoves me back as he draws his sword, swinging and narrowly missing—*purposefully* missing—the lightning-streaked human charging him. A second man launches himself at me, but Kyol's there throwing a fist into a face I recognize as Naito's one second before it hits. The thud of Naito colliding with the back wall echoes in the small stone prison.

"Sword-master?" Garrad rushes into the room, sword at the ready.

"It's under control," Kyol says. The guard glances between the two humans, nods once, then retreats back to his post.

It takes me longer to comprehend everything that just occurred than it took for it to actually happen. Now I'm staring at Naito, who's staring up at me, his right cheek already swelling.

"McKenzie?"

"Naito." I fall to my knees beside him and help him sit up. "God, I thought you were dead."

"Not yet," he says.

Relief floods me and I'm shaking because maybe I wasn't a complete fool. Maybe I didn't entirely misjudge Kyol. I peer over my shoulder. His sword is still drawn, the steel a barrier between the other human and me.

I turn back to Naito. "Are you okay?"

"I think my face is shattered but I'm alive."

"We have to get you out of here." I help him to his feet, then glance at the other human. "Both of you."

"That's not possible," Kyol says. He still hasn't lowered his guard.

"You can put your sword away," I tell him. When he doesn't budge, I stand and place my hand on his, making him lower the weapon. *Edarratae* thrum through my fingers.

Slowly, he reaches up and tucks my hair behind my ear. "If I hadn't taken him through the gate, *kaesha*, he would have been killed. If I hadn't later agreed to execute him, he'd be dead."

"Aren't you a fucking hero," Naito says from behind me. A muscle twitches in Kyol's cheek.

I glare over my shoulder. "You're not helping."

Naito crosses his arms and leans against the wall. "I want out of here. I'm not staying locked up for weeks or months like him."

The other human does look like he's been here awhile. A grungy shirt hangs over his lean frame and a scraggly beard covers a face that I'm sure would be pale if it weren't covered in dirt. But he's alive. They both are. Because of Kyol.

I turn back to him. "You can't keep them here forever."

"I don't plan to," he says. "Tell us where we can find the rebels, McKenzie. When we end the war, I'll send them both back to your world. I swear it."

The diamond necklace is heavy in my pocket, but the Court no longer has my allegiance. I won't help them, not ever again.

"I've told you everything I know."

There's a glimmer of something in his eyes. Pain? Disappointment? I can't be sure.

"Kyol, please," I try again. "They can't stay—"

"They're alive. That's all I can do right now."

Before I can say anything else, he pulls me from the cell. When he turns to pick up the torch from its groove in the floor, I catch Naito's eye. I hope the look I give him is reassuring. I hope it tells him I won't leave him imprisoned. I'll find a way to get both humans out of here.

I'M not qualified to plan a jailbreak, but I don't have a choice. As Kyol leads me out of the palace's basements, I'm plotting how I'm going to return. I'm going to need help breaking Naito and the other human out. That much is clear.

We don't say anything to each other as we walk, not until we stop in front of the door to a room I've stayed in before. He takes my hands in his. My gaze darts down both ends of the corridor, but no other fae are in sight.

"I love you, McKenzie," he tells me quietly. "Despite what you heard today, I meant what I said last night. I want to be with you. In your world or mine, it doesn't matter. But I can't abandon Atroth with the rebels still trying to overthrow him."

Edarratae dart down my arms, over my wrists and hands, and into him. Things aren't okay between us. He didn't kill Naito—thank God for that—but he's let me believe in things that aren't true.

When I don't respond, he lets out a sigh. "I have some things I must take care of today. Will you be okay by yourself for a while? It may be late before I'm able to return."

I nod, feeling like shit for what I'm about to do.

He starts to say something else, stops and squeezes my hands instead. Then he plants a kiss on the top of my head, turns, and walks away, back to his responsibilities as Atroth's sword-master. It still hurts, being second to his king.

I don't go inside my room after he leaves. Being alone with my thoughts? Not a good idea. Instead, I find my way back to the sculpture garden. What I'm planning is risky—I could be betrayed or end up imprisoned or worse—but I have to take the risk.

It doesn't take long to find who I'm looking for. He's here, sitting on a bench beside the statue of a *cirikith*, one not tethered to a merchant's cart, but wild and rearing, his stone scales intricately carved. When my shadow falls over the fae, he looks up from the document he's reading.

"My lord," I say in his language. *"Do you still want to earn your daughter's forgiveness?"*

TWENTY-ONE

•◆•

I F I DIDN'T have a prison break to distract me, I'd spend the rest of the day . . . Well, not crying in my room—that's not me—but definitely wallowing in some kind of despair. Instead, I all but pace a rut in the stone floor because I'm nervous as hell waiting for dusk. A million things could go wrong tonight.

Truth is, I think our plan sucks. It's Lord Raen's plan mostly. He thinks no one will stop him from dragging me through the basements because he's a high noble. I tried to tell him "fat chance" in Fae, but apparently that idiom doesn't translate. After he spent half a minute frowning in confusion, I finally just shrugged my shoulders. He took that as a stamp of approval.

And maybe his title will get us to Naito and the other human, but Raen wasn't so clear on how we're going to get them out. He just told me to trust him. He'd take care of it. Even though I'm having a difficult time taking people on faith these days, when the sun finally sets, I'm waiting in the corridor he designated, leaning against the wall and trying to look inconspicuous. Unfortunately, I can't control the *edarratae* on my hands and face, and even if I could, I'd still look human. There's just something different, something unexciting, about my race when compared to the fae.

Nervous, I take the imprinted necklace out of my pocket and fasten it around my wrist. It's comforting to have it against my skin again, and I hope it acts as a good-luck charm. I hope this jailbreak goes off without a hitch.

When the last rays of sunlight fade from the window across from me, Lord Raen approaches.

"Come," he says, walking by without so much as a glance. He doesn't check to see if I'm following, not until we descend a staircase. Halfway down, he stops and draws a dagger.

I freeze. Despite the fact that I'm standing three steps taller than him, it takes an effort not to scurry backward as he twists his wrist slowly back and forth. A menacing gesture if I've ever seen one.

"Poison," he says, and I see something wet glistening on the edge of the steel. *"Draw blood and your opponent will fall."*

"Dead?" I ask, heart thumping in my chest. I don't want to kill anyone, especially someone who's just doing his job.

"Unconscious." He slides the dagger back into the scabbard and holds it out. *"Don't cut yourself."*

Something moves behind Lord Raen. I hide the sheathed dagger behind my back, tucking it into my waistband. The fae climbing the stairs is dangerous. I sense it in his slow ascent, in the way his gaze slides from Lord Raen to me. The hilts of two swords rise up over his shoulders like demon's wings, but he's not a palace guard or one of the king's swordsmen. He's dressed in black, nondescript clothing.

Raen steps aside, but the fae doesn't pass by. He stops beside Raen and the corners of his mouth tilt up in a barely there smile. Maybe he intends it to be pleasant, but to me, it's just creepy.

"This is Micid, son of Riagar," Raen says. *"He's ther'rothi."*

I frown. *"Ther'rothi?"*

"It means," Micid says in English, "one who walks the In-Between."

I blink. The fae's smile widens.

"I visit *tjandel*," he explains.

I have no idea where or what that is. I glance at Raen, but he looks just as surprised as I am to learn Micid speaks my language.

"What's that mean?" I ask. "To walk the In-Between?"

Micid smiles. And disappears.

There's no flash of light. We're inside the Silver Palace so he couldn't have fissured anyway, but it can't be an illusion. I have the Sight; I'd still be able to see him.

When the fae reappears, I stagger back and nearly trip on the stair behind me.

"It means," he says, "I walk the In-Between."

I recognize the word Raen used now, *ther'rothi*.

"That magic is . . ." I was going to say extinct, but the impression I always got from Kyol was that it never existed in the first place. It's as impossible as bringing fae back from the dead. It's a myth, a legend. "It's . . ."

"Rare," Micid supplies, a gleam in his silver eyes.

Lord Raen climbs a step. *"Fae cannot conceal humans with illusion. This is the only way. Micid will take you into the In-Between. No one will see you. I will have Taltrayn's guards open the storage room. You'll direct Micid to where the humans are hidden. He'll open the door and, one by one, he'll take you out through the In-Between."*

I started shaking my head halfway through his explanation. *"No. I can't walk the . . . This wasn't the plan."*

"I changed the plan," he says, as if it's not a problem. Never mind that I didn't like his original plan; I *really* don't like him bringing another fae into this. The only reason I'm trusting Raen is because I'm convinced he'll do anything for Kelia's forgiveness. I have no reason to trust this Micid.

"I can't enter the In-Between without going through a gate," I say. *"This will kill me."*

"We're not traveling through *the In-Between,"* Micid says. *"We're merely wading into it like a shallow pool. I've done this with humans before."*

I don't like this. Maybe I shouldn't have gone to Raen for help. Maybe I should have found a fae to take me through Corrist's gate. I thought about it. Once I give Aren the location of the *Sidhe Tol*, he'll be able to fissure into the Silver Palace. I could draw him a map to Naito's cell. That's the problem, though. Once Kyol finds out I'm missing, he'll move the two humans. I'm sure of it. I can't leave without them.

I meet Raen's eyes. *"You trust him?"*

After a slight, almost imperceptible hesitation, he says, *"He will do as I've asked."*

That hesitation doesn't do anything for my confidence, but I have little choice now. *"Fine. Let's get it over with."*

Micid holds out his hand. When I wrap my fingers around his, he doesn't seem bothered by my chaos lusters.

"You're sure this won't kill me?"

"Positive," he replies. "You're not leaving this world. You'll be able to see it; it will not be able to see you. Fae can hear us, though, so you must remain silent."

He rubs his thumb across my palm, setting off every warning alarm in my head. I start to pull my hand away, but at that moment, everything goes black.

I gasp when the chill hits me. My vision returns a moment later, but everything—the stairs, the arcing stone ceiling, even Lord Raen—is bathed in a blue light. When I turn my head, the world ripples as if it's underwater. The air in my lungs is cold enough to threaten frostbite, but it's not quite as bad as fissuring through the In-Between. I can endure this. I think.

Raen says something. I can't make it out because his voice sounds muffled, but Micid gives him a quick reply, then escorts me down the stairs.

This is dizzying. Micid and I are apart from the world, moving through it at a different pace, it seems, even though we're following Raen and reach the entrance to the storage room just one moment after him.

"Unlock the gate," Lord Raen says to the two guards, his voice still distant, still hard to understand.

I expect them to protest, but the swordsman on the left asks, *"Is there something we can help you find?"*

"No."

The guards exchange a brief look at the curtness of Raen's response, but they open the door.

Raen enters. One guard follows him inside. Micid and I slip past the other, who frowns after Lord Raen.

"Perhaps I can shorten your search, my lord," the first fae says. *"What are you looking for?"*

"A sword."

The fae scans the hundreds of swords slanted in their racks against the wall. Cautiously, I urge Micid past him. I need to move before my teeth start chattering.

"Where's the inventory?" Raen asks.

"Inventory?"

"Yes." Raen's eyes narrow. *"You're guarding these artifacts. Certainly you have a list of the items stored here. How else would you know if something is missing?"*

"Artifacts?" the fae says, clearly seeing the contents of the storage room as discarded junk.

"Get me the inventory. Now."

The guard blanks his expression. *"Yes, my lord."*

I'm face-to-face with him when he abruptly turns. Micid pulls me to the side, out of the way just in time. His free hand goes to my waist. It remains there even after the threat passes. I manage to resist the urge to elbow him in the gut. Instead, I step away, putting as much distance between us as possible, and pull him toward the back of the storage room. *"There's another guard around the corner."*

The *ther'rothi* nods. As soon as Garrad comes into view, he releases my hand. I see Micid blur forward for an instant and then the blue glow of the In-Between vanishes. The Realm is hot, almost scalding, in comparison. I fill my lungs with air. It feels like I'm taking a breath in a sauna.

Garrad leaps to his feet. His sword is halfway out of its scabbard when it's suddenly rammed back in. The flesh at his throat splits open. Blood pours out the deep gash. It pours out of his mouth when he gurgles out a cough. He staggers into the wall, starts to slide down it, but vanishes into the ether before he reaches the floor.

A cold fist clenches in my chest as I watch Garrad's soul-shadow rise up.

Micid reappears.

"You didn't have to kill him." My words are barely a whisper. No one was supposed to die.

He wipes his blade clean on his sleeve. "He would have prevented me from opening the humans' cell. Where is it?"

"You could have knocked him out." Garrad was one of Kyol's men. Kyol trusted him. He trusted me.

Micid shrugs. "The humans, shadow-reader. Our time is limited."

My skin is clammy, my fingers prickling and numb. I can't tear my gaze away from the bloodstain on the floor. I can't forget the shock in Garrad's eyes, but I jab a finger toward the wall. I don't know what else to do. I'm committed now. I can't *not* go through with this.

Micid drags the cart out of the way. "Where is the trigger-stone?"

"Above you."

"Where?" He motions me forward. "Show me."

Heart stammering, I walk to the wall and stand on my tip-toes to touch the stone.

"Here?" he asks.

His hand brushes mine, and I jerk back. "Yes."

The stone glows blue with his magic. When I hear the first rumblings of the slab moving aside, I try to slip away, but Micid moves. I end up trapped between him and the cart. He bumps my shoulder—*not* accidentally—then catches me when I teeter off-balance. The way his hands grab hold of my hips is way too intimate. I panic.

I shove away, but somehow end up even closer to him. He laughs when I struggle, then stops when I manage to get my dagger out of its sheath. I spin out of his arms and hold it between us.

I cut him. His right sleeve is slit and there's a thin line of blood on his pale skin. Really, it's no more than a scratch, but apparently that's enough to piss him off. His expression darkens a second before he disappears.

Oh, crap.

I scurry backward. My arm goes numb when my dagger is knocked from my hand. Micid, still invisible, launches into me. I crash down on my back. His hand tightens around my throat. I pry at fingers I can't see, try to squeak out a call for help, but there's no air. The wall was sliding open, wasn't it? Where the hell is—

"McKenzie?" Naito stands above me. As my vision blurs, I see him scan me from head to toe. Then, *finally*, he kicks out.

Micid grunts. I suck in a breath and punch at where I think his head should be. I miss.

"Naito!" I manage a shout before a hand clamps around my throat again.

Naito launches himself on top of me. The other human joins him, striking at the space between us. I slide across the ground, away from the fight, and suck air into my lungs. By the time I'm breathing normally, the struggle's over.

"What is this?" Naito shoves Micid, apparently still caught in the In-Between, away.

"Ever hear of a *ther'rothi*?"

He scowls. "They don't exist."

"Apparently, they do," I say, climbing to my feet. The other human helps Naito up. "Lord Raen hired him to help get you out."

Naito, dusting himself off, stops midbrush and stiffens. "Lord Raen?"

I don't get a chance to explain. There's the sound of running footsteps, then the fae who was left guarding the door to the storage room rounds the corner. He skids to a halt, surveying the scene behind the blade of his sword. I follow his line of sight to the puddle of blood on the floor.

"We didn't kill him," I say, though guilt stabs through me. I'm at least partially responsible for Garrad's death. I brought Micid here.

"Back into the cell," the fae orders, taking a step forward. I back up. Naito stands his ground, but the other human moves to the left, bends down, and retrieves my dropped dagger.

"Back in the cell, Evan," the fae tries in English.

"No," Evan says. He has no hope of taking down a fae, especially one of Kyol's swordsmen, with that dagger. He must be desperate, though, because he strikes at the air with an aggressive—and almost comical—roar.

I frown, wondering if his time in captivity has screwed with his mind. Then, out of the corner of my eye, something moves.

The pole of a spear slams into the fae's head. He drops like a rock, Lord Raen standing behind him.

"Where's Micid?" Raen demands.

I wave a hand toward the floor behind me. *"Somewhere over there."*

His jaw tightens. *"He was your escort."*

"Looks like we're going to need a Plan B." I won't apologize for Micid. I don't think the *ther'rothi* is dead, just unconscious, either from my dagger's poison or Naito and Evan's attack.

"Plan B?" Raen asks. He doesn't get it, and I'm not going to explain.

Naito walks past Raen without so much as a glance and kneels beside the unconscious fae guard. He searches his clothing, finds a set of keys on a metal ring, and pockets them.

Evan belts a sword around his waist, grabs a crossbow off the wall, then surveys the rest of the storage room. "Nice of Taltrayn to lock us in an arsenal."

Naito takes the guard's dropped sword. When he rises, Lord Raen steps forward.

"Kelia. I must speak with her."

When Naito turns his back on the noble, a throb of sympathy courses through me. I don't know what Raen did to make Naito hate him so much or to make his daughter sever all ties. It has to be something worse than just disapproving of their relationship.

Lord Raen makes a noise, then steps in front of Naito. *"My daughter. I will speak with her."*

Naito's eyes are cold. *"She doesn't want to speak to you."*

"You will make her."

"No." He steps around Raen.

Raen puts his arm up, not letting him pass. *"You will make her."*

Naito's lip curls. *"I won't make her do anything she doesn't want to do."*

"There was another fae guarding this storage room," Raen says, his tone even more threatening than Naito's. *"He'll return, and when he does, I can delay him or tell him where you are."*

I step between the two men. *"I'll tell her to talk to you."*

Naito turns his glare on me.

"We're wasting time," I say. "We need to go."

Evan surveys the storage room. "We need to blend in if we're going to walk out of here. Cover up our skin."

While they search the room for some kind of disguise, I turn to Raen. *"Watch for the other fae. Please. I promise I'll talk to Kelia."*

At first, I don't think he's going to budge. Cold, silver eyes watch Naito. The animosity in the air is almost tangible. This is hard for him, helping the human who took his daughter away.

Finally, he sighs. He takes off his gloves one at a time, shrugs out of his robe, hands it all to me, then silently walks to the door to stand guard.

"That'll work," Evan says, nodding at the robe in my hands. Then he holds out the dagger Raen gave me. "We haven't exactly met. I'm Evan. I read the shadows for Aren before the Court caught me."

"McKenzie," I say, taking the dagger.

He nods. "The *nalkin-shom*. I've heard of you."

I manage not to roll my eyes. "Seems like everyone has."

He laughs and then helps me slip on Raen's robe.

We rummage through the room for another minute. Evan and Naito find armor that covers everything but their hands and faces. I end up giving Raen's gloves to Naito. They fit him better, and we decide he's the best swordsman out of the three of us—I wasn't really a contender. We find only one other glove. Evan pulls it on and settles for pulling his sleeve down over his other hand. I plan to keep both my hands beneath my robe unless I absolutely have to take them out.

Evan scratches at his beard. "That just leaves our faces."

"There's nothing we can do about them," Naito says. "Masks and hoods will draw too much attention."

"So what do we do when someone sees us?" I ask.

"We kill them."

I must make some type of disgruntled noise because Naito looks at me. "If we can escape without killing anyone, we will. But if we don't have a choice—" He shrugs.

I might be turning my back on the Court, but that doesn't mean I want anyone to die.

Anyone *else* to die. My gaze slides to the bloodstain on the floor, then to the glowing blue torch in the wall above it. I walk over and take it out of its holder.

"We'll carry these. If we keep the orbs in front of our faces, the fae might not see our chaos lusters."

"The light will draw attention," Naito says.

"So will the *edarratae*," I say, unwilling to back down on this. No more fae are going to die because of my decisions.

"We can't see in the dark," Evan puts in. "McKenzie, you carry it since you know the way. Naito and I will stay behind you. We'll take care of anyone who looks at us too closely."

Naito doesn't argue this time. Good. We've already lingered longer than we should.

Lord Raen waits for us by the exit.

"Kyol will know what you've done," I tell him.

He nods, his expression unchanging. *"But he won't be able to do anything about it, will he? Not without admitting who he was hiding here."*

And if the king or his lord general finds out Kyol didn't execute either shadow-reader, he'll be screwed. I don't want him to get in trouble for this. Radath will be pissed enough when he learns I'm gone.

I adjust my grip on the torch. *"Will you tell him I'm sorry?"*

Lord Raen gives me a grim smile. *"If you'll tell Kelia the same."*

"Let's go," Naito mutters behind me.

Raen steps aside. *"Quickly. To the left."*

Naito slides past us and exits without so much as a glance at the fae. Evan whispers a quick thank-you. I follow on their heels.

"Naito," Lord Raen calls.

Surprisingly, Naito stops.

"If Kelia's in Lynn Valley," Raen says, *"take her away from there. Please. The lord general intends to attack at tomorrow's dusk."*

Lynn Valley. Oh, God, that's where I'd been. That's where the rebels are, or were just a day and a half ago.

"But that's in my world," I say.

Raen's lips tighten. *"The king is that desperate."*

Desperate enough to launch an attack in a residential area? I don't want to believe it, but one look at Naito tells me I should.

TWENTY-TWO

· — ·

T HE CORRIDORS OF the basement are blessedly deserted.
I lead Naito and Evan through the narrow tunnels, hoping
I can get us out of here quickly. Both times I traveled to the
storage room I came from the other direction. I would have
turned right outside the door if Raen hadn't told us to go left.
I can only assume this way is safer, that the fae guard took the
other way out.

My torch lights the way, its glow bathing the stone walls in
its blue-white light. I listen for footsteps, for the rustle of cloth,
the creak of *jaedric* armor, or a soft inhalation of air. Anything to indicate someone's approaching. I hear nothing, nothing but the sound of my heart thudding in my chest and the
occasional shuffles of Naito and Evan.

Despite the cool air beneath the palace, sweat dampens my
forehead. I'm worried about Aren, about Kelia and Sethan,
and—maybe just a tiny bit—about Lena. I need them all to be
okay.

Another corridor, still no sign of the fae. This escape
attempt is going eerily well, a fact that makes my skin tingle
with apprehension as I lead us up a set of stairs. They curve
sharply to the right. I can't see anything around the bend.

I slow almost to a stop as I near the turn. God, I don't like
this. It's too easy, too quiet.

"What's wrong?" Naito whispers.

I shake my head to indicate nothing, force my paranoia aside, and round the curve.

No one's there. A gate is at the top of the steps, though. I hurry the rest of the way, praying it isn't locked.

It is.

"Let me try." Naito slides past me, taking from his pocket the ring of keys he confiscated from the unconscious guard. I wince when they clatter and scrape against the metal lock. Naito's trying to be quiet, but with the corridor so silent . . .

"Got it." He pushes the gate open. Its screech echoes off the stone walls.

Evan curses behind us.

"Wait here," I whisper. I'm barely able to squeeze through the narrow crack without opening the gate farther. I scan the empty corridor. I'm about to tell Naito and Evan it's clear when a fae steps into the passageway no more than twenty feet to my left. The blue-white glow from my torch highlights his face. It's Taber. Shit.

"Hi, Taber," I say, stepping toward him.

"McKenzie?" He frowns at the open gate. "What are you doing here?"

Think, McKenzie. Think!

"Kyol gave me keys."

Taber scans me slowly, head to toe. "Your robe doesn't fit."

I look down. "No . . . but it's, um, warm."

He cocks his head. "Perhaps I should escort you back to your room?"

"That would be great, actually." I move toward him, praying he'll turn around and walk with me, but his frown vanishes. He moves past me, shoving my arm aside when I try to block his path.

A second before he reaches the gate, Naito and Evan burst out. Naito rams his shoulder into Taber's chest, throwing the fae backward. Evan grabs his arms, holds him down while Naito grabs Taber's head and slams it once . . . twice . . . three times into the stone floor.

Taber lies still.

Naito stands, wiping the fae's blood off on his pants. Evan is slower getting to his feet—I think he's weak from sitting in that tiny prison—but neither human holds my attention for long.

"What's wrong?" Naito asks. "He'll be fine once a healer sees to him."

I start backing away, pointing the orbed end of my torch toward the three fae running toward us.

Evan turns, curses. He unslings his crossbow from his shoulder, arms it with an arrow, then sights the weapon down the corridor.

"Run!" he orders as the bolt *thrum*s from the bow. It strikes the leg of the fae in the center.

Evan nocks another arrow. The other two fae take cover in an alcove, pulling their injured comrade with them and calling out an alarm.

I chuck my torch aside—no need to hide our *edarratae* anymore—and run.

"Come on!" Naito yells.

Evan abandons his attack and follows. We fly past a set of stairs.

"There's an exit," I shout at Naito, who's edged in front of me. "Ahead and to the right." It'll get us out of the palace. If we can make it into the city, we might have a chance.

Fae rush into the far end of the corridor. We skid to a halt, lose precious seconds as we all seem to realize at once they'll cut us off before we make it to the intersection.

Naito shoves me the other way. The two uninjured fae emerge from their alcove at the corridor's other end, sandwiching us in.

Evan shoots off another arrow. Misses.

Naito draws his sword. "Up!"

I lunge for the staircase, fly up the steps two at a time with Evan and Naito on my heels.

We're going to have to hide, not run. I try the handle of the wooden door in front of me. Locked. I rush to the next one while Naito tries the doors on the left side of the hall.

Evan fires down the stairs.

"I can't hold them off," he yells, sliding another bolt into place. He fires again.

"Here!" Naito shoves open a door.

Evan reaches it first. I run through after him, an instant too slow. A fae grabs me, swinging me around as his two companions rush into the room. I brace a hand against the wall, manage to stay upright long enough to kick the door shut and slam the latch into place.

My captor launches me against the wall. My head hits hard. My vision blurs, blackens. I blink the spots from my eyes in time to focus on Naito.

He lurches forward, plunging his sword through the back of the fae holding me. It almost skewers me as well. The point of his blade stabs toward my stomach, just above my belly button. I flatten my back against the wall and suck in.

Naito pulls his sword free and then grabs my arm as the fae falls. He curses as he stares at my stomach.

"I'm fine," I assure him as the fae vanishes into the ether. I push Naito farther into the room, away from the door, which is now being pounded on from the other side.

The two fae who made it in circle Evan, their swords drawn, ready to strike as soon as he lowers his crossbow or shoots. Even if Evan kills one of them, there's no way he'll get another arrow nocked before the other fae cuts him down. I'm not even sure he has another arrow.

Naito pulls me to Evan's side. There might be three of us, but we're human. The Court has the advantage. They've spent years honing their skills. If we weren't in the Silver Palace, we'd already be dead. They'd fissure behind us and strike us down.

And time's on their side, not ours. They can wait for backup to break down the door.

We're in a parlor or some other type of sitting room. There's only the one exit and then three arched windows set into the wall on our left.

The windows. We're one tall story off the ground. The fall is likely to hurt, but it'll be better than a sword through the gut.

I don't pause to second-guess my plan. I grab a chair and launch it through the glass.

Evan shoots the same instant. The bolt plunges into the shoulder of the fae on the left. The other lunges forward. He slashes into Evan's forearm before the human dodges back.

Naito attacks, swinging his sword at the fae's head. The fae ducks, parries, and strikes out, seemingly all in one move.

I shove Evan toward the window. He dropped his crossbow when the fae cut into his arm. He tries drawing his sword, but his hand is slick with blood.

"Get out of here. Go!"

He drags in a breath, nods. "Don't leave him."

He hands me his sword. When he jumps, I turn back to the fight, swinging my blade at the fae who's still standing when he takes a stab at Naito. He blocks my attack easily, advances with a thrust of his own. I parry and stagger back. Alone, I'd be dead—alone, *Naito* would be dead—but together, we manage to keep the fae off.

"The window," I say. "Go!" I grunt when a particularly hard hit rattles through my sword.

"You first," Naito throws back.

I take a swing at the fae's head. Miss.

"He knows who I am," I say, not knowing if I'm telling a lie or not. "He'll turn me over to Kyol. You have to get back to Kelia. Go! Now!"

He wants to protest—I see it in his eyes—but invoking Kelia's name does the trick.

The fae curses when Naito makes a leap for the window. I put myself between them, forcing the fae to focus on me. He parries my attack and strikes back. The sword flies from my hand and clatters against the wall.

I draw my poisoned dagger. Throw it.

The fae raises his off hand in defense and bats the dagger aside. The throw wasn't hard or fast, but the blade is sharp and blood wells from a small cut on the top of his hand.

I don't wait for the poison to kick in; I lunge for the window.

He catches me. I swing back with an elbow, manage to catch his chin, but his hold doesn't loosen. He throws me to the floor, pins me there.

I shove my knee into his groin, but there's no momentum behind it. He slips to the side. His hands tighten around my wrists.

"Be still," he snarls in Fae.

A flash of pain bursts behind my eyes when I head-butt him. He grunts, but I'm certain I did more harm to me than to him. I can barely focus. His face wavers above me. I struggle, bucking and twisting and trying to squirm away.

He wavers again. This time, it's not just my vision. His arms buckle and he collapses on top of me. I lie there, gasping for air, then somehow I manage to shove him away.

Rolling to my stomach, I crawl on all fours toward the window, my arms shaking beneath me. I grab the window's edge, ignore the glass biting into my palms, and will my muscles to cooperate.

My upper torso drapes over the windowsill. Glass pricks my skin, but Raen's cloak protects me from too much damage. The street below is empty. It's going to hurt when I hit, but I need to get out of here. The fae are still beating on the door.

My weight is split between the room and the outside world. I'm about to slide over the edge when something grabs me. It's a Court fae, the one with the crossbow bolt through his shoulder. He drags me back inside the room as the door bursts open and the king's swordsmen charge inside.

I scream myself awake. Cold. Wet. Caught. My teeth clatter and someone throws a second bucket of water over my head.

I cry out again. My skin seems to freeze over my bones.

"Ah, there you are," Radath's voice croons just inside the reach of a hanging orb's blue glow. He overturns his bucket at the edge of the light and sits.

I wish I could remain unconscious. Everything hurts: my ribs and stomach, my back, and especially my shoulders and arms. My hands are shackled securely to the wall. There isn't a length of chain or anything between it and my silver manacles; I can't adjust my position at all.

"You need to start talking," Radath says. "You can start by explaining what you were doing last night."

I'm so damn cold it's a struggle to pull my thoughts together. I squeeze my eyes shut, open them, and search the shadows of my prison. How did I get here? How much does Radath know?

"Where did you get this?" Radath asks. He's holding something in his hand. A dagger, the one Raen gave me.

"I want to talk to Taltrayn." I try to keep my voice steady, but I'm shivering too much.

Radath laughs. "Of course you do."

Something moves in my peripheral vision. A tiny glimmer of hope rises in me. It's snuffed out an instant later when Micid, not Kyol, steps into the light.

Radath follows my line of sight. "I've brought along my *ther'rothi*. He asked to meet you."

The fae's gaze oozes over me. I'm already shivering, but a deeper tremble runs through my body.

"Micid is a rare breed," Radath continues. "Possibly unique. Show her what you do."

The *ther'rothi*'s lips stretch into a smile one moment before he disappears. I press back against the wall, afraid of what he'll do, but he reappears a few seconds later in the exact same spot. That's when confusion sinks in. Radath said Micid wanted to meet me, but we already met. And I already know what he can do. Why the demonstration?

Radath chuckles. "Does it bother you? Not being able to see him? I learned of his magic a few years ago and agreed to keep it secret—only the king and I know what he can do. In exchange, he works for me when I need him."

Someone's not keeping it a secret, but I'm not about to correct the lord general.

Radath leans forward, drops his voice to a whisper. "I also ignore his little trips to *tjandel*."

Tjandel. I recognize the word. Micid said he visited there.

"Unfamiliar with the place?" Radath inquires. He wants me to ask about it. I won't.

"It's a . . . What do your people call it? A whorehouse. Yes. It's a whorehouse in an unsavory district on the edge of Corrist. It's outside the silver walls, so its clientele can fissure in and out without being seen. I know of many nobles who have tasted the delights there. All would deny it, but not Micid. Micid is addicted to the whores. Addicted, in fact, to their chaos lusters."

It feels like Radath just dumped a third bucket of icy water over my head.

"Most of the whores are there willingly," he says, his voice saccharine. "Some of them aren't. They don't all have the Sight, and Micid has a fetish for humans who scream and thrash beneath him. He likes them slightly insane, grasping and clawing at the invisible demon they believe to be inside them. Since you do have the Sight, you'll understand what's happening, but I'm sure he wouldn't be opposed to breaking you in. You'd scream for him, wouldn't you, McKenzie?"

Micid watches me with a small, sadistic smile.

Then, suddenly, Radath gets to the point. "There were two others with you last night. Who were they?"

He doesn't know about Naito and Evan. Thank God. They must have escaped. At least I accomplished something last night. I sit straighter, trying to ease the bite of the shackles into my wrists.

Radath lifts the poisoned dagger. Carefully, he slides its blade under a damp lock of my hair, lifting it out of my face. He wants me to be scared of him—I am—but I won't tell him about the humans. It won't save me; it will only condemn Kyol.

Radath grips the left side of my neck in one big hand, laying the dagger flat against the other side, right over the puckered scar Aren left on my skin. His hand tightens, constricting my airway. "Who were they?"

I have to tell him something, something that will appease him and buy me time.

"Rebels," I choke out. "I was supposed to get them inside the palace."

Radath's grip loosens. Micid, smirking at the edge of the orb's glow, lifts an eyebrow. He doesn't deny my claim, though. He really doesn't want the lord general to know we met before.

"And what were these rebels supposed to do," Radath asks, "once they came inside?"

I scrape up the courage to pin him with a glare. "They were supposed to kill you."

Radath chuckles. "I'm as untouchable as the king, McKenzie."

A door creaks open. "Lord General."

I let out a shaky breath. Kyol's found me.

"I told Atroth I would handle her," Radath says without turning.

"I will handle her," Kyol says. I'm not sure if his coldness is directed at Radath or at me.

"You already had an opportunity to make her cooperate," Radath says, switching to Fae. *"You failed. She's no longer your pet."*

"You may discuss that with Atroth. He wishes to speak with you."

The lord general glares at me without rising. I don't think he's going to leave. He doesn't take orders from Kyol, and he seems to enjoy having me chained to this wall. My interactions with him over the years have been few, but I never thought he'd treat me like this. Of course, I never thought I'd give him reason to.

Radath's shoulders slump. Then, with obvious reluctance, he stands, turning to Kyol. *"She's betrayed our king, sword-master. Atroth expects her to be punished. I expect you to pry out the rest of her secrets. Understood?"*

"Understood." Kyol's expression gives away nothing.

Radath gestures to Micid. The *ther'rothi* leaves my cell first. Radath follows.

He smiles, then lets the door thunk shut behind him.

For a long time, Kyol doesn't move. A thousand different apologies make their way to my tongue. They die before they pass my lips. I'd do it over again to save Naito and Evan.

"How could you be so foolish?" Kyol demands. I flinch at his tone. "They were safe, McKenzie! *You* were safe!"

He strides beneath the orb, his fists clenched at his sides.

"I couldn't stay here, Kyol."

"So you were going back to *him*!"

"I—" My voice cracks. My chin quivers. I bite my lower lip, refusing to cry.

"McKenzie." His voice is pained now. He drops to his knees in front of me, his face drawn and shoulders hunched as if he's just lost a war.

My heart twists in my chest. Still, I swallow back an apology. Instead, I softly ask, "Can you get me out of here?"

He scrubs his hands over his face. "I don't know."

I don't really have a right to ask it of him. I got myself into this mess; he should make me get out of it.

"Sidhe." He cups my cheek in his hand and leans his forehead against mine. We stay like that for a long time, him warm, strong, and steady; me cold, wet, and shivering. I feel raw, like my emotions have been stripped away, layer by layer, leaving my soul pink with abrasions. Even the *edarratae* seem dull and distant.

"If you want out of here, McKenzie, you have to give me something. Atroth won't consider releasing you without information on the rebels."

I can't help the Court anymore. The rebellion might have done things I don't like, but the Court's manipulated and used me. Radath's ordered humans executed, and I'm certain he gave my name to the vigilantes hoping they would kill me. The king's done nothing to stop the lord general. Kyol's done nothing to stop his king.

"I can't," I whisper.

He lets out a long sigh and then, slowly, he slides his hand up my left arm toward the manacles. When he reaches my wrist, a part of me is convinced he's going to free me anyway, but then his fingers slip to the diamond necklace hidden under my sleeve. He tugs, and the necklace falls free in his hand.

He touches the center stone and then nods to himself. "This will buy your freedom."

Oh, God.

"No, Kyol, you can't!"

"Shh, *kaesha*." He places his fingers over my mouth. "It's the only way to save you."

I yank against my shackles. "No, wait. Listen. I'll tell you whatever you want to know. I'll do whatever you want, but please—*please*—don't do this. Don't trade my life for his."

His face is expressionless as he rises; only his eyes betray how much I'm hurting him.

"You'll hate me for this, won't you?" he asks.

I nod because I don't trust my voice. Aren trusted me with his life. He was confident I wouldn't betray him. If the Court fae show up at the anchor-stone's location, he'll think I care nothing for him.

Kyol slips the necklace inside his pocket. "I'm sorry, McKenzie. For everything."

TWENTY-THREE

◆

THE BLUE-WHITE ORB hanging from the ceiling is the only thing keeping back whatever I hear scurrying in the darkness. It doesn't keep back my nightmares, though. Some of them are old, recurring ones; others are brand-new. Every time my eyes close, I pray that when I open them, I'll discover these last few weeks have been a dream. The king's war will be uncomplicated, the rebels will be clearly bad, the Court will be clearly good. But the world doesn't work that way. War is never so simple.

Plus, I'd never have met Aren. His kiss doesn't seem like a manipulation anymore. All his gentle moments, the way he's looked at me . . . Maybe he really does care for me.

The scrape of a sliding latch echoes in the darkness. The door cracks open. The door shuts. In the darkness, I hear someone suck in a breath.

Please, don't let it be Micid.

A shadow moves to the edge of the orb's glow. The toes of two scuffed boots break the circle. The fae advances another step, then another. Light rises slowly up a pair of black pants pulled tight around muscled thighs to a hand gripping the hilt of a sword, to a strong, broad chest, then to an angry face framed by wild, disheveled hair.

"Aren," I whisper. *No, no, no.*

His jaw clenches. My chest constricts.

I shake my head. "No, Aren. Please. I didn't give Kyol the necklace, I swear."

His scowl fades as he strides beneath the hanging orb and then he kneels beside me. He cradles my face between his palms. "*Sidhe*, you're freezing."

Heat pours into me. I don't know if it's from my *edarratae*, from his magic, or just from being near him again. It doesn't matter. It feels good. *He* feels good.

That's when it registers he still has his sword. No way would the Court allow him to remain armed.

"Kyol didn't . . . ?"

He smoothes back my damp hair. "You're going to be okay, McKenzie. I'm getting you out of here."

I look beyond his shoulder. Kyol stands just visible at the edge of the orb's glow.

"He . . ." My throat closes up. "He brought you to me?"

Grim, Aren nods once. Without turning to the sword-master, he demands, "The key."

When Kyol doesn't move, Aren stiffens. Slowly, he stands. His hand moves back to the hilt of his sword. "The key, Taltrayn."

"Radath has the only key."

A moment passes where nobody moves, nobody even seems to breathe. When Aren's gaze shifts back to me, my stomach sinks. If I'm reading his expression correctly, he's horrified.

He turns back to the sword-master. "You're going to make me do this?"

"You can heal her," Kyol says without a flicker of emotion.

Aren's shoulders sag—just for a second—then he kneels once again.

"Aren?" I search his face, trying to figure out what they're talking about.

He tucks a lock of hair behind my ear. "This is going to hurt, McKenzie. I have to heat the metal, make it malleable so I can pull it off. I'll heal the burns as soon as you're free."

It takes a moment for that to sink in. Then I remember Tom. I remember how he screamed when Aren touched him.

I remember the smell of his burnt flesh and the blisters on his arms when Aren took his hands away.

"No. No fucking way. Are you crazy?"

"I'll do it as quickly as possible."

"No." I pin my gaze on Kyol. "Don't you have bolt cutters or something?"

Kyol doesn't so much as twitch.

"Listen," Aren says. "You can't scream, McKenzie. Tal-trayn has a fae loyal to him guarding the door, but other fae are on patrol. Here." He unfastens his belt and lifts it toward my mouth. "Bite down on this."

I shake my head.

"You can do this," he says. "You have to."

Damn it, damn it, damn it. I don't *want* to, but Aren would never suggest it if there was any other way. And Kyol would never let him hurt me.

I hiss a breath out between my teeth. "I guess it's better than chopping my hands off."

Aren smiles as if everything's going to be okay. I give him a skeptical glare as I take the belt between my teeth.

He reaches up to wrap his hands around my shackles. The metal warms. After shivering in this cell for so long, I almost welcome the heat. Not for long, though. The intensity increases, gradually at first. Then all at once it *hurts*.

My nerves short-circuit. The metal feels so hot it's cold. Then I hear something sizzle, smell an acrid burning. I jerk against the silver searing my wrists, but I can't break free. Biting down on the leather between my teeth, I squeeze my eyes shut. I scream, but it's too high in my throat to become a sound.

It's too much. I slam the back of my head against the stone wall as my wrists melt. I slam it again and again and again.

I'm barely aware of Aren prying the manacles off, of him wrapping his hands around my wrists. Nausea churns through my stomach because it feels like he's touching sinew and bone. I can't possibly have any flesh left.

"Shh," Aren soothes, sending his magic into me. "It's over. You're okay now."

The fire slowly subsides. My wrists grow cold, then numb, then warm again as Aren's touch stirs my *edarratae*.

He takes the belt from my mouth, hugs me to his chest, and

weaves his hand through my hair to cup the back of my head. He flares his magic again, heals whatever injury I caused banging against the wall. I tremble in his arms until he tilts back and wipes tears from my face. His eyes beg forgiveness.

I suck in a ragged breath and try to pull myself together. There's nothing to forgive. He did what he had to do to free me.

Lightly, he brushes his fingertips over my wrist. "See? No scars."

I look down to my pink but smooth skin, and my lips curve into a weak smile.

"Ah, there it is," he says, his gaze dropping to my mouth. "I haven't seen that in a while."

I manage a short laugh. My eyes meet his again and . . . Oh.

I catch my breath. A curl of sun-blond hair falls across his brow, crossing a faint white scar I've never noticed before. His silver eyes, with that glint I always found infuriating, shimmer with something more than his typical tease. I'm suddenly aware of my lips, of them parting as they remember the taste and feel of his.

He smiles, then raises my hand to his mouth and kisses my healed wrist. "We need to go. Can you stand?"

"I think so," I say.

He fastens his belt around his waist and then helps me to my feet. As soon as I'm up, the extent of my exhaustion hits. The last time I ate was breakfast at Shane's. It's been at least twenty-four hours since then. I'm weak and Aren has to do most of the work, setting me on my feet and keeping his arms around my waist until my knees decide to hold me. It takes a while. My body is tight and sore from shivering and my skin feels like it's been worked over with sandpaper. My wrists are the most sensitive. They don't exactly hurt, but I'm aware of where they were burnt.

"You okay?" Aren asks, his breath warm on my neck. I nod, and we turn toward the door, toward Kyol.

Kyol. He didn't give the necklace to his king.

I can't move, and not just because Aren's arm is around my waist, holding me tight to his side. Kyol has been everything to me for so long. He's the one I've always turned to, the one I've relied on, and I'm hurting him. The pain is so obvious in his eyes.

His lips tighten. His gaze slips from me to Aren. "You remember the path through the wards?" Aren nods. "The guards at the eastern entrance aren't mine, but they're inexperienced. I presume you can handle them."

"Of course," Aren replies.

"They need to be left alive to report to Radath."

Aren nods again. He tries to move forward, but I don't budge. Kyol can't mean to . . .

He does.

"You're not leaving." My words are more an accusation than a question. Kyol's face is as unreadable as ever.

I throw off Aren's arm and cross the room. The hell if I'm going to let him become a martyr because of me. "You can't stay. Radath will kill you."

"McKenzie," Aren whispers a warning. He hurries to the door, presses his ear against it.

"Shh." Kyol places his fingers over my lips. I slap his hand away.

"Why won't you leave?"

The most minuscule wince breaks through his mask. "The war isn't over."

"Don't bullshit me, Kyol."

"McKenzie, I—"

"You said you would leave."

"I can't, *kaesh*—"

"*Why!*"

"Because I couldn't live with myself!" he roars.

I flinch back and a sharp, almost debilitating pain lances through my chest. Is he so ashamed of his feelings? All these years, I thought only the king's decree kept us apart. I didn't think he despised himself for loving me.

Aren unsheathes his sword and mutters something about us drawing all the guards.

"McKenzie," he says, his voice low, controlled again. "Radath has been whispering in the king's ear for years, telling him how to fight this war. Atroth listens because the methods work. I've convinced him to forbid some of the lord general's more deplorable plans, but if I leave . . . I *must* stay, *kaesha*. I cannot allow Radath to control the king."

"That's why you want to stay?" I ask. Lies and truths have

been tangled up for so long, I'm not confident I can tell them apart anymore.

His jaw clenches. He nods. "If I leave Atroth to Radath's counsel, the war will end, but thousands of innocent fae will be killed in the process."

His words make me feel only marginally better. Kyol's putting the Realm before me again. I understand why he wants to stay behind—I respect it even—but I can't keep doing this. I accept who he is, what he stands for, but I'm no longer able to be the girl in love with the honorable hero; I need someone who's capable of forgetting his responsibilities for me. At least some of the time.

"I can reason with Atroth, McKenzie," he continues. "I *will* reason with him. I'll convince him to speak to the false—" He stops, draws in a breath. "To the son of Zarrak. We can negotiate peace."

Aren's caustic laugh cuts through the air. "We tried that once, remember? Your king won't loosen his control of the gates. He needs the *tinril* to pay off nobles and bribe his Inner Court."

"He needs the *tinril* to protect the Realm from you." Kyol's eyes flash. "He needs it to prevent another Brykeld."

Aren doesn't flinch, but I do. I know now he's not responsible for what happened. He regrets the massacre. He even set up the fae who led it so I could track him down, so the Court could capture him. I believe all that, but he's responsible for other crimes, crimes like turning Kyol's swordsmen into *tor'um*.

Damn it, why does this have to be complicated?

"McKenzie," Kyol says softly. "I'll end this war as quickly as I can."

"You could do more good with the rebellion." My words are barely a suggestion. I know what his response will be. He's too honorable a man to turn his back on his king, too honorable to abandon the Realm to Radath's brutality. It's selfish to ask it of him.

TABER'S guarding my cell. I stop short when I recognize him, worried he'll be pissed I allowed Naito and Evan to knock him out cold. When he does nothing except hand me a hooded cloak, I whisper an apology and a thank-you—it's the least I can do—then follow Aren down the corridor.

He knows the way out. We creep down the shadowed hall, hugging close to a rough stone wall covered in a fuzzy moss. I'm fairly certain we're not beneath the Silver Palace. This place is too big; there are too many other prisoners here. We pass more than a dozen thick wooden doors, some holding back the moans and cries of their cell's occupants and others holding back only silence. Most likely, Radath had me fissured to Chaer, a prison at the inside edge of the Barren. Fae can't fissure out of that stretch of land, not anymore. Not since the false-blood Thrain destroyed a gate in the Barren's core. No one knows how he did it, but when the gate collapsed, it created a void in the Realm. It's not the same as being handicapped by silver. It's still possible to open fissures in the atmosphere, but they're too hot to approach. It's like the loss of the gate damaged the In-Between.

Aren holds up his hand at an intersection, signaling for me to wait. When he disappears around the corner, I edge forward.

I peek around the bend in time to witness one of two fae collapsing in a heap. Aren deflects the other's attack, counters with swings of his own. The guard staggers under the brutal blows, almost slips. Before he regains his balance, Aren kicks his feet out from under him, then slams the hilt of his sword into the fae's temple.

The hair on the back of my neck stands on end. I scan up and down the corridor, looking and listening for running footsteps. The fight was brief—less than a minute—but the clash of steel on steel sounded loud as gunfire.

Aren glances over his shoulder, sees me standing here. "Clear?"

I listen for a few seconds more, then nod. If anyone heard anything, they'd be raising the alarm by now.

Aren holds out his hand.

"Taltrayn's kept his word so far," he says, intertwining his fingers with mine. "If he holds true, he'll make sure the guards on the roof are distracted, but we'll need to move quickly. Can you run?"

I nod. I don't have much of a choice.

He opens the door. The long shadow of the prison stretches across the dirt at our feet. The sun is setting somewhere behind us. If we could wait twenty minutes, we'd have the cover of darkness, but we can't just stand around here. Aren squeezes my hand and then we take off.

Cold air burns my lungs and a stitch in my side makes me want to double over, but I don't stop, not until Aren finally slows when we reach the first sprinkling of trees. He puts a hand under my elbow, keeping me upright. We're still in sight of the prison, though, so I force my legs to keep moving. I stumble once, regain my balance, then stumble again. If fae not loyal to Kyol look this way, they could see us. An archer could still hit us. I *have* to keep going.

I make it ten, maybe fifteen minutes before I take Aren's hand and make him stop. Not because I think we're safe, but because we're heading west, deeper into the Barren. The jolt of adrenaline that brought me this far has worn off and my mind has cleared. At least, it's cleared enough to know this isn't the way we should be going.

"We need to get to the gate in Belecha," Aren says. "Rokan is closer, but the Court will expect us to go there."

Belecha is across the Barren. Even if I could walk the entire way without resting, it would take me at least a day to get there. We don't have that much time.

"Radath's sending troops to Lynn Valley," I say.

A flicker of surprise. "What? When?"

"They may already be there. Lord Raen said something about 'tomorrow's dusk,' which is today." I glance back at the setting sun even though it's no indication of the time in Vancouver. "Maybe now."

"Lord Raen?" He frowns. "Kelia's father?"

"He helped me free Naito and Evan."

"Naito and . . . They're both alive?"

"Yes. I think so." I run a hand over my tangled hair. "Radath ordered Kyol to execute them. He didn't—I told you he wouldn't—but he refused to let them go. I was caught breaking them out."

He stares for a long moment, then, "Lynn Valley. You're sure about that?"

I wish I wasn't. "Yes."

"Okay." He turns his head left, then right, scanning the thin forest as if he might find a solution to the problem hanging from a tree branch.

"Okay," he says again. He takes my hand. We walk no more than a dozen steps when his fingers tighten and he increases our pace. Another half dozen steps and he curses.

He pulls me into a run, but we're still heading west. It's the wrong way. He needs to go east or he won't make it to the edge of the Barren in time to fissure out and warn the rebels. It might already be too late.

I pull my hand free from his. "Go. It's okay."

He shakes his head. "I can't leave you."

"You can't abandon them."

His eyes are pained as he turns to me. "McKenzie—"

"If the Court finds rebels there, if the Court attacks, the fight could spill over into human homes. You need to go."

His gaze drops to the ground. He shakes his head, but takes a small pouch out of his pocket, ties it around one of my belt loops, then unhooks a dagger from his belt. He slides his hands under my cloak and around my waist, tucking the sheathed weapon into the waistband at the small of my back.

He takes a half step back but leaves his hands on the curves of my hips and holds my gaze. "Keep going west. You should reach a road by morning. Turn right and head toward Belecha. You'll come to a crossroads on the way. I'll be there in the morning, waiting for you, but if I'm not . . ." He draws in a breath. "If I'm not, you'll have to continue on your own. Keep your hood up and your chaos lusters hidden. The Court will be looking for you. Wait until dark before you enter the city, then find a tavern, one that's crowded. Ask where you can find *saristi*. It's a bird from the Adaris Mountains. Everyone will tell you there aren't any in Belecha, but word will get back to Sethan's supporters—he has them in every city. Wait until one finds you. They'll take you somewhere safe."

I nod, trying to act calm and competent even though I'm dead tired and don't want him to go.

His jaw clenches; his hands tighten on my hips. "You're resourceful. You should be fine."

It's not me I'm worried about. His silver eyes drink in every detail of my face. That's not a good sign, him acting like he'll never see me again.

"*Sidhe*, I don't want to leave you." He grabs the back of my head and pulls me into a brutal kiss.

He tastes of the Realm, light and exotic. Addicting. My *edarratae* pulse in rhythm with my heartbeat. He's warm, strong. A small explosion goes off in my stomach when he shudders. He's good at this, teasing all thoughts from my mind but him. His tongue parts my lips, dances with mine, and the world spins. I'd let it keep spinning but Aren breaks away, grasping tightly to my arms.

"McKenzie." He kisses my lips again briefly, then again, lingering. "I'll be waiting at the crossroads. I promise."

TWENTY-FOUR

◆

H E'S NOT WAITING for me in the morning. I walked through the night, afraid that if I stopped to rest, I'd never get up again, and reached the road to Belecha just as the sky began to pinken. It took about half an hour to reach the crossroads. I planned on waiting until late afternoon, but an electric storm—something extremely rare in the Realm—was inching in. Besides, Aren told me to go to Belecha if he wasn't here. It's possible he might not make it here at all.

The thought makes my stomach hurt.

I turn north and watch the dirt pass beneath my boots. I'm not the only one traveling to Belecha. Merchants and their *cirikith*-drawn carts begin to crowd the road. I keep my cloak clutched around me, careful to make sure my hands and face remain out of sight. It's during times like this, when I'm walking through another world, surrounded by magic-users, that I wonder if I might be crazy. Maybe my mind is trapped in some kind of elaborate hallucination while my body is still restrained to a bed in Bedfont House. That's where my parents sent me. I was flunking all my classes, disappearing without explanation, and was caught more than once "talking to myself" and "having fits." It took Kyol a month to find me there, a month during which medications were forced down my throat and I was surrounded by the truly insane.

I ignore the old memories and trudge on. I don't expect to make it to Belecha—I expect Aren to fissure to me long before I get there—but as the sun descends behind dark clouds, the city's outlying buildings come into view. The stone would blend in with the gray sky if snaking green vines weren't covering the walls. By the time the dirt road turns into smooth cobblestones, those walls take on a blue hue. Night's fallen. Fae workers are sending their magic into orb-topped streetlights.

I've been here before—a few times, in fact—but Kyol always took me straight to the gate. Even if I had someone to fissure me through it now, we'd have to wait until morning. City gates are closed after dark to all but the Court fae, and the only reason they would need to use it is if they were escorting a human.

I wrap my cloak around me and hurry toward a squat building with an open door and boisterous conversation spilling out into the street. As soon as I step inside, see fae clutching fat mugs, and smell a pungent, stale odor, it's obvious I've found a tavern. A shady one, I think, because I'm not the only one here hiding my identity behind a hooded cloak.

I want to hole up in a corner to rest, but I force myself to walk just a little farther. The bartender, a gaunt fae with black hair falling well past his shoulders, asks me what I want.

I want food, but I say, *"I'm looking for saristi."*

My accent sucks. His eyes narrow. *"You're looking for what?"*

"Saristi," I say, hoping I'm emphasizing the right syllables.

"You're in the wrong province for that," he says. Then, *"What do you want?"*

From the scowl on the bartender's face, I won't be allowed to stay unless I order something. There's a menu on the countertop. Since I can't read it, I point to a random line of symbols in the middle.

And immediately snatch my hand back. I'm lucky. No *edarratae* flashed over my skin, but damn it, I can't be that careless.

"Fifteen tinril," the bartender says.

I have no clue how much that is, so I reach into the pouch Aren gave me and take out a few coins. Making sure my hand stays hidden, I drop the change on the counter.

He raises an eyebrow, then sweeps the coins into a pocket. I clench my teeth. There's no way I gave him the exact amount, but I'm not going to ask for change. I don't want him to figure out just how foreign my accent really is.

I'd like to hunker down in a corner or at least somewhere near a wall, but the only free table is right smack-dab in the center of the joint. It's better than standing, though, so I pull out a chair and sit. It doesn't matter that the chair squeaks and wobbles as if it's one wrong move away from falling apart; it's good to be off my feet. It would be even better if I had a bed. I'm certain not even my nightmares would wake me once I lie down.

A few minutes later, a fae sets a bowl in front of me. I don't know what's in it. Some mashed-up something covered in something yellow. I start with the flatbread since that's unlikely to kill me, eat half of it before I'm brave enough to dip a tiny corner into the sauce. I take a bite.

And try not to spit it out. Bitterbark. They turn that crap into a sauce?

Stomach growling, I scrape it off to the side and try a small spoonful of the mash left in the bowl. It tastes like orange-flavored eggs. Disturbing, but edible.

The fae packed into the tavern are louder than when I first entered, but I tune them out. It's easy to do since I lack the energy to translate their words. I finish off the rest of the mash—which tasted worse and worse with each bite—and debate asking the bartender for a drink.

My hood is wrenched off before I make a decision. I try to jerk it back up before anyone notices my chaos lusters, but it's too late. Everyone's staring—gaping, really—except for the fae who removed my hood. He's linebacker-heavy and almost a full foot taller than I am.

"Are you the one the soldiers are looking for?" he demands.

Heart pounding, I take a half step toward the door and say, *"No."*

He scowls. Whatever. He asked the question. Did he really expect me to say yes?

A fae from the crowd says something I can't translate, but my attacker wipes his hands off on his mud-stained pants and answers, *"I found her. I get the tinril."*

There's a reward out for me already? Great. I take another step toward the exit.

"Do you work for the rebels?" a woman asks. She's wearing fitted pants the color of red soil and a white top that flows past her left side but stops just above her right hip, giving her easy access to the dagger sheathed there.

"I don't work for anyone," I say. Technically, it's true. I haven't helped the rebels yet. Well, not unless you count the warning about Lynn Valley.

The bartender, clearly not liking my response, invades the circle forming around me. *"If you don't work for the king, then you work for the rebels. Get out."*

"We should give her to the rebels," someone from the back of the crowd shouts. There are a few murmurs of agreement, but the majority look interested in making some cash. I still have Aren's dagger hidden under my cloak. It won't do any good against the thirty-odd fae here, but if a single individual tries to hand me over, I might have a chance.

"I won't have the king's soldiers invading my place." The bartender eyes the fae who ripped my hood off. *"Get her out of here."*

I'd rather almost anyone else escort me outside. This guy's almost twice the size as the rest of them. And he stinks. Of alcohol and *cirikith* shit, I think.

"You can make twice as much tinril if you sell her," a fae standing between me and the exit says.

"Sell?" the linebacker asks.

The fae nods once. *"I know where."*

A chill settles over my skin. I scan the tavern, trying to find some other way out of this. But these aren't the sort of people who are going to offer help without getting something in return, and I don't know how much *tinril* I have in the little bag Aren gave me. I doubt it'll be enough. Besides, nothing would stop someone from just taking it. Best not to mention it at all.

My gaze settles on the bartender. He's still scowling, but I think his wrinkles are deeper than a moment ago. And maybe more disgusted than furious? At least one person here seems to have a problem with selling me.

"You'll give her to the Court, Delan," he says.

"You told me to get her out of here." Delan's words are so

slurred I have trouble translating them. *"I will. What I do with her after that is . . ."* Something.

"I have another option," a familiar voice says.

The group of fae blocking the tavern's exit shuffle aside to reveal the newcomer, Lorn, standing in the doorway. He doesn't look at me; he just tugs at the cuffs of his sleeves as if he's already bored with this scene. I don't know if I should be relieved to see him or not.

"I'll take her," he says once he's satisfied his attire is in order.

"For how much?" Delan demands.

Lorn just laughs and says again, *"I'll take her."*

"Not without paying." Delan makes a move to grab my arm.

I jump back, then jump again when a knife plunges into his chest. Delan frowns at me as if I'm the one who threw it. I didn't. I have no clue who did. It wasn't Lorn. He's still standing in the doorway, looking as unconcerned as ever.

Delan's gaze drops to the hilt. He wraps his hand around it, wavers, then pulls it free.

A mistake. His eyes widen as blood gushes from the wound. He cups his hand to his chest to catch the flow, then scans the tavern, but no one offers help.

His knees buckle. He lands on all fours, makes an effort to rise, then disappears into the ether. The rest of the fae search one another's faces—undoubtedly trying to figure out which one of them threw the knife.

"Now that that's settled," Lorn's voice cuts through the silence. "McKenzie."

I tear my eyes away from the wet blood on the wood floor. Clenching my teeth, I step past it. Lorn flicks up my hood when I reach him, then we both step outside.

A cloaked figure waits for us. I let out a breath when I catch a glimpse of Kelia's face, not only because she's alive but also because she's here. I trust her more than I do Lorn.

"Aren's okay?" I ask.

She nods. "Naito?"

He still hasn't turned up yet. That can't be good, but I tell her, "He was fine a day ago. He made it out of the palace. A shadow-reader named Evan was with him."

Lorn breezes by us. "No time to talk, my dears. The gate is quite a ways off."

"No one's allowed to use the gate after dark." This is his world; he should know that.

"True," he says without slowing. "But I own the guards."

I alternate jogging and speed-walking to keep up. Who is he? The Godfather of the Realm?

Kelia keeps pace with me without breaking from a walk. "If they made it out of Corrist, they'll be okay." She sounds mostly confident. "Naito knows where he can go for help."

Lorn glances over his shoulder, heaves out a breath when he sees how far behind we are. "It's bad enough we have to go through a gate to fissure but must you walk so slowly? Really, Kelia, I don't know how you tolerate Naito."

Kelia rolls her eyes.

We're silent the rest of the way to the gate. Fortunately, we manage to avoid running into any Court fae, though it's not an easy feat. Belecha's entire garrison seems to be searching for me, and I hate it, this feeling of being hunted. I'm constantly looking over my shoulder as Lorn weaves us through the city. I just want to get to the damn gate and get back home. I can handle myself on Earth. I know the way things work there. Here in the Realm, I'm practically helpless, and I'm sick and tired of relying on other people.

It's the thought of going home that pushes me on, so when we reach the bank of the lake and see no fewer than a dozen swordsmen guarding the gate, I look at Lorn, praying he's bought off every single one of them.

He sighs dramatically. "There were only two here before. If we'd found you sooner . . . Kelia, go fetch Aren. If he wants his shadow-witch alive, he's going to have to leave the *tor'um*."

She fissures out. I watch her shadows twist and thicken into the topography of what I presume is Lynn Valley.

"Aren's still there?" I ask Lorn, pulling my cloak tight as a strong, cold wind barrels down the narrow pathway where we're hiding.

He leans against a stone wall. "He's healing the *tor'um* who managed to escape into the woods. There aren't many, but their injuries are severe. If you're lucky, Aren hasn't burned himself out yet."

"Were you there? During the attack, I mean."

"Taking care of Kelia, yes. Her depression is . . . Well, it's bringing even me down."

Not an easy feat, I'm sure. I lean against the wall opposite him. "You have a life-bond with her."

"Uh-huh," he murmurs, fingering his sword's hilt while keeping watch down the street.

When he doesn't elaborate, I ask, "Why Kelia?"

"I needed a life-bond with someone."

"She wasn't seeing Naito?"

Lorn chuckles. "Oh, she was seeing him—nightly, I presume." He glances my way and smirks. "The sons and daughters of Cyeneanen have . . . How would you say it? Reserve? Magical reserves? The bond allows me to access it. My magic requires a lot of energy, especially when fae object to my little mental incursions."

"She agreed to—"

I flatten against the wall when two fissures slash through the darkness. Kelia and Aren. God, Aren looks ragged. He's smeared with dirt and blood. I don't see any serious injuries, but he looks like he might be having just as much trouble standing upright as I am.

He greets me with a smile that doesn't touch his eyes. "Are you okay?"

"I'm fine," I lie. I'll be fine when I get out of the Realm. "The gate's guarded. There's about a dozen swordsmen."

He nods, then walks to the end of the narrow alley to peer around the corner.

"Too many," he says as if talking to himself. "I'll need help, but we're scattered. Hurt." He runs a hand through his hair.

I've never seen him like this before. He seems . . . not quite disoriented. Maybe at a loss? Like he has no idea what he's going to do. I'm still trying to figure out what's wrong when Kelia whispers to Lorn, "Sethan's gone to the ether."

A block of ice settles in my stomach. Defeated, that's how Aren looks. Aren might be the fae who works out the logistics of the war—when and where and how to strike against the Court—but he's not a Descendant. He can't replace Atroth; only Sethan could.

Shit. Has the rebellion just lost the war?

"The Vancouver authorities are there," she adds. "There were fires. Stray arrows. Human casualties. We don't know yet what they think happened."

It's like someone's taken an ice pick to my eyes. I press the heel of my hand to my forehead, trying to relieve some of the pressure. A part of me didn't believe Atroth would authorize the attack. His fae have always gone out of the way to *not* involve normal humans.

"I'm sorry," I say when Aren ducks back into the shadows.

He gives me another fake smile. "We'll get you out of here."

"That's not wh—"

"Against these odds?" Lorn shakes his head. "I think I'll take Kelia and go. I've already contributed much more time and energy than I should to your crumbling rebellion."

His crumbling rebellion. A muscle in Aren's cheek twitches. I'm sure it hurts, seeing everything he's fought for fall apart with one fae's death.

"I'm staying to help," Kelia says. Lorn rolls his eyes, but doesn't look surprised by her offer.

He has to help now if he wants to be sure she's safe.

"Don't you have people you can bring here?" I ask, remembering the dagger that killed Delan. Somebody in the tavern threw it.

"Lorn's too concerned about his neutrality to involve his people." Aren edges back to the building's corner.

Lorn shrugs. "I'm doing just fine under Atroth's rule. My associates have no reason to want a new king occupying the Silver Palace."

This is why I don't trust Lorn—he clearly only helps when there's money to be made. Or Kelia to protect.

Aren ducks back into the darkness. "More fae. And they're moving."

"Organizing patrols of the lakeside?" Lorn asks. At Aren's nod, he adds with a dramatic sigh, "It was only a matter of time."

"We have to move," Aren says. "I'll keep as many of the swordsmen away from you as I can, but, Lorn, you'll have to take care of the ones who slip past me. Stay with McKenzie and Kelia until they use the gate."

He meets my gaze, still faking confidence. "You have the dagger I gave you?"

I pull it free from my waistband.

"Good. You shouldn't need to use it."

Lorn snorts and rearranges his sword-belt. Somehow, I doubt his blade's drawn blood in decades.

I'm shaking as we inch toward the edge of the building. Aren's exhausted. Even if he were fresh, he'd have trouble taking on a dozen fae at once. I don't see how he's going to make it through this, not unless that number is cut by half.

"Ready?" he asks.

No, I'm not ready. There's no way this will end well.

He presses an anchor-stone into my hand.

"Wait," Kelia says before we move.

Lorn peers sideways at her. "Having second thoughts, my dear?"

Without glancing his way, she says, "I can work small illusions." She holds out her hand. I stare at it for a good five seconds, wondering what she's doing, when a small smile bends Aren's lips. He pulls her into a hug.

"That will help." He steps back and turns to me. "She's mimicking your *edarratae*. It's not perfect, but it'll be enough to lure the Court fae."

A decoy. It's a good idea.

"She'll fissure out when the fae close in," Aren says. "I'll try to draw the others' attacks while Lorn takes you through the gate."

Lorn heaves a sigh.

The knots in my stomach loosen a little. This might work. I nod to signal I'm ready and then Kelia and I both pull on our hoods.

We start off casually, just four people strolling down the street. The guards spot us immediately. We're heading toward the group at the gate. There are *more* than a dozen of them now. If half don't follow Kelia when she runs, we're screwed.

Aren waits until the silver plating is almost underfoot before he orders, "Go!"

Kelia's hood flies off when she runs. There's a second of stunned silence before five Court fae take off after her. Aren and Lorn draw their swords. I unsheathe my dagger.

The guards fissure after Kelia as soon as they step off the silver. We run onto it. Aren's in the lead. He takes down one fae before he can draw his sword, blocks the attacks of a second and third while Lorn and I sprint for the gate.

Two fae block our path. Lorn mutters something under his breath but parries their attacks.

I throw off my hood—they've figured out I'm human, I'm sure—and see someone charging at me out of the corner of my eye.

I swing my dagger. The fae's sword crashes against it, flinging it from my hand and sending a sharp explosion of pain through my wrist. He has ample time to finish me off. He doesn't.

He grabs my arm. I slam the heel of my palm into his nose. He's pulling me toward him, so I hit twice as hard. He clutches his bleeding nose, but lunges after me as soon as I run.

Aren steps between us. Kills him quickly.

I escape toward Lorn, toward the gate, retrieving my dropped dagger on the way. The soul-shadows rising into the air prove Lorn's a hell of a lot better fighter than I took him for. He dispatches another fae, then dips his hand into the river.

I lose sight of him when a swordsman blocks my path. Aren's beside me. He pushes me to the right as he charges forward.

There are too many. Two more approach, swords at the ready, but inching forward more cautiously than the one whose nose I broke. My little dagger isn't going to do much good against them and . . . and, shit. They've sent for reinforcements.

A dozen fissures slash through the air at the edge of the silver plating. Fae step out of the light. In the midst of their twisting shadows, a crossbow rises.

"Aren!"

The fae fires.

Aren's not able to fissure out of the way, but the arrow doesn't slam into his chest. It plunges into the back of the Court fae he holds in front of him like a shield. The fae doesn't disappear into the ether. His *jaedric* armor stopped the bolt from going all the way through. He's alive, so when the archer looses a second bolt, Aren uses the fae's body to block it as well.

I wrench my attention back to the two swordsmen in front of me. One of them has a deep, ugly scar carved from temple to jaw. I swipe at the air when he lunges. They want me alive; it's the only advantage I have.

The scarred fae moves to the right, begins to circle. The other one waves his sword. He's toying with me, the bastard.

I back up to keep them both in front of me. No need. Lorn's here. He intercepts the scarred fae, manages to knock the sword out of his hand in time to meet the attack of the other guard.

"To the gate, please, McKenzie," Lorn says, striking high at his opponent twice before attempting a low blow.

The cold night air burns my lungs as I dodge around them. Lorn's fissure is still open at the gate, but I can't go through it without a fae.

Oh, shit. There are plenty of fae around. The guard Lorn disarmed glances between me and the gate. In his eyes, I practically see his plan take shape.

He charges me.

I slash. I don't expect to cut through anything except air, but he's faster than a human; he reaches me too soon. My blade slices into his belly, gets stuck on something inside him, then rips the rest of the way through.

I put up a hand to keep him from barreling into me. My palm presses against hot blood and—and, oh God, I think it's his intestines—before he collapses.

I'm still staring at him when Lorn grabs me. Still staring as Lorn drags me to the gate. Staring, still staring, as Lorn dips his hand into the river and opens a gated-fissure. The swordsman disappears into the ether the moment we disappear into the In-Between.

TWENTY-FIVE

.-◆-.

I RETCH INTO the toilet, clutching the porcelain lid. I don't know whether to keep my eyes open or shut. If I open them, I'll see the bright red blood my hands smeared across the white seat. If I close them, I'll see the pale, pain-stricken face of the fae I killed.

The fae I killed.

My stomach lurches again. I already threw up the minuscule meal I ate at the tavern. Dry heaves wrack through my body now, and I'm shaking. I can't stop. I've seen fae die before, but I've never felt a blade carve through flesh like that, never pressed my hand against someone's insides. I've never been directly responsible for a death.

I should be tried for murder. Yes, it was self-defense but even so, a judge would sentence me to . . . to *something*.

"Is she hurt?" Aren's voice behind me.

"She's fine," Lorn says from his post by the door. "It's just a bit of queasiness. She managed to kill one of the guards."

Aren lays his hand on my shoulder, turns me away from the toilet. "McKenzie?"

My vision unfocuses. Seeing. Remembering. My stomach churns, and I want desperately to go back into the In-Between where it's too bright to see and too cold to think.

"I'm quite impressed, actually," Lorn says. "I didn't know human girls were capable of killing."

"Shut up, Lorn." Aren takes my chin in his hand. "Look at me, McKenzie. *Look* at me."

I force myself to meet his silver eyes. I try to ignore the smear of red across his jaw, ignore the fact that the hands touching me have killed so many more fae than I have.

"McKenzie?" Aren smoothes my hair away from my face. I'm not crying. Why am I not crying? I just *killed* a man.

"It's okay, McKenzie."

It's not okay. "Where are we?"

The skin at the corners of Aren's eyes tighten. "We're in Colorado. Naito lives here."

"Is he here?" I ask. I manage to stand without his help.

"We haven't found him yet."

I can't take the way he's looking at me, like I'm fragile and one second away from falling completely apart, so I nod and walk out of the bathroom.

He follows me to the living room. The rebels have made themselves at home, the few who are here, anyway. Lena's sitting on a camel-colored couch in between Trev and another fae—I think his name is Nalst. Three fae sit to her right in chairs stolen from the dining table. They all look out of place here, and not just because chaos lusters flash across their skin. They're too haggard and dirt-smeared to belong in a house like this. It's not a mansion like Shane's place, but it's put together just as well. Either Naito has a talent for picking out drapes and accent furniture or he hired a professional decorator.

Bottles rattle in the kitchen. Since the house has an open, spacious floor plan, I can see it from the hall's exit. It's separated from the living room by a granite countertop. Kelia's on the other side, peering into the open refrigerator. I think the fridge might be the only working appliance in this house. The lamps are all unplugged, there's no television in the living room, no phone or other appliance anywhere in sight.

"You should eat something," Aren says.

"A drink would do her more good." Lorn strides by. He stops where the dark cream carpet meets the tiled kitchen floor.

"Kelia, my dear. Could you please step away from the cold machine?"

"Refrigerator." She holds out her hand without turning to look at him. "And my *edarratae* barely register it."

"But it *does* register," he says. "Really, sometimes I think you're damaging your magic to spite me."

"Here." She hands him a bottle of white wine, then looks at Aren. "There's nothing to eat. We'll have to go out to get food."

"I'll go," I say. Too quickly. Aren gives me a look that I haven't seen since the last time I plotted an escape attempt, though this time, there's no amusement in his eyes. He thinks I'm going to run. I'm not. At least, I don't think I am, but I need time to think. I need time to be alone.

"Perhaps you'd like to take a shower first?" he suggests.

I glance down. Hell. I can't go out in public like this. My clothes are stained with blood; I'd be arrested for sure.

I *should* be arrest—

No. I won't think about that.

"Yeah," I say. "I'll shower."

Kelia sets a couple of wineglasses on the counter. "I have extra clothes in Naito's closet. Someone else will have to go to the store."

"Kelia," Lorn's voice holds a warning.

She gives him one quick scowl, opens a fissure—

"Kelia!"

—and disappears.

"Nom Sidhe," Lorn curses. "She could have at least . . ." He stops. Out of the corner of my eye, I see him turn toward me. "You, shadow-witch. Read her trail."

I'm already staring at it. The dancing shadows might as well be magnetized, they capture my attention so fully. She's fissured to the Realm. To the north. Corrist, I'm guessing, because I'm sure she's searching for Naito.

Lorn thrusts an open magazine into my left hand and a pen into my right. I map the contortions shading my vision, turn the page when I zoom in on the southern quarter of the city and scratch down those shadows, pinpointing her location as well as I can.

"Corrist," I say to make the magic work.

Lorn peers over my shoulder. The map is drawn over a

diagram of some atom/nucleus thing. Hopefully there's not too much text obscuring my lines.

"Thank you." His fissure slices through the air a moment later. I focus on the magazine in my hand so I don't get sucked into staring at his shadows. It's *Popular Science*. There's a photo of a corpse in the story highlights. It peeks out between my bloodstained fingers.

My hands itch. I toss the magazine on the counter. Fisting my hands at my sides, I hurry to Naito's bedroom to grab clean clothes.

I linger in the bathroom long after I finish showering. My skin is clean, but not my conscience. If anything, the guilt is worse than before. When the warm, humid air grows heavy, constricting, I rise to crack open the door. I don't intend to leave, but somehow, I end up at the end of the hall. The living room is packed with fae. Aren's speaking to a black-haired man who's shaking his head. In black pants and a richly embroidered jacket, he has to be a noble. Plus, he's brought an entourage of guards—four of them—all armed and standing ready to defend their employer.

My gaze is pulled toward the door. Kyol told me years ago that this isn't my war. I should have listened; I can listen now. I can leave this all behind and start living a normal, human life, a life where I won't be put into a situation where I might have to kill to survive.

I close my eyes, draw in a breath. No. Retiring isn't an option anymore. Maybe the Court fae were the good guys when I first entered the Realm, but they aren't now. I have to undo all the harm I've done these last few years.

I'm about to force my feet to move, to walk into the living room and join the rebels, when twin flashes of light strike outside the back windows. Shadows twist through the backyard. Naito and Evan move away from them along with two fae I've never seen before. Evan stumbles.

"Aren!" I call.

He grabs his sword.

"Naito and Evan," I say, gesturing toward the door as the humans stagger inside.

"He's hurt," Naito says, a needless statement since there's an arrow protruding from Evan's chest.

Aren drops his sword and helps Evan into a chair. He's pasty white beneath his beard, and his lips are dry and cracked.

Lena rises from the couch. "Hold him," she says. "I'll heal him."

Aren grabs one of Evan's shoulders. Naito grabs the other. Then Lena wraps her hand around the shaft of the arrow and yanks.

My stomach lurches, but I can't tear my eyes away from him, away from the blood that gushes from his chest, from between Lena's fingers as she presses her palms over the wound.

Evan's sweating. He stops fighting Naito and Aren and goes still. When his eyes close, I half expect to see his soul-shadow rise up. He's not fae, though. He's human and . . .

I exhale when he nods and mutters a thank-you. He's not dead. Not yet, at least.

Naito straightens. He steps back to scan the living room, glancing at the black-haired noble and his guards, then looking into the kitchen. He walks past me to peer down the hallway before turning back. "Where's Kelia?"

"She's looking for you," Lena says, accepting a towel from Trev and cleaning her hands. "She's fine. Or she was when she left."

"Lorn went after her," I add.

"Lorn?" Naito mumbles something under his breath, then, "She won't listen to him."

"I'll send someone to bring them back," Aren says. He exchanges words with Trev, who opens a fissure and disappears. "What happened to you two?"

"Archers," Naito says, walking to the kitchen. He picks up the bottle of wine Lorn didn't have time to open. "We had to make a run for the gate. He was hit just before we fissured here."

"Could you have been tracked?" Aren asks.

Naito glances into the backyard, then back to Aren. "No. We looked for humans before we made our move."

Aren relaxes. The fae noble says something to him, but the

*shrrip*s of opening fissures drown out his words. He and his guards disappear a moment later.

Naito steps to my side and hands me a glass of wine. "You look like you need a drink."

Not as much as he does. Trev's been gone less than two minutes, but Naito keeps glancing into the backyard as if they should have returned hours ago. Seriously, if he and Kelia aren't reunited soon, their story might become a little too Romeo and Juliet.

I sip my wine while he downs half his glass. A heavy silence settles into the living room. Aren sinks onto the couch beside Lena as if he's giving in to the weight of the atmosphere. Nalst and the other fae take seats as well.

"The fae who left," Naito says, his voice just above a whisper. "He was Shyer, son of Asray. His father's the high noble of Criskran. They support the rebellion. Or they did. He just ended his association with us. What happened at Lynn Valley?"

"The fight spilled over to the *tor'um*'s neighbors. Some humans died." After a pause, I add, "Sethan died."

Naito closes his eyes. When he opens them, he drains the rest of his glass and pours a new one. I hold mine out for a refill as well. I need something to dull the realization that I've just joined the losing side of the fae's war.

TWENTY-SIX

◆•◆

"**N**AITO!"
   Kelia's cry jars me awake. My head thumps back, hitting the wall.

   "Kelia!" Naito leaps to his feet beside me.

   Kelia launches herself into his arms. He stumbles back, nearly falls over the couch. He doesn't seem to mind, though. He balances on its back and wraps his arms around her. They kiss and jagged blue lightning strikes across her cheek. It leaps into Naito's lips and then skates down his neck to disappear beneath his shirt collar.

   Watching the *edarratae* play across their skin makes me aware of the chill in the room. My gaze shifts to the couch, but Aren's not there. Only Lena. She doesn't so much as twitch despite the makeout session going on behind her. She stares at the tiled top of the coffee table. For once, I don't hate her. She's just lost her brother, and I feel like shit for having worked for the people who killed him.

   The blinds on the back door rattle. Lorn swings it shut, then heaves a dramatic sigh. "Could you two please restrain yourselves in my presence? I can only tolerate so much."

   Naito and Kelia separate. About an inch.

   I swallow the sip of wine at the bottom of my glass, then stand to set it on the counter. Aren comes out of the hallway with

Sosch perched across his shoulders. I haven't seen the *kimki* since Aren took me through the gate in Germany, so I'm glad he's here and safe, but he seems just as weary and defeated as the fae.

Aren's gaze slides from Naito and Kelia to me. God, he looks tired. He hasn't showered or rested. He hasn't had time. He's been trapped in conversations all afternoon. Shyer isn't the only fae who's come by to confirm Sethan's death. The Court's announcing their victory across the Realm, and each time the news is passed on, the rebellion's supporters fall away. The whole thing's teetering on a pedestal that won't hold it anymore.

Aren sets Sosch on the floor, then gives me a smile that doesn't reach his eyes. I can't stand seeing him like this.

"Kyol said he'd talk to the king," I tell him. "Atroth might be willing to negotiate a truce."

Apparently, it's the wrong thing to say. Aren's face hardens. He walks past me to go sit beside Lena on the couch.

What? I can't even mention Kyol's name? Whatever. Aren needs to consider all his options. Even with Sethan dead, Radath won't stop hunting the rebels.

Lorn's staring at me. So are Naito and Kelia, but less obviously.

"Have a seat, Lorn," Aren orders, picking up a sheathed dagger from the coffee table. He grips its hilt, point down, between his palms.

I frown as Lorn walks into the sitting area and drops down on a sofa-chair. When Naito and Kelia take the matching chair, I sink to the floor in front of the fireplace and loosely wrap my arms around my knees.

"We have to find someone else to take the throne," Aren says quietly. "A Descendant whose lineage can't be questioned."

For some reason, everyone looks at Lorn.

Lorn takes in all the stares, laughs. "Oh, no. Not me. I'm perfectly happy ruling the Realm from the shadows. I have no desire to be king."

"Your bloodline is the next purest after Sethan's," Aren says. "The nobles would support you."

"My bloodline is the next purest after Sethan's *and* Atroth's," Lorn counters. "Besides, my reputation would taint the entire rebellion."

Lena shifts beside Aren. "Half the Realm already knows you've helped us," she says. There's not much life in her voice, but at least she's here and participating, and if she throws her support behind Lorn, maybe Sethan's backers will consider him. If he lets himself get talked into this.

He shakes his head. "No, they know I'm connected to Kelia and all they know about her is she's an eccentric."

"Hey!"

"You are, my dear." He smiles at her. "Your infatuation with everything human is unnatural."

She rolls her eyes, a very human gesture that pretty much proves Lorn's point. Naito leans forward and whispers something into her ear. She laughs and snuggles closer to him.

When her *edarratae* strike up Naito's arms, my skin tingles, and I can't stop myself from looking at Aren. He's watching me. There's still a dark edge in his expression. I don't like seeing him so grave and distant.

I'll probably regret my next question for the rest of my life, but I just admitted to myself moments ago the rebels needed to consider all their options. I might as well put the idea out there. "Why can't Lena be queen?"

The Realm's never struck me as a place where women's rights are violated. As far as I've seen, women are treated with the same respect as men. So why not?

"It's never been done before." It's Lena who answers, and to my surprise, she doesn't look like she wants to slash my throat. I wouldn't call her expression friendly, but it's a definite improvement over the last time she acknowledged my existence. She's willing to step up. If she can get the support.

"It's not a bad idea," Lorn says after a moment.

Nalst speaks up from his spot beside the fireplace. "The high nobles might consider her over Atroth *if* they believed the Zarrak line contained more of the *Tar Sidhe's* blood. They don't."

Lorn glances at me, hesitates. After a quick look at Aren, he says, "With Taltrayn's support behind Lena, they'd consider it."

I sniff. If only. "I already tried to get him to leave the Court. He won't abandon his king."

No one says a word. That's odd. What's even odder is,

when I scan the faces around me, no one meets my gaze, not even Aren, who's staring, jaw clenched, at the hilt of his dagger.

Something twists through my stomach. "What?"

Kelia shifts in Naito's arms. She knows something I don't. They all do.

"The king's ordered Taltrayn to be executed," Lena says.

A chill sinks into my bones. No. Atroth wouldn't execute Kyol. They're *friends*, have been for decades. I wouldn't have left Kyol if I thought he'd be hurt. Lena has to be misinformed.

But no, Aren's expression confirms it. There's a defensive glint in his eyes, but they're sharp, almost threatening, too.

"You weren't going to tell me."

His face is like a stone. There's no remorse there, no apology.

"Did you think I wouldn't want to know?"

"You didn't need to know." He chunks his dagger down on the coffee table; it slides off the other side.

I suck in a shallow breath. The air isn't cold enough to quell the hurt burning in the pit of my stomach, and I'm too pissed to do anything but stare. He stares right back at me.

"So sorry to interrupt what I'm sure will be an interesting little quarrel," Lorn says from the sofa-chair. "But if Taltrayn abandons the Court, the nobles will take note. They trust him. They know he'd never change his allegiance without reason. They'll consider your cause. They may consider Lena."

A muscle twitches in Aren's cheek. "We don't need him."

"We do," Lena says.

"We don't!" Aren's eyes flash. "Besides, he's in the dungeons beneath the Silver Palace. We can't get to him."

"We could if we knew the location of a *Sidhe Tol*." Lena looks at me.

I grab a sketchbook off the coffee table. I found it last night and started drawing all the shadows I could remember. Flipping through the pages, I find the map I'm looking for. It isn't my most accurate map—I sketched it in the dirt while I waited for Kyol to speak to the *Sidhe Tol*'s guards—but the rebels have Sosch. The shadow-reading will take them close enough for the *kimki* to find it.

"Moldova," I say, jamming my finger down on the center

of my sketch. I'm with the rebellion now. There's no reason to withhold the gate's location.

"Moldova?" Naito says. "That's in this world."

It is. Aren doesn't seem to care.

"You give me the *Sidhe Tol* now," he all but snarls. "For him."

"I would have given it to you anyway."

He laughs.

I dig my fingers into my knees, attempt to hold on to my temper, but I'm too tired for this. "Don't be an ass, Aren. You need him. If he's going to be executed, he knows he can't reason with the king."

"So that's how it is," he says. "You want me to risk my life for his."

"I—" I stop. Jesus, that's what I'm asking, isn't it? With the *Sidhe Tol*, Aren has surprise on his side, but he still has to get out of the Silver Palace. It won't be a simple rescue. He might not make it. How can I even ask him to try?

"Aren—"

"I'll talk to our other supporters. I'll make them listen." He stands and abruptly opens a fissure.

"Before you go," Lena says, "you should shower and change clothes."

Her suggestion comes out more like an order. Aren stiffens. I'm certain he's going to ignore Lena and step through the slash of light, but then his shoulders relax. He lets his fissure disappear. "I won't change my mind on this."

Lena returns his stare, but says nothing. The living room is silent for a long, tense moment before Aren finally heads to the hallway.

"Somebody is short-tempered today," Lorn says when he's gone.

He has reason to be. He's exhausted and frustrated. He's lost friends, the rebellion is falling apart, and I just asked him to save the life of one of his enemies.

I scrape my fingers through my hair. I don't want to hurt Aren, but Kyol would do anything to save me. I can't abandon him. There has to be a way to help him without Aren being involved.

I look up, and my eyes find Lorn. Maybe?

"No," he says, preempting my question. "I'm afraid you've lost your advantage, McKenzie. The *Sidhe Tol* isn't useful to me if others know its location. Besides, you still owe me for saving your life in Belecha."

"Then I'll owe you again. *Kyol* will owe you." I hear the desperation in my voice, but I'm too worn-out and shaken to try to hide it.

"Now you're offering favors that aren't yours to give away," he says. "No, I've done far too much already. My people can't be involved in a raid on the palace. If Aren has no interest in freeing Taltrayn, then this rebellion is over."

He sounds so nonchalant. He really doesn't care about the rebellion.

"I need to speak to McKenzie alone."

All eyes turn to Lena. She doesn't look eager to talk to me. In normal circumstances, I wouldn't want to talk to her either, but, well, things have changed.

Lorn stands. "It's past time I leave, anyway. Kelia, you will stay out of trouble, won't you, my dear?"

When she doesn't answer, just raises an eyebrow, he sighs. "Then do send for me *before* you do something foolish."

He's the only fae who fissures out. I watch his shadows bend and shift as the others go out the back door. It's quiet when it closes behind them. The only sound is the squeak of the shower being turned on. Not wanting to remain sitting on the floor for this conversation, I move to the chair Lorn vacated.

Lena still doesn't say anything. I hate the silence. I hate sitting here not knowing if Kyol's alive, not knowing if I can get to him in time or if I can get to him at all. But it seems wrong and selfish to bring him up right now, so instead I say, "I'm sorry about your brother."

She looks up. I don't think she believes me. She doesn't look skeptical, exactly. Her eyes are a muted silver, not bright and sharp, and her expression is as neutral as I've ever seen it. It reminds me of Kyol, and I have to wonder if she's hiding as much as he does behind her mask.

"I didn't think you would support me," she says.

I would support Sethan if he were here. Of course, Sethan

didn't advocate killing me. He didn't break my arm. He didn't have an obvious vendetta against me. But Lena is the only option we have now. I'm willing to put our past aside and start over if she is.

"Can you get Kyol out of the palace?" I ask.

"Can you convince him to support me?" She doesn't blink. I want to lie. I want to assure her Kyol will do anything I ask, but he won't. He'll do *almost* anything, and as much as I want to believe his pending execution will erase that "almost," I don't think it will. There's a reason why his support could win Lena the throne: the fae respect him. They trust him. They know honor is etched into his soul. Even though his honor has kept us from being together, I don't want that part of him to change. Kyol has been the only constant in my life these last ten years. I need him to stay the same.

I need him to stay alive.

"I don't know," I say. God, I hope those words don't get him killed. Lena doesn't owe me anything. She might not take action without a guarantee, but I can't give her one. If Kyol doesn't think she's good for the Realm, he won't help the rebellion.

"Sethan didn't want this," she says quietly, her gaze settling on the coffee table. I relax some. It has to be a good sign that she's thinking about what Sethan would do. Sethan would take this risk.

"When the high nobles chose Atroth as king, he could have protested. He could have complained about the remapping of the provinces. There was a quiet outcry, but that was to be expected. What he didn't expect was Thrain."

Thrain. Of course this would lead back to him. I might be oblivious to the existence of the fae if he didn't discover me.

"There have always been false-bloods," she continues. "But none were as successful as he was. He scared Atroth, and Atroth reacted . . . badly. He started making decisions based on how to keep his throne, not how to protect the Realm. Sethan . . ." Her voice cracks and, hell, I almost—*almost*—want to put an arm around her shoulders. "Sethan decided to overthrow the king only after Krytta."

Krytta. The ghost town in the middle of what became the Barren. A magical implosion killed every one of its inhabitants when its gate was destroyed. Their essences, their souls, were ripped from their bodies. More than two thousand fae—they hadn't gone into the ether—rotted in the sun for weeks before a caravan reached them. But that wasn't Atroth's fault.

"Thrain destroyed the gate," I say. "Not the Court." It sounds like I'm defending the Court. I'm not—not really—but the king and his fae did do some good things. They saved my life, got rid of Thrain, and have been trying to keep peace and order in the Realm. Plus, if the king was a tyrant or truly, thoroughly evil, Kyol would never have fought for him.

"It was Thrain's fault," Lena acknowledges, "but the fae in Krytta were protecting him. He wouldn't have had that support if Atroth made different decisions. Krytta's merchants couldn't afford the gate taxes. They lied when they told inspectors what they were transporting, and the king responded by invading their businesses and confiscating their goods. Fae who fought back were imprisoned or killed, things escalated, and *then* Thrain destroyed the gate." She meets my eyes again. "Do you think Taltrayn will see the damage his king has done?"

He's already seen it. That's why he stayed behind: he thought he could reason with Atroth. I'm sure he knows now how wrong he was to believe that, but whether his new perception of his king will translate into support for Lena, I have no idea.

That's not the question she's asking, though.

"Yes," I say, putting confidence in my voice.

Maybe too much confidence. Lena's lips thin. She looks like she's about to stand when she moves to the edge of the couch. Then she goes still again. After another long moment in which I seriously consider dropping to my knees and begging for her help, she lets out a breath. She doesn't look happy, but some of the tension ebbs out of her posture.

"I need you to talk to Aren."

I frown. That's not what I expected her to say.

"Talk to him about what?" It might be a stupid question, but Lena was here when Aren all but said he'd rather see Kyol dead than have him help the rebellion.

"You need to convince him to save Taltrayn."

Maybe she's hard of hearing or was totally spaced out during that conversation. I shake my head. "Aren *hates* Kyol.

You're going to have to send someone else. With the *Sidhe Tol* they can—"

"No one else will go," she cuts me off. "Not without Aren."

"I already tried—"

"You didn't try," she snaps. "You gave in. You gave in because you didn't want to hurt him."

The fact that she knows me this well annoys the hell out of me. Add to that annoyance a shovelful of exhaustion and I'm close to saying something I'll regret. The deep breath I take in doesn't do much to calm me, but I exhale, reminding myself that I can't afford to piss her off.

"You saw how he acted," I say. "He won't listen."

Her lips twitch into a brief, bitter smile. "Aren sent you to the Court with an anchor-stone. In all the time I've known him, he's never done something so careless, so foolish, before. He acts on instinct, but his instinct isn't always right, and he's angry and tired now. He's not thinking clearly, but if you push him—if you really try to make him see reason—he'll listen to you."

I pinch the bridge of my nose. It feels like someone's slamming a hammer against the backs of my eyes. "I need some time to think."

"You don't have time," Lena says. "If you care about either of them, you'll make Aren do this. He won't give up on this rebellion until he's dead or we've won. The only way to win is with Taltrayn's help."

The shower squeaks off in the bathroom, and snakes coil in the pit of my stomach. Lena knows Aren better than I do. Maybe he will listen.

"Can Aren do it?" I ask.

"If he can put a sword in Taltrayn's hand, I believe so."

Aren and Kyol fighting side by side? It could work. If they don't kill each other.

"Okay," I say. "I'll talk to him."

AREN'S alone in the study, sitting in a black swivel chair with his back to the door. He stares at the center of a redwood desk and doesn't turn when I enter. I'm not being stealthy, though. I'm sure he hears me.

This is going to go so well.

Light streams in through the window's open blinds. On the wall to the left, two tall bookcases are crammed with atlases, loose maps, and spiraled sketchbooks. My shelves back home are the same, though Naito's look like they're much better organized. His desk is in order, too—clean, with all his pens in the holder beside a blank legal pad. There's a jar of anchor-stones sitting there, too. I walk over, pick it up, and study the two world maps—one of Earth, one of the Realm—pinned to the wall. Naito's marked the gates on both with red pushpins.

I rotate the jar in my hand, making the anchor-stones clank against the glass. "Aren?"

No response.

I bite my lower lip, trying to decide how to reach him. "Taltrayn can help you."

A short, caustic laugh, and his silver eyes slide to mine. "You think calling him by his family name will change my mind?"

Okay. Bad strategy. "This isn't about him. It's about the rebellion."

"It's about you." He stands, sending his chair careening toward me.

I catch it, grip its back, trying to think of a way to do this without hurting him. "That's the problem, Aren. It shouldn't be about me. You have a chance to end the war."

"I can do it without him."

"How?"

He stares out the window.

"I'd really like to know. Sethan's dead. His supporters are abandoning you."

His jaw clenches.

"Think about it, Aren. Kyol knows the king. He knows General Radath."

Not even a twitch at those words.

"He knows the locations of the other *Sidhe Tol*."

"Damn it, McKenzie!" Aren spins. "He lost you! He can't have you back!"

My heart gives an angry thud. "I left him—"

"Because you had to."

I dig my fingers into the chair's leather. "I was leaving him before Radath tossed me into Chaer."

"Because you had to," he says again, acid dripping from his voice. "He wouldn't compromise his honor for you."

"He was going to tell the king about us!" I shove the chair at him.

He swipes it out of the way and storms forward. "He's had ten years to make you fall in love with him. I haven't had ten weeks! Tell me how that's fair!"

I back away, my heart pounding.

"Do you know what he's been doing these last few weeks? Do you?"

"He—"

"He's invaded the homes of every fae *rumored* to be connected to the rebellion. He threatened their families, knocked around anyone who didn't answer his questions. If he didn't like what they had to say, he arrested them. If they fought him, he killed them. Do you have any idea how many of my friends he's murdered?"

"He wants this war to end just as much as you do." I hate that Kyol has to kill. I hate that Aren has to, that I had to.

He rams his fist into the open door. It slams shut. "You'd say anything to make me save him."

"Aren—"

"Go ahead," he snarls. "Lie to me. Tell me you don't still have feelings for him."

Edarratae flash over his face. The blue lightning seems to buzz with his fury. The only time I've ever seen him close to this angry was when I called the cops with the vigilante's cell phone, but after the initial blowup, he turned cold and indifferent. He's not indifferent now.

I shift my gaze to his chest, watch it rise and fall with his furious breaths. He's right: I'd be lying if I said I don't still have feelings for Kyol—I do—but I'm not doing this just to save him. I'm doing it to save Aren, too.

"What happens afterward?" he demands. "What happens when Taltrayn puts his hands on you?" He grabs my hips. "When he begs you to forgive him?" He pulls me against his chest.

My hands go to the hard muscles of his forearms. Lightning leaps up and down his arms, heating my palms.

"Aren," I whisper.

His mouth is close enough for my lips to pull a chaos luster across the air. I shiver when it sparks over my tongue. Aren doesn't close those last few millimeters, though. He hovers there, his eyes daring me to initiate the kiss.

All thoughts of Kyol disappear. Aren's hands clench on my hips when I slant my mouth over his. He's stunned only for a moment and then he kisses me back, pressing the length of his body into mine. The *edarratae* pour out of him, into me. My muscles turn molten. They quiver. I slide my hands up his chest to grip his shoulders. I dig my fingers into his muscles as he dips his tongue into my mouth.

A moan. *My* moan. Warmth coils in my stomach, sinks lower. Aren hooks his hands behind my knees, lifts. I wrap my legs around his waist and weave my fingers through his disheveled hair. Everything's moving too quickly, not quickly enough.

He sets me on Naito's desk, then slides his hands under my shirt. Lightning bolts around my rib cage and I arch into him. He kisses my jaw, my throat, the scar along the side of my neck. He murmurs something in Fae, but my body is too full of *edarratae*, my mind too full of him, to translate.

I kiss him again, sucking chaos lusters from his lower lip. They taste so good, so tantalizing. *He's* tantalizing. I press my hips forward, needing to feel him against me. I wrap my hand around the back of his neck to pull him closer, but this time he doesn't budge. He removes my hands one at a time.

"Fine," he says, his words coming out breathless. "I'll save your precious sword-master, McKenzie. But I will never, ever give you back to him."

TWENTY-SEVEN

•◆•

"WOULD YOU *PLEASE* stop pacing?" Kelia says. Again. I ignore her. Again.

Pacing is the only way I can stay awake. The one time I closed my eyes I dreamed UPS delivered Aren's and Kyol's heads to the front door. When I tore the tape off the box containing Aren's head, rage-filled eyes of red, not silver, glared up at me. I jerked awake, a scream lodged in my throat, when he accused me of killing him.

No. There will be no sleep for me, not until I know they're both safe.

I walk from the back door toward the front, glancing at the time on the oven along the way. It clicks to 3:04.

They should be back by now. Aren took every fae but Lena and Kelia with him when he fissured out five hours ago. I shadow-read for the Court long enough to know the king's men usually come out the victors of any battle that lasts more than half an hour. The rebels have always executed quick, surprise attacks, hitting their target and fleeing before the Court sends reinforcements. This isn't good, Aren and his men being gone so long.

"You're making me dizzy," Kelia says.

I'm making myself dizzy. Not my fault. There's not enough space to pace.

I reach the back door, see no fissures splitting the darkness on the other side of its glass window, and pivot. Straight into Naito's chest. He puts his hands on my shoulders, steers me toward the sofa-chair, and forces me to sit.

"Aren's broken people out of prison before. Relax."

"He's never broken anyone out of the Silver Palace." I try to stand.

Naito pushes me back down and gives me a small smile. "You managed it. I think he might be okay."

Not funny. I never should have convinced Aren to go. What the hell was I thinking? What the hell was *he* thinking to agree?

Naito waits a moment, undoubtedly making sure I don't try to get up again. When he's satisfied I won't, he drops down on the couch beside Kelia. "The Court doesn't know we have the location of a *Sidhe Tol*."

"That gets him into the palace, not out of it." I eye the arm he drapes around Kelia's shoulders, wishing Aren was here to do the same. Just wishing he was here.

"It's a covert operation," Naito says. "He's good at this type of thing. The Court fae won't know he's been there until it's too late."

Kelia rolls her eyes when I stand. I can't stay still, though. I've been shaking for the last few hours, and more than once, I've made a run for the bathroom, certain I would throw up. I didn't. I haven't since I first got here.

On my trek toward the front door, I grab the camo-colored lighter off the kitchen counter. The candles placed throughout the living room and kitchen are already lit, but my hands need something to toy with. I flick the wheel and let the flame burn a few seconds before extinguishing it.

"How long until that runs out of fuel?" Kelia mutters.

I'm about to tell her I saw another lighter in a drawer when Naito launches to his feet. "They're back."

I spin toward the back door just as Aren slams it open. He stalks by without meeting my eyes.

Lena rises from the table when he enters the kitchen. She intercepts him, grabbing an arm that I'm just now noticing is stained red with blood. He savagely shakes off her hand, takes a glass out of the cabinet, and jerks on the water faucet.

The back door rattles again. I wrench my gaze away from Aren in time to see Kyol stagger inside.

Oh, God. His face is bruised and bloodied, his left eye almost entirely swollen shut. Beneath the tatters of his cotton shirt, bright red slashes snake around his ribs and over his shoulders. My chest constricts, imagining his back covered in a meshwork of ugly lacerations.

His good eye focuses on me. He leans heavily on a sword and takes another step inside. He stops. He wavers.

I'm there before he collapses. He hisses out a breath when I grip his arms to lower him to the floor.

"Shit. I'm sorry." Jesus. There's not a safe place to touch. His skin is ripped to shreds.

He's still clutching the sword in his hand. I pry at his fingers.

"Kyol," I whisper, urging him to let it go. He tries to answer but coughs instead, and the wet, gurgling rasp tears at my heart.

Lena drops down beside me. "Move!"

Shaking, I climb to my feet and back out of the way. I don't breathe until she puts her hands on him. Kyol's body lurches, absorbing her magic. She's healing him, thank God. The shallowest lashes begin to seal shut. He's going to be okay. He and Aren both are going to be okay.

I wait until Lena's finished before I return to him. He looks so tired. I must as well. His brow lowers in concern. He reaches up to touch my face.

"Kaesha."

"What happened?" I ask, ignoring the lightning striking through my core and putting a little distance between us because I don't want to test Aren's temper.

Kyol's mask wavers for an instant. "I wouldn't allow my men to fight in Lynn Valley. I tried to prevent the attack."

"You failed," Lena says. Behind her, Aren's eyes are a sharp, angry silver. His body is so rigid I'm certain he's one second away from an explosion.

Then, without warning, his shoulders relax. I'm not sure what to make of the transformation until I remember Amy's wedding reception. As soon as Aren spotted Kyol, the tension slid out of his muscles. The change hit me as odd then, but I understand it now. Aren hides his emotions behind his half smiles and his nonchalance as completely as Kyol hides his behind his impenetrable masks.

"We need to talk," Lena says. "Clean up. Quickly. Then join us in the kitchen."

Kyol and I help each other rise.

"You're sure you're okay?" he asks.

"I'm fine," I say. Or I will be so long as he and Aren don't kill each other. Aren's doing his best to pretend like nothing fazes him, but his hand tightens around the hilt of his sword. "Go on." I point him in the direction of the bathroom.

Aren watches me as I walk to the table. Lena steps between us, insisting he let her heal him, but his gaze never wavers. It's almost tangible, and an electric tingle rushes through my body. I glance down at my arms, assuring myself that his *edarratae* haven't found some way to leap across the distance between us. No. Nothing but goose bumps on my skin.

I take a seat at the table. When she's finished healing Aren, Lena joins me. So do Naito and Kelia, but Aren bypasses us and enters the kitchen. He returns a few seconds later carrying a glass of something red. I frown because I swear he's almost grinning. Then I realize why.

When he sets the *cabus* down in front of me, I push it away. "No, thanks. I'm fine."

"You're not fine. I'll force it down your throat if I have to, *nalkin-shom.*"

If it wasn't for the small, almost imperceptible smile tugging at the corner of his mouth and the way he called me *nalkin-shom*, I might be pissed. Instead, a pleasant warmth spreads through me.

"I just need coffee."

He sinks into a chair and pushes the glass back into my hands. "It's this or nothing."

"Nothing is fine with me." It feels good, arguing with him like this again.

"McKenzie," he scolds.

I lean back in my chair and cross my arms.

"You should drink the *cabus.*"

I stiffen at Kyol's voice. I didn't hear him approach at all. By the look on Aren's face, he didn't either. We were both completely focused on each other.

"It will make you more alert," Aren says, his smile gone now.

I pull the glass closer, but only because I'm uncomfortable with the way everyone is watching me.

The only empty chair is to my left, so Kyol walks over and takes a seat. He's close enough that I can feel the slightest warming of the air and smell a hint of soap. He's wearing the same black pants he had on when he got here, but he's borrowed a shirt.

"Good," Lena says. "Now that you're here—"

"Before we speak," Kyol interrupts, his attention completely focused on me. "I would take you away from all of this, McKenzie. I'd make sure the fae never found you again. You'd never have to read another shadow." He touches the scar on my throat. "You'd never be hurt again."

A chaos luster zigzags down my neck, and my stomach clenches tight. It's disorienting, having my emotions pushed and pulled like this. I'd be happy with Kyol—I know I would. He's what I've always wanted.

I look at Aren. *Edarratae* careen through my stomach at the way he drapes himself in his chair. He may look all haphazard and careless, but there's a certain alertness, a certain readiness, to his posture. Behind that façade, he's watching me. There's a hint of tension in the skin around his eyes, almost as if he's bracing for a blow. I don't want to hurt him any more than I want to hurt Kyol.

"I've decided to help the rebellion." I slump down in my chair and stare at the table. I don't have to look at Kyol to know a dark cloud has moved in above him. I feel it settle about his shoulders, weighing him down in a torrent of sorrow. If he joins the rebellion, his betrayal of Atroth will be complete.

Lena unfolds a map of the Realm on the table. "The other *Sidhe Tol*. You know where they are."

I bite my lip through the heavy silence. Kyol's not just betraying his king; he's betraying his friend.

"Putting you on the throne will only start a new war," Kyol says.

My mood plummets. Of course, he's right. Atroth's supporters aren't going to go away just because Kyol throws his support behind Lena. Some will convert because they respect and trust him, but a significant number of the others will fight.

"I will make you my lord general," Lena says. "You'll decide how the war is fought. Any strategy you don't like, we won't implement. Any swordsman who serves in my court and doesn't live up to your standards, you'll have the authority to discharge. You will be able to go through the rolls of the current king's troops and decide which fae will be loyal to us and which fae will need to be sent away. I will listen to your counsel, Taltrayn."

With reluctance, I have to admit Lena's not just a pretty bitch; she's smart, too, and perceptive enough to see that Kyol's real issue is with Radath, not with his king. But Kyol's not concerned about titles. If he agrees to this, it will be because he decides it's in the Realm's best interest.

Kyol turns to me. "This is what you want?"

One last chance to walk away from all of this. God, I want to. My life would be so much simpler, so much *better*, if I walked away and let the fae deal with their own problems. And Kyol would walk away with me, *for* me, but I think a little part of him would die if he left the Realm with Radath commanding the king's swordsmen. Joining the rebellion is the best chance he has of getting rid of the lord general.

"It's the right thing to do," I say. For better or for worse, I've just sealed all of our fates.

TWENTY-EIGHT

•◆•

"THE *SIDHE TOL* are all in this world," Kyol says.

Aren, whose chair is rocked onto its two back legs, levels out with a thud.

"No wonder we've never found them," Naito mutters. "We'll need to study the terrain. I'll get an atlas."

"How many are there?" Lena asks.

"The *Tar Sidhe* created twelve," Kyol responds, referring to the fae who ruled the provinces after the *Duin Bregga*, the war that wiped the locations of the Missing Gates from the minds of the fae. "But we've only found three. Radath will move his troops to secure them and to protect Atroth."

Aren's eyes narrow. "If he does that, their locations won't be secret anymore."

"He has no choice. He can't allow you to fissure into the king's bedchamber."

I don't move a muscle. I barely breathe because they're having a conversation and they don't look ready to kill each other.

Aren seems to weigh something over in his mind. "We have to assume Radath's already moved his people, then. That's a problem. We've never had enough fae to take on the Court when they're ready for us. We have even less now, and without surprise on our side . . ."

Naito returns, handing an atlas and pen to Kyol. "Mark the locations. Then I'll print out more detailed maps."

Kyol opens the book to the world map, then looks at me. "You drew him the map to the *Sidhe Tol* in Moldova?"

"It was the only way to get you out of Corrist."

I'm not sure how he feels about that. He's not mad. He's more . . . pensive?

"I don't regret it," he says quietly.

The memory of the *Sidhe Cabred* floods my mind. I can almost smell the sweet scent of the garden's flowers and hear the waterfall's soft rain. When I meet Kyol's eyes, I'm certain he's picturing it, too, the moonlight on our skin and the chaos lusters coiling around our bodies. There's something else in his expression, though. Regret? Maybe he's wishing he made love to me that night. I wished it for years.

I tear my gaze away from his.

"Radath has to protect all three *Sidhe Tol*," Lena says. "We only have to attack one."

"No," Aren says. "We need to keep their forces split as long as possible. We'll attack all three, then fissure to the *Sidhe Tol* we choose at a designated time."

"How many fae can you gather?" Kyol asks.

Aren shakes his head. "Not many."

"Just mark the *Sidhe Tol*," Lena says. "We'll decide where and how we'll attack later."

I scoot my chair closer to Kyol to help him read the countries and page numbers in the index. He tells me the countries the other two *Sidhe Tol* are in. Since I've never been to them and haven't seen the shadows of anyone who has, I can't draw a map to their locations. Kyol will have to imprint anchorstones. That might take a while.

Well, it might take a while if he had thousands to imprint. I don't know how many fae Aren can scrounge up. He's staring off into space. Plotting, I presume. He's been in charge of the rebellion's offensives for almost three years. He'll come up with some way to pull this off.

I return my attention to the atlas. It takes less than five minutes to mark the approximate locations of the *Sidhe Tol*. When Kyol's finished, he pushes the atlas toward Aren.

"I think Montana is the best option," he says.

Aren doesn't so much as glance at the map. He's staring at Kelia, whose chair is so close to Naito's, she's practically sitting in his lap.

"I think you should contact your father," Aren says.

Kelia scowls. I told her Lord Raen's role in helping Naito escape. She listened, but didn't seem to care.

"My father—"

"Not your father," Aren cuts her off. *"Yours."*

Naito's eyebrows go up. "Mine?"

"The Court used the vigilantes to hurt us. We'll use them to hurt the Court."

"The vigilantes," Kyol says, his head tilted slightly.

Aren meets his gaze. "Yes. Giving them McKenzie's name almost got her killed."

When Kyol looks at me, there's a flicker of confusion in his eyes.

"They attacked us in Germany," I say. "They knew my name and used it to track my cell phone."

He shakes his head. "We've never contacted the vigilantes."

Aren lets out a caustic laugh.

"It was probably Radath," I say quickly, before this discussion turns into an argument. "I'm sure they'll go to the *Sidhe Tol* if Naito tips them off to its location."

"No," Naito says. "I don't want anything to do with my father."

Aren leans forward, resting his forearms on the table. "You don't have to see him. Just make a phone call. Give him the location of the gate and tell him fae will be there."

"He'll question my motivation."

"Tell him Kelia's left you for someone else."

Kelia makes a face at this, but says nothing.

"We'll find some other way," Naito grinds out.

"I can call him," I say.

Naito argues, but in the end, he has no choice except to agree. He gives me his father's phone number with the caveat that I can't call him from anywhere close by. He doesn't want Nakano to know where he lives. I think it's overkill, but Aren has Nalst fissure me to a pay phone in New York.

The call is short, partly because I don't want to say anything that will make Nakano suspicious, but mostly because I'm worried about Kyol and Aren being in the same room together. Within twenty minutes of arriving in New York, we're at the city's only gate. I don't realize the short turn-around time is a bad idea until Nalst takes me through the second fissure.

As soon as the In-Between releases me, I collapse to my knees in Naito's backyard and draw air into frozen lungs. Knives of ice slash my stomach to shreds. I cough, expecting to see blood splatter on the dew-covered grass, but Nalst lifts me back to my feet. He half drags, half carries me to the back door and shoves it open.

"Aren!"

By the time Aren reaches me, the world levels out. The sharp cramps in my stomach ease, leaving behind a dull ache and some queasiness.

Aren lays the back of his hand against my cheek. "*Sidhe*, you're cold. I should have made you drink the *cabus*. Can you walk?"

At my nod, he leads me to the kitchen table. Kyol is there, sitting with his back to the wall, watching me. I give him a smile to tell him I'm fine. His jaw clenches, but he returns his attention to the maps spread out before him. Lena is sitting to his left, studying the maps, too. Most of her hair is pulled back into a loose ponytail, but she's left the front sections framing her face. With her head tilted downward, those honey gold locks brush the edge of the table.

Aren lowers me into the chair across from her, then continues on into the kitchen.

"Did you reach Nakano?" Lena asks without looking up.

I glance to my right at Naito, who's sitting with his arm draped around Kelia's shoulders. He toys with the name-cord braided into her hair and doesn't give any indication to show he's listening.

"Yeah," I say. "I couldn't tell if he believed me. He didn't say much."

Naito doesn't weigh in with an opinion. I guess it doesn't matter if the vigilantes show; Lena is planning on going through with this no matter what.

"McKenzie." Aren sits beside me, putting a fresh glass of

cabus on the table. I didn't drink any of it before. I guess I should have. Because I'm feeling weak and shaky, I raise the glass to my lips, and tilt my head back.

I intend to down it without stopping for a breath, but I only manage two swallows before I gag. I swipe the back of my hand across my watering eyes. I'd rather chew on bitterbark for a week than take another sip.

"How's the plan coming?" I ask, a diversion designed to keep Aren from insisting I drink more. I'll finish the glass. Eventually.

Kyol's eyes meet mine, linger. When he glances at the *cabus*, I realize I must look awful—pale, probably—and I have the distinct feeling he wants to walk around the table and take me in his arms.

He doesn't, of course. His face expressionless, he turns to Aren and asks, "How many humans do you have working with you?"

"Five," he answers, matching Kyol's neutral tone. "Trev will bring back our other three. They're not shadow-readers, just humans with the Sight. We'll split them between the *Sidhe Tol*. The fae who attack in Montana will have to do with just one."

"You have six humans," I say, ignoring the tension between the two fae. I frown at the map in the center of the table. The Court will probably have three or four humans at each location. We'll still be at a disadvantage. "You can send me to Montana."

"We'll make do with who we have," Aren says.

"You need me—more than me, actually."

"No." His tone makes it sound as if everything is settled.

My knee-jerk reaction is to snap that he doesn't control me, but I manage to choke back the words. He's just trying to protect me. I get that.

"What if Radath or some of the king's other officers show up? You'll need shadow-readers at each *Sidhe Tol* to track them."

He pulls a map of Montana closer.

I turn to Kyol. "Tell him he needs me."

"You're in no shape for this, McKenzie." He says it so simply, so evenly, so goddamn gently.

"So both of you would rather be distracted by illusions? You want the rest of the rebels to be distracted by them? That's bullshit. Fewer fae will die if I'm there."

"I won't let Naito go if she doesn't," Kelia says.

Naito cocks an eyebrow at her.

She shrugs. "I won't. If they're going to make McKenzie stay home because they're worried about her getting hurt, then I'll make you stay home, too."

Naito just shakes his head with a smile, pulls her to him, and gives her a loving kiss on the forehead. "I'll still go, but we need the *nalkin-shom*. If Radath or the king's other officers *are* there, McKenzie can identify them. She can track them if they try to escape, and we do need the extra pair of eyes."

Kyol's fists clench on top of the table. It's a small sign of his anger, but from a man who's an expert at concealing his emotions, it's as significant as a bomb exploding.

"I'll be fine, Kyol."

He shakes his head. "Radath will order his men to target you."

"They . . ." Oh. That's what this is about. Radath knows how Kyol feels about me. He knows he can use me to get to the sword-master. I can't let that stop me from helping, though, so I scan the others at the table, trying to find some support or inspiration. My gaze rests on Naito, the only person here besides me who doesn't have *edarratae* flashing across his skin. "They won't know who I am."

Kyol draws in a breath. "You're very noticeable, *kaesha*."

An ache twinges through my heart. I push the pain aside, focus on our problem. "If we all wear camouflage, they won't be able to tell us apart."

Aren makes a noise that's half harrumph, half laugh. Before I can stop him, he kisses my cheek. A chaos luster bolts from his lips to my skin, sending a shock of tingling heat down my neck.

"You're brilliant," he says. He leans forward to see past me to Naito. "The vigilantes will be wearing it, right? Can we get enough uniforms in a day?"

Naito gives me an appreciative smile. Not only will the camo allow me to blend in; if Aren and the rest of the rebels wear it, it'll make it more difficult for the humans to tell them apart from the rest of the vigilantes. Sure, they'll eventually notice the rebels' swords and *edarratae*, but with the camo, it might take the humans two or three seconds longer than if they went in wearing only their *jaedric* armor. Two or three seconds is enough time for the rebels to fissure out of the way.

"It shouldn't be too difficult," Naito says. "I can look up the locations of a few army surplus stores."

"We need a fourth front," Lena says suddenly, looking up from a map. There's no preamble to her announcement. It's the first time she's spoken since I sat down. "We need to attack the palace itself."

"We don't have enough fae for that." Aren rests his hand on my thigh.

I catch my breath. My jeans protect me from his *edarratae*, but the natural warmth of his hand seeps into me. He's leaning on his opposite elbow, which rests on the table. I don't think anyone else notices we're touching.

"We won't need many," Lena says. "Just enough to force Atroth to keep guards on the wall. Taltrayn can suggest places to attack."

Is Aren staking a claim or something? Letting me know I'm his? That he's going to keep his promise not to let Kyol have me back?

"There are weaknesses to exploit," Kyol admits. "But the guards will be on alert."

I like kissing Aren. I like his teasing smile, his haphazard appearance, his loyalty to Lena and the rebellion, but do I like *him*? I barely know him.

"It will be worth the risk," Lena says. "Once we fissure inside the silver walls, we'll have men attack the guards from behind."

Aren rubs his thumb along my outer thigh. It's distracting, and now is *not* the best time to sort out my feelings, not with Kyol sitting across from us, not with a battle looming on the horizon.

Aren's thumb stops its caress. "Strategic assassinations might work. We need to control the entrances to the inner city. Taltrayn?"

"I can list sentries to neutralize." There's no emotion in Kyol's voice. He stares at the center of the table and doesn't look up. I want to crawl into his arms, tell him he's doing the right thing, and that everything's going to be okay, but I can't. I can't do any of that.

"Good," Lena says as she rises. Realizing she'll definitely notice where Aren's hand is if she's standing, I beat her to my feet.

Naito straightens out of his chair, too. "I'll look up those surplus stores."

"I'll help," Kelia pipes up.

"I'm not going to let you touch the laptop, baby."

She tilts her head to the side. "I'll have to find other ways to occupy myself, then."

Naito grins and takes her hand.

Kyol's gaze follows them when they leave the table. He has to know they're a couple. He has to see they're happy together, good together. If Kyol was a weaker man, if he'd given in to his desires, we could have been like that, too.

Aren and Kyol both rise when Lena steps into the living room to talk to Nalst. When Aren turns toward me, I grab the glass of *cabus* and use it as a shield between us. There's a faint smile on his lips. It doesn't last long, though. It disappears as soon as Kyol steps to my side.

"Are you sure you want to do this?" he asks, ignoring Aren. He's still trying to take care of me, to give me a way out of this war.

My hands tighten around my glass. "I have to do this."

I'm worried he's going to argue that point. I take a sip of *cabus*. I don't know why. To buy some time? To show my determination? Whatever my motivation, I regret it immediately. Trying not to make too much of a face, I gulp the liquid down, then set the glass aside.

"I choose to do this," I tell him.

He looks into my eyes. If we were still working for the king, this is the type of battle he'd shelter me from. He only tolerated the risks to my life before because they were minimal: he and a contingent of his best swordsmen were always with me, and we ambushed the fae I tracked. Tomorrow will be different. The Court knows we're coming. There will be a lot of death, a lot of violence. This could be as bad as Brykeld.

Kyol takes my hand. Warmth spreads through my palm and

a chaos luster spirals to my elbow. "You'll stay by my side and do as I say. You'll fissure out when and with whom I tell you to."

"Except," Aren interjects, taking a small step forward, "she'll be with me."

Kyol squeezes my hand. He lets it go before addressing Aren. "She and I have worked together before."

Aren gives a lazy shrug. "In the past. She's not your puppet anymore. I'll keep her safe."

"*I'll* keep her safe. I've protected her for ten years."

"You didn't protect her from me."

Kyol's fist launches Aren into the wall.

Nalst rushes forward, drawing his sword, but Kyol snarls something I can't translate and doesn't slow down. He strides through the living room and out the back door.

"*Sidhe,*" Aren groans on the ground. He gingerly touches his jaw.

"You deserved that," I tell him.

Lena scowls and adds, "You should have seen that coming."

"I *did* see it coming. I just didn't have time to duck." He sits up and stretches his jaw, working it to the left, then to the right.

I don't feel sorry for him. Aren was an ass. There was no reason to provoke Kyol.

"McKenzie," he calls out when I turn to leave. I ignore him and go outside.

It's a warm evening. Humid. A half-moon hangs low on the horizon, half obscured by thin wisps of clouds. Kyol's sitting to my left, his back against the brick wall, his forearms resting on his bent knees.

I sink down beside him. "Are you okay?"

He doesn't say anything for a long time. He's staring at his clasped hands. His *edarratae* are bright out here. In the past, I'd trace their paths on his skin. I miss doing that. I miss the heat of his touch, the familiar comfort of it.

"I've lost you, haven't I?"

His pain tears me into pieces. My throat closes up, and I can't answer him. I don't know how to. I've been avoiding this conversation, this decision, for far too long because I thought it would end with me alone and heartbroken. Now . . . now it doesn't have to end that way. Lena's made him her lord general, but if Kyol and I both survive tomorrow, he would abandon that position. He'd abandon the Realm if I ask. Ten years ago, one year ago, maybe even a month ago, I would have asked.

He lets out a sound that's so very close to a single, choked sob. "I dedicated my life to my king. I should have dedicated it to you."

I swallow against a raw throat. "I shouldn't have had to wait ten years for you."

"I . . ." His voice breaks. "I've wronged you all this time. I knew how you felt, how *I* felt, and I did nothing."

I bite my lip, taste blood, but the pain isn't enough of a distraction. The tears fall.

"*Kaesha,*" Kyol breathes out. "Don't cry. Please. Come here."

He drapes an arm around my shoulder and pulls me into his embrace. I close my eyes, selfishly soak in his scent and his warmth.

"I came out here to comfort *you*," I whisper.

His arm tightens around my shoulders.

"This comforts me," he says. "This comforts me very much."

TWENTY-NINE

◂◆▸

THE VIGILANTES' JET landed in Great Falls about three hours ago. It will take them almost four hours to drive and then hike to the stream the Court fae are guarding. We won't fissure out until Aren's scouts report they've arrived. It's nearly time to go, but I've never had to wait this long for an operation before. It's nerve-wracking.

Not for Aren, though. He's sitting in the living room cracking jokes. It's annoying, how collected and carefree he seems. I finally ate a decent meal so, physically, I'm doing better. Emotionally, though, I'm stretched thin. Every time I'm in the same room with Kyol, I feel like I'm ripping his heart from his chest, especially if I'm anywhere near Aren. Because I can't stand hurting him, I'm doing my best to stay away from both fae.

I choke down a few swallows of *cabus*, chase it with almost half a can of Dr Pepper. I told Kyol he didn't have to help the rebellion, but he said he'd never forgive himself if anything happened to me. Besides, he's determined to send Radath to the ether. That doesn't make me feel any better. If anything happens to Kyol, *I* won't forgive myself.

"McKenzie."

Naito holds out a belt with an empty holster. Reluctantly, I push my chair away from the kitchen table and stand, taking the belt and putting it on.

"This is the safety." He flicks up a little lever on the right side of the gun in his hand. "Press here to change the magazine." He pushes a button on the grip, lets the black rectangle drop an inch, then clicks it back into place before holding it out. "There are extra magazines in the bag with your sketchbook."

Fabulous. I slip the gun into the holster at my hip.

Before I'm able to sit back down, the back door swings open. I step into the living room in time to see one of Aren's scouts stride in. A wave of uneasiness washes through me. I don't have a good feeling about this. I feel like my luck has run out, that if we go through with these attacks at the *Sidhe Tol* and the invasion of the Silver Palace, someone I care about isn't going to return.

Lena gives orders to the gathered fae. Fissures rip through the air and most of the rebels disappear. Naito follows Evan and Kelia out the back door, leaving just me, Lena, Aren, and Kyol inside.

"You two will work together?" Lena asks them. I think she really wants to know neither of them will be stabbing the other in the back. I'm not worried about Kyol losing control. Aren on the other hand . . .

"We'll sort out our differences later," he says.

Lena doesn't look entirely satisfied with that answer, but she nods and fissures out. When Kyol exits the back door, I return to the kitchen to grab the army green satchel with my sketchbook, pencils, and, apparently, extra magazines. I'm praying I won't need the latter. I might not need the sketchbook either. Even if Radath shows up in Montana, odds are against me being within shadow-reading distance when he fissures out. But maybe I can sketch out the locations of one or two other officers if I'm nearby when they flee. Better to be prepared.

Aren blocks my path when I turn. He's not smiling, but he doesn't seem angry either. He knows I've been avoiding him, and I'm surprised—and maybe disappointed?—he hasn't cornered me before now.

"I'm sorry about earlier," he says. "I shouldn't have provoked Taltrayn."

He's apologizing? He has a hard time even acknowledging Kyol's existence. "He's still taking me through the gate."

Lena made that call earlier, agreeing with Kyol that we'd be more efficient together than Aren and I since we haven't exactly cooperated on anything since we've met.

"I know," Aren says. "But I wanted to apologize. I don't want Taltrayn to convince you I'm the bad guy."

At that, I give a short laugh. "You *are* the bad guy, Aren."

He frowns, and I realize he's taking my words the wrong way.

"What I mean is you're the . . . well, the rebel. Kyol's the good guy. He's made mistakes, yes, but he loves me."

He cocks his head to the side. His gaze makes my skin tingle. The step he takes toward me is hesitant, careful, and when his silver eyes peer down at me, I stop breathing. His lips are so close. I remember the way they felt pressed against mine. I remember his taste, the heat of his *edarratae*.

The smallest distance separates us when he whispers, "You don't think I'm in love with you?"

"I . . ."

I don't know, and I can't answer him anyway because he lowers his head. I raise mine. His kiss is gentle, tentative, like he's afraid of breaking this moment and breaking me. It takes only a heartbeat before I really do break. I grab the back of his neck, pulling him hard against my mouth until he responds. Chaos lusters fire from his lips and from the hands cradling my face. The lightning sparks across my skin, buries itself low in my stomach, and I moan.

His fingers clutch at my shoulders. He gasps my name as he separates his mouth from mine. "If you keep making noises like that, we'll never get out of here."

I don't want to go. I want to stay here with him. I want to see if we could work, if we could be something together.

"McKenzie," he breathes out when I pull him back for another kiss. He presses his forehead against mine. "You're killing me. We have to go. Or you can stay but I . . ." He swallows. "*Sidhe*, I have to go."

He's right. Damn it, he's right. I bite my lower lip, then nod. "I'm sorry."

"Don't be," he says. "It's nice, you letting yourself want me." His fingers graze my cheek and then diamonds glitter in his silver eyes. "Ah, a rare smile. I could die happy right now."

I laugh. "I smiled a lot before I met you."

"I'll make sure you smile a lot more." I shudder when he kisses my palm. "A whole lot more. Right after we overthrow the king."

IT'S too fucking quiet. The vigilantes and the Court fae are both supposed to be here. I should hear gunfire and the sharp *shrrip*s of fissures ripping through the air, not my thumping heart and the wet *plop* of rainwater dripping from the trees.

Kyol pulls me to a crouch on the soggy ground and cocks his head to listen. Thunder rumbles in the distance. It's supposed to rain off and on all day. Aren's counting on it, actually. If the vigilantes deploy silver dust again, a good, hard shower should take care of it. Right now, though, a sticky humidity thickens the air, making it hard to breathe. The Kevlar vest under my camo clings to my torso, and my sweat-soaked undershirt rubs against my skin. With their *jaedric* cuirasses under their fatigues, the rebels have to be sweltering just as much.

Kyol lowers his mouth to my ear.

"Two Court fae. Ahead and . . ." His lips graze my ear. A chaos luster reverberates down my neck. It pools in my stomach.

"Ahead and to the right," he finishes, his voice strained.

Ignoring the ache in my chest, I bite my lip and nod, confirming that the two fae aren't illusions. They creep forward without moving the underbrush. We stay frozen as they silently stalk by, passing between us and Aren and Nalst, who crouch twenty feet to our right. Kelia and Naito are on the other side of them, and the rest of the rebels assigned to this *Sidhe Tol* are spread out behind us and on the opposite side of the stream, less than a quarter mile ahead.

A sharp crack of thunder vibrates through the forest. The thick canopy protects us from the rain for a few short seconds before the downpour penetrates it. The air cools, but I'm quickly soaked through and even more miserable than before. I want this over with. If Radath hasn't sent more than a few fae to protect this *Sidhe Tol*, it shouldn't be difficult to get a sizable number of rebels into the Silver Palace.

A patch of brown and green detaches from a tree. I wait for a bolt of blue lightning to indicate the moving bush is a rebel, but something big and black and barrel-like slips out of the foliage. Not a rebel. A vigilante. He stuffs a can inside something that looks like a launcher, then aims at the two Court fae.

The canister thumps from the barrel and then explodes.

I throw myself on top of Kyol to shelter him from the fall-out. The black cloud doesn't hang in the air long; the rain washes the dust into the earth.

Kyol grips my shoulders. "McKenzie!"

"The silver." I run my hand over his hair, sloshing off dark-ened rainwater. Most of it's on me. He *should* be able to fissure.

"You don't protect me," he grates out, rolling me to my side. I cry out when something stabs into my right hip.

Kyol curses under his breath and jerks the piece of metal free. Then he fissures away, leaving me gasping for breath. Christ, it hurts. And all at once, more pain registers—from another piece of metal in the back of my left arm. It's deep, cutting into the muscle. The vigilantes stuffed shrapnel as well as silver into the coffee cans this time.

I don't have a chance to pull it out before Kyol reappears, blood dripping from his sword. He grabs a fistful of my shirt and drags me to a thick tree as gunfire and fissures rip through the air. Bark and splinters burst from the trunk above my head. Kyol fissures again and again at my side, keeping up an almost constant shield against the attack. He can't maintain this pace, though. He'll burn out.

"Jorreb!" Kyol shouts during one of the few instances he's visible in this world. A second later, Aren takes out the vigi-lantes firing on us, ending the assault.

But it continues elsewhere. Everywhere. I fling rainwater out of my eyes and scan the forest. It's almost impossible to see anyone unless they're moving. Kyol spotted the two Court fae before I did. Maybe I'm missing others, others he can't see because they're hidden by illusion.

But no. All the fissures—every single one of them—are camo-clad rebels. Where the fuck are the rest of the Court fae? The plan's gone to hell. We're not supposed to be the ones fighting the vigilantes.

Kyol's breathing hard at my side. I grab his wrist when he starts to rise, silently plead for him to remain. He pulls me to his chest. His arms are warm but they're trembling. He fissured too much too quickly.

He squeezes me tight. "There's no reason for you to be here if the Court fae aren't."

"How far to the *Sidhe Tol*? Maybe they're there."

Bullets strafe the ground to the left, and the air erupts with earth and wet leaves.

Kyol presses me into the tree trunk. "No. They'll stay away from the silver plating."

"Maybe they removed—"

"They're in the trees!"

Kyol and I aren't the only ones who hear Naito's bellow. The second I spot a Court fae perching on a thick limb, he's riddled with holes. A flash of light and he disappears. Dead. His soul-shadow dissipates into the rain-drenched canopy.

The vigilantes bombard the treetops, and the foliage erupts with fissures. Fissures and shadows. Only a few of the latter are white. The rest are all black.

"What do you see?" Kyol asks.

"They're out of the trees," I report, scanning the scene around us. The Court fae are everywhere now, fissuring in and out to dodge the vigilantes' attacks. Kyol will see the fissures, so I search for fae who aren't disappearing. They're the ones most likely to be hidden by illusion.

"Female archer by the moss-covered tree."

He follows my gaze. "Visible."

Another rebel will take her out.

"Straight ahead. A swordsman coming up the hill."

"Visible."

"Two swordsmen walking past the exploded coffee can."

"I see three. Describe them."

"The one on the left is male, crouching down now. The one on the right—"

"Is his sword bloody?"

"Yes."

Kyol vanishes in a flash of light. He reappears behind the two fae, dispatches the first before they know he's there, meets the spinning attack of the second and counters. Three swings later, that one enters the ether, leaving behind nothing but his fading soul-shadow.

Kyol fissures back to my side. I describe the scene again. Then again and again, sprinting from one tree to the next at Kyol's command. There's something synchronous about the way we work together. He knows where I'm looking, understands the details that capture my attention like that rotting limb a fae not visible to Kyol steps over, or the area of ground I describe as a giant's footprint. He stays close when I whisper locations to him, touching my shoulder, my arm, placing an encouraging hand on the small of my back. To show he's there for me. He'll take care of me, keep me safe.

His warmth is comforting and the horror of what's going on around us isn't as sharp as it will be later in my nightmares. It's as if I'm watching it from a distance. This is a scene from a movie, nothing more.

Nothing more until something hits me. I'm slammed to the ground a second after Kyol fissures away again. Pain explodes through my left shoulder blade and radiates across my back.

I gasp as I roll to my right side.

Something moves in front of me. A man. A vigilante. Vaguely familiar eyes widen in surprise. Not Naito's eyes. His father's eyes. They narrow, undoubtedly realizing I'm not one of his people, then his mouth thins into a resolute line. A pistol rises out of his camouflaged netting. It aims at my chest.

"Dad!"

The vigilante whips his head toward Naito's voice.

I roll away as Kyol fissures between us, swinging his blade at Nakano.

The gun goes off. Something wet splashes across my face.

"Kyol!" I cry out, terrified he's been shot. A second later, I see a severed arm clutching a pistol and hear Nakano's scream.

"Dad!" Naito skids to his knees beside his father.

"McKenzie!" Kyol's hands are on me.

Before I can say anything, Aren fissures to my other side. "Are you hurt?"

I shake my head. There's too much going on. Too many gunshots and fissuring fae. And there's an arm on the ground in front of me and a man bleeding and cursing and trying to push away his son, his son, who—even though he hates him—is trying to save his father's life.

Naito cinches his belt around the stump of Nakano's arm.

"Help him." I push Aren toward the humans.

"You're not hurt?"

"No." A bullet in the back is what knocked me to the ground, but I don't think it penetrated my vest. Adrenaline's numbing the pain now.

"Get her out of here," Aren orders. He scrambles across the forest floor to Nakano.

As Kyol's pulling me to my feet, a shadow captures my attention. I would just let it go, but it nags at me like an itch that needs to be scratched. It's a Court fae. I can't see his face, but I'm certain I know him. He's . . . Holy shit, it's Radath.

I yank my sketchbook out of my satchel as he fissures away. "He's running."

"Not now, McKenzie."

I push Kyol's hands away and take the pen out of the spiral. "It's Radath."

Kyol freezes. I take advantage of his indecision and scratch the first twist of shadows across a blank page. The trail's fresh enough. I think I can map his location to within a couple hundred feet.

"He's gone to the Realm." He'll double fissure so I *have* to be accurate. A deeper shade of black narrows into a curving line. The river leaks out into the Jythia Ocean.

I focus. The shadow's scale changes, grows more precise. I flip to the next page to narrow my map down as well. He's fissured into a rocky field. It's nowhere near a town, just a place in the middle of nowhere.

"Criskran." I shove the sketchbook in front of Kyol's eyes. "You can catch him."

His jaw clenches.

"Stay with Jorreb," he orders. He takes my gun out of its holster, presses it into my hands, and something flickers in his eyes. I don't realize what it is until he fissures out. He doesn't expect to see me again. Why? He can take Radath in a fair fight.

In a fair fight.

Fear drives the air out of my lungs. It's a trap. It's the only explanation for Radath being here, *right here*, where Kyol and I both stood.

God, what have I done?

I press my back against a tree and scan the forest for anything, anyone who can help him.

Aren's stopped Nakano's stump from bleeding. He fissures away to fight a trio of Court fae, leaving Naito at his father's side.

"Get away!" Nakano roars at his son.

Naito complies. He picks up the gun from his father's severed hand and takes aim at one of the fae Aren's fighting.

I scramble in the direction of the *Sidhe Tol*, slipping on wet leaves as the battle roars on. I have to find someone willing and able to help Kyol. *I have to.*

I spot Nalst running past Nakano. Before I call the rebel's name, Nakano moves. My heart thumps in my chest as he pulls a gun out from behind his back. He aims.

"Watch out!" I scream, swinging my gun up to aim, but Nalst is in my way.

Two shots ring out. I spin in the direction Nakano shot, making sure he hasn't hit any rebels.

He has.

Kelia cries out, sinking to her knees. She has armor under her camo, though. She'll be okay. She'll get up. She'll . . .

A wet stain grows across her breast.

Oh, God.

I run to her. I drop my gun, placing my hand over her heart to try to stop the bleeding. Her cuirass is in the way. The blood's leaking out the gap on the side, too. It's leaking everywhere, staining her clothes. I can't put enough pressure on it.

She cries out when I yank at her shirt, ripping it so I can get to the strings holding the *jaedric* together.

"I'm sorry. I have to . . . God. I have to get this off you."

My hands shake. Blood tightens the knots at her side. I can't get them undone.

"Naito," she chokes out.

Shit. She's going to die. She can't wait. She needs help now.

"Aren!" I yell.

I scan the forest, spot him slaying a Court fae. He turns toward me the same instant Naito does.

"Kelia!" Naito flies across the forest floor almost as quickly as Aren fissures here. He drops to his knees, takes his hand in hers. "Baby, hang on."

"Naito," she whispers, focusing on his face.

Aren takes out a knife, cuts through the bindings on her side. He flings the cuirass aside and places his hands over Kelia's bullet wounds. His hands glow blue as he flares his magic. The tension floods out of Kelia's body. An instant later, she vanishes.

I stop breathing. No. She couldn't have died. Aren was healing her. He was . . .

A spasm wracks through Naito. An anguished scream rips from his throat.

"No!" He reaches for her rising soul-shadow, clutching at the air as if he can keep it in this world. "No!"

The white shadow dissipates.

"No!"

I back away. Kelia's dead. Kyol's gone. Fae are still dying around us. I don't know if any rebels have made it to the *Sidhe Tol*. Don't know how much longer until the reinforcements from the other attacks arrive.

Naito screams again. His pain brings tears to my eyes.

God, we shouldn't be here. We shouldn't have come.

I take another step back. My tears stream down my face, mixing with the rain.

Another step back and I hit something. I put a hand behind me to balance against the tree, only it's not a tree.

I start to turn, but something wraps around me. Something invisible.

The forest blurs, darkens, then reappears in a shade of blue. A hand covers my mouth. I can't suck in enough air to scream.

I shiver. Not from the icy grip of the In-Between but from the wet tongue that slowly licks up my neck.

THIRTY

◆•◆

I TWIST AND I thrash and I try to scream, but no one sees
Micid drag me to the *Sidhe Tol*. No one hears his sick
chuckle when he bites my ear, and the battle's too loud, too
chaotic, for anyone to notice the spray of water my kicking
legs send up when Micid reaches into the stream and opens a
gated-fissure. He presses an anchor-stone into my palm, covers my fist with his hand, then pulls me into the slash of white
light.

My rain-soaked clothing freezes to my skin. Pain stabs
through me, stealing my breath and cramping my muscles—
all my muscles: my stomach, my calves, my bruised back.
Everything hurts.

Then the In-Between vanishes and I stumble into the
Realm. My lungs aren't working right. The air filling them
doesn't seem to contain any oxygen. Shadows creep into my
vision, blurring the gilded doors to the king's hall. The shadows aren't all from our fissure, though; most are from my fading consciousness. My knees buckle, but Micid's hand tangles
in my hair and he drags me through the open doorway.

I recover enough to lock my knees, forcing Micid to stop
walking. He slides his hand down the side of my neck, agitat-
ing my *edarratae*. When he puts his arm around my shoulders, I slam my elbow into his stomach.

He hisses and grips the back of my neck in one hand, then places a knife against my throat with the other.

"Bring her here, Micid," Atroth says, rising from his throne. Four guards stand at the foot of the dais, hands ready on their swords, and more than a dozen archers stand with their backs against the room's long walls. Arrows are already inserted into their crossbows. Everyone is silent and alert, ready in case any rebels make it through the *Sidhe Tol*.

Micid places his mouth against my ear. "I will tame you when this is over."

His knife cuts into my skin as he leads me down the length of the blue carpet. I'm cold and shaking, but my clothes are just wet, not frozen like I thought, and the muscle cramps are gone now. Unfortunately, I'm all too aware of my thudding heart and the anxiety pooling in my stomach. If I wasn't holding out hope to find some way out of this, I'd force Micid to slit my throat. I'd rather be dead than in his whorehouse.

Atroth gazes at me as if I'm a child who's disappointed a parent. When he walks down the platform's steps, his four guards part to allow him through.

"Put away the knife, Micid."

"Of course, my king." He makes the blade disappear.

I swipe my hand across my neck. It's only bleeding a little—the shrapnel stuck in the back of my arm is a worse injury—but Atroth scowls, unties a blue sash from around his waist, then dabs at the shallow scratch. I don't know why he bothers. My clothes are stained with Kelia's blood.

Kelia. She's dead. Kyol probably is, too. And Aren?

My gut twists. The fight at the *Sidhe Tol* wasn't going well, and Aren didn't see Micid take me. Naito and I told him about the *ther'rothi*, but will he realize what happened?

Atroth folds the sash several times before he slides it into a pocket of his embroidered jacket.

"You've become a problem, McKenzie."

"What do you want?" Somehow, I manage to sound angry, not scared and exhausted.

Atroth's eyebrows go up. "What do *I* want? McKenzie, you've done this to yourself. When we rescued you from the rebellion, *I* intended to carry on as usual. I've always thought you were smart, strong-willed. I never thought you'd allow yourself to be manipulated by a false-blood. What's worse, you've used your chaos lusters to manipulate Taltrayn as well."

"I didn't—"

Micid gives me a shake, making me swallow my words.

Atroth heaves out a sigh. "I suppose his actions are partly my fault, though. I knew how he felt about you, but I believed him when he swore he wouldn't act on those feelings. Still, I shouldn't have allowed you to work so closely together for so long a time." He shakes his head as if he's had this discussion with himself a thousand times before. "But I needed you protected, and Taltrayn was my sword-master. It made sense. You were effective together."

I scan the length of the throne room, looking for some way to save myself. There are too many archers between me and the door. I study their faces, hoping to see Taber or someone else who might be more loyal to Kyol than to Atroth, but I don't recognize any of them.

"*Sidhe,*" Atroth curses, regaining my attention. "You have no idea how difficult this is for me."

I focus on him and feel my eyes widen.

"For you?" My voice is so soft, so cold, the nearest guards loosen their swords in their scabbards.

The king frowns. "You don't think I'm enjoying this, do you? I've known Taltrayn longer than you've been alive. I never wanted to hurt him. When my guards discovered you helping the rebels infiltrate my palace, I should have had you executed. I didn't because Taltrayn begged me to spare your life."

"So you planned to give me to *him* instead?" I jab a finger toward Micid, who smiles in return.

"Of course not," Atroth says. "It was a threat only, for both you and Taltrayn. You knew more about the rebels than you told us. I needed you to talk."

"I could take her now, my lord."

"No, Micid. She won't become one of your whores." He says this as if he's doing me a favor, as if he's the most reasonable and tolerant king to ever rule a world. He's not. He's obviously aware of the *ther'rothi*'s fetish. Atroth's a bastard for ignoring it. Besides, Micid's sick smile doesn't waver. He still thinks he'll have me.

I shiver. When I cross my arms over my chest, the shrapnel embedded in the back of my left arm stabs deeper. I focus on that pain instead of the panic threatening to tangle my thoughts. Atroth hasn't ordered his guards to kill me yet. There must be some way out of this.

"I'm not the only reason Kyol helped the rebellion," I say, trying to buy time. Aren will end up here eventually. If he's alive. "He disagrees with the way you're running this war. If you didn't let Radath—"

Atroth holds up his hand. "The rebels started this. I'm doing what I must to protect the Realm. Taltrayn understood this until you began whispering in his ear."

"I didn't know what was going on until I was abducted."

"You still don't know what's going on. No. Don't say anything else. I hate to let your talent go to waste, but I can't trust you anymore."

"So you're going to have me killed?" I say the words like they're an accusation. I don't know if he notices the way my voice cracks.

"We'll see," he says, staring past me. When he drops into his silver throne, I turn.

Lord General Radath enters via the huge gilded doors. A silver-threaded ceremonial cape is hooked to his *jaedric* cuirass. He may have briefly been at the fight at the *Sidhe Tol*, but he doesn't have one smudge of dirt, one bead of sweat, or one speck of silver-dust on him. He couldn't have engaged any of the fae or humans in Montana. He couldn't have fought with . . .

Kyol. My heart stutters when I see him. He's bruised, bloodied, and bound, but he's alive. He holds his head up and is composed as he strides behind Radath. Composed, until he sees me.

His mask shatters and a look of helpless horror crosses his face. One of his two guards has to shove him forward. He stumbles, then quickly shutters his thoughts and focuses on the king.

He's alive. I close my eyes and draw in a breath, but his presence doesn't mean I'll make it out of this. It doesn't mean either of us will.

I glance back at the gilded doors, praying Aren and an

entourage of rebels will charge through them, but I hate this, standing here waiting for somebody else to save me. I need to find a way to save myself.

Radath ignores me and bows to Atroth. "The son of Tal-trayn, my lord."

The king and his former sword-master lock eyes. The silence in the throne room is deafening, the atmosphere heavy. Even though Kyol's hands are tied in front of him, Atroth's guards shift their attention from me to him. I'm just a human. I'm not a threat; Kyol is.

"My lord," he says after a long moment. "She shouldn't be here."

Atroth's frown deepens. "She shouldn't be here like this; you're right. Neither should you. I've been lenient with you, Tal-trayn. I allowed you to continue seeing her. I believed you when you said you had no hand in her escape. I *trusted* you, and you repay me with treason?"

Kyol's jaw clenches. "I lost her because of my loyalty to you."

"Lost her? To Jorreb?" Atroth's temper cools. "Taltrayn . . . Kyol, you never should have lost your heart to a human. They're fickle creatures. They don't understand loyalty like we do, like *you* did before she bewitched you. McKenzie was with the rebels for a handful of weeks. She couldn't possibly have felt the same way for you as you did for her, not if she's given herself to another fae so soon."

Something in Atroth's tone catches my attention. I glance from him to Kyol, then from Kyol to Radath. Kyol's here. Kyol's alive. If Atroth intends to kill him, why the hell is he taking so long? Why didn't he order Radath to kill Kyol on sight?

The only plausible answer is that Atroth doesn't *want* to kill him. He's searching for a reason to forgive his sword-master. If Kyol plays this right, he might be able to survive.

Radath mutters something under his breath, then, more clearly, says, "My lord, this has gone on far too long. We should have executed him before. We should execute him now."

Atroth sits back in his throne, taps his fingers on the sleek, silver armrest. "He's my friend, Radath."

"He's a traitor. He has been for a while. We've only

discovered his deceit recently, but he's been working against me, against *us*, for years. If he hadn't opposed every plan I had, we could have ended this war a thousand times over. You cannot trust—"

Atroth holds up a hand. "Kyol, don't you see she doesn't care about you? Maybe she never has."

I keep my mouth shut because he might be able to survive this, but my heart's pumping adrenaline through my veins and my mind is scrambling for an idea, some spark of enlightenment that might save both our lives.

"If she lives, she'll aid the remnants of the rebellion," Atroth continues. "If we destroy it today, the next false-blood will find her. I won't allow her to hunt down my officers. You can give her a quick death, Kyol."

Kyol's gaze doesn't waver from the king. I swallow, trying to wet my throat. I need to tell him it's okay, there's no reason for us both to die, but I'm too damn scared to force the words out.

"I'm willing to forgive you if you do this," Atroth says. "Everything can go back to the way it was." He draws a dagger from his belt, holds it out toward his sword-master.

"Did you ever love me?"

Kyol's words are so soft I barely hear them. I certainly have a hard time comprehending them. He's listening to Atroth, doubting how I felt? I waited for him—for ten years, I waited. Does he think that's normal behavior for a human? I can't tell. His mask is in place. There's not a glimmer of emotion in his silver eyes.

"Take the dagger," Atroth urges, sounding sympathetic.

"Did you?" Kyol demands, facing me squarely. "Or did you use me, McKenzie? Did you meet Jorreb before he abducted you?"

It feels as if the In-Between steals my breath away. My throat is raw when I manage to swallow. I shouldn't have to deny his accusations. He should know me better than this.

"Kyol," Atroth says again.

"I want to know," he says. "I want her to tell me."

"I . . ."

"They're stalling." Radath draws his sword. "My lord, it's foolish to let him live one moment more."

Kyol's expression doesn't change, the muscles in his face

don't twitch at all except when he blinks, but something in that one action is more a wince than an involuntary movement. He *is* stalling.

Atroth sighs. "You've sealed your fate, Taltrayn. Kneel."

"I'm sorry, *kaesha*."

Radath walks forward. My heart thumps when he raises his sword and . . .

No, I can't watch Kyol die.

Time blurs. My thoughts tangle. The Realm grows small and distant and I'm no longer standing where I was. I've leapt onto Radath's back. I've torn the piece of shrapnel from my arm. I've drawn it across the lord general's throat.

The metal is small, blood-soaked. My grip isn't firm enough to really slice, so I bring it around again—

Radath grabs my wrist and twists. Something cracks. Then something slams into my face.

"McKenzie!"

Two people, three, maybe a dozen scream my name. I can't separate the voices or the shouts or the whistles of flying arrows.

Blood drips from my face, splatters on the floor beside a leather boot, a leather boot that disappears. At first, I think my vision's failing. Then the noise filling the throne room registers.

"McKenzie!"

I recognize Aren's voice this time. He made it through the *Sidhe Tol*. He's just inside the throne room, hiding behind the body of a Court fae. Arrows bounce off the fae's *jaedric* armor, but puncture his throat and arms. When he vanishes into the ether, Aren dives back out the doors.

Half the fae follow him; the other half . . .

The other half target Kyol, who's managed to free himself from the ropes binding him. He holds a dagger—the one Atroth offered him moments before—to the king's throat. The muscles in Kyol's arm quiver, and my heart breaks at the bleakness in his eyes.

"Taltrayn," Radath grinds out, holding a hand to his bleeding neck. The lord general doesn't move, though. He doesn't have to, not with Micid moving . . . somewhere.

I throw myself across the floor, searching for the *ther'rothi*.

My elbow hits something. I swing my arm around, ensnaring what have to be Micid's legs. He stumbles, falls.

I scream when pain explodes through my injured wrist, but shouts from the other end of the throne room drown out my cry.

Somehow, I'm underneath a still-invisible Micid. I lock my arms around what I think is his waist, then wrap my legs around, too, as a fae screams behind me. The sound of metal striking metal becomes a steady percussion. I catch a brief glimpse of Aren and a dozen rebels fighting Court fae.

I lose sight of him, and I can't see Kyol because Radath's in the way. I can't help either of them. All I can do is hang on to Micid. Hang on while he strangles me.

Black shadows creep in from the corners of my vision. My body tingles, demanding that I unlock my arms from around Micid and pull his hands from around my neck, but still I hold on. If I let him go, I'm dead. Aren and Kyol and the rest of the rebels are dead. No one will see Micid's attack.

I can't let go.

I can't . . . let go.

I can't . . .

Something wet spills across my chest. Air snakes inside my lungs, just enough to allow me the strength to blindly swing my fist. It's no use, though. Something heavy weighs me down, stealing my breath again.

"McKenzie."

I desperately try to shove Micid away.

"McKenzie, it's me. It's okay. He's dead. The *ther'rothi* is dead."

I stop struggling. Sometime later—seconds, millennia—my vision clears. Aren smoothes damp hair back from my face. He kisses me and then hugs me tight. I say nothing when my body screams in protest.

"I thought I lost you," he says.

Edarratae warm my skin, then his magic seeps into me when he presses his fingertips to my swollen cheekbone.

I want to tell him I'm okay, but my throat refuses to work.

He glides his hands lightly down my neck. I manage a quiet moan as he heals the bruises Micid left behind. I swallow, try to sit, but only manage to roll to my side.

The fight's not quite over, but some of the Court fae are dropping their weapons. A few of them are actually helping the rebels. Taber's here and two or three others who I know Kyol trusts.

Kyol.

I look behind Aren to see him still standing with the dagger to Atroth's throat. Radath . . . As I watch, Radath stalks this way, sword raised.

"Aren," my voice cracks.

"Jorreb!" Kyol shouts. His gaze locks with mine, and in that one brief moment, I know. I know he sprung Radath's trap and came here to die. He didn't come prepared to kill his king. The horror of his choice, of his decision, is reflected in his eyes, and a part of him shatters when he draws the dagger across Atroth's throat.

Aren turns toward Radath, but he's too late. He can't get out of the way, not without leaving me exposed. He presses me to the ground as Radath lunges forward, sword raised.

No!

Radath smiles.

No!

The smile's still there when Kyol's blade plunges into his back. Radath's eyes widen. His mouth contorts into a sneer. With his last breath, he swings his sword down, but Kyol shoves him forward.

The lord general stumbles over us, his blade narrowly missing Aren. He vanishes into the ether the moment he hits the ground.

THIRTY-ONE

_{•—•—•}

SOMETIME LATER—MINUTES, hours, days, I have no concept of time—the battle is over. Supposedly, it's a victory. It doesn't feel like one. I'm in the sculpture garden, sitting on a marble pedestal. Two stone fae rise up behind me, the shadows cast by their swords crossing at my feet. The blade-shadow on the left points to a smear of blood not too far away. There are a lot of those throughout the palace, a lot of them in my memory, too.

Naito's rampaging somewhere nearby. Lena won't let him leave the palace. At least for a while. Until the pain and anger subside. Until he's no longer determined to hunt down his father. It's for his own good, she says. She's worried about the vigilantes killing him. I'm worried he'll end up imprisoned for murder.

Something shatters, and Naito's shouts end. I close my eyes, sympathizing with his pain, his need for vengeance. I doubt he'll ever be able to go home.

I've only caught glimpses of Kyol and Aren since they left the king's hall. They've been occupied securing the palace. The rebels have blocked off the residential wings. Every other room and corridor has archers—both rebels and the handful of Court fae Kyol trusts—standing ready to kill. Word has been circulated that they're to shoot anyone who fissures here as soon as they step out of the light. So far, the strategy has worked. The Court fae have almost completely stopped using the *Sidhe Tol*.

I lean back against the legs of one of the stone fae. It's a beautiful day. The sun is just now beginning its descent from the bright blue sky. Without Naito screaming, it's quiet. If I keep my gaze away from the bloodstains, it's peaceful even. There's something very wrong about that. A day like this should be filled with darkness. It should be filled with clouds and the threat of violent weather.

"McKenzie."

Lorn stands a few paces away. I've never seen him look so disheveled. His white shirt is wrinkled and dingy, his shoulders are slumped, and his silver eyes seem darker, duller, than normal.

My throat closes up. It did the same thing earlier when Lord Raen found me. I couldn't say anything then, but I didn't have to. Kelia's father took one look at my face and paled. Tears blurred my eyes. By the time my vision cleared, he was gone.

Lorn sits beside me.

"I hired fae to protect her," he says.

I look at him, but he's staring at the floor.

"I haven't heard from them," he continues. "I assume they entered the ether before she did."

"It was chaotic."

There's something pensive in his soft *hmm*. We sit in companionable silence for a while. Then a stream of curses comes from nearby. Naito again.

Lorn looks in the direction of the subsequent crash. His Adam's apple bobs once before he thins his lips and straightens his shoulders.

"*That* must end," he says, almost sounding like his normal self. Almost.

He stands, starts to take a step away, but a flash of light cuts through the air. The Court fae is in this world for all of a half second before three arrows pierce his chest. I watch, not even flinching, as his soul-shadow rises into the air.

This time, Lorn's *hmm* is heavy with perception. "You're not doing well."

"Nobody's doing well." Him included.

"True. But everyone else here reacted when that fissure opened. You didn't. You would be dead if it wasn't for the archers." When I don't respond, he sighs. "You're not going to recover here. You should go back to your world."

"I'm fine," I say.

"You just pointed out nobody is fine. If you're staying for them, you shouldn't. Seeing you like this will not cheer either of them up."

"If a fae uses illusion—"

"By the time you reacted, your warning would be far too late." He shrugs. "Do what you will, but if you do decide to take my advice, I can have a fae fissure you to a safe place."

"I'm fine," I say again. If I keep repeating it to myself, maybe one day it will be true.

IN the end, Lena orders me to go back to Earth. She claims she wants me fresh and alert in case the remnants of the Court fae launch an organized attack. I don't want to admit it, but she and Lorn are both right. Being back in my world helps some. I can almost pretend I'm normal, that I know nothing of the Realm and the fae and the war that has taken too many lives. Almost.

I switch off the television. The channel has been running the same story over and over again even though the Canadian authorities have no new information about what happened in Lynn Valley. Half a neighborhood caught fire—so did a portion of the forest behind it—and three humans died. The thing that perplexes the investigators the most is that the residents in four of the homes are missing. They can't find the *tor'um* despite the fact that some of the neighbors are certain they were there when the blaze erupted.

I hate that the fae's war spilled over into my world. A month ago, I would have sworn if that happened, it would be the rebels' fault, but they were careful when they abducted me from campus. Aren didn't allow his people to use magic that would be visible to humans, and he made sure they were careful when they aimed their bows—every arrow the rebels fired hit either a fae or a fissure. The Court fae weren't as cautious, and the Canadian authorities don't know what to make of the half dozen arrows they found during their investigation.

I rise off the couch. I'm staying in a suite in Las Vegas. Apparently, this is Lorn's idea of a safe place. With all the tech infused throughout the city, he's probably right. No fae is going to want to stay here more than a few minutes.

I'm heading for one of the three bedrooms, determined to sleep for more than two hours this time, when my skin tingles. I feel him, a familiar warmth I'll never be able to forget.

"How are you?" Kyol asks.

I don't know why his question brings on the tears—I haven't cried since I saw Lord Raen—but my chin quivers and the dam I built to hold back my emotions shatters completely. I spin toward him and then throw my arms around his neck. His arms tighten around me, and he holds me like nothing has changed.

Everything's changed. Nothing will ever be the same between us.

"Kaesha."

I lay my head against his chest, hear his heart thumping. Somehow, it manages to sound heavy and broken. Or maybe that's my heart.

"You're okay," I say.

"Yes." He smoothes a hand over my hair. "Lena's had me speaking with the province elders."

"Will they support her?" I ask.

"Some might."

His words are a whisper, and I know this isn't the conversation we should be having right now. I have things I need to say, things I need to tell him.

"Kyol—"

"Shh," he says. "I know." He draws in a breath and takes a step back to look at me. "I wish . . . I wish things had turned out differently. I wish I hadn't been such a fool."

"But—"

"No. It's okay. I understand why you're leaving me. You've made the right decision. I've made so many wrong ones."

The pain and regret in his voice kill me. I don't say anything because I can't. My throat burns too much. If there was a way to do this without hurting him, I would. He's my protector, my first love, my best friend. He's the one person in my life who's always understood me, but what I said in Naito's backyard is true: I never should have had to wait ten years for him. I should have respected myself more than that, known I deserved to be treated better. I should have *demanded* to be treated better. Maybe if I had, he would have given in. We would be together. But I was a coward. I never gave him an ultimatum because I was afraid he'd choose his king over me.

"I should go," Kyol says. "The remnants are still attacking the palace and Lena is . . ."

There are a number of ways I could fill in that blank, but I raise an eyebrow, waiting.

"She is reckless," he finishes. "She insists on being part of the guard rotation. We need more fae to keep control of the palace, but it's foolish for her to risk herself." He draws in a breath. "I just needed to make sure you were okay before I speak to her again."

"I'm fine," I say, but tears pool in my eyes. I try to hide them, but Kyol sees. He takes me into his arms again. I should push him away because I don't want to make this good-bye any harder. I'll see him again, but we won't be like this. We'll be . . . just friends. Acquaintances. Colleagues.

A sharp *shrrip* cuts through the air. Kyol tightens his arms around me, then focuses on something over my shoulder. "If Jorreb hurts you, I'll kill him."

He kisses my hand, lets his lips linger, drinking in my chaos lusters one last time. Then he steps back, lettings my fingers slip through his as he opens a fissure. A moment later, he's gone.

Before I turn, I wipe the tears from my cheeks.

Aren stands a few feet away. His hands are shoved into his pockets, and his hair is a wild, disheveled mess, but he's no longer covered in blood, sweat, and dirt. He looks tired, though. Tired and maybe a little apprehensive.

He speaks before I'm able to make my voice cooperate. "If I were a good man," he says, "I'd acknowledge that Taltrayn is an honorable fae, that he loves you and would take care of you. I'd step down and let you have the man you've always wanted, but, McKenzie, I'm not as good as Taltrayn. I never will be, and I can't step down. I'll fight for the chance to be with you."

Those are words I waited a decade to hear from Kyol. But in all that time, I never prepared an answer to them. I don't know what to say. I don't know how to tell Aren that I need to see if we can be something together.

The way he draws in his next breath seems strained and his gaze flickers to the wall before returning to me. "I know we didn't get off to a good start." He lets out a laugh. "I know you hated me and I threatened you and provoked you, but we could start over. I wouldn't hurt you again. *Sidhe*, I swear I'd never hold a sword to your throat. I'd protect you. I'd make sure you never had to jump out another window, and I'd . . ."

I'm tempted to let him continue, but he's rambling, and that's so unlike him I can't help but smile. He stops midsentence.

"McKenzie?"

"I might give you another chance," I say.

His gaze moves from my eyes to my lips. He focuses on them as if he's not sure he heard me correctly. Then a grin pulls at the corner of his mouth.

"Might?" He laughs. "I've always said you were stubborn, *nalkin-shom*."

He approaches me then. There are still issues between us, things we need to discuss and disagreements we need to work out, but my heart thumps when his fingertips graze my cheek. It's a light, tender touch, there just long enough to warm my face. He moves closer. I feel the heat of his body, smell cedar and cinnamon, and my lips suddenly ache to feel his. They're so close. If he lowers his head one millimeter more . . .

"I love you," Aren whispers.

I shiver when something hot strikes through me. Not an *edarratae*; it's something deeper, more potent and powerful. He must feel it, too, because he captures my mouth in the next instant. The kiss is possessive, desperate, and delicious. He doesn't hold back or let it end. He pulls me up in his arms until only the toes of my shoes touch the ground. I hold on, return his kiss, and flush with heat as chaos lusters fire through my skin. They coil around us both, melding us together, as the world fades away.

FROM *NEW YORK TIMES* BESTSELLING AUTHORS

ILONA ANDREWS
YASMINE GALENORN

AND NATIONAL BESTSELLING AUTHORS

ALLYSON JAMES
JEANNE C. STEIN

HEXED

Four of the bestselling names in romance and fantasy come together in this collection of thrilling novellas featuring powerful women who know how to handle a hex or two . . .

PRAISE FOR
Ilona Andrews

"Andrews blends action-packed fantasy with myth and legend, keeping readers enthralled."　　　　　*—Darque Reviews*

PRAISE FOR
Yasmine Galenorn

"The magic Galenorn weaves with the written word is irresistible."　　　　—Maggie Shayne, *New York Times* bestselling author

PRAISE FOR
Allyson James

"One of my favorite authors…Will keep you enthralled until the very last word!"　　　　　　　—Cheyenne McCray,
New York Times bestselling author

PRAISE FOR
Jeanne C. Stein

"Stein's plotting is adventurous and original."
　　　—Charlaine Harris, #1 *New York Times* bestselling author

From the #1 *New York Times*
Bestselling Author
PATRICIA BRIGGS

RIVER MARKED

Car mechanic Mercy Thompson has always known there is something unique about her, and it's not just the way she can make a VW engine sit up and beg. Mercy is a different breed of shapeshifter, a characteristic she inherited from her long-gone father. She's never known any others of her kind. Until now.

An evil is stirring in the depths of the Columbia River—one that her father's people may know something about. And to have any hope of surviving, Mercy and her mate, the Alpha werewolf Adam, will need their help . . .

Now available from Ace Books

penguin.com

Explore the outer reaches
of imagination—don't miss these authors
of dark fantasy and urban noir who take you
to the edge and beyond . . .

Patricia Briggs	Anne Bishop
Simon R. Green	Marjorie M. Liu
Jim Butcher	Jeanne C. Stein
Kat Richardson	Christopher Golden
Karen Chance	Ilona Andrews
Rachel Caine	Anton Strout